398

THERE AT THE FOOT
SHONE TWO GREEN FIRES . . .

They burned close together, with an uncanny radiance that made the short hairs on the back of my neck stand up and quiver. In the heart of each emerald glow was a dagger-blade shape of utter blackness, and as I stared I heard a strangely familiar voice come from out of the demonic flames, demanding:

"Are you naked?"

"Ha?" I managed to say.

"Son of a Siamese, you are! Well, get some clothes on and put wheels on it! I don't know how long Creepo the Wonder Wizard will be gone, and we've gotta get you out of here before that. Now *move!*"

You don't argue with demons. If you lose, it's bad, and if you win, they eat you. I grabbed my small-clothes, yanked them on, and stumbled into my shoes.

"Great, super. Now take those pillows and the spare blanket, and bunch them up and cover them with the quilt so it'll look like someone's still under it. Got that? Come *on*, sweetie, time is tuna . . ."

Ace Books by Esther Friesner

DEMON BLUES
HERE BE DEMONS
HOORAY FOR HELLYWOOD
GNOME MAN'S LAND
HARPY HIGH
UNICORN U.
MAJYK BY ACCIDENT

MAJYK BY ACCIDENT

ESTHER FRIESNER

ACE BOOKS, NEW YORK

If you purchased this book without a cover, you should be aware that this book is stolen property. It was reported as ''unsold and destroyed'' to the publisher, and neither the author nor the publisher has received any payment for this ''stripped book.''

This book is an Ace original edition,
and has never been previously published.

MAJYK BY ACCIDENT

An Ace Book / published by arrangement with
the author

PRINTING HISTORY
Ace edition / August 1993

All rights reserved.
Copyright © 1993 by Esther M. Friesner.
Cover art by David Mattingly.
This book may not be reproduced in whole or in part,
by mimeograph or any other means, without permission.
For information address: The Berkley Publishing Group,
200 Madison Avenue, New York, NY 10016.

ISBN: 0-441-51376-X

Ace Books are published by The Berkley Publishing Group,
200 Madison Avenue, New York, NY 10016.
The name ''ACE'' and the ''A'' logo
are trademarks belonging to Charter Communications, Inc.

PRINTED IN THE UNITED STATES OF AMERICA

10 9 8 7 6 5 4 3 2 1

chapter —————————— 1

"SO *THERE* YOU ARE, YOU WORTHLESS RATWHACKER!"
Velma Chiefcook's heavy hand fell on my shoulder like a sack of
potatoes. The great hall of Thengor's Academy of High Wizardry
echoed with her harsh voice, the huge chandelier overhead
swaying, the timid fire-sprites inside their separate glass cells
flickering with fear. Even the tall brass-bound doors guarding the
mighty Master Thengor's apartments shuddered on their hinges.

"What d'you think you're doing up here, eh?" Velma demanded, shaking me until my teeth rattled, then jerking me within
a thumb's width of her ruddy nose to bawl garlic breath right in
my face.

"Please, ma'am, the call came for all of us students to report to
the hall and wait for word," I gasped. Velma was not satisfied.

"A fine pile of peelings that is! Only time you ever call yourself
a student around here, Kendar Gangle, is when you use it as an
excuse to escape your chores. You're a disgrace to the whole
Academy of High Wizardry, you are, you talentless, clumsy
hexfumbler. You're kept on just out of the goodness of Master
Thengor's heart, is what! Well, I'm not no such of a pushover as
the master. Think you can slip away from *me* when there's honest
work to be done below? A bad day you were born and a worse
you'll die, you loathsome little—"

"Woman, do you think it is entirely wise to speak of death so
freely in this house, considering?" A deep, commanding voice,
smooth as a waxed weasel, filled the hall. Velma Chiefcook knew
that voice—as did all of Master Thengor's servants—and she
feared it. At the sound, her jowls paled and she loosed her grasp
on my shoulder. I looked up in gratitude as an impressively robed
figure detached itself from the ranks and glided towards us.

1

I've often wished I were somebody different. That's not so hard to understand when you've been stuck being Kendar Gangle for sixteen hopeless years of your life and no end in sight. Ever since Mother sent me to the Academy, not a day went by that I didn't think, *I'd give six weeks' allowance to be Juvee Lowfloater,* or *I'd give all my pocket money plus my genuine dragontooth charm to be Siv Skinshifter,* or *I'd give anything to be Malicondor Lovelucky for just one night!*

Well, forget all that. I'd have given everything I owned, twice what I could borrow, seven times what I could steal, plus all the Gangle estates besides to be Zoltan Fiendlord for just an hour. I figured it would be the only hour of my life when people would be afraid of me. I knew that being respected is, you know, a lot more *respectable* than being feared, but I'd be willing to settle.

Just look at him! I thought, feeling years of envy well up in my belly. *Anyone on the street sees Zoltan and right away, no question, they know he's a mighty wizard. Even if he's not. Even though he's still just a student, like me.*

It was true. Everything about Zoltan screamed WIZARD!, from the top of his conical hat, decorated with whole galaxies of stars, moons, suns, and planets, to the tips of his curly-toed black velvet slippers. He was too young to have the proper wizardly long white beard, of course, but he did have a very nicely pointed, neatly trimmed black beard with matching moustache. There was also that certain way his dark brows slanted up from his fiery black eyes that made most people speak to him very politely and in general do whatever he wanted them to do. It was hard to give that expression a name; it just seemed to say, *I wonder what you'd look like as a toad?* He could even get Master Thengor's owl, Rosco, to sit on his shoulder without pooping on his robes.

I rubbed my own whiskerless cheeks ruefully. The only roughness I found was the start of a new crop of pimples. I didn't even like to think about what had happened the first (and only) time I'd tried my luck with Rosco.

Velma Chiefcook sank to her knees before Zoltan, wringing her fat hands wildly. "Oh, please, kind sir, I didn't mean no harm. Nothing personal to our good lord an' master in what I said at all, no harm meant, no ill-wishing intended, no need to tell him, now is there?"

"*You* ill-wish *him*? A mere radish-twiddler like you ill-wish Master Thengor?" Zoltan laughed loud and long. Velma dared to utter one nervous giggle and he was on her like the king's tax-collector on a loophole. "*I suppose you think it's funny?*" he snarled. Poor Velma shriveled up into a plump bundle of moans and whimpers.

The other students in their color-coded robed ranks observed the chief cook's torment and exchanged approving whispers. Some of the boys in the lower grades of wizardly studies even snickered. Whatever our individual opinions of Zoltan, splendid and self-important in his midnight-blue gown of senior student rank, all of us hated Velma. She had served us creamed squash once too often. Some crimes cry out for blood!

Zoltan paced back and forth before the writhing cook, a frown creasing his high forehead. With a little shock of recognition, I realized that the top student in the Academy of High Wizardry looked just like our top—and only—teacher. It was like watching a much younger Master Thengor in action, which was pretty scary. At least when the old Master Thengor tried to smack me one for my latest goof-up, I had a sporting chance of outrunning him. Master Thengor didn't like to use his magical powers for something as simple—and frequent—as punishing my mistakes, but I had the feeling that Zoltan wouldn't think twice about zapping me on the run, just to practice his aim.

"I don't know, Velma, I just don't know," Zoltan said, shaking his head solemnly. "These are dark days which linger over our house. Ill omens have been recorded. Strange portents have been seen."

"That's so, sir," the cook quavered. "I had three pots o' cream turn on me, just like that, and half our supply o' squash has gone all—"

A glare from Zoltan silenced her before she could babble on. "I am not talking about spoiled cream, woman!" he thundered. "I am speaking of the imminent death of the greatest wizard Orbix has ever known!"

A peal of thunder rumbled through the vast hall. Five of the chandelier fire-sprites fainted and went out. All of the other students did their best not to tremble at the sound. I didn't even bother trying; I just yipped and curled myself up into a little ball, even though I knew the thunder was just Zoltan's way of emphasizing his words.

Theatrical wizardry—stuff like thunder and fireworks and invisible trumpets and exploding pigeons—is the easiest course in the whole Academy, simple enough for charlatans and mountebanks to master. I got an F all three times I took it, but Master Thengor promised me a D-minus this term if I signed a blood oath afterwards that I would never, ever, under pain of being torn apart by gryphons, even *consider* using it in public.

Velma Chiefcook burst into tears. I felt like doing the same thing. With Master Thengor dying, there went my promised D-minus. And Mother would've been so proud!

The great brass-plated doors groaned and swung open. A small, weary woman shuffled out. Though I'd only seen her once or twice before, on special occasions like when King Steffan visited the Academy, I immediately recognized Lady Inivria, Master Thengor's wife.

As long as I was on the floor already, I pressed my face to the cold tiles of the great hall and covered my eyes. Even so, I wasn't sure if I was showing the Master's wife enough respect, so I peeked through my fingers to check on what everyone else was doing. To my embarrassment I saw that the rest of the Academy students were limiting themselves to graceful bows from the waist. The more advanced pupils who had already been awarded their pointed caps removed these and used them to make elegant, sweeping gestures before the lady. Zoltan simply nodded and gave her a mysterious smile.

"Sure of yourself, aren't you?" Inivria sneered.

"Sure enough," Zoltan replied smoothly.

She laughed at him, showing a perfect set of teeth that looked all the whiter against her dark brown skin. Once upon a time she might have been beautiful. Many of the lower-ranked students claimed that she was fairly young, but that marriage to Master Thengor had aged her ahead of her time. She was dressed in layer upon layer of the most expensive silks, colored like the sunset, until she looked like a gigantic cocoon and it was anyone's guess if she had a good figure.

"Well," she said, "maybe you'll find out that the old blister's still got a surprise in store for you. A nasty one, I hope. Come in. Come in, all of you. It's almost time. He's losing more and more control by the minute. The stuff's turning visible every so often. That means the end is almost here." She didn't sound unhappy about it at all.

Before I could scramble to my feet, the rest of my fellow-students vanished through the brass doors which were beginning to close slowly after them. I heard the heavy panels slam shut behind me just as I slipped through. I wasn't very quick at my studies, but I was fast enough on my feet. I grinned when I realized that I'd left Velma Chiefcook on the other side of those doors and that now I wouldn't have to do whatever task it was she'd found for me in the kitchens.

"Wipe that stupid smirk off your face, you fool ratwhacker!" someone beside me hissed, and followed up the suggestion with a sharp slap to the back of my head. "Our master's not dead yet. What do you think he'll do to you if he catches you smiling at his deathbed? Do you want to find out whether he's still as ornery as always?"

"Oops." I snapped my expression from smug to sorrowful at once. All around me, the room echoed with the sound of sobs, groans, wailing, and other cries of grief. I wondered how much of this was real and how much was being done because alive or dying (or even, possibly, dead), Master Thengor scared everyone.

I tried to rustle up a few tears, or at least a whimper of sorrow, but it was no use. I never liked my teacher much when the old wizard was in full health, and the only thing I felt now that Thengor was dying was a vaguely guilty sense of relief.

No more teacher, no more books, I thought. *And no more hanging on tenterhooks. There's no other magician as mighty as Thengor in all the lands of Orbix, nor any so greedy for gold. So greedy he'd even hold onto a student as rotten as I am, and not out of the goodness of his heart. I just don't have any talent for magic. Mother will have to understand that I'm simply not cut out for the life of a great sorcerer and let me come home.*

It was a comforting thought. It comforted me for about ten seconds before a second idea hit me right under the ribs: *If I'm not cut out for the life of a great sorcerer, what sort of life* am *I cut out for?*

What *was* I good at? Now there was a thought to conjure with, if I was any good at conjuring, which I wasn't. It was the sort of thought that got down the back of my tunic and itched, making me twitch and fidget until Poldi Flamesinger turned around and whispered, "Look, Gangle, it's crowded enough in here without you making it uncomfortable for all of us. Everyone's hot to be near Master Thengor's bedside when he makes his final bequest, and everyone's shoving, but you can leave off. There's no way short of a miracle he'll ever leave anything to *you.*"

"Don't want anything," I mumbled, wishing I could tell Poldi that he was fat enough to be a crowd all by himself. Not that I would. Poldi was called Flamesinger because of the mastery he had shown in summoning fire-sprites. One word amiss to him and a fellow could wind up with sparks in the most painful places.

"Well, then, stop jigging like a gutted frog, you idiot rat-whacker, or I'll turn you into one."

"You and whose books of spells, Tubby?" demanded Yro Frogsnapper. He was one of the senior students who, like me, had been in imminent danger of failing Master Thengor's course of High Wizardry until the fateful day he discovered that he had a particular talent for snapping his fingers and turning his enemies into frogs. It wasn't much of a talent and it was his only one, so Yro was rather jealous of it. Now he brought the first three fingers of his right hand into the "ready" position, curled his lip at Poldi, and asked, "Feeling lucky?"

"Try it and broil," Flamesinger snarled.

"Mmmm, broiled frog's legs are my favorite," Yro shot back.

"Try snapping when I've fricasseed your fingers off."

"Try singing when you're small, green, and squashed under the heel of my boot."

"You're not wearing—"

Neither one of them heard the warning rumble, but I did. Ever since my family's money had bought me admission to Master Thengor's Academy of High Wizardry, I'd saved my skin at least once a day by keeping a sharp eye peeled and a keen ear pricked for the signs of approaching danger—and believe me, there were plenty of them at the Academy!—then running like a rappid in the opposite direction. There was nowhere to run in Master Thengor's apartments, but there were plenty of places to hide. I spied a silver-legged divan against the nearest wall and dived beneath its thickly cushioned shelter just as an ear-splitting *crack!* shattered the solemn peace of the death-chamber.

When I dared to peer out, I saw that where Poldi Flamesinger had stood there was now only a slowly cooling heap of ashes. I wasn't entirely sure, but I'd be willing to bet that the dead frog lying on top of the ashes had once been Yro.

From somewhere high up towards the center of the domed chamber, the creaky, raspy voice of an immeasurably old man wheezed with laughter, then croaked, "I may be dying, but I've still got it!"

Slowly I dragged myself out from under the divan. It was the safest place in the room, but for once curiosity got the better of me. This would be my first and last chance to get a really good look at the private apartments of the greatest wizard the world of Orbix had ever known. It was also likely to be my last day at the Academy of High Wizardry, and when Master Thengor's successor sent me home in well-earned disgrace, I figured I'd better bring *something* back for Mother, even if it was only a description of how the masters of magic did their interior decorating.

Following the little incident with Poldi and Yro, there was plenty of room for me to look around and get an unobstructed view. All of the other students were giving the recent blast-site a wide berth, for some reason, even though everyone knew lightning never struck twice in the same place. Not even wizard's lightning. Putting on an expression of deepest mourning, I was free to stare at anything that struck my fancy.

It really was a very impressive room, built in the shape of a tremendous circle. Though the entire student body of the Academy was a trifle crushed and crowded as we milled about on the richly carpeted floor, there was actually space to spare in the wizard's bedchamber. The trouble was, most of that spare space was vertical.

Master Thengor was fond of his comfort, and his chief comfort was getting a good day's sleep. I guess that's why he'd built himself the world's most impressive bed, a bejeweled, silk-strewn monument to the goldsmith's art. It was only fair that such a magnificent gem of furniture have a worthy setting, so Master Thengor placed his bed in the very center of the room at the very top of a towering platform of seven levels. The first of these was planted with a forest of tall jade stems, each topped with a crystal sphere that seemed to give off its own soft radiance.

I leaned over to nudge the nearest student I could reach and asked, "Where are the fire-sprites? I can't see them."

"There are none." His name was Tolly Cursetrader, and although we'd entered the Academy at about the same time, he was almost ready to step up to the blue-robe rank. I didn't even rate a robe at all. He didn't like to talk to me much if he could help it, unless he saw the chance to make fun of me.

"No fire-sprites?" That was silly. I could *see* the glow! "How can there be light without fire-sprites?"

Tolly merely snorted. "That shows what *you* know, you fool ratwhacker. Think our learned master would use such primitive means to light his own private rooms? Ha! Those spheres each contain a filament of a most rare and precious substance created solely by Master Thengor's art. He calls it *illuminum*. There's nothing lighter."

"Wow." My eyes went on to the next level of the dying wizard's bed. Here a second ring of stemmed spheres rose up, but these contained more familiar captives. Even as poor a student as I am could recognize fire-sprites, water-willies, earth-glums, and wind-puffers, the four basic breeds of elemental on Orbix. A great wizard always kept a good supply of assorted elementals on hand, in case he might want their services at any moment of the day or night. There were also one or two different sorts of creature in some of the globes—not elementals, and nothing I could identify from my schoolroom lessons. I didn't think any more about them.

The third and fourth levels of the bed contained Master Thengor's children and their servants. *Contained* was the right word. If I squinted, I could just see the outline of a faintly golden transparent barricade sealing in the wizard's horde of children. Just the way the second-level elementals were kept quiet and out of the way in their crystal globes, the children fought and tumbled and pinched and squealed and howled without a single sound escaping or anyone but their nursemaids and tutors having to suffer. Well, it was what they got paid for.

Judging from the looks on the nursemaids' and tutors' faces, they weren't paid nearly enough.

"See it, do you?" Tolly remarked. "That yellowish glassy stuff keeping them in? It *should* be invisible, but it's not quite. That means the end's almost here."

"Oh, yes, definitely." I agreed with Tolly quickly, so that he couldn't guess that I had no idea what he was talking about. Lady Inivria too had said that *something* was growing visible, and that meant that her husband's death was near, but what that *something* might be . . . Don't ask me.

"And we're not the only ones who know it," Tolly went on. "Just look at *them*, next two levels up from the brats under glass. *They* know."

He nodded and I looked. On the fifth level, Master Thengor's twenty-three official mistresses and concubines sat bewailing their lord's approaching death. I had to admire the way they managed to do it without smearing their eye makeup or mussing their hair. While they wailed—never too shrilly—they artfully ripped their bright veils just enough to show off their best features. I had to admire that, too.

All of this was for the benefit of the gentlemen one level higher up. These black-gowned worthies were the great wizard's closest professional associates, summoned to witness his death. (Master Thengor had no friends. The one lesson he taught us over and over and over again was that the word for a wizard with a lot of friends is *corpse*.) The men of magic paced majestically around and around their special level of Master Thengor's bed, muttering darkly. They only paused to exchange a grim nod with one another or a flirtatious "Yoo hoo!" with the soon-to-be-unemployed ladies one level below them.

Finally, at the pinnacle of the seven-layered platform, just under the cavernous chamber's stained-glass dome, stood the great wizard's bed itself. This topmost level was wide enough to support Thengor's bed, his wife, and six attending physicians from the six schools of healing: herbal, thermal, crystal, mental, dermal, and chiropractic. All of them were staring aghast at the dying wizard's still-smoking handiwork down at ground level.

"My lord, you should not tire yourself so." Lady Inivria sounded tired enough for the both of them. After so many years, she had to know that the acoustics of the great apartment were good enough so that her smallest, most private whisper could be heard by everyone in the room. Maybe she didn't care. "A simple reprimand would have been enough. You will wear yourself out before you have settled all of your affairs."

"What? What's that, wife?" Death or no death, Master Thengor still had enough cantankerousness in him for a herd of bulls with bedsores. "Telling *me* what to do, are you? Do you recall what happened to the last woman who tried to tell *me* something?"

The lady Inivria sighed. "The last woman who tried to tell you something was Mistress Jeska Reapercheat, the finest physician in all of Orbix. She told you not to eat so many stewed lampreys."

Thengor turned sullen. "I like stewed lampreys."

"Too bad that they didn't like you, or you wouldn't be dying of them now. My love," she added without much feeling. "Nor would poor Mistress Reapercheat be scattered all over five kingdoms."

Thengor chortled. "Couldn't cheat her way out of *that*! Ha! Just like all these squizzle-headed doctors: Go against their advice and they fly all to pieces. Nerve of the woman. I told her I *like* stewed lampreys."

Inivria sighed again. "Yes, dearest. You also said that you'd like to see all of your students once more before you died. I've brought them in, just as you asked. Now what do you want me to do with them?"

The old wizard's black eyes twinkled. "Have 'em line up," he said. "Put 'em in order of accomplishment and let them come past me, one by one."

Inivria's eyes narrowed with suspicion. "You're not going to kill them off, are you?"

"Really, wife, the very idea!" Thengor made a rude sound with his tongue. "Why bother? We've already collected their tuition for the full year, and the Academy rules say no refunds. No, let 'em live, let 'em live. I just want to tell the lower grades where they can sign up to continue their studies, recommend a few of the upperclassmen to become apprentices to old Master Gurf, Master Dwimmermet, Master Whatzisbeard there—the one playing winkies with Brinda Sweethands and—Hey! I see that! Stop it, you two! I'm not dead yet, Brinda my girl, and if you think you and that old goat are hot stuff now, you'll learn that I've still got a little lightning bolt tucked away for a rainy day and it's got *your* names on it!"

His anger exhausted him and he sank back amid his pillows in a coughing fit. The six healers buzzed around him like green-gowned bees. And then, while they applied their potions and their hot compresses and their stones of power and their therapeutic massages, it happened.

"Look! There it is!" Tolly Cursetrader forgot our widely different ranks in the wonder of the moment and grabbed my arm while he pointed eagerly.

"There's what?" I asked. I gazed up to the very top of Master Thengor's bed in bewilderment.

Something extremely strange had happened. Without warning, from out of nowhere, an enormous cloud the color of fresh honey appeared above the wizard's bed. It turned and tumbled, knotted itself up small, and spread out like a big, fluffy quilt. Sometimes it seemed to form a whirlpool ready to suck up Master Thengor and all his household into another world and sometimes it looked as if it had a gigantic face.

Not a very friendly face, either.

I gasped and trembled. "What *is* that?"

"What is that?" Tolly echoed. "Did I hear you right? Do you honestly mean you don't know what that is?"

I shook my head miserably, ashamed. In all the years since Mother decided I should become a wizard, my closest companion at the Academy had always been my ignorance.

Tolly didn't even bother to lower his voice when he laughed in my face. "Why, you thick-skulled ratwhacker, that's pure Majyk!"

"Magic?" I repeated. Because that's what I thought he said. (Both words sound alike to most people, like *bear* and *bare*. They sure sounded alike to me. Of course, as everyone from Master Thengor on down to Velma Chiefcook was fond of telling me, what did *I* know?)

"Majyk," Tolly said, making the word sound as if it tasted

delicious. Somehow I got the idea that he wasn't just talking about pulling-rappids-out-of-a-hatch tricks.

"You want to spell that?" I suggested. He did. I didn't know what to say, so I didn't say anything except, "Huh?"

He frowned. "You really don't know what—? Oh. Yeah. I guess you wouldn't. They never tell us anything about Majyk until we've shown ourselves to be worthy." He didn't have to add, *That lets you out.*

"I don't understand," I said. So what else was new?

"I can't believe one of Master Thengor's students doesn't know beans about Majyk. I mean, *I* was told the day after I was named Most Likely to Raise the Dead in the yearbook. I don't mean the Dead *in* the yearbook—that was Gil Zombificator, and he was killed when he raised old Master Fortslop, the one who was always such a pain in the robes about all wizards keeping their hair a decent length, down to the shoulders minimum, and it was summer and Gil had just had a haircut and Fortslop got one look at him with his ears sticking out the way they did, and dead or alive, the old slug was still able to yank away enough of Gil's Majyk so he could blast the poor fellow all the way to—Oh, never mind all that."

"I still don't get it." What I really didn't get was how Tolly spewed out so many words at a gulp.

"No? You really must be as big a ratwhacker as the other fellows say you are. Hmmm." Tolly considered. "I don't think it would hurt anything if I gave you the basics. You couldn't do any harm with the knowledge, and since you're likely to be booted out of the Academy as soon as Master Thengor's cold, it won't be like I'm telling tales out of school, so to speak. Ha, ha."

"Ha, ha," I repeated dutifully. Part of me wished I'd paid more attention when Dad tried to teach me how to use a broadsword. For once in my life there was something I *wanted* to chop up into small, gooey slices.

"Majyk," Tolly breathed. He stared at the golden cloud above Master Thengor's bed, and his beady blue eyes began to shine with greed. "It's the stuff that puts the spunk in our spells, the energy in our enchantments, the charge in our charms, the can-do in our cantrips. Without it, we wizards are nothing. We could wag our wands until the unicorns come home, but if we didn't have a little Majyk, we wouldn't be able to turn snakes into snacks or cats into catsup!"

"Cats are mythological creatures," I said, reciting one of my earliest lessons from Elementary Bestiary. I was desperate to show

Tolly that I knew *something*. "They have nine lives, they wear boots, they steal the breath from sleeping babies, they always land on their feet, their only natural enemy is curiosity, and they don't really exist."

Tolly gave me a sharp jab in the arm. "*I* know that! I only meant—Oh, forget it. No use explaining anything to *you*." He thrust his hand into his robes and pulled out a crumpled piece of paper. "See?"

"Gosh!" I was impressed. "When did you get your poetic license, Tolly?"

"Oh, it's easy enough to come by if a man's got a little drive." He looked mighty pleased with himself as he tucked it away again. "So, think you understand Majyk *now*, ratwhacker?"

I lowered my head. I hated the way Tolly talked down to me, but why should he be any different from everyone else? And what could I do about it, anyway?

From the first day I came to Master Thengor's Academy of High Wizardry, I learned that it never paid to talk back to anyone inside the ivory-covered walls. If I tried it with the non-magic-using servants, they were all bigger than me and quick to hit. If I tried it with the other students, most of whom I could've beaten in a fair fight, they all had more magical talent than me and they weren't shy about using it to make my life miserable.

Once, when a senior turned me into a mouse and I went to complain to Master Thengor, the old wizard told me it was my own fault for not having mastered a simple shielding spell. Then he sicced Rosco on me. I spent the rest of the week in a mouse hole until a letter from my mother reminded Thengor that no one paid tuition to educate a rodent and the wizard changed me back to human form.

Only now . . . What was it that Tolly had said? How no magician could do anything if he didn't have Majyk? "That's not fair!" I exclaimed.

"What's not fair?"

"Majyk, that's what. I mean, here I've been going to classes and memorizing ten gazillion gobbledegook spells until my tongue's in a knot, and practicing mystical gestures and arcane hand-signs and necromantic finger-wiggles until I look like an idiot, and all along I couldn't have done *anything* magical unless I had some of that Majyk-stuff!"

"Kendar," Tolly said with a big, oily grin on his face. "Kendar, were you ever taught how to use a sword?"

"Sure, I was! I'm a Gangle!" I stood tall, proud of my

lower-upper-middle-noble-class heritage. "I was just five when Dad got me started."

"And tell me, did your father give you a *real* sword to start with?"

"Well . . . no. Of course not. I told you I was only fi—"

"When *did* you get to use a real sword?" He was enjoying this, the toad.

"Why, just as soon as Dad could tell that I was ready to control it and that I wouldn't hurt myself or any innocent bystanders with—with—with—"

Damn!

Tolly chuckled. "Control, that's the key. That's why we can see all of Master Thengor's Majyk now that he's dying. The greatest wizards keep their Majyk invisible. After all, it's no one's business but your own how much of it you've got, right? Silly to tempt a more powerful wizard into trying to take it away from you. Although I hear tell that there's some wizards great enough to *sense* when there's wild Majyk about; they can dowse for it, like."

"Is that how you got your Majyk, Tolly?"

"Me? Naaahh. It was a gift from Master Thengor. He gives all his students some seed-Majyk for starters, as soon as he thinks we're ready to handle it. If we want to get any more, it's up to us."

"You mean a wizard can just *give* Majyk away?"

Tolly nodded. "I hear there's more to it than that, but I'm only halfway through my Principles of Majyk course."

All of a sudden, I felt nervous. So that was why we'd been called in! Master Thengor was going to divvy up all his lifetime of accumulated Majyk before he died and give it to us. I'd finally have what it took to work spells, perform enchantments, lay curses, and do all of those other wizardly things Mother wanted me to master.

Mother wanted it; did I?

My dad, Sir Lucius Parkland Gangle, was always going on about how the only thing prettier than a big fat inheritance was a big fat stag with an arrow through its heart, but I could see nothing pretty about the gift that Master Thengor was going to give away before he died. The longer I looked at the massed and visible load of Majyk floating over his bed, the more it frightened me. All that power, and once I had some—even the littlest bit—no more excuses.

Up on the platform, the golden cloud began to fade until it was a ghost of itself. Master Thengor made an effort and sat up straighter against his pillows. The Majyk vanished from sight.

"All right, all right, that's enough, let a man die in peace, can't you?" He swatted at the healers until they withdrew a few paces from the bedside. "Well?" he demanded of the lady Inivria. "Are you going to bring me my students or am I going to give you purple scales again?"

"By your leave, my lord." Inivria reached down the front of her silks and pulled up a small silver whistle on a matching chain. "All right, all of you robes, line up by rank!" she bellowed. To her husband she said, "I'll just get the windows open, shall I, so your soul can fly out in whatever direction it likes? When you die. It's going to be soon, you know. Darling."

"Purple scales," Master Thengor muttered. "Stewed lamprey with purple scales." But he didn't try to stop her when she commanded the servants to open all of the stained glass panels on the big dome over his bed.

Tolly moved away from me fast, making for his place near the front of the line as we students arranged ourselves. While we shifted around, a path was cleared for us all the way up to the seven levels of Master Thengor's bed. Zoltan Fiendlord was in the lead, as always.

You can guess where I was. Unfortunately, so could Velma Chiefcook. I don't know who let her in, but there she was, standing between me and Orton Spoonbender, the *second*-worst student at the Academy.

"Not so fast, you slippery ratwhacker! You've got no business here. Our mistress said the *robes* was to line up by rank. I don't see you wearing any such of a thing as a robe, do you?"

She was right. Even Orton Spoonbender was a good enough student to have earned a robe, any color robe. After six years at Master Thengor's Academy of High Wizardry I was still stuck in the tunic-and-trousers stage.

I let her grab me by the scruff of the neck and march me out double-time. She was right: I didn't have any business being there. Majyk wasn't something you gave away to just *anybody*; I knew that now. And to tell you the truth, even if Master Thengor did give me a crumb of Majyk from his deathbed out of pity, I wasn't too sure I wanted it. If I hadn't earned any Majyk on my own in six years, it was too late to have any now.

Dad liked to say, "A Gangle never gives up! A Gangle never quits! A Gangle never throws in the towel!"

On the other hand, he also said, "Of course if you're no good at something, lay off. There ain't no sense being a damn fool about things. Stick to what you can do best."

I guess we all want to do what we're best at, and among wizards we usually earn a name that lets other people know our specialty. Throwing curses, turning folks into frogs, flying through the air, making demons do anything you want—none of that seemed to be it for me, with or without Majyk. That didn't mean I hadn't earned a name for being good at *something*.

"Here," Velma said when she'd gotten me down to the kitchens. I took the heavy stick from her work-roughened hands. "There," she said, pointing to a little three-legged stool in the corner. I sat down and saw the hole in the wall right away. It was a big one. I held my weapon in both hands and got ready.

They called me Ratwhacker for a reason, you know.

CHAPTER ——————— 2

THE GREATEST THING ABOUT RATWHACKING IS—
  The best thing about ratwhacking is—
  Why I Love Ratwhacking, by Kendar Gan—
  Why I Like—
  Why I Don't Really Mind—
  Why I Don't Actually Wish I Were Dead All the Time I Have to Waste Squatting in Front of Rat Holes With a Big Stick Down Here in These Big, Smelly Kitchens, Ratwha—
  All right, all right, the least rotten thing about ratwhacking is, you get to hear some pretty good kitchen gossip. Master Thengor always taught us that knowledge is power, especially if you can get your hands on knowledge you weren't supposed to have in the first place. The student wizard who could use his skills to eavesdrop and bring back a juicy piece of news from the women's quarters got a big fat A.

  Then there was the sad case of Thelfel Leatherwing, who could change himself into a bat. He used to hang upside-down from the rafters just outside Lady Inivria's rooms, hoping for that A by learning something nasty about our master's wife. I remember him coming back into the dormitory one night, bragging about how he was *almost* sure that Lady Inivria had a lover and that he was *this close* to figuring out who it was.

  "She got a gift today," he said. "It was a golden cage with a robin in it. I'll bet *he* sent it. And I'll bet my life he shows up tonight, which is when I'll find out who he is. Then I'll tell Master Thengor."

  "I wouldn't do that if I were you, Thelfel," Orton Spoonbender counseled. "What if he's a wizard, too? What if he catches you and—?"

16

Thelfel scoffed at the thought. "These wizards are a superstitious, cowardly lot. I have nothing to fear." So saying, he leaped to the windowsill, slid down the drainpipe outside, turned into a bat halfway down, and glided off into the night.

That was the last time we saw him alive. The head gardener found the mauled body of a bat under Lady Inivria's window next morning. I was ratwhacking again, which was why I heard him tell Velma Chiefcook, "Strangest thing you ever did see. Looked like the poor critter'd been torn all to pieces by a giant bird."

"Birds don't kill bats," Velma sneered. "This your notion of a joke?"

"A fine joker I'd make! Tell that to the big pile o' robin feathers I found all over the body," the gardener shot back. He might've said more, except he was interrupted by the arrival of the blacksmith who Master Thengor had hired to put bars over Lady Inivria's windows.

So anyhow, there I sat, as I'd sat so many times before, waiting for some luckless rat to stick his whiskered nose out of the hole and get his skull bashed in. While I waited, eyes on the hole, I kept my ears pricked for any useful servants' chatter behind me. I didn't have long to wait.

"—called all the young robes up there to his deathbed," said Bini, the girl Velma was training in the art of slow poisoning—I mean, cookery. Bini hadn't been with us long enough to have earned any kind of a name. She did too many different tasks about the kitchens for any one specialty to stick out yet. (If somebody'd asked me, I could've told them that Bini had *two* specialties that were sticking out just fine, but that's the way to get your head walloped with a ladle.)

Velma snorted. "That's old news, Bini m'girl. When I was up there, I saw 'em lining up to get their share of the old man's Majyk."

She pronounced the word as if she knew what she was talking about. Did *everyone* in this entire sprawling household know about Majyk but me? That hurt.

"Won't be no shares about it," Bini said. She sounded confident.

"Here! What d'you mean by that?"

"Oh, nothing." I didn't dare turn around to look at her, but I could guess that she was probably wearing a smug I-know-something-*you*-don't-know expression. Then I heard a sharp *whap!* followed by a sharper "*Ow!* Why'd you hit me for, Missus Vee?"

"For being a pesky little closemouthed twit, is why! You know something, you spit it out so's we can all know." A chorus of agreement went up from the nine or ten other servants in that part of Master Thengor's kitchens. When you spend your whole life peeling spuds or cutting up meat or taking care of the treadmill dog who turns the roasting spit or fetching firewood and water, you want every scrap of entertainment you can get.

"Orright." Bini gave in fast. I bet she liked all the attention. "Well, these past few weeks, I been walking out with that nice young Master Zollie, and—"

"What 'Master Zollie' is this?" Velma sounded angry and suspicious. "You don't mean Zoltan Fiendlord, do you?"

"He said to call him Zollie," Bini said in her own defense.

"I don't care did he tell you to call him a palsied woodchuck! Around here we don't call no student *Master*, no matter how big a head full of wind he's got, until he's officially promoted and given his own silver wand by the Council! Hmph! *Master* Zollie, my trembling rosy aspic."

I heard one of the meat-choppers make a rude noise and say, "Aw, Velma, you're just mad 'cause he took the bone outa yer brisket in front of all the students. Talk of how you was on yer knees afore him, sobbin' fer mercy, got down here faster'n creamed squash through a goose."

"*Walkin' out* with Zoltan Fiendlord, was she?" came another man's voice—it sounded like the head gardener again—followed by crude laughter. "How much *walkin'* you do, Bini?"

I stole a quick glance over my shoulder in time to see the fellow stoking the fire grin and say, "Onliest girl I ever knew could walk with her feet kickin' up bareheeled in the—"

"Zollie wouldn't like to hear you talk about me that way," was all Bini replied, very softly. Everyone got suddenly quiet. "Like I was saying, Zollie told me there ain't gonna be no silly peel-and-chop when it comes to Master Thengor passing on his Majyk. Oh, there might be one or two small parcels of the stuff handed out to some of the other wizards—a courtesy, like—but when simmer comes to seethe, Master Thengor's gonna give the whole hog's load to just one man."

No one had to say another word or mention any names. They knew.

"But—" Velma Chiefcook's quavery voice was the first to break the shocked silence. "But—but why?"

The meat-chopper laughed nervously. "Thought you heard all them tales 'bout how Zoltan's the old man's son."

"Aye, but not legal. Born out of wedlock, he was, and never once did old Master Thengor say out in public that he's Fiendlord's dad," the fire-stoker replied.

"That's don't mean nothin'." The meat-chopper's cleaver rose and fell after every second word. "Don't take no hawk to see that them two's as alike as one short rib to the next."

"Two peas in a pod," Velma agreed.

"Twigs off the same branch," the fire-stoker put in.

The wine steward nodded. "Two cups of the same vintage."

"Two rats from the same hole," I mumbled, and hoped no one heard me.

"Master Thengor can't leave Zoltan the lion's share of his Majyk," Velma objected. "He's got kids he ain't even used yet, some of 'em legal, born to his true wife, Lady Inivria."

"And all of 'em too lazy to study wizardly lore, or too interested in other things, or too young to care." The meat-chopper hacked off a big, bloody hunk from the slab in front of him and tossed it to the servant manning the roasting spits.

There was a lot of cooking going on lately, more than usual. Besides all of the visiting wizards and doctors called in to attend the old man's deathbed, there were also lots of other guests in the palace for the occasion: courtiers sent by our good King Steffan, to honor the death of his chief wizard; famous wandering minstrels from a dozen kingdoms who had come to write *The Ballad of Wizard Thengor* just as soon as there was no more Wizard Thengor around to turn them into worms if he didn't like what they sang about him; creditors who'd been too scared of the old man to demand that he pay back every copper he owed them, but who wouldn't be too scared to help themselves from Thengor's treasury once he was dead. (I bet they were in for a surprise when Zoltan got all of Thengor's Majyk and used it to hold onto all of Thengor's treasure.)

Anyway, according to the sacred laws of hospitality, they all had to be fed. A tremendous feast would take place in Master Thengor's palace as soon as the old man's soul took flight. The feast was supposedly to celebrate the freedom of the wizard's spirit, but we all knew whose freedom we'd really be celebrating. As chief cook, Velma should have been overseeing the work of the other servants in the seven other kitchens. Instead, Bini's calm announcement about "Master Zollie" left her frozen where she stood.

"But he—he—Zoltan—Master Zoltan—if he gets nigh all

Master Thengor's Majyk and adds it to what he's got of his own,
then he'll be—"

"The greatest, most powerful wizard on Orbix." Bini said it for
her. "More powerful, even, than Master Thengor ever was."

"And the most dangerous," the meat-chopper muttered. He
lifted his cleaver again, then screamed and jumped onto the
chopping block.

A fat black rat scampered across the floor, a chunk of liver in its
teeth.

The kitchen was a riot of yelling women and running men. The
meat-chopper stood on top of his block waving his cleaver and
shouting things like, "There he goes! Get 'im! I'll stay up here
so—so's I can see 'im better an' tell you where he's got to!" The
treadmill dog stopped running and began to bark furiously,
lunging on the leash that tied him in place. With the treadmill at
a standstill, the roasting spits stopped turning and the meat began
to burn. Velma threw a squash. Bini grabbed a broom and chased
the rat, but he ducked under her skirts and vanished into a hole on
the other side of the woodpile.

I didn't move; I just hunched up my shoulders and closed my
eyes. I knew what was coming.

WHAP!

"You empty-headed idiot!" Velma shook the ladle at me, ready
to let me have another smack. "What're you doing, daydreaming?
That's not what you're here for, Ratwhacker, and don't act like
you don't know it!"

"But that rat didn't come out of *this* hole, Velma, honest!" I
protested.

WHAP!

"And how would you know if it did? *I* saw you! I saw as how
you was woolgathering, spying on honest, hard-working folk
when you should've been minding your own chores."

"But you know this isn't the only rat hole in the kitchens." The
back of my head was smarting something awful. Velma had a
heavy hand with that ladle. "It's not my fault if the rats decide not
to come out of the one hole I'm watching."

WHAP!

"Ow," I said. "You want to take it a little easy with that
ladle?"

"You hear me, Kendar Ratwhacker, and you hear me good and
proper." Velma loomed over me like a brick wall. A really ugly
brick wall. "Down here, your excuses don't cut no carrots. I give

a lad a job, he'd best do it, and do it right. Everyone says as how you're going to be beating road dust back to that fancy-prancy family of yours as soon as Master Thengor's dead, but until that happens, you're *mine*. I don't give two poppyseeds *who* your old man is; long as you work for me, you either show some results or you'll *pray* for this ladle!''

''But—'' I started to say. Velma raised the ladle again. ''Uh, what sort of results, exactly?'' I asked meekly.

''If I don't see a dead rat on my worktable by the time Master Thengor's funeral feast gets under way, you'd best crawl into that hole yourself and pull it in after you.'' With that, Velma stalked off to help the meat-chopper down off the butcher-block.

I turned back to the rat hole, rubbing my sore head with one hand and holding my ratwhacking stick awkwardly with the other. The next set of whiskers that popped out of that hole would belong to the unluckiest rat on Orbix.

I tried to concentrate on my work, but it was hard to do. Staring at a big black hole is boring. There were too many distractions. Upstairs servants kept running down into the kitchens with fresh news about what was happening in Master Thengor's apartment. Once Lady Inivria had the students in line and told them to march up to the topmost level of the great bed, the dying wizard had seemed to change his mind. Instead of handing out bits and pieces of his Majyk, he began to give a farewell speech. He was still giving it. The latest report was that a couple of the lowest-ranking students had fallen asleep and tumbled down several platform levels. Even Zoltan Fiendlord had summoned up one of his smaller demons and made the monster pinch him every few moments, just so he could keep his eyes open.

''Just like the old lemon,'' Velma grumbled. ''Always did like to make a body suffer.''

''Well, he can't keep it up forever,'' the gardener said.

I knew the feeling. There's something about staring at a rat hole that gets to you, after a while. This one in particular had a funny effect on me. It looked different than any other hole I'd ever watched. Blacker. Deeper. Colder. The edges weren't all rough, the way a proper gnawed-out rat hole is. It didn't look like it had been gnawed out at all; it looked—I don't know—as if something worse than rats had put it there.

That was a silly thought, and I told myself to snap out of it. *This is a regular rat hole, Kendar, you jerk*, I thought. *It's just—just made by neater rats, that's all.*

And as if to prove me right, at that very moment the biggest, boldest, *weirdest* rat I'd ever seen stuck his whiskery pink nose out of the hole and stared at me with huge green eyes.

I'll say it was weird. Rats don't have pointed ears. Rats don't have fur on their tails and paws. Rats don't have triangular heads and short noses. Rats don't open their mouths to hiss at people, and they don't have white, needle-shaped teeth instead of big yellow chisels. If I didn't know any better, I'd have said it wasn't a rat at all.

But what else could it be? I mean, it was coming out of a rat hole. Yes, no doubt about it, this was definitely one weird rat; and weird or not, I knew my duty.

"Heeere, ratty," I cajoled, tightening my grip on the stick. "Niiiiice ratty. Come on out all the way and Uncle Kendar's going to introduce you to Mister Stick so Auntie Velma won't hit me in the head with Mister Ladle anymore. Cooooome, ratty, ratty, ratty."

"*Meow!*" said the rat, and dashed out of the hole.

Fast? Don't ask. Most rats are fast, but this one had them all beat. It darted under my stool and out the other side so quickly that I fell over backwards trying to hit it. I didn't waste any time on my backside, I just picked myself up and took off after my quarry.

The rat ran straight across the kitchen floor; I ran after it. The rat bounded up the stairs to the feasting chamber with me in hot pursuit. The rat zipped between the feet of an upstairs servant and I knocked him out of my way, gasping an apology. We raced the length of the feasting chamber and out into the great hall in half a breath. I was swinging my ratwhacking stick while I ran. I kept missing.

Well, I kept missing the *rat*, but I did a mighty good job on three vases, one crystal ball, and the nose off a plaster bust of Master Thengor.

On we ran, right for the brass-bound doors of Master Thengor's bedchamber. I backpedaled, afraid we'd crash, but just as we were a stick's swing away someone opened the left-hand door. It was one of Master Thengor's mistresses, Brinda Sweethands, cursing up a bonfire. She had poor Rosco by the throat and was choking the life out of the old man's owl-familiar. I got just a glimpse of what Rosco had done to Brinda's expensive silk robes before the rat slipped between the open doors and I sprinted after.

The rat streaked straight through the forest of legs inside, heading for the high ground; I had to take the harder route. The servant who tried to stand between me and the old man's seven-layered bed got whammed in the ribs with my stick. It was an accident. I shattered two of Master Thengor's rare illuminum spheres on the first level when I tried to whack the rat. It was an accident. I took out two globes holding fire-sprites and one containing a water-willy on the backswing. It was an accident. A dense cloud of steam went up when the freed water-willy grabbed both of the fire-sprites, blinding everyone nearby, so it wasn't really my fault when the rat and I smashed through the glassy shields around Master Thengor's kids and trampled one of the tutors. I'm telling you, it was an *accident*!

You'd think my fellow-students, waiting in single file all the way up the seven levels, would see what was going on and either help me or get out of the way, but nooooooo. They just stood there, so I couldn't help it when my stick sort of kept knocking them down. Some people!

And when three of Master Thengor's mistresses jumped off their knees and started screaming as the rat zoomed past them, and when they all grabbed hold of the wizards on the next level up and hollered for them to *do* something, and when the wizards *and* the ladies got so tangled in each other's long robes that it only took the teensiest little touch of my stick to send them all rolling down the stairs, picking off some more of the Academy students on the way down—

Oh yeah, right, sure, blame *me*. I was just trying to do my job. After six years of everyone saying "Ratwhacker never pays attention," you'd think they'd be pleased with the change. For once in my life I was concentrating on something, paying so much attention to whacking that rat into the next kingdom that nothing else mattered. Where the rat went, I went; what the rat did, I did. Only the rat was smaller.

I didn't *want* to knock that doctor of thermal medicine off the topmost level. I couldn't *predict* he was going to scream that loud or bounce that high. I didn't *know* that all the fuss he made would frighten that weird rat so badly. I couldn't *swear* the beast was going to run around and around Master Thengor's bed so that I kept bumping into the other five healers plus Zoltan and Lady Inivria while I tried to whack it. I couldn't *tell* that it was all going to get Master Thengor so furious that his face would go all purple like that. Hey, I could hardly see Master Thengor's face, because the thick golden cloud hovering over his bed was getting thicker and darker and lower and lower and—

The rat leaped. So did I.
BANG!
Or maybe SPLORSH! I don't remember.
It wasn't my fault. Honest.

CHAPTER ——————— 3

"IT WAS AN ACCIDENT," I MUMBLED, FLAT ON MY BACK with my ratwhacking stick lying across my stomach. I tried to sit up, but I could only make it onto my elbows. My legs weren't listening to me. They felt like a bear had fallen on top of them.

My eyes weren't doing too well, either. The lids were down and wanted to stay down. Every time I tried to open them, the smallest sliver of light stabbed itself all the way through to the back of my skull like a spearhead. All I wanted to do was keep my eyes shut, lie back down, and go to sleep until I felt better.

I would have, too, if not for all the screaming.

I forced my eyes open. There was too much light, and I was looking right straight up into it. That was funny. I could've sworn there used to be a huge domed roof covering Master Thengor's bedchamber. I distinctly recalled Lady Inivria ordering the servants to open up the stained-glass windows in the dome so the old man's soul could fly out one of them when the time came.

Now there were no windows and no dome, just the jagged teeth of broken stone and shattered glass. The screaming was still there. I flicked a couple of pieces of stained glass off my tunic and used my stick to help me stand up.

My legs bent under me. The floor felt lumpy and it kept bouncing and shifting under my feet. Even when I leaned on my stick to steady myself, I didn't feel secure. Had the same disaster that blew away the roof of Master Thengor's bedchamber also done something horrible to the floor? I looked down.

Oh. It wasn't the floor I was standing on; it was Master Thengor's bed. That explained why it felt so springy. Master Thengor was still in it. That explained the lumps.

"I'm sorry, Master Thengor," I said, trying to hide behind my stick. I waited to die. Master Thengor had zapped two students just for bickering at his deathbed. What would he do to me for standing on it?

Nothing, apparently. Master Thengor just lay there with his mouth open and his face gray. I stopped cringing, but the screaming kept right on going strong.

Carefully I climbed off the dead wizard's bed and got my bearings. From where I stood, I could see everything, and most of that was people running away. They weren't all screaming—just the kids and the mistresses and three of the healers and one show-off wind-puffer and Master Dwimmermet. The tutors and nursemaids kept telling everyone, "No running, no pushing, don't forget to take your partner's hand, we'll be counting noses once everyone is safely outside, no need to panic, don't shove, *I* saw that, Sali, and it's two demerits on your record—"

The tutors and nursemaids were also getting pushed, shoved, and trampled by my fleeing fellow-students. Any noses they'd get to count outside would probably be broken ones, and nobody was taking anyone's hand except to yank them away from the doors and get out first. I saw Tolly Cursetrader skewer one poor man with a quill-thin shaft of sizzling green light, just to get him out of the way.

"Wedwel's teeth!" I swore. It wasn't a big oath or a really bad one—Dad would have sneered and Mother would have sent me to my room for uttering our god's name so lightly—but I had to say something. "Why are they running? Why are they screaming? What was it, an earthquake? A tornado? What happened here?"

"You did."

I wasn't expecting an answer, so I jumped as high as my ratwhacking stick when I got one. When I came down, I saw Lady Inivria scowling at me. Her multicolored veils were all tattered and tangled and there was so much plaster dust in her hair, I couldn't tell whether it was black or gray. She was flanked by two of the remaining black-robed wizards. Behind them, Zoltan Fiendlord sat at the edge of the topmost platform, his head in his hands. He was crying. I supposed that he really must have loved his father.

I looked from Master Thengor's wife—I mean widow—to the two wizards. "What did *I* do?"

Lady Inivria gestured at the missing roof. "Guess."

I raised my eyes. There was a nice fresh spring breeze blowing into the room through the ruined dome. I wish I could've enjoyed it. "Me?" I squeaked. "I did tha—? But how could I—? I never— You don't mean it."

She meant it. Her arms were folded across her chest, her feet were planted firmly apart, and she was glaring at me with enough fire in her eyes to turn King Steffan's whole capital city of Grashgoboum to ashes. You can't get any more sincere-looking than that. "Home-wrecker," she growled.

"My lady, I—I'm sorry." I fell to one knee before her, holding my stick in both hands. "Master Thengor was my favorite teacher—" My *only* teacher. "I would never harm him on purpose!" Not and live to tell about it afterwards. "If anything I did caused his death, you have to believe me, it was an accident!"

"Really?" She unfolded her arms slowly. "What a pity. For any deliberate damage you might've done to my late husband, I'd have given you a reward. I was talking about how you've wrecked my *home*." She took a step towards me. "Young man, you will use what you've got to repair it at once."

One of the two wizards—the handsomer one, Master Benidorm—caught the lady's elbow and murmured, "Inivria, do you think it's wise? The power he has—"

"Oh, stop worrying!" She jerked her arm away. "I know this puppy. He's called Kendar Ratwhacker, which should give you some idea. Look, he's not even in his first robes yet, not after six years with us! He'll do as he's told, if he wants to live, then you and Master Gurf can take it all away from him, send him packing, and we'll be free to sell it in pieces to the highest bidders." She gave poor Zoltan a disdainful smile and added, "How much pocket money do *you* have, Zoltan darling?"

"It was *mine*!" Zoltan shouted, his angry face wet with tears. "It was supposed to come to *me*!"

"Did you ever hear the story of the three eggs?" Lady Inivria asked sweetly. "Two bad."

Zoltan said something so foul that even my dad would've been impressed. The lady shrugged it off, all her attention on me. "Well, I'm waiting," she said. "You've got the means; fix it."

I looked at the gaping roof, then at the stick in my hands. Either the lady had bizarre ideas about the proper tools for the job or she knew something I didn't know. Again.

Master Benidorm sidled up to her. "I don't think he knows what he's got," he said softly.

"Ratwhacker? He never did." A cold smile curved her lips. "You're right, love. I thought it would save you some energy to have him do the dirty work of spellcasting, but if he's that ignorant—Well, no use wasting any more time. Take it away from him and let's get things back in order."

Master Benidorm nodded. "Right, then." He pushed his sleeves back up to the elbows and started mumbling a long string of those odd-sounding syllables that are every great wizard's warm-up exercises for some really spectacular enchantment. The pointed tip of his hat twitched like a lizard's tail, wiggling faster and faster the longer and louder he went rolling through his recitation. The stream of sound pouring from his lips all sounded like "Arglebarglegarfnongwizwozzleblat" to me.

"I beg your pardon, old man," said Master Gurf, laying a hand on Master Benidorm's arm. "I think you meant to say 'Arglebarglegarf*ning*wizwozzle*blot*,' didn't you?"

Master Benidorm's hat stopped twitching. His eyebrows came together in a murderous frown. "I know what I'm doing, Gurf," he growled.

"To be sure, to be sure." The older wizard twiddled his thumbs and was jolly enough for a whole wagonload of tax-collectors. "And what a shame that would be, if I'd have to tell the Council that you were trying to remove young Ratwhacker's Majyk while deliberately using the first person *singular* form of the spell. Our noble colleagues wouldn't like to hear that at all. It would look as if you were trying to keep the whole of Master Thengor's Majyk for yourself." He stopped twiddling his thumbs and plucked off his own hat. Underneath the star-strewn black silk cone sat a miniature goblin. It was the color of rotting mushrooms, except for a fine set of grinning green teeth.

I'd grin too, if I had a loaded crossbow aimed at Master Benidorm's heart.

"It would also mean that I was within my rights to have my familiar slay you on the spot. The Council doesn't like pigs, Beni. Now, shall we try that spell again, from the top?" Master Gurf suggested pleasantly, popping his hat back over the goblin. "This time we'll do it together, just to make sure you don't wind up weighed down with all of this poor, unlucky lad's burden of Majyk."

"Majyk?" I squeaked. No one heard me. People have to listen to you before they can hear you, and they have to realize you're there before they even bother listening.

The wizards joined forces, their voices rising and falling in perfect unison as they ran through the spell. Their hands traced eerie patterns on the air, patterns that seemed to glow with pale blue fire before they vanished. The tip of Master Benidorm's cap was twitching again, and the tufted ends of the black cord cinching Master Gurf's robe rose up and swayed back and forth like twin serpents.

I tried to make them stop. I was afraid of what they were going to do to me. What was all this talk of Majyk? Majyk and *me*, no less? I didn't have any Majyk! No one at the Academy ever gave me the smallest crumb, speck, or droplet of the stuff—probably a good thing, too. How could they take something away from me I didn't have?

Very painfully, I bet.

(I remember one day, early on in my career at the Academy, when Master Thengor needed some blood for a demonstration and the storeroom was fresh out.

"Kendar," he said, "go fetch me a rock from the garden."

I did as I was told, bringing back a big chunk of granite. "Are you going to show us a different spell, Master Thengor?" I asked.

"Why should I?" he replied.

Like a fool, I said, "Well, because you said we needed blood to make the first spell work, and we don't have any blood, and all you've got there is a rock, and my dad, Lord Lucius Parkland Gangle, always did say that you can't get blood from a—from a—from a—"

I was still stammering like that as Master Thengor wrung the last red drops from the stone in his hand and tossed the dried-out husk aside. "It works with turnips, too," he said.)

So maybe a little casual Majyk had rubbed off on me after so many years at the Academy—you know, like lint—and Master Benidorm and Master Gurf *could* squeeze it out of me if they tried hard enough. Never underestimate a stubborn wizard. I didn't want to find out how hard they'd try; I sure as anything didn't want to end up like Master Thengor's rock. There had to be some mistake. I had to make them see, before all that was left of me was a handful of bone-dust and the few sorry splinters of my stick.

"Masters, you have to listen—!" My words were drowned out by the swelling volume of their chant. The hazy outline of a pair of monstrous, taloned hands formed above their heads. They were perfect, those hands. You could count every wart and hair on them. You could even read the future in the lines on their palms. (I didn't need to read anything to tell what *my* future was going to be if the wizards didn't call off their ugly creation.) The hands reached out for me, closing in on either side.

I picked up my ratwhacking stick, ready to defend myself. I knew it wouldn't do any good, but I refused to just give up. Maybe

I wasn't smart enough to be a wizard, but I was stubborn enough. "Get away from me!" I shouted, waving the stick at them. "Get away or—or you'll be sorry!" I never knew that a pair of disembodied hands could chuckle.

The hands clapped together.

The walls flew apart.

CHAPTER ———————————————— 4

"HALLOOOO UP THERE!" ZOLTAN FIENDLORD CUPPED his hands to his mouth and hailed me. I never thought the day would come when I'd find myself so far above the best student at the Academy of High Wizardry. It only goes to show you that if you live long enough, you'll see everything once, and creamed squash too many times.

"Halloo yourself," I replied, trying to sound dignified. *You* try hanging by the back of your tunic from the top of a shattered stone column just a few handspans below where the roof used to be, pretending that you're doing it on purpose, and see how dignified you can sound! The worst part is keeping the *front* of your tunic from strangling you while you hang there.

Zoltan tilted his head back and regarded me closely. "That was quite a display of sorcery," he said. "I'm impressed. I never knew you had it in you."

Neither did I.

"Oh, it was nothing," I said, looking modest. Inside, I was jumping up and down with glee. Zoltan Fiendlord was impressed with *me*? Bring on the firecracker-breathing dragons, this was a reason to celebrate! If I didn't choke on my tunic first.

"Nothing?" Zoltan repeated. "I wouldn't call it nothing. Such grace! Such artistry! Why, when you blasted those ghostly hands apart, one of them scooped up Master Gurf and launched him like a catapult's payload, clear through the hole in the roof! I wouldn't be surprised to hear he flew all the way to Vicinity City. Inspired, positively inspired. And as for Master Benidorm and Lady Inivria—" He nodded towards one of the few walls left standing. There was a peculiar-shaped hole in the plaster that looked like it

31

had been made by a two-headed, four-armed, four-legged monster. A wizard's hat lay in the dust.

"I didn't—I didn't kill them, did I?" I had to ask, dignity be damned. "You see, I—I meant to use a fairly mild spell—more control that way—and—and—"

Zoltan spread his hands. "You were magnificent. Pure control, unlike any I have ever seen. After you punched them through the wall they were alive enough to run like rapids clear out of the palace. I think they must still be running. You should've seen Inivria." He chortled in his beard. "I didn't know a woman could move that fast while wearing so many veils."

We shared a good laugh, although my half of it came out as a gurgle. Zoltan cocked his head at me again. "I guess you like to breathe the clearer air up there after such a strenuous exercise of your powers."

"Oh, yes," I replied, wishing I could gulp down more air than my ever-tightening tunic-collar allowed. "It's very refreshing."

"Were you, ah, planning to come down any time soon? Talking to you this way is giving me a stiff neck."

A stiff neck? I could give him lessons! "Urrrh—"

"I would consider it an honor, sir, if you would allow me to use my own poor and inadequate measure of wizardry to help you down from your noble perch. If you don't mind."

"Help yourself," I wheezed. Zoltan made a slight, one-handed gesture and I felt something solid slip beneath my feet to lift me up and off the broken column. Very gently the invisible platform brought me back down to the top level of Master Thengor's bed where Zoltan Fiendlord waited. As soon as I had my feet on firm ground once more, the senior student bowed before me. He never bowed so deeply to Lady Inivria. I should have felt flattered.

I didn't. I felt awful. I felt like a miserable little fake.

"Don't do that!" I cried. "I don't deserve it." I grabbed Zoltan's shoulders and made him stand up straight. "I didn't do anything in here on purpose—not the dome, not the hands, not the wizards, nothing! I can't. I don't know how. I'm still not robed, and I never even heard about Majyk until today because—because—" It hurt to admit it, but I had to speak. "Because Master Thengor never thought I was good enough to have any!"

Zoltan Fiendlord smiled. It looked friendly enough, but there was something else lurking behind those curving lips that gave me the cold shivers. It was as if he'd known all along that I had nothing to do with the magical happenings in Master Thengor's bedchamber. His whole song-and-dance about what a wonderful wizard I was had been done just to make me confess what he already knew. Yes, that was it: It was the smile of a man whose greatest pleasure in life is making other people squirm. He was half a head taller than me, too, and it was very disconcerting to see that strange smile bearing down on me like a headsman's half-moon axe.

He sounded pleasant, though, as he said, "Well, Kendar, good enough or not, now you've got it all."

A little while later, Zoltan and I were down in the kitchens hunting up something to eat. "Good thing you didn't destroy the whole palace," he said as he came out of Master Thengor's private pantry with a platter of cold mutton and leftover stewed lampreys. He dropped it to the tabletop in front of me with a dramatic clatter, then pulled up a stool opposite. All of the servants had run away, and we were on our own. "It'll give you somewhere to hide until we can get you fixed up."

"Hide?" I stared at the mound of eel-like fish on the plate. They stared back. I didn't feel hungry. "Why would I want to hide?"

"Think about it." Zoltan snapped his fingers and a dagger appeared. He hacked off a slice of mutton and offered it to me on the point. I declined. "You've got the greatest supply of Majyk that has ever been amassed in the history of our world. That makes you the most powerful wizard on Orbix. Some people might envy you. Some people might be afraid of you. Some people might want to have you working for them, whether you want to or not. Some people—and I'm not mentioning any names—might be a little annoyed that you wrecked their house and threw them out right through the wall. Some people"—he stabbed a lamprey and munched its tail—"might want to complain about you to the Council."

My blood turned to jelly. Even Master Thengor spoke in awe of the Council. Wizards don't work together well, but the Council was made up of those wizards least likely to rip each other's throats out. When an individual wizard made trouble, the Council members pooled their powers and took care of the problem. Then everyone got a day off to go to the funeral.

"I don't get it," I said, waving my hands helplessly. "Why do *I* have Master Thengor's Majyk? I never wanted it. I never asked for it. From what Tolly Cursetrader told me, Master Thengor would sooner die than give me any of it!"

"He did," Zoltan reminded me.

"So how come I've got—"

"It was an accident." He polished off the first lamprey and went to work on a second, delicately spitting out the teeth. "I know it wasn't your fault, Kendar. I was right there; I saw what happened. Master Thengor was about to bequeath his Majyk to—to the proper parties. Poor man, he had sunk very low, very low indeed, and his Majyk was at its most tangible and visible. All for the best, I suppose. It's easier to parcel out visible Majyk, and no arguments later about who got how much."

"Why didn't he use his Majyk to save his life?" I asked.

Zoltan gave me another of those condescending smiles. It was almost like old times, except he hadn't called me "Ratwhacker" once. Yet. "If it were only that simple! As our beloved late teacher told us in Advanced Theoretical Majyk, the amount of abstract research still to be done in the field is astonishing."

"You don't know either," I stated.

That got me a black scowl from Zoltan, but just for a second. The smile came back fast and he replied, "No one knows, not even Master Thengor. Some illnesses respond to treatment by Majyk, and some do not; there's no way of telling which. It's almost as if the Majyk itself decides."

"It's—alive?"

"Don't be silly. No one has ever seen or isolated a Majyk elemental. Now, what we *do* know about Majyk is that it can be tamed and governed by wizards like ourselves. Over the centuries we have learned the words and gestures that make Majyk our servant. Servant, not slave! *That* was a mistake our ancestors made, and it nearly cost us our world."

He nodded towards the kitchen fireplace. There, carved into the mantel, were the words which every householder on Orbix must always have hanging above every fire in his home as a grim reminder of that ancient catastrophe:

LET THAT BE A LESSON TO YOU

I shuddered. Maybe Master Thengor had never taught me about Majyk, but he made sure that every student who entered his Academy of High Wizardry learned the greatest, most fearsome lesson in all the history of Orbix. If nothing else, it taught us that power should never be taken lightly.

"Uh, Zoltan?" I was embarrassed to hear how badly my voice was shaking. "You said we were going to . . . to fix me up? What—what exactly did you mean by that?"

Zoltan slapped his thighs and stood up. "My, my, it is true what they say about stewed lamprey. Excuse me, Kendar, I'll be right back." He strode briskly from the kitchen.

I waited for him, chin on fist, stomach in a knot, and in my case stewed lampreys had nothing to do with it. Master Gurf and Master Benidorm had wanted to fix me up, too. I didn't even know I was broken, but I had the feeling I would be, sooner or later. I looked around the deserted kitchen and felt terribly lonely. I even missed Velma and her ladle. "Why do I need to be *fixed*?" I moaned aloud.

"Got me," said a small, distant voice. "You spray the furniture or what?"

"*What?*" I shouted, jumping from my seat. The empty kitchen threw back the echoes of my cry. "Who's there?" *There . . . there . . . there . . .* came the fading answer. "Where are you?"

"Calm down, Kendar, I'm right here," said Zoltan, coming out of the shadows to rejoin me at the table. "Sorry about that. It took me a while in the close-closet to realize that your little, ah, demonstration of power scared away every last living elemental in the palace. The first thing we ought to do after we take care of your problem is summon up a team of water-willies or forget about flushing that—"

"What is my *problem*?" I shouted.

Zoltan's teeth showed in a thin white line between black moustache and blacker beard. "For one thing, I'd say temper. Sit down, please." I did. "But there, I'd say you already know what your problem is: You've got Master Thengor's Majyk."

"I do *not*." Even as I said it, I knew I was wrong. The evidence was scattered all over the ruined palace. "I mean, if he didn't give it to me, how did I get it?"

"Think," said Zoltan, and waved his dagger over the leftovers. Immediately the lampreys began to twist and writhe, forming themselves into a braided frame around the edge of the platter. In the center, the scraps of cold mutton vanished beneath a slowly spreading pink mist, and at the core of the gently swirling fog I saw Master Thengor's bedchamber as it had been not so very long ago. There lay my teacher, there hovered the golden cloud of Majyk, there stood his wife and attendant healers, there waited the students, and there—

There went the rat, there went me, there went the two of us right through the heart of the Majyk, and *there* went the roof as the whole bright cloud exploded in a hundred different directions!

I raised my eyes from the vision. "Oh."

"Funny stuff, Majyk," Zoltan mused. "The oldest texts tell about how it was before we wizards learned to make it obey us. Back then, Majyk was wild. Sometimes you could see it, sometimes not. There are many stories about travelers, on a lonely road at night, seeing a glowing cloud through the trees and mistaking it for the welcoming fire in some peasant's hut. But when they ran towards it, sometimes it ran away, sometimes it shattered at their touch, and sometimes . . . it stuck. After that, in the cases where it stuck, the traveler discovered he was able to do the most wonderful things, but only when he said certain words and made certain motions. The fellow who first figured out the connection between the glowing cloud, the special words and signs, and the right results, became the father of all wizards."

"So you're saying that when I ran into Master Thengor's Majyk, it . . . stuck?"

"Well, I'd never say that you *took* it from him." Zoltan winked. "Although Majyk can be taken, or stolen, if the wizard who wants it is stronger than the wizard who's got it." I know, I know: That left *me* out. "Married wizards have combined their individual portions of Majyk and used it to work cooperative spells. Divorcing wizards have gotten into some mighty ugly battles of sorcery over who gets how much of the Majyk they held in common. There have even been cases of it being held in trust for years by the Council, until a wizard's chosen heir could learn enough sorcery to master his parent's store of Majyk."

"But why did it stick to *me*?"

For once, Zoltan stopped smiling. Instead he wore a half-compassionate, half-pitying expression that made me check to see whether I'd fastened my breeches correctly. "Is that important?" he asked, leaning across the table to rest one hand on my shoulder. "I think we must agree that what *really* matters now isn't 'How did I get this?' but 'How am I going to get rid of it?'"

I screwed up my mouth, thinking it over. "Zoltan, what if I'm not sure I *want* to get rid of—?"

"Can you control it?"

"No."

"Can you use it to protect yourself from any great wizard who finds out you've got Master Thengor's hoard and wants to take it away from you?"

"No . . . But I did all right with Master Gurf and Master Benidorm!"

Zoltan flicked away my words like so many dead flies. "A fluke. A lucky happenstance. A freak accident. Can you truthfully believe you will be so fortunate every time someone tries to help themselves to your Majyk?"

"Uhhhhhh . . . no."

He got up and strolled casually around the table until he was standing right behind me. "Do you want to find out what will happen when some greedy wizard tries to *rrrrrip* the Majyk out of you?" he whispered in my ear.

Next thing I knew, I was down on my knees begging Zoltan Fiendlord to use all of his own powers to take away my Majyk as painlessly as possible.

"Don't worry," he assured me. "You won't feel a thing."

CHAPTER ———————— 5

I COUNTED THE SILVER TASSELS ON THE BED CANOPY
for the fifth time and sighed. The sum came out the same, and so
did the result: I still couldn't fall asleep.

"Zoltan?" I called into the darkness.

"Aren't you asleep *yet*?" came the impatient reply.

"Sorry. I'm trying."

A sigh a lot like my own answered me from the doorway. "If
you're not comfortable, we can move to another room. Perhaps
you don't feel able to relax, knowing you're in Lady Inivria's
bed."

"No, this bed is fine." It was comfortable, no denying that.
After six years of sleeping in the student dormitory beds, a sack of
broken pottery would be comfortable.

What wasn't so comfortable was the feeling I got every time I
rolled onto my side and saw the iron bars over the windows. I tried
telling myself that Zoltan knew best. He suggested that I sleep in
Lady Inivria's room specifically on account of the barred windows. *So no other wizard can come sneaking in on us this night,*
he said. *Iron's the only thing that slows down the slickest spell.*

I should've felt safe. Zoltan had thought of everything for my
comfort and security. He'd even volunteered to stay up all night
and keep watch while I slept. Any wizard who wanted to get at me
would be stopped by the bars at the window and Zoltan at the
door.

He'd done so much for me; too much. As for the one thing I
could've done for him—No wonder I couldn't sleep.

"Zoltan, I'm sorry," I said. "About the Majyk."

"Oh, forget it." I heard him shifting on his stool. "I should
have anticipated this. There was just too much in Master Then-

gor's hoard for all of it to have stuck to you. Go to sleep and don't think any more about it.''

I made an obedient little sound and rolled onto my other side. No good. ''Zoltan?''

''*Now* wha—? I mean, what is it, Kendar?''

''Why didn't all of Master Thengor's Majyk stick to me?''

''Maybe some of it liked you and some of it didn't.''

''Do you really think—?''

''Oh for—! I'm *joking*, Kendar. Majyk's not alive. Master Thengor acquired his over many years, from many different sources. Only a wizard of his powers was strong enough to hold it all together. It's only natural that when he let go, some of it would go shooting off to freedom.''

''I guess . . . Well, g'night.''

''Good night already.''

I flopped onto my back and there was the canopy again, silver tassels dangling. I wished for a night-light, but all the fire-sprites had run away with everyone else in the palace and the only thing Zoltan had been able to kindle up was a dish of cold sheep fat with a twist of cloth for a wick. It gave a bad, smoky light and it smelled. We put it out as soon as we reached Lady Inivria's bedroom. If I'd have had a night-light, maybe I could've counted the individual silver strands on each tassel, but as it was—

''Zoltan?'' I suppose a strangled scream counted as a response. ''Zoltan, if some of Master Thengor's Majyk shattered and flew off when I hit it, and some of it stuck, why couldn't you remove just the part that stuck? I mean, why is it still sticking to me?''

This time Zoltan's sigh got mixed up with a groan. ''If I could answer that, I'd be a Master in my own right with my own wand by now, plus a seat on the Council. Sometimes it doesn't matter *why*. Sometimes we've just got to take care of business first and figure out the reasons after. My guess is that Master Thengor's Majyk hung together so long that now it won't respond to any outside wizardry until the original mass is reunited. If we're going to remove your Majyk, we've got find the rest of it first. We'll get started tomorrow.''

''Oh.'' I tried rolling onto my stomach, but the pillow was too fluffy and it stuffed up my nose. I tossed it off the bed. ''Uh . . .''

''Spit it out, for Wedwel's sake!'' Zoltan shouted. ''Just say whatever's on your mind, get it over with, and go to *sleep*!''

''I just—I just wondered how we were going to find the rest of the Majyk," I said quietly. "I mean, there's a lot of it out there. How will we know which Majyk was Master Thengor's?"

"We won't," Zoltan replied. "But your Majyk will. You'll see. Tomorrow we'll leave the palace and set out on the road. Before too long, you'll feel a force pulling at you. When you do, give yourself up to the attraction. Majyk calls to Majyk, the way nibs of iron fly to lodestones, and there's a stronger, more special call between bits of Majyk that were once kin. I've heard of more than one wizardly divorce that got reversed when the partners' split-up Majyk pulled them back together. With all the Majyk you've got now, it shouldn't take us long to attract the rest of Master Thengor's hoard, and with your Majyk there to help, it won't be hard to remove the smaller portions from wherever they've gone. Remember how easy it was to pry that little bit off your old broom handle?"

I did. We'd discovered that my ratwhacking stick had picked up its own share of Majyk shortly after Zoltan determined that he couldn't de-Majyk me until the entire original cloud was reassembled. It was very strange, watching Zoltan mumble and wave his hands over the staff, stranger still to see a golden ghost of Majyk in stick-shape rise up from the wood and fling itself at me. I tingled and burned all over when it hit, but it wasn't an unpleasant feeling.

"Yeah, I remember," I said.

"So, see how you haven't got anything to worry about?"

"Uh-huh." I turned onto my side and squeezed my eyes closed. That lasted three heartbeats. I opened my mouth to speak.

Zoltan must've heard my jaw creak, because he spoke first. "What is it this time, Kendar?"

"Nothing. Just—I'm sorry."

"Again? You're sorry too much. Why do you keep apologizing? What are you so afraid of? Of me? Do you think I'm going to get angry at you for some trifle and fry your eyebrows with a little wizard's lightning?" He chuckled. "A fine way that would be to treat a friend! Even one who asks so many annoying questions."

I could hardly believe my ears. "I'm—I'm your friend?"

"I hope you are." The voice out of the darkness sounded warm and sincere. "When you stop and think about how far we may have to journey together, seeking the rest of Master Thengor's Majyk, we'd do best to be friends. Besides, I've always liked you, Kendar."

"Gosh." I felt the corners of my mouth stretching so far out in

a smile that I thought my face would split. "Well, good night."
He answered me with a grunt, but I was too happy to care. The one
person I'd always admired and envied just told me he'd always
liked me. *Me!* That made up for all the years of being Kendar
Ratwhacker. I settled down under Lady Inivria's quilted coverlet
and set my mind on going to sleep. I didn't want to annoy my good
friend Zoltan any further. I like to think I drowsed off for a while.

Still . . .

"Zoltan?"

No answer. I sat up in bed and peered towards the door. There
was a full moon-and-a-half sending bars of silver-blue light into
the room, but not enough for me to see that far that clearly. Had
he fallen asleep at his post? Or was he gone? You know how it is
with stewed lampreys.

"Zoltan, I just wanted to say I'm sorry for—for what happened
to your father," I whispered. Still no reply. I got out from under
the coverlet and crept nearer. "I said I'm—"

The words froze in my throat. There at the foot of the bed shone
two green fires. They burned close together, with an uncanny
radiance that made the short hairs on the back of my neck stand up
and quiver. In the heart of each emerald glow was a dagger-blade
shape of utter blackness, and as I stared I heard a strangely
familiar voice come from out of the demonic flames, demanding:

"Are you naked?"

"Ha?" I managed to say.

"Son of a Siamese, you are! Well, get some clothes on and put
wheels on it! I don't know how long Creepo the Wonder Wizard
will be gone, and we've gotta get you out of here before that."

"Who—?"

"I'm your worst nightmare. Now *move* or I'll prove it!"

You don't argue with demons. If you lose, it's bad, and if you
win, they eat you. I grabbed my smallclothes, tunic, and breeches
from the bedside chair, yanked them on, and stumbled into my
shoes. The green fires bobbed up and down, as if nodding
approval.

"Great, super. Now take those pillows and the spare blanket—
there, it's all folded up at the foot of the bed—and bunch them up
and cover them with the quilt so it'll look like someone's still
under it. Got that? Come *on*, sweetie, time is tuna!"

I did as I was told, without question. The fires narrowed to slits.
I could feel them burning into my skin. "Not bad, not bad. It'll
have to do. Okay, sport, now you think you can follow me without
knocking over everything between here and breakfast?"

"Follow me?" I didn't like the sound of that. Where would a

demon want to go? "Listen, if it's all the same to you, O Great One, I'd rather—"

The twin green fires uttered a horrible rasping sound and I felt needles pierce my left calf. "It's *not* all the same to me, dimbulb, and it shouldn't be all the same to you! When I tell you to move, I want to see some *action*!"

"Yes, O Great One," I murmured, saying a private prayer to Wedwel that Zoltan would return before this fiery fiend could take me anywhere really unpleasant.

"This way," said the demon, and the green fires led me into Lady Inivria's wardrobe.

Once inside the scented, silk-hung darkness, I expected my diabolical guide to keep leading me further and further in, until the back of the wardrobe melted away and we emerged into some fantastic world. I thought I would never see Orbix again, or Mother or Dad or my sister Lucy or my brother Basehart or—well, come to think of it, I didn't much care if I never saw my brother Basehart again—or my new friend Zoltan.

I didn't think I'd bash my nose on the back wall of the wardrobe.

"Turn around, idiot," said the demon. "And don't make such a fuss about a little bump on the nose. If he hears you, it's all over." I felt something small and solid nudge my leg. "Turn around and peek out, but don't open the door any wider, okay? That crack's good enough for what you've got to see. And whatever you do, keep quiet."

Keep quiet? Hardly. I had it all planned. As soon as Zoltan came back, I was going to yell my head off and he'd be able to use his powers to capture this crazy demon. He wasn't called Fiendlord for nothing. Until then, I would pretend to go along with what the demon wanted. Like my friend Zoltan said, sometimes we've just got to take care of business first and figure out the reasons after.

I heard the hush of a slippered foot on stone. The wardrobe was near enough to the doorway so that I could see Zoltan's unmistakable outline even in the poor light. It's kind of hard to miss someone who's wearing a wizard's hat. How many people are pointy on top? He stood leaning against the doorjamb, hands pressed together, eyes gazing at the pillows-and-blanket lump in the bed. I thought I saw the gleaming hint of a smile and figured he was pleased to find me asleep, finally. I took a deep breath and got ready to holler for rescue.

He flung his hands apart and a crackling sheet of white fire fell from the tasseled canopy over the form in the bed, burning it to ashes in a flash.

I was still gaping when he strode over to the smoking remains and made weird gathering-in motions with his hands. "Where is it?" he muttered, poking at the charred black flakes that used to be the quilted coverlet. He jerked his head this way and that, avidly searching the air for something. "It couldn't have just flown off. There's iron barring the windows, no way out but the door." He dropped to the floor and stuck his head under the bed. "It should've been freed when he died. Where is it?"

"Ahem," the unseen demon murmured, giving my leg another nudge. "Would you have any use for this?" A familiar, hefty wooden shape fell into my hands. "So we can be on our way without being disturbed by your pal, there." The green fires seemed to slue in Zoltan's direction.

I crept out of the wardrobe as silently as I could and tapped Zoltan on the shoulder with one end of my ratwhacking stick. I wish there'd been enough light to see the expression on his face when he looked up and I clipped him under the chin with the other end. His eyes rolled up and he toppled over, but I was out the door before he hit the ground.

I heard the demon yelling after me to wait. Wait for a demon to catch up with me? Right. I kept running—down four straight flights of stairs and three corkscrews, falling over chests and tripping over footstools, skidding on throw rugs and hooking my feet on heavy carpets, tromping on soft, squishy things I didn't want to name and skinning my shins on hard, sharp-edged things that I called every name in the book. I didn't stop until I was out of the palace, over the drawbridge, across the moat full of hungry slimegrinds, and well into the surrounding grounds.

Like all wizards, Master Thengor liked to live with a lot of elbow room. Not only did he need space enough for a really big structure to house the ever-growing numbers of his family, students, and staff of servants, he also wanted enough land around it so that he would have plenty of time to see any approaching enemies, spies, creditors or salesmen and make the appropriate preparations for their reception. The moat full of slimegrinds wasn't the half of it.

You can't have a home that big inside the city walls, so Master Thengor built his modest abode far from the noise and smell and confusion and salesmen of the capital. When King Steffan wanted the services of his chief wizard, he had to send envoys to bring Master Thengor to Grashgoboum. (The slimegrinds didn't scare them; they worked for the government.) Sometimes Master Thengor didn't want to be brought. That was when he ducked into the maze.

That was where I wound up too. I don't know what I was thinking of—I knew I had to get away, I knew I didn't want to be found, I knew I needed time to be alone to think about what the greenfire demon had showed me—but I'm pretty sure I didn't want to die just yet. Master Thengor's maze was famous all over Orbix. Every Wenchpinch Eve he would open it to the public as a special treat. Every Wenchpinch Day he would make a small fortune in finder's fees paid by friends and relatives of the people who had gone into the maze the evening before and hadn't come out since.

I was safe in the maze. If Zoltan woke up any time soon and searched for me, he'd never think to look in here. On the other hand, if I'd just taken to the road and headed for Grashgoboum, he'd be able to spy me easily from any of Master Thengor's observation turrets and then—*zzzzit*! Fricasseed Ratwhacker. If I stayed hidden in the maze long enough, he would assume I had somehow found the way to use Master Thengor's Majyk to fly far away or turn invisible or tunnel unseen through the realm of the earth-glums. Then he'd give up and go away and I could come out. I wouldn't starve while I waited, either: Master Thengor had very kindly planted his maze with cheerberry bushes.

So that was my plan and I was proud of it. Just wait until Zoltan was gone and then come out and—

And what? Go home? That would be the first place he'd look for me. He wouldn't be the only one. Other people knew what I had, and wanted it; people like Master Gurf, Master Benidorm, Lady Inivria. Others? Probably. Every single wizard who'd been present at Master Thengor's deathbed knew the old man had a lifetime's hoard of Majyk to give away, and they'd be wondering where it had gotten to. I doubted that it would take them too long to find out, and then it would just be a question of who found me first and how much they'd hurt me before they let me go.

If there was anything of me left to *be* let go.

Suddenly it looked as if I'd be spending a whole lot of my life eating cheerberries.

"Great!" I growled at the full moon-and-a-half. "I don't even *like* cheerberries!"

I paced the narrow paths of the maze, thinking hard. The cheerberry bushes grew tall around me. In some places their prickly branches met overhead and wove themselves into a canopy cutting off nearly all the moonlight. I stubbed my toe on something in the path and gave it a vicious kick. It rolled ahead of me and I kept kicking it, cursing my rotten luck as I went.

I was so intent on thinking up a way to get home without being hunted down by every Majyk-hungry wizard on Orbix that I didn't notice where I was going. Right turn, left turn, doubling back out of a dead end, it was all the same to me. The branches above gradually thinned out and erased the dappled shadows little by little. I gave my improvised kickball one last shot so that it rolled all the way into the clear moonlight.

The skull tumbled to a stop and came up grinning right at me. I guess I wasn't the only one who didn't like cheerberries.

CHAPTER ———————————— 6

THE HALF-MOON WAS ALMOST DOWN BEHIND THE TOP of the cheerberry bushes, and the full moon was following it when the skull said, "Stop crying."

I kept my head down on my knees. "'Mnot crying," I mumbled.

The skull didn't believe me; I could tell without looking. I thought you needed a tongue to make that rude noise. "*Sure* you're not. And I'm an aardvark. Okay, have it your way, you're not crying. So what is it you're *not* crying about?"

"I want to go home," I said. By now I was convinced that I'd fallen asleep out of sheer exhaustion and this conversation was all part of a bad dream. No harm in talking to skulls in your dreams, is there?

"Well, that makes two of us, Einstein."

"Ratwhacker," I corrected. You'd think a skull would get your name right in your own dreams. You can't count on anything, these days. "Call me Ratwhacker."

The skull made a sound of disgust. "What I'd *like* to call you isn't fit for a lady's ears. Hmmm. No ladies around." And it called me a name that sent all the blood rushing to my cheeks and made me jerk my head up in shock.

"Now, look, this is *my* dream and I'm not going to have anyone, dead or not, calling me—!"

The words died one of the quicker deaths. I think they had their heads chopped off or something. The moonlight was almost gone, but there was still enough to see by. What I saw was the old skull and, sitting on top of it, the same unearthly rat I'd chased all the way from Velma's kitchen to Master Thengor's bedchamber and through the cloud of Majyk.

He winked at me with the invisible demon's own glowing green eyes.

My hands groped for the ratwhacking stick, but he switched his strange, striped tail and said, "Ah-ah-ah! Is that any way to treat someone who just saved your life?"

"You—?" I let the question fall unasked. There was no use denying it: I recognized his voice right away, and who could ever forget those baleful green eyes? Yes, he had saved me from Zoltan, but how far could I trust a demon's good will? I was at his mercy. I owned enough Majyk to awaken the greed of every wizard on Orbix, but if I didn't know how to use it, how could I hope to save myself from this fiend in rat's clothing?

I couldn't, and I knew it. I bowed my head. "What would you have of me, O Great One?"

The demon leaped lightly off the skull and approached me. I prepared myself for the worst. The creature was uttering an alien, rumbling sound that made his whole black-brown-and-white body vibrate. He rubbed his head against my hand, looked up into my eyes, and said, "Breakfast would be nice."

"Very well." A Gangle knows when to surrender. (That was the motto Grampa Urien Waterrights Gangle adopted right after the Battle of Skivi's Gulch.) I rolled up one sleeve of my tunic and extended my left arm. Turning my face away, I tried to sound brave as I said, "Will this be all right for starters, O Great One, or would you prefer dark meat?"

Shortly later I added, "*Ow!*" and crammed a badly bitten hand in my own mouth. "What was that for?"

"For being a jerk and thinking I'd ever eat something as scrawny as *you*," the demon said, pointy ears flattened back against his sleekly furred skull. "And for me being a bigger jerk and saving you from Merlin the Short-Order Fry-Cook in there. What *is* that brick pile, anyway? A mall?"

I had no idea what the demon was talking about, but I was afraid if I said something else he thought was stupid, he would bite me again. No, thanks; once was plenty, especially since he'd said he didn't want to eat me. No sense giving him any sample tastes that might change his mind. I checked out the damage the fiend had done to my hand. Four tiny holes, little bigger than pinpricks, oozed blood from the fleshy part between my thumb and first finger.

"I should be grateful," I muttered.

"That I saved your skin?" The creature's whiskers curled up into a self-satisfied leer. "Yeah, I'd say so."

"I should be grateful that your teeth aren't like an ordinary rat's, O Great One. A bite that hard from one of them would've torn my hand clean open."

"A rat?" the fiend repeated, stiff-legged, the fur on his back lifting. "A *rat*?" His tail bushed out, and I could swear I saw yellow sparks shooting from his green eyes. "Did I hear you call me a *rat*?"

"Uh—" That was all I got to say before a ball of hissing, spitting, clawing fury launched itself at my face. I threw my arms crossways over my eyes and tried to roll aside, but the cheerberry bushes caught my tunic.

"—live to see the day one of *my* mother's kittens would hear himself called a *rat* and take it lying—!" the demon swore as he flew through the air right at me.

I braced myself for the impact of fangs and talons.

ZVIT!

"Ow!" someone yowled. For a change, it wasn't me. "Ow, ow, ow, my tail, my tail, my tail's on fire, help, help, help me, help me, put it out, throw water, spit on it, do *something*!"

I dropped my crossed arms and saw the fiend running in desperate circles, smoke rising from the tip of his tail. If I'd had a brain, I would've grabbed the chance to escape. Instead I scooped up the demon-rat with one hand, spat on the fingers of the other, and pinched out the smoldering tip of the poor beast's tail.

The fiend lay quiet in my arms awhile, panting. I could feel his heart beating rapidly as I held him. After a moment or two, the rumbling sound came back. This time I didn't find it so unnerving. In fact, it was kind of nice.

"What happened to you?" I asked.

His whiskers twitched. "What are you, a wiseguy? You set my tail on fire, you son of a—"

"Me? I didn't do it."

"Yeah, right, I always go around bursting into flames at this time of ye—Say, wait a minute." The creature looked thoughtful. "Well, swat me with a broom and call me a dust-bunny! Looks like I *am* the biggest jerk after all. Serves me right for not remembering what you did to those other trick-or-treat rejects."

He grinned when he saw how completely confused I was. "In there," he said, indicating the towering walls of Master Thengor's palace. "When they tried to have those neon Frankenstein hands tear you open like a junk-mail envelope."

"You mean Master Gurf and Master Benidorm? But what happened next—I didn't—not on purpose—I—"

"Purpose, shmurpose," said the demon. "Purpose don't cut no notches on the Uzi. I'm no Funk and Wagnalls, but I'd say that there's *something* protecting you, and I don't mean a deodorant."

"O Great One," I said. "For all I know, you are the biggest funkin' wagnalls from whatever oozy notch spawned you, but what *are* you talking about?"

The fiend showed me his pointed teeth. "Hey, yeah, that's right!" he said. "I *am* talking, aren't I? And you're not running around like some sitcom extra who thinks he's going nuts just because his cat's talking. Talking cats s.o.p. around here, or—?"

"Cat?" I threw the creature off my lap as I scrambled backwards up the cheerberry bushes. "You can't be a cat!"

"I can't, huh?" The beast's scornful gaze went right through me. "Why not? You're a turkey."

"Cats aren't—they don't—everyone knows there's no such thing as a cat. Cats are legendary animals!" I was babbling with fear. This was worse than when I thought I was facing a demon. At least I'd been taught the basic safety procedures for dealing with demons—don't argue with them and don't sign anything without a lawyer present—but cats were anybody's guess.

"Well," the beast said in a remarkably calm tone, "if I'm not a cat, what am I?"

I thought about it. "You did come out of a rat hole—" I began. A scowl from the beast made me drop that train of reasoning.

"Where I come from, cats go into rat holes to kill the rats," he informed me. "After the rats are dead, we come out of the rat holes. See? Makes sense, doesn't it?" I nodded. Speaking half to himself, the creature added, "You know, what *doesn't* make any sense is that last rat hole I went into. I couldn't seem to turn around and go back out the way I came in. I wonder why—?"

"Cats—cats kill rats?" I asked, distracting him.

"Rats, mice, voles, Boston ferns, cockroaches, shoes, Chihuahuas, all kinds of pests," the beast replied cheerfully. "Listen, swifty, I'm no M.I.T. grad, but I get the feeling that was no ordinary rat hole I stuck my nose into. Do all the animals around here talk?"

"No. None of them do; not normally. Well, sometimes frogs and toads, but only the enchanted ones, and sometimes familiars, but the others don't, as a rule." A memory struck me. "Neither did you, when you first came out of that hole. Unless 'meow' is another one of those weird words you've been using that I don't understand."

The beast sat up proudly. "'Meow' is the ultimate word, bozo.

You skinballs gotta use hundreds of words to get what you want, but all we cats gotta do is go 'meow' and we get food, shelter, fresh kitty litter, doors opened, our ears scratched, you name it. So all I said when you first saw me was 'meow,' huh? Hmmm.'' He was thinking.

So was I. "Majyk," I said, snapping my fingers.

"Say what?"

"That's the answer: why you can talk, why everything! That's what happened to both of us. When you stuck your head out of the hole and I chased you—"

"—with a big fat stick, you lousy—"

"—we both jumped right through the middle of Master Thengor's Majyk. That's it. That explains everything."

Not to the cat, it didn't. The moons were down and the first stains of sunlight were seeping through the cheerberry bushes by the time I finished telling him all about Majyk and what it had done to us.

"Gotcha," the cat said. "So that's what that yellow stuff was? Far out. And I thought the smog in L.A. was bad. You got most of it, huh? No wonder Rasputin was trying to nuke your shorts."

"*Who* was trying to do *what* to my *which*?"

"That yoho in there." Again he nodded towards the palace. "The skinball with the black beard. See, the way I've got it figured, when you're awake this Majyk stuff you got is armed and dangerous. Anyone makes a move against you, it automatically goes into attack mode and zaps them."

"So that's what happened to Master Gurf and Master Benidorm," I mused.

"And my tail," the cat reminded me. "But when you're asleep, it's like turning off the alarm system. That was what your pal with the beard was waiting for."

The thought of Zoltan's false friendship and real treachery still hurt. "Why did he do that?" I asked the air. "We were going to find the rest of Master Thengor's Majyk, and once it was all together, he could've taken it off me. I never asked for it; I never wanted it; I'd have *given* it to him. Why did he try to kill me?"

"Some people got no patience." The cat licked one white paw. "Why wait for you to *give* him your Majyk when he could just *take* it when you died? And once he had your share, he could use it to find the rest of the old boy's hoard, solo. Two can't quest as cheaply as one. Eliminate the middleman."

"Take it when I die—" Saying the words aloud helped me make the mental connection. "Sure, that's right! When a wizard's dying, he uses his last bit of control to give it to someone specific. But if he dies without passing his Majyk on—''

"Or if he gets run over by some clodfoot geek with a big fat stick who's trying to score a home run off a poor, innocent kittycat's head—'' the cat put in.

"—then it's free for the taking!" Just a little detail *he* "forgot" to remind me of. I shook my fist at the palace. "Zoltan, you bastard—''

"He was, wasn't he?" The cat licked his other front paw. "The wizard's favorite bastard. The old man's Majyk was supposed to fall right into his lap. Then you came along and left him holding an empty bag. I heard him tell his grubby little girlfriend that he was going to get what was coming to him, no matter what. You didn't see her, but she was lurking around the kitchens for a while, hiding out in the pantry.''

"Bini's in the palace?"

"She was. Maybe she still is." The cat tried to shrug. "Who do you think fixed up that platter of leftovers? Laughing Boy? He told her that if he had enough sorcery and enough skill, he'd fight you man-to-man, but until he knew for sure just how good you were at commanding your Majyk, he was going to play it safe and—''

"How do you know all that?"

The cat set down his paw. "I was in the kitchen. You can pick up the most interesting things in kitchens.''

"And they didn't see you? Gosh. Invisibility's one of the harder spells. How did you learn to use your Majyk so quickly?"

"Cats don't need Majyk to be invisible." He started work on his left hind leg. "Anyway, I wanted to keep tabs on you, buddy-boy.''

"Why?"

"First off, I was waiting for my chance to pay you back for that little heart attack you gave me, chasing me with the stick. But after I watched you some, I noticed how you could work some pret-ty slick tricks with that Majyk stuff. Whether you wanted to or not.'' He lowered the leg. "Not that *I* knew enough to call it by its right name, then, or to know it was taking care of you on autopilot, but I got eyes. I always say it's better to throw in with the winning side, and I could see you had *some* kinda muscle behind you.''

I turned around. "Where?"

The cat sighed. "I could also see pretty quick that you could use a few extra bytes in the mainframe. And now that I *do* know about Majyk, I'm just what the programmer ordered for you!''

He looked so friendly, so eager to help me out. So had Zoltan, before. At least Zoltan spoke a language I could understand. I didn't trust this . . . cat.

I wasn't born yesterday. I'd heard the stories.

"What do you want from me?" I demanded, giving him the narrow eye.

"Bottom line?" He wasn't smiling anymore. "Okay, tough guy: I want what you want. I want to go *home*."

"So go," I said. "You don't need Majyk for that. I'll take you back to the hole."

"Weren't you listening? I *can't* go home that route. I tried. Strictly a one-way street. But a smart kid like you with a load of Majyk like you got and a pal like me, hey! It's just a matter of time until we figure out how to make it jump through hoops. Then we use it to find me a way back to my world."

"I don't *want* to learn how to use it," I said. "I just want to get it all back together, get it off my back, and get on with my life."

"Okay, don't have a cow," the cat said. "So we get the rest of the Majyk together for you, if that's what floats your boat."

"I don't have a cow," I told him. "Or a boat."

"No? You look like the kinda guy who's always been a little dinghy, but—Ahhh, forget it. A lump of Majyk like the old man owned will be more than enough to buy us any wizard around. We offer him a deal: your Majyk for my ticket home, *capeesh?* Everyone's happy."

I folded my arms. "What is this *we* offer him a deal with *my* Majyk?"

The cat winked. "Thought you said you didn't want it. I'm trying to do you a *favor*, chum. Sort of like the favor I did you last night? Or do the words 'extra-crispy' mean nothing to you? Oh, how soon they forget!"

He was right. "I do owe you one," I admitted.

"You owe me several, but who's counting?"

"All right, I'll go along with your plan." By now two of the minor suns were up, with one more to come and the biggie still below the horizon. The light cast disturbing shadows on the skull, shadows that made me think of disturbing possibilities. "Uh, cat? The other wizards—they're pretty mad at me."

"I'll bet." The cat seemed unconcerned.

"The other pieces of Master Thengor's Majyk—they could be anywhere."

"Everything's got to be somewhere, skinball."

"I don't know how far we'll have to go to find the rest of the Majyk, or to find a wizard who doesn't want me dead."

"Travel is supposed to be educational."

"I've never been anywhere except my home and the Academy here."

"What! You mean all your charm, wit, and sophistication are strictly do-it-yourself? Will wonders never cease."

"Cat . . . none of this might work. It's dangerous on the road, especially when we don't really know what's out there." *I could tell you stories!* the skull seemed to say. *Nasty stories.*

"Maybe—" I went on, "maybe we should try to adjust to the way things are. If my Majyk protects me while I'm awake, you could keep an eye on me while I sleep and we could both make it to my parents' place safely. My mother would be happy to give you a home right here on Orbix. It wouldn't be so bad."

The cat gave me a funny look. "Strange as it may seem, Captain, I don't *want* to explore strange, new worlds, to seek out new life and new civilizations."

"No?" My face fell. *Trapped!*

"Not when there's no other cats around to share it with. Female cats, that is. A tom gets lonely."

"Is that your name?" I asked. "Tom?"

"Uh-uh. Mittens was my slave-name. Call me Scandal," said the cat. "Nothing runs faster, nothing can keep up with me, and I'll tell you all you'll ever need to know. You lick my ears, I'll lick yours."

I made a gagging sound. "Have a hairball?" he asked brightly.

"No, thanks. Couldn't we just shake on it instead?"

He laughed. "Ratwhacker, there's hope for you yet! Now, about breakfast . . ."

CHAPTER ——————— 7

IT WAS CLOSER TO LUNCHTIME WHEN WE FINALLY found the way out of the maze. At least our time wasn't wasted in helpless wandering, or blundering down dead ends and into blind alleys. The cat told me that he found me by following my scent, so getting out just meant following our double scent-trail in reverse.

"No sweat," he said. "Not mine, anyhow."

The three minor suns of Orbix's present incarnation were scattered across the sky like red pearls, and the great sun stood almost directly overhead when Scandal led me to the last gap in the cheerberry bushes.

"That has got to be the biggest damn maze since the Pentagon!" he swore, shaking his head. "Thought I'd wear my nose out before I got us backtracked all the way."

"I think it's laid out more on an octagonal plan than a pentagon," I said. "At least that's how it looks from up high when you're in the palace towers." I lifted my foot to take the first step back into the blessed world outside the cheerberries.

It's hard to move your foot when a big cat hooks himself onto it with all four paws and hangs there.

"What are you *doing*?" Scandal hissed.

"I thought leaving would be nice."

"Har-har-*har*-de-har-har, Norton. Aren't you forgetting something?" I thought about it. After a while—a *very short* while—he snorted. "Don't burn up the *whole* woodpile at once, skinball; I mean your old playmate."

"Zoltan?" I smiled. "Let him try something! My Majyk will protect me."

"Think he doesn't know that?" Scandal dropped from my leg

54

and paced the grassy path. "That's why he waited until you were asleep before he tried anything, remember? Heck, it'd be a blessing if he were as stupid as you and *did* take a potshot at us. Then the Majyk could zap him and we'd be sure he was out of the picture for—"

"What do you mean, 'if he were as stupid as—'?"

"Shut up, I'm thinking." Scandal's striped tail twitched worse than the tip of Master Benidorm's hat. "If he's still in that palace, up one of those towers, he's probably watching the grounds to see which way we'll run." He stopped pacing and surveyed the palace. "No good, no good, not a chance of us sneaking out on his blind side; he doesn't have one. At least two of those towers are high enough to give that guppy a three hundred and sixty degree view."

"Master Thengor did like to know who was coming to visit," I said. The cat sounded good and worried, which didn't do a thing for my morale. "He said it cost less energy to man a sentry tower than to run a crystal ball."

"What a good little conservationist he was," Scandal sneered. He started pacing again. "So Zoltan lies low but keeps an eye out for us and he sees which road we take away from here. Then he comes after us at his leisure and waits for his moment to strike. The road's long, the going's rough, most of the time I'm stuck playing nursemaid to a kid who couldn't find his way out of a closet with a road map—"

"What kid—?"

"Clam it, skinball, I'm on a roll. At last the villain sees his chance! We've made camp for the night, you're sleeping, I'm off somewhere answering the call of Nature, Zoltan comes slithering nearer, nearer, *nearer*—!" The fur on Scandal's back was standing up like bushpig bristles. "He checks the bases, tests the wind, gets the nod from home plate, it's the windup, the pitch, and—zammo! *Arrivederci*, Ratwhacker."

I swallowed hard. "I don't think I want my derchy reaved," I said. "I don't even know what it is."

"Trust me, you don't wanna know." Scandal sat down. "If only we could *provoke* him into an attack. The protective reaction we'd get from your Majyk would take him out of the game for a little while, maybe even bench him for good."

"I don't want him dead."

"Why not? He wouldn't mind seeing you that way."

"I'm not Zoltan." I scuffed my foot over the grass. "And I never want to be."

"It's out of my paws, kiddo." Cats have the oddest way of shrugging; it's done more with the tail than the shoulders, mostly because they don't have too much by way of shoulders. "That Majyk of yours does what it wants when it wants and how hard it wants, especially when it comes to saving your hide. Zoltan tries to hurt you, he's just gonna have to take his chances."

I looked out of the maze at the wide world beyond. "So will we. Come on, Scandal, we're going."

"What, you like to go deaf for a hobby? You thinking of running for Congress or something? You heard what I said about Zoltan tailing us!"

I hunkered down and stroked Scandal's head. It seemed to calm him. "I heard. But if you're smart enough to plan on making him attack me first, he's smart enough to not do it. We could starve to death in here while we tried to come up with a foolproof way of provoking him." As if on cue, my stomach rumbled.

Scandal's whiskers twisted into a wry expression. "See whatcha mean. If we play a waiting game, he wins. And I can't even eat these stupid berries. Okay, we're outa here. We'll just have to be real careful about keeping our backsides covered for a while." He stepped out of the maze and I followed.

"Hey, where is it?" he said all of a sudden, stopping in his tracks.

"Yipe!" I fell over him and got the wind knocked out of me. Lifting myself painfully, I growled, "Where's what?"

"The skull, Yorick, the skull! That spooky soccer ball you've been booting along ever since I found you. Go back and get it." He wrapped his tail around his paws. "I'll wait."

I brushed dirt and grass clippings off my tunic. I thought I could hear the slimegrinds in the moat laughing at me. "Why do we need the skull?"

"I want a souvenir and I don't like the postcards—Why do you *think* we need the skull?" Scandal spat. "Just do it."

I shook my head but I went back into the maze and brought out the skull. It wasn't too far from the entrance. Like Scandal said, I'd been kicking it all the time he was tracing our way out. I guess I was bored; I sure wasn't thinking about what I was doing. "Here," I said, offering it to the cat.

"Put it in your pouch," he said coolly.

I checked. "I don't have a pouch."

"Uh-huh, big surprise. No pouch to put things in, and we're about to set off on a God-knows-how-long journey. Nothing to put in it, either. No food, no matches, no knife, no rope, no water, no way to *carry* water, no money, no weapons—''

''I've still got my stick,'' I replied.

''Wonderful. Use it to thwack yourself upside the head when you get hungry, see how you like the taste.''

I looked at the cat, then at the skull. ''I think I understand now,'' I said in a voice made soft by awe. ''I'm a fool. The tales all tell of the wisdom of cats, and the tales tell the truth. You wanted me to pick up the skull so that I would always have a reminder of the dangers awaiting us and every man's need to plan for the future.''

Scandal made a sputtering sound. ''Fetch me my boots and shovel, Ma, it's getting deep out here. Look, pal, all I wanted you to bring that headbone along for was in case we *do* find breakfast, we'll have something to eat it out of. Drink out of, too. Who knows? Maybe we'll run into some heavy-metal geek who'll pay us cash money for—''

''Armored knights can find their own skulls,'' I told him.

''Going by the level of smarts I've seen around here so far, I bet they couldn't find their own rumps using both hands. Come on, Ratwhacker, let's make tracks.''

We headed down the main road away from the palace. I could've sworn I felt Zoltan's eyes burning into my back with every step. Even with my Majyk protecting me, that thought gave me the chills. Pretty soon the road forked off into two branches. Scandal stopped.

''You're the native guide here, Bwana. Which way?''

''Follow me,'' I said, taking the left-hand branch. ''I know right where we're going.''

I did, too. New arrivals at the Academy of High Wizardry are always thoroughly instructed on how to find their way around the palace and the grounds. It wouldn't do to wander into the women's quarters or stumble into one of the wizard's private laboratories or take a wrong turn outdoors and wind up face-to-yuck with a slimegrind. Master Thengor would've been very upset if anything happened to us: Live students pay higher tuition than dead ones. I knew everything there was to know about the place.

Master Thengor's estate was girdled by a huge wrought-iron fence with only two gates. The one that opened onto King Steffan's royal highway was also made of iron and never unlocked except on Master Thengor's say-so. The road from this gate to the palace was wide, smooth, and flanked by fragrant gardens. The other gate was made of gold and opened onto a narrow, rocky goat-path that was always mucky, no matter what the weather. This gate was never locked and never guarded—who would be fool enough to try stealing a wizard's gold? Any visitor who wanted to enter Master Thengor's estate from the goat-path gate had to walk up a long, winding, potholed track that took them through evilly brooding forests, bleak moors where unseen beasts howled eerily, and stinking swamps. My choice was obvious.

"Well, I *guess* that's breakfast," Scandal said, looking down at the purple, prickly thing he had just killed. Yellow blood trickled out of its torn throat and it looked back at the cat with its single, glazing, orange eye.

"No, it's not," I told him. "Voondrabs are poison in months with no R. The rest of the year, they just taste awful."

"Ugh." The cat made a face and batted the dead voondrab into the swamp. One of the flowers floating on top of the brown ooze gobbled it up. "Ratwhacker . . ."

"Yes, Scandal?"

"If you wanted me dead, you could've used that stick when my back was turned. I don't think I've got enough Majyk to put up much of a fight."

"You're going to help me, keep watch while I sleep, and be on the lookout for Zoltan. Why would I want you dead?" I was honestly puzzled.

"Oh, I don't know. Little things. *Little smelly purple things covered with sharp, wicked spines that drop out of trees with no warning and try to bite my ears off!*"

Nobody in his right mind actually *likes* voondrabs, but I thought Scandal was making rather a big fuss about it. "That voondrab couldn't have killed you. Not unless you ate it. It couldn't even have bitten your ears off. See, the voondrab's teeth fall out during the mating season—"

"Your teeth aren't so safe, either, believe me," the cat shot back. "Why in the name of Saint Morris did you get us into this awful place? Don't tell me the other road led to something worse!"

"It certainly did." I told him all about the two routes to Master Thengor's palace, then waited for him to praise my choice.

"A wide, clean, smooth, level road?" Scandal repeated. "Leading to a major highway? With gardens on either side? Pretty gardens? Gardens that *don't* smell like two weeks in a gorilla's gym socks? Gardens where maybe, just maybe, a cat could catch himself a nice mole or two for breakfast? Not a purple, smelly, prickly mole, but a real, normal, plump, juicy—?''

I nodded. He called me *that* name again.

''Gee, Scandal, take it easy!'' I protested. The cat was still swearing at me; just as well that most of the words were foreign. ''We couldn't take the other path. It leads to the iron gate.''

''Let me guess: Iron makes your skin break out?'' he mewed. ''Where've you been sleeping, baby, on an anvil?''

''Iron and Majyk don't mix,'' I answered, touching my cheeks self-consciously. They weren't *that* lumpy, were they?

I guess they were.

''So what if they don't mix?'' Scandal demanded. ''I'm not asking you for a cocktail, just a way out of this dump where we won't get attacked by Gorgonzola, Queen of the Zombies.''

''Zombies are democrats,'' I corrected him, rather proud that I'd managed to remember something from Master Thengor's non-necromantic lessons. ''They don't have queens.''

(According to the royal decree of our lord, King Steffan, all schools in the kingdom had to teach their students about other forms of government, so we'd realize how good we had it. We were encouraged to talk about whether it was better to have a land ruled by a king, a council of nobles, or the common people. There was even a year-end contest sponsored by the king himself, with a prize given for the best composition on the theme of *The Ideal Government*. My old roommate, Grendel Trevus, showed me the brilliant essay he'd written in praise of democracy. It was very persuasive. Funny, the day after he turned it in, I got a new roommate.)

Scandal growled. ''I don't care if zombies have queens, Manhattans, Brooklyns, or—*Rrryah!* I just want to know why we couldn't go out the other gate!''

''It's locked. And the key's still somewhere in the palace. And the gate's iron. And Majyk can't do much when there's iron around. And it's too tall to climb. And there are spikes all across the top. And—''

''Okay, okay, I get your drift.'' Scandal was discouraged. ''You don't need to beat a dead horse.''

''You do if you want to work the spell for keeping werewolves from digging up the flower beds,'' I said.

He let out an awful yowl and took off just like that, don't ask me why. I had to run hard to catch up to him, and running's not easy when you're carrying a big stick. I know, because it just sort of accidentally got in the way of my feet and I kind of tripped and almost fell headlong into the swamp.

I was sitting in the mud, pulling voondrabs out of my tunic, when I heard a familiar voice say, "There you are, Ratwhacker. Tsk. What took you so long? This ain't the nicest place to keep a girl waitin'. Like a hand? Or is this some sort of great wizardly thingie, a what d'you call it, a ritchool? Annual blessing of the voondrabs, maybe?"

I brushed mire-dripping bangs out of my eyes and saw Bini laughing at me. Funny, it didn't seem like she intended the laughter to be mean—just as if she wanted me to laugh too so I could feel less embarrassed. I started to haul myself out of the swamp and she offered me a helping hand.

"Here," she said, taking off her old kitchen apron and giving it to me when I was standing on dry land again. "Wipe your face and—wait, hold still . . . ah!" She reached up and pulled a baby voondrab out of my right ear. "Much better, ain't it, now?"

"Bini, what are you doing here?" I asked while I scrubbed off as much of the swamp goo as I could. I looked around, hoping to see Scandal lurking somewhere, but no luck. I did catch sight of the big covered basket Bini had on one arm. It looked mighty heavy. "Going on a picnic?"

"A swamp picnic?" She laughed. "Oh, that's a good one! No, you take it, love. It's for you, for the road. Just a few odds an' ends, not too much, but enough to fill your belly a time or two before you'll need to find more eats. And a nice bottle of Missus Vee's famous cheerberry cordial. If you don't care for the taste, it's good for keeping off mousekitters."

She stood there smiling, holding the basket out to me. I just eyed her, not making one move to take it. Finally she put it on the ground; her smile vanished. "It's not none of it poisoned, if that's what got your nobblies in a jangle. If you don't believe me, reach in, cut off a chunk of whatever you like, and I'll eat it myself."

"That's no test," I replied. "*He* could've given you the antidote."

"He who? Auntie what?"

"You know who: Zoltan."

This time when she showed me her teeth, it wasn't in a smile. "So that's it. You don't trust me 'cause you think I'm in with Zollie, ain't it so?"

"What else should I think?" I returned self-righteously. "You were never this nice to me in all the years I had to work down in the kitchens, and you've been walking out with Zollie—Zoltan

Fiendlord, and I heard you say that he was going to get nearly all of Master Thengor's Majyk.''

"You got ears on you big enough for a wolf," Bini said through gritted teeth. "Know what happens to wolfs?"

Silly question; everyone knows what happens to wolves. They're worse than lemmings, some ways. The poor dumb animals are always getting themselves killed falling down the chimneys of brick houses, into big pots full of boiling water. If not that, they sneak into old ladies' homes, dress up in the grannies' flannel nightgowns and crawl into the bed until someone finds them, panics, and calls a woodchopper to come in and take care of the beast. It's an awful mess. Bloodstain-resistant sheets, pillowcases, and flannel nightgowns are the most popular Grandma's Day gifts on Orbix, followed by Wolf-B-Gon chimney filters.

"You don't look much like a woodchopper to me," I said.

To my surprise, Bini burst into tears.

I didn't know what to do. Had I insulted her? I'd never heard of a girl who *wanted* to be told she looked like a woodchopper. "Look, Bini, I'm sorry, I—" I tried to put my arm around her; she let me. It felt nice, so nice that I stood there for a while just enjoying it and not trying to find out what was wrong.

It didn't last. Bini snatched her apron back from me and used the least muddy corner to blow her nose. "You great hulking clods of wizards, you think you know it all, don't you? Secrets of the universe, mysteries of nature, riddles of life and death and all that trash? Well, you don't know spoolshells about women, you don't!'' She sobbed, making a gargling sound in her throat so loud I thought she'd choke.

"Oh yes, I know how you've got it figured," she went on. "A girl the likes of me goes walking out with someone the likes of Zollie and you think she'd do anything she could to make sure he gets all of Master Thengor's dirty old power."

"Well . . . wouldn't you?"

She sobbed again. Voondrabs heard and left the swamp in squishily galloping droves. They're very sensitive during the mating season.

"Oh, *sure* I would!" Master Thengor could have taken sarcasm lessons from Bini. "And slit my own throat after, just to have something to do. Don't you see, you fool ratwhacker? *I love him!*''

No, I *didn't* see. "I thought that when you love someone, you want them to have anything they want. Zoltan wants this Majyk bad." Real bad. I had the death-attempt to prove it.

Bini stopped crying long enough to snort. "Hmph! As if a man was smart enough to know what it is he *really* wants. That's where us women come in. Now, was Zollie to have got all that Majyk, what then?''

"He'd—uh—he'd be happy?"

"Oh, he'd *think* he was happy, to be sure. At first. He'd be the most powerful wizard Orbix ever knew, he would. Folks would come from all around, over mountains, across seas, up King Steffan's toll road, just to ask him for help. They'd heap great, huge, tall, uh, *heaps* of gold and jewels at his feet. They'd bring their children to learn wizardry from him. Other wizards would always be comin' 'round, cap in hand, just to tell him how much they always did admire him and was there anything they could do to please him, like feed the slimegrinds or take out the garbage or anything.

"And then there'd be the women." Her face got hard. "Perfumed an' painted an' powdered an' all wrapped up in them silky veils like they was walking birthday presents for *my* Zollie to be unwrapping. Dancin' like they'd got a nest of tiggies in their unders. Singin' their nasty-minded songs about the lamprey and the knothole—"

"I never heard that one," I said. "Do you think you could teach me how it—?"

Bini ignored my honest question. Like Scandal would say, she was on a roll. "And then, the worst of it!" she shouted. "The day when the king hisself calls my Zollie into his castle and tells him, 'M'boy, I got a little gift for you, in recognition of blah-blah-blah,' and he claps his hands together smart-like, and his servants bring in this rolled-up rug, and they give it a push, and when it's all unraveled there's the king's own daughter, the lovely princess, all dressed up and ready to be—to be—to become my Zollie's *briiiiiiiide!*''

She hit that last word so shrilly that I wished she'd left the baby voondrab in my ear. After I made sure she hadn't made me deaf I pointed out, "King Steffan doesn't have a daughter. He's not even married."

"That won't stop 'im." There was no talking her out of it. "I know all about these kings. Whenever they've got to win over a mighty hero, *snap!* they develops daughters just like mushrooms after a rain."

"And they wrap them up in rugs? How uncomfortable. Couldn't they just send someone to bring the princess in to meet Zol—her future husband?"

"Shows all *you* know." Bini stuck her hand down the front of her blouse. I held my breath. She pulled out a small book, cheaply made, printed on flimsy paper, without even a decent set of hardboards to protect it on the outside. She waved it at me. "Says right here in Raptura Eglantine's newest book, *How Wild My Wizard*, how handsome young Master Brad first meets up with the high-spirited Princess Carmine when she's whipped out of the rug that her older sister was supposed to be rolled inside of," Bini gazed at the tattered cover and sighed fondly before pressing it to her bosom.

"Can I see that?" I asked, reaching out. She swatted my hand away with the book.

"Try to take advantage of a girl, will you?"

I hung my head. "I just want to help."

"If that's what you want, then take this basket and go away!" she commanded me. "Take all your wicked, awful, veneminen—venomominous—*poison* Majyk with you! Take it far away, so far my Zollie won't never be able to find you and kill you and take all that Majyk for hisself and—and—" She was crying again, probably thinking of rugs and princesses and lampreys.

I picked up the basket. It was as heavy as it looked. Bini was still crying when I knelt beside the swamp and used my ratwhacking stick to fish out the old skull. I didn't know if I'd ever see Scandal again, but in case I did, I didn't want him mad at me for forgetting it. I shook most of the mud out of the skull and stuck it on top of my stick so it could dry out. Then I said goodbye to Bini.

"And don't come back," she told me between sobs. It wasn't quite the sendoff I expected after six years at the Academy of High Wizardry, but it was all I was going to get.

I walked out of the golden gate and down the goat track. It was a long, hard road, with a lot more stones than I thought were really necessary. My feet were hurting badly by the time the goat track ended in a thick forest to the west of Master Thengor's estate.

A few raw stumps stood like broken teeth just inside the forest's border. Woodchoppers had been there, but they hadn't ventured too far into the wild woods. I wondered why not. It didn't look like a dangerous forest. I couldn't recall it being shown on any of Master Thengor's maps as a place to avoid, like the Forest of Fear to the north, or Manglegrove to the south, or Ye Timberland of Ye Staggering Headless Brainsucking Corpses to the east, or Slaughterwood—wherever Slaughterwood was supposed to be.

(My best grade in Geography was an F-plus, and I only did that well because I was finally able to find my way back from the student latrine to the classroom without getting lost.)

I sat down to rest on one of the stumps, the basket between my feet, my skull-topped stick leaning against my thigh. Two of the minor suns were well on their way down the sky; the afternoon was dying. I still hadn't had a bite to eat, but I didn't have much appetite. All along my lonesome road, I'd kept a sharp eye out for Scandal. Every step I took, every sharp stone I treaded on, every pothole I tripped over, I didn't care about the pain if it let me catch up with the cat. All I got was the pain.

I'd even tried using my Majyk to find him. Hadn't Zoltan said that Majyk attracts Majyk, the greater calling to the lesser? Surely if I put my mind to it, I could make my Majyk seek the cat's. It would be a pulling sensation, I just knew it, or maybe a glow. I closed my eyes, concentrated my thoughts, and hoped.

Not a twinge, not a spark, not a sliver of difference.

"Stupid cat," I said out loud. The trees rustled. "Why'd you have to run off like that?" I grabbed my ratwhacking stick and shook it angrily until the skull spun and rattled. "Fine! Run away! Leave me alone! See if I care! You need me more than I need you! You don't know a thing about Orbix. You'll never find the hole that'll take you back to your own world without me to help you. You could die a dozen different ways first. You—you—" Something was starting to choke off my words before I could force them out; something too much like tears. "*You didn't even know voondrabs are poison in months with no R!*"

"Maybe not," said the cat, poking his head out from under the cloth covering Bini's picnic basket. "But when you've got a whole roast chicken for a roommate, who the hell needs voondrabs?"

CHAPTER ———————— 8

"YOU LOOK LIKE SOMETHING THE CAT DRAGGED IN," Scandal said. "You shouldn't excuse the expression."

"Did you have to eat the *whole* chicken?" I pawed through the picnic basket and all I came up with to prove there'd ever been a chicken in there was a handful of bones.

"I left you the wishbone. I thought a big-deal magician like you would appreciate it. It's the thought that counts." His whiskers were shiny with grease. "Hey, quit your whining. There's plenty of other stuff left in there for you to eat."

"Plenty," I agreed. "If you like cold leftover stewed lampreys and cheerberry cordial."

"You will," Scandal said. "When you get hungry enough, you'll love 'em!"

The worst part was, he was right. Now that Scandal was back, so was my appetite. Bini had packed a couple of loaves of bread—day old, but bread—and before long I was devouring a cold lamprey sandwich. When I was done, I packed away the rest of our supplies very carefully.

"Hey, skinball, aren't you forgetting something?" Scandal pointed a paw at the remains of the roast chicken.

"First the skull, now this. What is this thing you've got for saving bones?" I asked.

"Next time we've got us a locked iron gate, you'll be ready with a skeleton key, nyuk, nyuk, nyuk." I glared at him. "Nyuk. Okay, so I'm no George Burns. You never know what'll come in handy on the road, buddy-boy—even bones have their uses—and it won't kill you to carry 'em; where's the beef?"

"There was beef in there and you ate all of that, too?" I couldn't believe my bad luck. "Boy. I walk for Wedwel knows

65

how long over the worst roads in the kingdom, all upset because I don't know what's become of you, and all the time you're snuggled up inside the basket *I'm* carrying, eating everything that isn't nailed down!''

''Kiddo, if you gotta nail it down before you can eat it, it's not worth the trouble.'' Scandal licked his paw and used it like a face-cloth to tidy up. ''The way I see it, we've got bigger fish to fry than worrying about your stomach. And if you ask me if I ate the fried fish, too, I'll bite you.''

''What *do* we have to worry about?'' I asked, pulling my feet up onto the stump. ''Aside from where we're going to sleep tonight, what we're going to eat in a couple of days when this food's gone, and where we're going to find fresh water to drink. Cheerberry cordial doesn't quench your thirst, but I hear it's good for keeping off the mousekitters.''

Scandal wiggled his eyebrows at me. ''Oho! Do I hear you worrying about practical things? You, the kid who was all set to hit the road with only dumb luck and a little Majyk going for him?''

''I wish now I'd had the dumb luck to pack a spare tunic.'' I hugged myself tight and shivered. It was cooler in the forest and my swamp-soaked clothes hadn't dried out completely yet, no matter how long I'd marched.

''Cold, pal?'' Scandal cocked his head. ''Yeah, you do look a little blue around the whiskers. Well, like I always say, anyone who can freeze to death in the middle of a forest deserves it. You get the big pieces, I'll get the kindling.''

It didn't take us long to get together the makings of a good-sized fire. Once Scandal dropped the last twig from his mouth, the two of us sat down on opposite sides of the woodpile and waited.

And waited.

And waited.

Scandal was the first to speak. ''Well? You like freezing? Make with the Boy Scout training already! Strike a match, break out the flint and steel, rub two teenagers together, do *something*!''

I looked sheepish. ''I don't know how to start a fire. I was kind of hoping you did.''

''Me? Where I come from, it's your kind who make such a godawful big deal over how *you* get to be the boss of all the other animals because *you* are Man the Toolmaker, Man the Beast Tamer, Man the Firemaker! So make us a fire or I'll report you to the union for impersonating a human being.''

I shook my head sadly. ''I never made a fire in my life; not from nothing. I could do it if I had a live coal from another fire, but if not—Master Thengor never taught me how to summon a fire-sprite.'' I shivered again and coughed. This time it felt as if the swamp water had seeped all the way into my bones.

''You sound terrible,'' Scandal said.

''I feel terrible.'' I coughed some more. Then, as pathetically as I could, I added, ''I think I'm gonna die.''

That was all I needed to say at home to get plenty of attention and fuss made over me. Mom would rush me off to bed, make one of the servants stand by to bring me anything I wanted, wake our cook out of a sound sleep to make me hot soup, you name it. Even at the Academy of High Wizardry, these words were good for getting some special treatment (Dead students don't pay as much tuition as live ones, remember?) and being excused from class. Just one whimpery *I think I'm gonna die* and whoever was in charge of my life at the moment would jump right in, take care of me, and take care of any little sideline problems I was having at the time, too.

The cat just said, ''Good, then after you're dead I get to eat your share of the lampreys.''

I stopped wilting right away and started to broil. ''You selfish—! I'm dying and all you can think of is—! You mangy—!'' I wasn't thinking, I was just mad. I picked up a small stone from the forest floor and chucked it at Scandal.

I've got a good eye and usually hit what I aim for, but I wasn't aiming to hit him—only to teach him a lesson. The stone struck a finger-width away from his haunches. He let out an explosive hiss and rose straight up in the air, legs stiff, claws out, fur on end—

—Majyk sparking like mad.

I gaped, but not for more than an instant. Then I moved faster than a flying crossbow bolt, tearing up a handful of dry grass and leaves, holding it close to the thousand tiny stars of fire leaping from the cat's fur. The many sparks that missed the outstretched tuft of tinder burned my bare skin, but the few that landed on the dry leaves began to smoke and smolder nicely. By the time Scandal landed, I had the seed of a fire in my hands. I knelt and puffed it into flame, feeding it with bits of bark and small pieces of twig. Little by little I coaxed it into fully crackling life.

''There!'' I threw a bigger branch on the fire and sat back on my heels, proud of myself. ''I did it!''

''*You* did it?'' Scandal stopped smoothing down his ruffled fur long enough to give me a dirty look.

"All right, you helped," I admitted. "But it's not as if you knew what you were doing."

"Did *you*?" the cat returned. "Face it, me proud beauty, we're both up to our alligators in something incredibly powerful, a force that can give its master almost anything he wants, and because we can't control it, it's doing us about as much good as a hat to the Headless Horseman. *That's* the problem I was trying to tell you about before: We've got to learn how to use our Majyk, or else."

"Why?" I asked. "I just want to give mine away—not to Zoltan Fiendlord, or Bini will kill me if he doesn't first—and you don't need it, because you just want to go home. I thought we agreed that—"

Scandal threw himself over his back, all four paws stretched out and his white belly showing. "Go ahead, kid, help yourself."

"Huh?"

"My Majyk. It's yours for the taking. You can't get rid of the load you're carrying until it's all in one handy-dandy family-sized economy pack, so get started by collecting mine. I didn't give at the office. Take it away!"

My mouth opened, then closed. I always knew it was smarter than me. Scandal lay there a while longer, then rolled onto his side and said, "Can't do it, can you?"

"I thought—I thought that when my Majyk found some more of Master Thengor's original supply, it'd just come leaping onto me like puppies."

"What a disgusting thought." Scandal wrinkled his nose.

"If that was true, though," I went on, "then your Majyk should've jumped off of you and onto me the first time we met. And if the Majyk doesn't just come to me when I find it, then when I *do* find it, what am I going to do to *get* it?"

"Pree-zactly, Einstein," said the cat.

"Scandal, what'll we do? How can I learn about controlling Majyk?"

"How's it usually done around here?" he asked.

"You sign on with a wizard and he teaches you."

"We can forget that. Too much of a chance of running into another Zoltan. Any do-it-yourself books on the subject you could get? *From Wimp to Wizard in One Week*? *The Self-made Magician*?" I let him know there weren't any. I also asked him what "wimp" meant.

"It's a cross between a wyvern and an imp," the cat said quickly. "Very dangerous. Okay, no teacher, no books, exactly how things must've been around here when the first cave-geek discovered Majyk. Am I right or am I right?''

"You're right enough. Zoltan told me almost the same thing about the ages when Majyk was still wild.''

"Zoltan could've told you to fly off the top of the tower and you'd've given it a whirl. What I want to know is: How did that first yangadang learn how to use the stuff without blowing his own head off?''

"Trial,'' I said. My lips were dry. "And error.''

"Right! And what's good enough for your cave-geek wizards will be good enough for us. Ah, the sweet siren song of pure science! How I do love it. The rapture of raw data, the thrill of theories, the ecstasy of experiments—!''

He was so excited that he appeared to be rising from the ground. Then I blinked, and if it was an illusion, it was gone.

"Hold on!'' I objected. "You've got *me* tagged for all this rapture, thrills, and ecstasy, don't you?''

"Eminently logical, Captain.'' The cat raised one eyebrow. "You've got the most Majyk, so you've got the most that can backfire on you. You'd better learn how to master it before something goes kapow.''

"What if something goes kapow during the experiments?''

"Relax, Jack; your Majyk will protect you.''

"From itself?''

"Hmmm, fascinating.'' Again the single eyebrow lifted. How did he *do* that? "In theory it should . . . Well, I guess we'll find out.''

"That's impossible!'' I protested. "It takes years to master Majyk! There are thousands of spells and gestures to learn, and if you make a mistake and combine the wrong word with the wrong gesture—''

"Yeah, yeah, yeah, kapow.'' Scandal was calm about it. Why not? It wasn't his neck on the line. "Hey, kiddo, listen to your old Uncle Scandal: These big-deal magicians on your world ain't no different from the con artists we've got back on my home turf. All that whoop-de-doo about studying for years, memorizing the right words, the right hand-jive, that's all smoke screen, ya know? Give you a f'rinstance: Some girl wants to take off a few pounds, she just eats less and exercises more; anyone could tell her that! But the kind of wizards we got, they tell her, 'If you read *only* the words in this diet bible I have written and eat *only* the special, magic meals I have prepackaged for you, then and *only* then you will lose fifty pounds in five days *plus* you will wind up married to the rock star of your choice.'"

"You worship rocks?" I asked.

Scandal sighed. "Only for entertainment. Is that *all* you got out of what I told you?"

"You mean that controlling Majyk is really simple, but the wizards just claim it's hard so they can get rich."

"Bingo! Give that boy a cigar and a paid-up health insurance policy for lung cancer. Listen, cuddles, if it'll make you feel any better, once you know how to boss your Majyk, I'll give you some mystic words and gestures of power you can use to impress the suckers. I used to live with a computer wizard before I came here, ya know. You shoulda seen him make with the mystic words and gestures whenever the hard disk crashed."

My head was spinning. Scandal's words were turning into a loud buzzing in my ears. I ducked, dodging invisible mousekitters, then got taken with a new set of the shakes. With teeth chattering I asked, "C-c-c-could this w-wait until morning? I th-th-think I'm gonna d—uh—I'm sleepy."

"Sure, buddy-boy, sure. You still don't look so hot. A good night's sleep oughta help." He yawned, showing off the ribby inside of his mouth. "Go on, I'll be on the lookout for Zoltan."

I didn't need him to tell me a second time. I curled up beside the fire, with the cloth from the picnic basket my only cover. The forest floor was no feather bed, but I was sound asleep almost immediately. My last waking memory was of something warm and furry cozying up against my stomach, and that nice rumbling sound coming from it.

"You wanna turn out that light, bozo?" Scandal poked me sharply under the chin with his wedge-shaped head.

"What? Where? Who? Is it Zoltan? What's happening?" I sat up quickly and looked all around. It was full night, our campfire just embers, and I couldn't see much of anything.

"Never mind," said the cat, tucking his tail closer to his body. "It's off now. But man, was it ever bright! Thought I'd never be able to sleep with that much light on."

Now that I was fully awake, I was annoyed. "You're not supposed to sleep. You're supposed to be on guard."

Scandal had one forepaw covering his nose, so his words came out muffled. "Zoltan's nowhere, not for miles. My bet is that that little cupcake, Bini, is using her female wiles on him to give us a good head start. Now shut up and let a feline sleep."

"How do you know Zoltan's not nearby?" If I couldn't trust Scandal to keep watch, could I trust his word at all?

"Trust me," Scandal said. "I looked. *Nada.* No one."

I had a right to be skeptical. "How could you see anything at night with the fire so low?"

"I'm a cat. We can see in the dark, you know? Although . . ." He got thoughtful. "I don't remember being able to see *this* well in the dark back home. I mean, we are talking *miles*. All the way back to the palace, almost. Better than I see in full daylight, which is another reason I didn't like it when you started making like a nuclear meltdown."

"What in Wedwel's name are you talking—?"

I didn't get to finish. I lit up. Just like that. My whole body, clothes and all, began to shine with a bright golden light. Clouds of mousekitters came zooming out of the deep woods, attracted by the glow. When they tried to bite me, my Majyk zapped them. They died making little sizzling sounds. All that was left of them were their long pink tails.

Then, with as little warning, I went out.

"What was *that*?" I exclaimed.

"One of two things, Sherlock: Mexican food or Majyk. Brother, we'd *better* get started learning how you can control the stuff. Lighting up like that could be dangerous."

"Aw, don't be silly, Scandal." Now that I knew it was just my Majyk kicking up, I wasn't too worried. I figured it wasn't any worse than having the hiccups. In fact, I felt a funny, bubbly sensation in my belly that made me suspect I was in for a case of them, too. "What kind of harm could it really do?"

The fizzing inside me got stronger. I hoped I wasn't going to burp. I took a deep breath, hoping to keep both the burps and the hiccups at bay. Sometimes a good scare—

I got one.

"Yaaaaaaiiiiiiihiiiiiiii!" The brawny shadow burst out of the trees and right into the middle of our campfire, broadsword flashing. "Aaaaaaiiiiiiiioooooowwwww!" It burst right out of the fire again, hopping from foot to foot while the two of us stared, too shocked to move. There was a flicker of light as the sword came up in a graceful arc and leveled off just under my chin. "Weak-blooded city-dweller, prepare to meet thy doom!" the shadow sneered.

My knees started to fold under me. Then I felt Scandal butting my leg and heard him whisper, "Hey, buck up, skinball! This dingdong wants to try something? *Let* him! *You* know what'll happen to anyone who tries to lay a finger on you."

I whispered back, "But I don't want to kill—"

"Didst speak, slave?" the swordsman thundered. "By Buxomia, I gave thee not leave to loose thy tongue. Dost thou but tryest that again and I shall loose thy tongue from thy head of a certainty, thy head from thy shoulders also. So swears Grym the Great!"

"Oh yeah?" I countered. "Well, I'm—I'm Master Kendar, greatest magician on all of Orbix, speaker to fire-sprites, rider upon the winds from whatever quarter they might break, fiendlord, expert in all the wizardly arts, personal court mage by royal appointment to His Extreme Highness, King Steffan of Grashgoboum, and if you don't leave me alone—"

"Oh, puttest thou a buskin it, thou wizardly windbag," said my opponent, and gave me a smack on the side of the head with the flat of his sword. A whole lot of pretty stars came out for an instant before it all went black.

My Majyk didn't do a thing.

CHAPTER ————————— 9

I WOKE UP NOT DEAD. IT WAS A GOOD START.

I also woke up hurting. The left side of my head felt like it would fall off if I leaned over too far, so I just lay where I was, my eyes half shut, and prayed that the throbbing would stop soon.

My vision was kind of blurry. The first thing I could focus on made me wonder if maybe I *had* been killed and this was the famous Pit of Eternal Guilt, Misery, Punishment, and Woe where Wedwel sent all bad little boys who wouldn't wear the nice sky-blue velvet tunics their mothers spent *so* long sewing just for them.

I wished I had a nice sky-blue velvet tunic right then. I'd have used it to cover my eyes so I wouldn't need to see Grym the Great sitting on *my* tree stump, holding the skull in one hand and his sword in the other.

"To slay," he intoned, "or not to slay. That is the question. Whether 'tis nobler in the mind to keep a sissified city-dwelling wizard in our service, or to take arms, and legs, and ears, and other choice cuts off his body and by disjointing rend them."

I closed my eyes, but Grym's image stayed with me. I had remained unconscious until well after the suns were up, so there was no possibility of *not* seeing what he looked like. The brawny shadow of the night before looked even brawnier by daylight. Grym had muscles where I didn't think you could grow muscles. Even his nose looked like it could win a fair fight on its own. He had a body to be proud of, so he didn't waste much money keeping it under wraps. All he wore was a leather loincloth, a wide silver-studded belt, a traveler's pouch, and sandals. If his clothing wasn't enough to shout BARBARIAN! at anyone he met, his speech was.

"To slay, to kill—to kill, perchance to maul. Aye, there's the fun stuff! For if we chop off some strategic portion of yon wizard, might we not assure ourselves of his being unable to run away from us in the future?"

"Don't move," hissed a well-known voice in my ear. I stiffened. "I said *don't move!* Cheez, you want another whack in the head before you'll listen?"

"Scandal?" I ventured, keeping my voice as low as possible.

"Don't move includes the tongue, numbskull."

"I only wish it were numb." I stole another sideways peek at Grym the Great. He was still asking the skull about whether or not to kill me. It's rude to interrupt other people's conversations. "What happened?"

"You got a knock in the noggin, what do you think happened?"

"I mean, what happened to my Majyk? Why didn't it protect me? Why did it let him—?"

I gasped. That fizzy feeling was back. So was Grym. This time his sword chunked down into the ground right before my eyes, narrowly missing the bridge of my nose.

"Livest thou, O wizard?" he asked. He followed up his kind inquiry by poking a sandaled foot into my ribs.

I sat up fast, even if it did mean that half my head ran away to howl at the moons. "I livest," I replied.

"Then hist, rally straightaway onto thy feet, O sage, that we may have parley."

I tried to stand but my legs didn't want to help me. Neither did Grym. I made it up as far as hands and knees while the swordsman loomed over me, sneering, both hands folded over the pommel of his mighty blade.

"Up, thou puling city-dwelling scum!" he roared. "Toyest thou at thine own risk with the patience of Grym."

"Whatever happened to 'O wizard, O sage'?" I grumped. My head was hurting worse than before, and the bubbles in my belly weren't helping. There comes a time when you hurt so bad that death seems like the lesser of two evils. This was my time. He wanted me to stand up, I needed something to help me to my feet, and he wouldn't give me a hand? Fine. I'd help myself. Let him kill me if he didn't like what I was going to do.

I grabbed the long cross guard of his broadsword and pulled. I expected Grym to growl, yank the sword away, and slice me open from moonrise to midnight, or at the least to give me another smack. Maybe this time I'd get lucky and it would kill me.

No such luck. The moment my hands closed over Grym's

sword, the vague churning in my gut turned into an explosion like a waterspout. I let out a whoop that was part pain and part pure excitement. My legs shook, but not from weakness. Fact was, as soon as I got my hands on that sword, I felt revived, renewed, ready for anything. I heard Grym scream—funny, you never expect to hear barbarians do that—and saw the sword between us engulfed in a sheet of golden flame. He dropped it, I grabbed it, and with one heroic swing of the blade—

—I fell over.

"'Tis all in controlling thy backswing, O wizard," said Grym, squatting beside me as I lay flat on my back. "Mine trusty blade, Graverobber, hath a tendency to pull to the right when thou wouldst slice therewith. Thou needest must keep thy shoulders straight, thine eyes upon thy chosen target, and swingest thou from the hips. Here, takest mine hand, that I might show thee."

I rolled onto my side with no help from him and gave him a hard look. I was still holding the sword, though I had the feeling he could've taken it back any time he wanted. "Why are you so helpful all of a sudden?" I asked.

"Who would not hasten to make an ally of so powerful a mage? My mother raiseth she no fools." He straightened up and pulled me to my feet, sword and all. The weight of the blade nearly pulled my arms out of their sockets, but he could tweak the pair of us around like we were straw.

I stuck the sword into the ground the way he'd done before. It was easier for me to use it as a prop than a weapon, though there was no need to let Grym know that. "So you want to be my friend, huh?" I said, pretending to be casual about the whole thing.

"Thou hast hit it, O wizard."

"Why?" I sounded almost as cynical as Scandal. Speaking of whom . . . Where was that cat? I scanned the surrounding woodland and couldn't see a trace of him.

"By Zaftigus and Tumidia, much as I do hold you mush-gutted city-dwellers in contempt, and do foully scorn and mistrust the cowardly use of magic in honest combat, still I would be proud to name thee, O Master Kendar, mine own blood brother and boon companion because—because—"

He paused, tense, his eyes darting to every forest shadow. Then, in a voice low enough for a master-assassin, he said, "It's my face."

It certainly was.

Since I was no longer in peril of my life, I had the chance to study the barbarian at close range. (Maybe too close. Baths are for mush-gutted city-dwellers.) Now that I got a good look at him, I realized there was something wrong, dreadfully wrong.

That same nose that looked able to fight its own battles was not only the most muscle-bound nose I'd ever seen, it was also—could it be?—the *cutest*. Though the scars of a hundred frays and twice as many tavern brawls crisscrossed Grym's round, well-tanned cheeks, it still wasn't enough to suppress the sudden urge I felt to reach out and pinch them. The sprinkling of freckles didn't help. Next thing I knew, my hands stopped wanting to pinch his cute little cheeks and started wanting to smooth out all the cute little tousles in his curly red hair.

"Alack!" he exclaimed, a look of the cutest sorrow in his twinkly blue eyes. "Woe also. Thou hast gazed too long upon my cursed face, hast thou not? Yea, I can see it in thine eyes that thou hast. Not even thy sorcery is proof against it." I know he *wanted* to look miserable, but his lips parted into such a cute, gap-toothed smile.

"Awwwwwww," I said. I couldn't help it. He reminded me of my little sister Lucy when she was just a kid. She could spend the whole day bashing me over the head with her toys—and that little girl liked to play with rocks more than dollies!—but all I had to do was tiptoe into her room once she'd been all tucked into her little bed for the night, gaze down at her sleeping face, and I just couldn't think about anything except how cute she was.

Just as cute as a barbarian. "You want me to get the J.P.?" asked Scandal, sticking his nose out of the underbrush. "Or you want to hold out for a church wedding?"

"What witchery is this?" cried Grym. He snatched the sword out from under my hands and swung it at the cat. Scandal jumped as high as the barbarian's knees, his whiskers shooting stars. Grym's mother didst not raise no fools indeed; he let the sword drop to his side and knelt before the still-sparking Scandal. Even on his knees, he was nearly as tall as me.

"Mercy, O wondrous beast!" he cried.

"Uh, this is my familiar, Scandal," I said.

"Hi, cutie," Scandal greeted the barbarian.

Poor Grym moaned. "It was ever thus! Oh, this face! This remorseless, treacherous, kindless face! Master Kendar, peerless magician, thou canst not turn thy back upon my suffering!" He flung himself at my feet. It was like having someone chuck a log at you. A *big* old log.

"Well, um, sure. I shalteth not turneth mine back unto thy

mickle great, whatzit, woe. Okay?'' I tapped him on the shoulder.
I swear I heard a metallic ringing sound.

"Is't so?" He lifted his face, and again I had to fight down the
desire to pinch those cheeks. "Shalt thou useth thy great wizardly
powers to lift this curse of nature from my visage? Dare I hope to
waken to a face more suited to my chosen calling in this world?
Wilt thou truly do this thing for me?"

"I said I would, didn't I?" I would've promised him anything
to cheer him up.

"Oh, masssssterrrr." Scandal was beside me, his tail switching.
"Could I have a word with you, pleeeeease?"

"Excuse us," I told Grym. He tried to give me back the sword,
but I motioned him to hold onto it for me.

I followed the cat a little ways deeper into the forest before he
spun around and spat, "Are you crazy?" I tried to answer, but he
was on another roll. "Tell me you didn't just promise Babyface
the Barbarian a quickie job of plastic surgery. Because if you did,
and you try, and you fail because you don't know which end of
your Majyk is loaded, he is not going to be a happy camper. And
if he's not happy—" Scandal made a slashing gesture with his
forepaw and a coarse sound in his throat like Dad always made
just before he fired one of the servants.

"Scandal, have a little pity on the guy," I pleaded. "He's a
barbarian! They loot, they sack, they pillage, they rampage across
the countryside. They take what they want and they want anything
they see. You have anything like that where you come from?"

"It's an election year, I could name names, but why bother? All
right, so he's a barbarian; so what?"

"So you can't strike fear into the hearts of the helpless peasants
if you've got a face that makes them want to go *awwwwwww* and
pinch your cheeks."

Scandal clicked his tongue. "You saw his sword. How many
times do you think he let anyone pinch any part of his body?"

"Barbarians like to move fast," I said. "Zip-zam, into the
village, grab the loot, hit the road. Cutting up the locals takes time.
Anyhow, after a while, I bet it seems pretty hopeless to him. You
can't chop off *everyone's* hand. That face just doesn't go with that
job."

"Get him to change jobs," the cat growled. "Or he'll get you
to change genders when you can't change his face, you mark my
words."

"He won't do anything to me." I sounded so positive, I
surprised myself.

"He did plenty already," Scandal reminded me. "I think he knocked your brain off the blocks. I don't like this world of yours—nothing's logical! Your Majyk should've shielded you from his sword, but it didn't. If we can't keep the same rules for the whole game, we're licked."

"There's a perfectly logical reason why my Majyk couldn't protect me from Grym's sword," I said. "Grym's sword *is* my Majyk."

When cats gape, they look like they're going to bite you, so I quickly added, "It's true. Whenever that sword gets near me, I feel like my blood's bubbling, and you saw what happened when I grabbed it."

"Yeah. Pretty fancy fireworks there. So how did you manage to suck the Majyk out of the sword?"

I shook my head. "I didn't. I don't know how."

"Oh, great!" Scandal said, lashing his tail even faster. "Just great. As long as that sword's around and in working order, there's one weapon on this world that can harm you. Hmm, maybe more than one. We don't know where the rest of your Majyk went. It might be in other swords. Or spears. Or daggers. Or Saturday night specials. Or—"

"I get the idea," I said. "I don't want to end up looking like a porkerpine before we find a way to fix everything. That's why I promised Grym I'd help him with his face. I want him on our side."

Scandal cast a casual glance back to the stump where the big barbarian still waited faithfully. "Better on our side than behind us," he agreed with me. I *think* he agreed with me. "And he would be handy to have around if we do find the rest of your Majyk sticking to some heavy stuff. A strong back and a weak mind . . . well, that's one better than a weak back and a weak mind." Why was he looking at *me*? "Okay, let's go welcome our newest Mouseketeer."

"Mousekitter? Where?" I gasped, swatting at the empty air. (The bite of the mousekitter is big, nasty, and smells like old cheese.)

"Is't resolved, O noble Master Kendar, mayest thou live ten thousand years and thy loins beget many sons?" Grym asked when he returned.

"Put down the shovel, pal, you're in," Scandal told him. "Now if you want to *stay* in, there's a few simple house rules you're gonna have to follow. You savvy 'house rules'?"

Grym turned to me, bewildered. "What's a house?"

"Those things with the pointy tops that you empty out first and burn down after."

"Ah! 'Tis well. Yea, O enchanted beast, I doth well savvy house rules."

"Great; you're beautiful," Scandal mewed.

"I know." Grym was downcast. "But Master Kendar shall fix that eftsoons, by Graverobber's glittering blade!" He brandished the Majyk-soaked sword.

"Put your eftsoons on ice, kiddo," said the cat. "No one likes a pushy barbarian. Master Kendar said he'd fix your face, he'll fix it, but when he's good and ready and not a moment before. You got a problem with that?" He puffed up his fur and walked stiff-legged around the barbarian.

"I hath none," said Grym, watching the cat warily. "Woe worth the man who would meddle in the affairs of wizards, for they are—"

"Yeah, yeah, we all know how that one goes. Spare me. While we're waiting for Master Kendar to get in the mood to help you out, you've gotta show us you're worthy of this big fat favor he's gonna lay on you, *capeesh*?"

"I *capiche*-eth." Grym whirled Graverobber over his head until the air hummed. "I, Grym the Great, late of the Devouring Horde of Uk-Uk the Unspeakable, do hereby take sword-oath! I swear by all mine household gods—and anyone else's household gods I might have stolen on the road—that I will protect and defend the constitution of my new lord, Master Kendar, with my life!"

The tree stump blasted itself apart into burning splinters. Flames roared up from its center, blackening the branches of overhanging trees. There was a horrible, thick stench of brimstone in the air. Scaly arms dragging the ground, dirty yellow eyes narrow with hate, huge mouth open wide so that you could count every single fang, out of the fire came the most hideous monster I'd ever seen since the time I caught a look at Velma Chiefcook without her girdle.

"Grym," I said. "That thing about protecting me with your life?"

"Aye?"

"This looks like a good time to start."

CHAPTER ——————— 10

"I WOULDN'T BOTHER WITH SWORDS IF I WERE YOU," said Zoltan, emerging from the trees to stand behind the monster. The fires died away abruptly, leaving only a ring of charred wood where the tree stump had been. "Swords just make Pthrubwl irritated. He's in a good mood right now."

"How can you tell if something like *that* is in a good mood?" Scandal whispered. The cat crept as close to me as he could, pressing his furry body against my leg. I could feel him trembling.

"He didn't tear us apart the minute he got here," I replied just as softly. "Fiends do that."

"What did you say, Ratwhacker?" Zoltan glowered at me.

"I said they have a lot of weather in Grashgoboum at this time of year." I tried to nudge Scandal away. I didn't want Zoltan getting his hairy paws on the cat. My old "friend" was plenty smart—smart enough to figure it was Scandal who'd saved me back in Master Thengor's palace. I didn't know what he might do to poor Scandal for that, and I didn't want to find out.

No good; the cat stayed put.

"Who is't who dares address the great and awesome wizard, Master Kendar, so boldly?" Grym bawled, striding to stand between me and the fiend. The big barbarian acted as if Zoltan's little scale-covered buddy was a piece of cheap furniture, not worth a second look. The only one he scowled at was Zoltan. "Thou art ugly and thy mother does dress thee funny."

"Ixnay! Ixnay!" I whispered urgently, calling on the help of Ixnay, god of fools and drunkards. (We Gangles have always been strictly Orthodox Wedwelians, believing in no other gods except Wedwel the All-Compassionate Destroyer, but when you're in a tight corner you always hedge your bets.) "That's Zoltan Fiendlord, Grym. He's not even a fully wanded wizard yet, but he can call up terrible demons to do his bidding. If you don't believe me, there's the proof."

The proof roared again, and a league-long blackish-green tongue whipped out of its mouth to snare a fat rappid that had gotten too close to the clearing for its own good. The fuzzy little critter squealed horribly as the fiend reeled it in, then crunched it up and spat out the floppy blue ears.

Grym deftly picked up one of the discarded ears on the point of his sword and flipped it into the air. He caught it with his teeth and devoured it in two mouthfuls, spitting bits of fur. With his mouth full (well, he *was* a barbarian!) he said, "A pox upon him and all his fiends. Yea, a murrain also. Distemper and the spavins take him. May mumps consume his manhood. What do all his Hell-spawned pets matter to a wizard of your power, noble Master Kendar?"

You don't really know you're in deep until you see the stuff floating up around your ears.

"Uh, right," I said, trying to pretend like I wasn't shaking in my tunic at the sight of Zoltan's creature. "They don't matter at all to a wizard of my power. Right. I laugh at them. Ha, ha." It was a bleat, not a laugh, but it was good enough for Grym.

"So I thought." The barbarian gave Zoltan a look of utter contempt. "Thy paltry illusions impress me neither. Thou canst not slay the mighty Master Kendar with such trumpery beast-lings." He hawked up a really huge hairball right at the fiend's taloned feet. I heard Scandal say "Wow!" with real admiration.

Yes, the fiend ate *that*. Luckily it didn't spit out any leftovers or I bet Grym would've munched *those*, spat something back at the fiend, and the fiend would've chomped on *that*, and we'd be stuck there all day watching two big beasts trading spit. (A little like the time I caught Velma in a lip-lock with one of the butchers, but not so nauseating.)

Zoltan stroked his black beard and chortled. "Maybe I can't kill the—hrrrmph—'mighty Master Kendar.' But I can certainly kill *you*, whoever you are."

"I am Grym the Great!" my protector declared, slashing the air with his sword. "I fear you not. I have taken sword-oath by this, my faithful blade Graverobber, to defend Master Kendar's life with mine own." He made another dramatic gesture with the sword and accidentally cut off the fiend's head on the backswing. It bounced across the clearing until it hit a tree, where it promptly changed into a rabid badger and scuttled off, foaming at the mouth.

"Tsk," said Zoltan, looking over the dead fiend's headless body. It was slowly transforming into a hippopotamus, but he put an end to that with a single stroke of wizard's lightning. An extremely ugly little lap dog jumped out of the ashes, yapping furiously, peed all over Grym's sandals, and ran away before the barbarian could chop it in two.

Zoltan made a nonchalant gesture, and seven brand new fiends erupted from the forest floor. "As I was saying," he continued, "before I was so crudely interrupted, maybe I can't kill you, Ratwhacker, but your Majyk won't give a bat-herder's damn if I try to kill your friends." He leered at Grym, who called him a user of perfumes and a jelly-boned city-dweller who would even *have polite conversations with women.* Zoltan ignored the ultimate insult. He was staring at Scandal with an evil smirk.

The cat bushed out his fur and hissed loudly at my former fellow-student. A low growl started deep in his belly, which sounded more like a bloodthirsty yowl when it came out. His tail stood straight up and he raised one forepaw, claws extended.

It was the weirdest thing. Suddenly I realized that Scandal wasn't doing all that because he was *afraid* of Zoltan and his fiends. Fear had nothing to do with it; Scandal was *angry!* Angry and ready to fight. So angry that if I didn't do something fast, he'd leap right for Zoltan's throat and get sliced open with one slash of a fiend's talons, Majyk or not.

"Well, well," Zoltan said, his smile twisting like a snake. "And what sort of freak do you have there, Ratwhacker? I've never seen anything like it, even while browsing through the deepest pits of Hell. Did you try to use your Majyk and have it backfire?"

Scandal muttered something like "Freak yourself," but Zoltan didn't hear. Apparently he didn't remember the cat from Master Thengor's deathbed fiasco. Why should he? Scandal had been just a furry blur zooming through the wizard's bedchamber.

I put on the biggest, slickest, shiniest grin I could and said, "I've got a surprise for you, Zoltan: Majyk's not so hard to manage after all. *That* happens to be my familiar, Scandal. I called him up myself." I made my own smile wriggle around as much as his, then added the clincher: "He's a cat."

"A cat!" Zoltan was stunned; I'd played it right. For once. "But cats are legendary beasts!"

I blew on my nails. "Not if you've got the right connections.

Any wizard with half a crystal ball can summon up the fiends of Hell, but how many of us can break through to the land of legends and bring back a cat?''

Zoltan turned sullen. "No one could learn to control that much Majyk that fast. You didn't even know there was such a thing as Majyk until a few days ago!"

I shrugged.

"Still, I suppose that might explain why you have taken this road," he murmured, half to himself. "None but the greatest wizards and the greatest fools would ever dare to choose a path that leads straight through the heart of the fearsome Forest of Euw at this time of the year. It is spring, when the flowers bloom and the nectar rises. Spring, when the moonbeams fall most prettily. Spring . . . when *they* come out in search of prey."

"They who?" I asked, and knew the instant after I asked that I'd blown it.

"You don't know who *they* are?" Zoltan's startled look quickly turned to gloating. "I'll bet you didn't even know you were in the fearsome Forest of Euw until I told you, either."

"I did so!" My protest was in vain.

"In fact, I'm willing to risk everything on the chance that you're still the same incompetent idiot Ratwhacker you always were and that you've been lying about being able to master Majyk."

"Fine." I clenched my fists and felt the sweat beading on my brow. "Bet away. It'll only cost you your life if you lose."

"Oh, I don't think it will." Zoltan looked cool as a toad's to-sit-on. "That's what fiends are for." He turned to the seven monsters he had summoned up and said, "Get them, boys."

Six of the fiends charged, filling the air with their blood-freezing howls. I scooped up Scandal, holding the cat close to my chest. I hoped that if I kept him that close to me, my Majyk would look out for us both, but . . . where did that leave Grym?

I should worry. The barbarian watched the rush of the attacking fiends with a diamond-hard smile and a ready-and-waiting stance that seemed to say *Cometh thou to Papa*. Two swift slices of Graverobber's Majyk-enhanced blade took one monster's legs out from under him as he raced past. He kept going on sheer momentum until he hit a tree. A twist and a tickle of the sword left a second fiend trailing his guts after him like war-banners. He looked rather embarrassed when he realized what had happened, and blushed himself to death.

Our third and fourth assailants sneaked past Grym, only to be barbecued by short, rapidly pulsating bursts of my Majyk. Bits and pieces of smoldering scales flew through the air. Zoltan cursed loudly and yelled at fiends numbers five and six to forget about me and destroy the barbarian first. "And don't just jump in without thinking, boys! Wait your chance, then make your move!"

The seventh fiend hadn't moved at all. I wondered why.

The other two surviving fiends paid heed to their master's instructions. Keeping out of sword-reach, they circled Grym slowly. The barbarian made a few lunges, which they easily dodged. Step by step they herded him away from Scandal and me until they had him at bay with his back against an oak tree. Their taunting laughter sounded like someone stomping a bag full of grasshoppers.

"Scandal, what'll I do?" I whispered. "They're going to kill him!"

"You're gonna hope they don't swallow his sword after, that's what," the cat said. "If they do, no way you'll be able to collect the Majyk off it."

"Majyk doesn't matter!" I cried. "We're talking about a man's life."

"A man who whomped you one upside the head." The cat looked at me, eyes like burning gold. "I take it you don't bear grudges?"

Funny, but I couldn't answer. All I could do was stare into Scandal's eyes. If I looked up, I knew I might have to watch poor Grym getting his innards ripped out, and I didn't want that. More than I'd ever *positively* wanted anything, I did *not* want that. The cat's eyes were huge and glittering, all except for the black slit pupils, like two chasms in the earth. If I stared into them hard enough, maybe I could tumble right in and take everyone else along with me. Far, far underground, far away from Zoltan and his pet fiends where we'd be safe . . .

"What's with you?" the cat asked. I wish I could've said. His eyes were bigger now. They'd gone from huge to vast, with big waves of gold washing out from the centers. Now I thought I could see solid objects floating in the golden sea: rings, arrows, books, more, all just waiting for me to dip my hand in and pick out the one I wanted.

"Ow!" yelped Scandal when I dropped him and plunged my hand into the golden sea too big to be held in a cat's eye.

The two fiends harassing Grym froze as a bright light fell on them heavier than a granite slab. I saw them turn slowly, like every movement cost them in blood, and couldn't believe my eyes when they fell to their knees before me.

"Aaaiiiieee!" shrieked one, gesturing with a knobby, clawed hand. "Behold! He has found the Sacred Sword of Sassafrax!"

I glanced at my own right hand. Yep. There was a sword in it, all right. Darned if I knew how it got there, but there it was. The scarlet hilt was encrusted with gems, the blade gleaming with inlaid silver runes, the pommel shaped like an emerald-eyed dragon sleeping on top of a mountain of sapphire skulls. It was a pretty spiffy sword, if I did say so myself.

"Oh woe!" the first fiend wailed. "We are doomed. No being of the netherworld may hope to stand before the Sacred Sword of Sassafrax!"

"What are you, nuts?" the other fiend snapped. "We're doomed, of course, but only because he has brought forth the Blessed Blade of Blindish, against which no creature of dark sorcery may triumph."

The first fiend got up off his knees—if they were knees—and glowered at his pal. "That's the Sacred Sword of Sassafrax, and you'd know it if you weren't half-blind from reading funnytale books under your blankets after infernos-out."

The other fiend got up too, paws on slithery hips. "There's nothing wrong with *my* eyes. The Sacred Sword of Sassafrax does *not* have a dragon-shaped pommel. The Blessed Blade of Blindish does. What's more, the Sacred Sword of Sassafrax can only be wielded by a virgin!"

"*None of your business!*" I shouted before either of them could ask me the obvious question.

"Whoooo, boy, are *you* ever turning red!" Scandal chortled nastily.

"Who cares *what* it's called?" Zoltan shrieked, jumping up and down beside the one remaining fiend not yet dead or quarreling. "It won't change the fact that Ratwhacker doesn't know one end of a sword from the other! He can't hurt you with it!"

"Sassafrax!" the first fiend bawled, ignoring him.

"Blindish!" the other bellowed.

"Call it *Blindafrax*, if you want!" Zoltan yanked out handfuls of his beard, frustrated beyond belief.

"Do you *mind*?" the first fiend asked frostily.

"Yes, this is important," his opponent confirmed.

"How important could it be?" Zoltan demanded. "How important if it causes you to ignore the commands of your master?" He stood up to his full height and tried to look imposing.

"Important enough for me to open your belly like a melon and scoop out the seeds if you don't give us a little time to get this settled, *Master,*" the first fiend said in a very reasonable tone.

"Oh." Zoltan's voice came out like a new-hatched chick's first peep. He shrank down inside his robes. The monsters went back to their battle.

"Sassafrax!"

"Blindish!"

"Sassafrax!"

"Blindish!"

"Sassafraxsassafraxsassafraxsassafrax-*infinity*!"

"Blindishblindishblindishblindish-infinity *plus one*!"

"Call it a cab!" Scandal suggested cheerfully. "Call me Ishmael! Let me call you sweetheart!"

"Call it anything," my old school-chum moaned, "only get *on* with it! Call it Fred, but *somebody* kill *something*!"

"All right," said Grym. He sliced one fiend in half lengthwise, right through the sassafrax, then cut the other one's blindish off. The two mangled bodies toppled over, washing the barbarian's sandals with blood.

"Verily do I hope this will get the stench of dog pee out," Grym remarked, studying his gory footwear.

I laughed so hard I dropped the sword. It shattered into a thousand pieces when it hit the dirt. Try as I would, I couldn't call it back together again. Hey, I couldn't even figure out how I'd managed to get my hands on it in the first place! I closed my eyes tight and concentrated until I got a headache. Nothing. I made a whole lot of silly motions with my hands and said all sorts of nonsense, hoping to trip over the right spell for summoning swords. No luck.

I looked up at Grym. "I meant to do that."

Zoltan's eyes lit up like a pair of rogue fire-sprites. He grabbed the one remaining fiend by its oozy elbow and said, "I don't know why you didn't attack when the others did, but I'm glad of it now."

"Of course I didn't attack," the fiend replied. "You said, 'Get them, *boys.*'" The monster primped its scales. "My name is *Pthrubwle*, with a final *e*. I'm a lady."

"And a very wise lady, too," Zoltan cooed. "So wise to have waited, to study our foes' defenses and weaknesses. But the hour to strike has come! See what a wonderful feast awaits you!"

He waved at us. Grym went into his fighting crouch; Scandal

puffed out; I started chanting "Sword, sword, don't go 'way, I need you right here today." It didn't work.

Zoltan got behind the fiend and gave her a gentle shove. "Go! Why do you wait? They are all yours for the eating! A banquet fit to glut the belly of a demon queen! You shall stuff yourself on their flesh until the juice drips down your—You *do* have a chin somewhere, don't you?"

"I'm on a diet," said the creature primly.

We relaxed.

"But I could kill them and not eat any. Maybe just a bite." The fiend shrugged. "I guess I could use the exercise."

While we watched in horror, she began to grow. Her shoulders burst through the topmost branches of the trees before you could say *Help!* "Is it all right if I just step on them?" she asked Zoltan.

He bowed. "By all means."

"Stand close, Grym," I ordered. "Maybe if we're all together, my Majyk will shield you, too."

"Forsooth, 'tis no affair of mine to teach a great wizard like thineself thy trade," the barbarian rasped, eyes on the still-growing fiend. She lifted her right foot and aimed. "Yet might I point out that whatever the protective properties of thy power, does thou know of a surety just how far 'twill go?"

"Meaning?"

"Meaning your Majyk might not be strong enough to take out something that big," Scandal translated. "For all we know, maybe the worst it'll do will be to give the lady a bad hotfoot one second before she gooshes us all into jelly. In other words—"

"RUN!" Grym shouted. We all took off for the trees just as the monstrous foot came crashing down.

CHAPTER 11

WE DIDN'T STOP RUNNING UNTIL WE CAME TO A WIDE, wildwater stream. Then we fell into it, so we had to stop running and start drowning.

Scandal was the only one able to stop before he hit the water. In fact the reason I fell in was because I tripped over Scandal. He threw himself down on the bank and watched Grym and me as we thrashed about. His furry sides were heaving rapidly. I don't know whether he was panting for breath or killing himself with laughter.

"Help!" cried Grym, brandishing his blade above the spray as his head dipped below the rushing waters. He came up in time to add, "Aid! Succor! Assistance in time of—*blub!*" He went under again, only his sword-arm sticking out above the flood.

"Don't worry, Grym!" I gasped, kicking my feet madly and paddling for all I was worth. "I'll save you!" I stood up in the stream, which only came up to my knees, and flung myself in a gorgeous dive towards the floundering barbarian.

I was already airborne when it hit me: *The water's* shallow, *you moron!* Then I plunged headfirst into the current and it *really* hit me: the rocky bottom of the stream, I mean. Ouch.

My eyes were still crossing and uncrossing when Grym fished me out by the collar of my tunic and tossed me onto the far bank to dry. Most of the pretty blinky-lights went away in time for me to see him wade across the water and carry Scandal over. The three of us sat there for a while in a thick bed of frilly blue flowers.

Finally Grym looked at me and said, "What then is the truth of thy life, O lowly mountebank and deceiver?"

"Huh?" I responded. Scandal rolled his eyes.

"Give it up, bud; he's wise to you. He knows you're no more a big-time wizard than I'm a liverwurst."

"In very sooth, 'tis so," the barbarian agreed. "Albeit a liverwurst might thou yet be, O beast, if a liverwurst be something edible." He eyed Scandal meaningly.

"That's a matter of opinion," the cat replied, but he looked a little nervous.

"Thou art as guilty of falsehood as thy master," the barbarian went on. He scowled at me. "The folk of my tribe do esteem truth above all things. Thou hast trespassed on mine trust, O thou naughty fibber. My people have a simple yet effective way of dealing with such double-tongues as thou."

He had Graverobber across his knees and was wiping the blade dry with fistfuls of satiny grass. I never saw grass that green and shiny at Master Thengor's, or at home, or—or anywhere. It smelled sweet, too; sweeter than whole garden beds of rosebushes in bloom; almost sweet enough to let me forget that Grym was going to demonstrate his tribal "simple yet effective" cure for liars on me any second now.

"Don't waste your time trying to teach Kendar a lesson, Arnold," said Scandal, yawning a big pink yawn. "It won't work; his power will protect him."

"His power." Grym's lip curled. He looked adorable. I had to sit on my cheek-pinching hand. "The power he promised would change my accursed face. Ha! I see now that he can no more control this *power* of his than I may command the moons."

"Okay, try something with him. Just try. No fur off my tail if you get fricasseed for it." Scandal started to groom himself.

Grym waved Graverobber a little too close to my nose for comfort. I felt captive Majyk bubbling off the sword, tickling me all over. "I swear by this blade, it is not because I fear him that I do not strike! Yea, on the honor of mine good arm in battle, was't not this very steel which rendered the vile quacksalver senseless?"

"Oh, sure, *senseless*." Scandal was unconcerned. "Yeah, like his power couldn't tell the flat of an incoming sword from the edge! It's lucky for you that the stuff only gets riled enough to fight back when people are trying to kill Kendar, not just trying to hurt him."

"What do you mean 'just' trying to hurt me?" I yelped.

Scandal was too busy working up a temper at Grym to answer me. "I've got news for you, Citizen Kane," he snarled. "The stuff that's watching out for Kendar *and* me *and* that tin-plated frog-gutter of yours is called *Majyk*, and if you had the smarts God gave little green apples, you *would* be afraid of him!"

Grym sniffed. "And why might that be, prithee?"

"Because Majyk is this cockamamie world's answer to a nuclear meltdown waiting to happen, and the only guy at the switch is this *bozo!"* the cat shouted, jerking his head at me.

I didn't know what a nuclear whatzit was, but maybe my Majyk did, and translated. I got a huge pain right in the middle of my chest, the same kind of hurt that always burned there whenever I heard someone I liked say how stupid and clumsy I was. I could take a hundred *You fool Ratwhackers* from people like Velma—people who didn't count—but when the words came from Mom, or Lucy, or even this crazy cat, so did the burning. A hard, bitter lump settled where my heart should be.

Grym was saying, "Still do I fear him not. But I have given him sword-oath, the which I may not break upon peril of mine honor."

"In other words, you're stuck with him," the cat commented.

I stood up, glaring down at the pair of them. "Why don't you say 'stuck with him *too*,' Scandal? It's what you're thinking," I spat.

"Amazing, Kreskin," the cat purred. "Now you're reading minds. Touchy, touchy. What anthill did you sit on?"

"I'm not deaf. I heard what you said about me."

"Oh, for—!" The cat made a little sound of impatience and switched his tail. "And you took it *seriously*? Gah! If you lived on my world, you'd probably be one of those ningnongs who spies on us cats every waking minute and any little thing we do gets interpreted to death."

He was on his feet, tail still lashing. "Do you know how annoying it can be?" He raised his voice to an irritating whine and threw himself into the part. "'Oh, pussums didn't eat'ums din-din. Pussums must be mad at us because we bought that other brand of cat food. We're so sorry, pussums, we won't ever do it again.' And—'Oh mercy!'—we put precious kitty-cat's kibble in his canned-food dish! Now pussums will hate us forever.'" Scandal eyed me scornfully. "It's right about then that I go piss in their sock drawer."

"I don't have a sock drawer," I told him.

"Stop the presses," he drawled. "Now if you don't mind, Nature Boy and I were having a polite conversation." He glanced at Grym and added, "Well, a conversation, anyhow."

"Our parley be ended," Grym declared, hoisting himself to his feet. "The oath that binds me—"

"You want to know where you can stick that oath?" I sniped.

Grym was bewildered. "By the laws of my people, I am barred from giving mine oath where I would not willingly give my sword.

This ban doth likewise extend to where I might stick both oath and sword, I fancy. Where, then, wouldst thou have me stick it?''

Before I could answer, Scandal said, ''Well, if there was ever a place where the sun don't shine, I'd say we've found it.'' For the first time since we'd outrun Zoltan's tame demon, we actually looked around to see just where our flight had taken us.

Grym was the first to speak. ''Dark, is't not?''

Dark it wast—I mean, *was*. The trees surrounding us seemed to breathe darkness. The grass underfoot and the thick patches of flowers everywhere were bright enough—they gave off their own unnatural candy-colored light—but the trees themselves were brooding, evil-looking, and *big*. Their towering crowns didn't let a single ray of sunlight through. If there *was* any sunlight. Suddenly I realized that I'd lost all track of whether it was day or night outside the forest.

The fearsome Forest of Euw, Zoltan had called it. I was just starting to get my first taste of what made it so fearsome.

''Flowers need sunlight,'' I said shakily, pointing to the thriving blossoms.

''Aye, if they be earthly flowers,'' Grym said. He cocked his head, then added, ''Hast thou heard the song of any bird, else the rustle of any small forest creatures, since we did enter this uncanny wood?''

''Not a peep.'' I bit my lower lip and observed, ''Zoltan didn't follow us.''

''No kidding.'' Scandal's fur started to rise on his back. ''He didn't even set that queen-sized demon on our trail.''

''Perchance he could not.'' Grym's eyes weighed every shadow under the trees. ''I have heard that there are some orders not even fiends will obey.''

I tried to put a happy face on things. ''Well, at least we don't have to worry about them bothering us anymore. I say we go through the forest, and once we're out the other side, we can—we can—'' I stopped. I wanted to say, *we can all go home to my place,* but I wondered what Mom would say about me bringing a barbarian into the house. She was pretty fussy about rude, uncivilized people who didn't wipe their feet and killed things willy-nilly. People besides Dad and my brother Basehart, I mean.

''Never mind what we'll do after we get out of the woods, Little Weird Riding Hood,'' Scandal said. ''First let's see if we can get *out*, period.''

''I say we go that way.'' I pointed in a random direction.

Grym snorted. ''I have given thee sword-oath, O Kendar. That is all that prevents me from saying thou art a muddle-headed ninny who could not find his way out of a ripped sack. But I have in sooth given oath, so I will not say that.''

"I guess you could do better?" I challenged him.

He simply gestured at the stream. "It floweth as all waters do, in but a single direction, seeking the sea. Let such become our own quest. With such a guide, we cannot miss our way. And there are fish in there to eat as well.''

Scandal's ears perked. "Fish?" He licked his chops and rubbed up against Grym's ankles. "I always said Tarzan here was a born leader.''

It stung, but I had to admit it, Grym had a good idea. If we followed the stream, we'd never have to blaze a trail or hunt for drinking water or go hungry. There were fish in the water, sure enough, and also patches of mushrooms clinging to the roots of the trees nearby. They looked normal enough—except for the blue-spotted ones—but I'd have to get really hungry before I'd risk eating them.

I don't know how far we marched. Scandal scampered along beside us until he got tired, then Grym and I took turns carrying him. He kept us entertained by telling stories about the life he used to have in his old world.

"You guys think the wizards on this world got power? Ha! They're small potatoes next to my old human. Now there was a wizard. A computer wizard. I remember one Columbus Day when he was just hacking around and he fixed it so one of those big electric news banners on Times Square kept on scrolling 'You mean it's NOT flat?'—signed 'Ronald Reagan.' ''

"What's not flat?" Grym asked.

"The world, dope. The world's round.''

The barbarian and I stopped in our tracks and exchanged a spooked look. Scandal squirmed in my arms. "What's wrong with you two skinballs?" he demanded. "Was it something I said?''

"This land whence thou dost hail—'' Grym began. "It do be—it do be—''

"Doo-be-doo-be-doo, Sinatra. My world's round, I said. All worlds are round. You got a problem with that?''

For a second, Grym and I didn't know whether to laugh or cry. We settled for laughing. Scandal didn't have a sense of humor when the joke was on him. He bit me and sprang to the ground.

"Right, next thing you'll tell me, this orbiting loony bin is flat,'' he hissed.

"Flat?" Grym stopped laughing long enough to think it over.

"Nay, by my sword, flat it has been but once, in the long-vanished Pewter Age when my people dwelled in cities and ate refined sugar. But that was centuries agone."

"No, no, no!" I had to correct him. "Master Thengor always insisted we learn history—something about not making the same mistake twice—and Orbix was flat twice: once in the Pewter Age when it was flat and round, and once in the even older Age of Very Large Pointy Animals, when it was flat and square."

"*Was* flat?" Scandal stalked up to me stiff-legged. "Don't mess with my head, man. Whadaya mean, it *was* flat? You guys get your own bargain-basement Columbus to prove it's round or what?"

I squatted down beside the stream and dug up a handful of soft clay. Next I scouted up and down the bank until I spied a clump of reeds, and yanked out a young one. I divided the clay into four portions and made a round pancake, a square pancake, a blobby shape stuck full of holes like a potooto, and a simple cube. Then I beckoned Scandal to come close for a good look.

"Orbix in the Age of Very Large Pointy Animals," I said, pointing to the square pancake. "It happened shortly after the Big Accident. For a while it seemed as if all Majyk had been destroyed in the disaster. The wizards could hardly find any and we lived under shockingly primitive conditions. Then Master Pasmoddle the Great discovered that most of the wild Majyk had been gathered into the cheek-pouches of the herds of giant horned hamsters that terrorized the land. There was a short, ugly war until the wizards perfected the giant wire-wheel trap. When they captured enough of the giant horned hamsters and harvested the Majyk they hoarded, the wizards regained the upper hand, and civilization returned.

"You know, I bet I would've gotten a much better grade if I'd known they were talking about *Majyk*, not magic. I mean, how can a giant horned hamster hoard *magic*? But when it's *Majyk*—"

"I can give you the name of a really good shrink, you know," Scandal suggested. "You just get me back to my world and I'll—"

I let him talk, even if I didn't know what he was talking about. I was trying to tell him what I remembered from Master Thengor's history lessons, and I knew if I got distracted, I'd forget everything.

I moved on to the reed, flat and long and green on the grass, and picked it up. "Next came the Age of Traffic and Shoving, when Orbix was shaped like this. It was a time of hardship. Whole tribes of people would pack up and leave their old hunting grounds''—I indicated one end of the reed—''and go off in search of fresh lands. Of course they ran into other tribes who they shoved out of *their* original hunting grounds''—I moved my finger down the reed a span—''and those tribes nudged the next tribes over out of *their* territory''—my finger moved down another notch—''and *they* had to push the next set of tribes off of *their* land''—I was almost to the end of the reed by now—''and when push came to shove—'' My finger skidded off the other end of the reed and plummeted to its death in the cosmic abyss.

''Aye, 'twas a bitter time,'' Grym agreed. ''It was then that my people turned to the worship of Ribok, god of the long march.''

''Have either of you two space cadets ever heard of a little thing called gravity?'' Scandal asked.

''Then came the Mellow Age.'' I picked up the lump of clay and tilted it back and forth so the cat could see all the holes.

''Orbix settled into this shape.''

''It looks like a vegetable.'' Scandal sniffed at the lump. ''Planets should definitely not look like vegetables.''

''You're right,'' I said. ''It does look like a vegetable: a potooto.''

The cat tried to cup one pointed ear with a white paw and didn't quite make it. ''Beg pardon?'' he asked in a cracked, wheezy voice. ''The old ears bin gittin' a mite persnickety on me, youngster. Thought as how you said po*too*to.''

''That's what I said.''

''The potooto is a root vegetable.'' Grym backed me up.

''Takes one to know one,'' the cat commented.

Either the barbarian didn't hear him, or he took it as a compliment. '''Tis a most tasty food. It doth grow in profusion, immune to insect pests. Yon holes which thou behold'st serve as traps for the vermin, which do plunge into them and all the way through the plant. Each time they do attempt to feast upon the potooto, they fall down another hole therein. In time, they grow discouraged. Thereat they pick themselves up and stalk away in disgust, muttering vile curses. Nor is the potooto useful only to stave off hunger.'' He took the clay model from my hands and blew softly across the holes. A gentle *poooot* filled our ears.

I took back the model. ''They say it wasn't too bad, living on a potooto-shaped world, but the surface was full of these big craters. They were pretty handy if you had a lot of garbage you wanted to dump and forget.''

"My tribe lost a whole royal dynasty that way." Grym shook his head over the Good Old Days.

"The only problem with the holes was whenever a wind blew over them—even a breeze—you heard music. It wasn't great music, but the way it wandered up and down the Ichthyonic Scale was kind of hypnotic. Entire civilizations fell under the music's spell. Healthy men and women would just sit around in white rooms staring at shiny crystals and telling everybody how they were really Master Pasmoddle the Great from the Age of Very Large Pointy Animals so they didn't need to go out and get a job."

Scandal scowled at Grym. "And I bet your tribe decided they were the giant horned hamsters, huh?" The barbarian tried to look *Who, me?*

I picked up the cube. "This is what Orbix looked like in the Age of Teen Death Ballads, the one that came just before the age we're in now. It didn't last too long—we never know when the next shape shift's going to come—but we got a lot of good music out of it."

"And what does this world look like now?"

I picked up the green reed again, gave it a twist in the middle and joined the ends.

Scandal pointed his nose at the treetops and yowled. "The pain! The pain!" he cried, rolling on the ground.

"What's wrong? What hurts?" I asked, feeling helpless.

"My brain! My brain!" the cat wailed. "All the logic is being sucked out of my brain! If you don't say something that makes *sense* real soon, I'm going to turn into one of *you* idiots!"

"I could help," Grym offered, raising his sword.

Scandal got better at once. "Let's not be hasty, Dr. Kildare," he commanded, springing to his feet. "We come in peace. All I want to know is how in the name of Steven Hawking did you people wind up living on a planet that changes shape like a politician changes promises?"

"What is amiss with that?" Grym asked. "For that matter, what is a politician?"

"Something slippery enough to eat a potooto and just leave the holes."

Grym scratched his head. "Doth not thy place of origin likewise transform itself?"

"No, back home we're all kind of attached to living on a round world."

"Round?" Grym's mighty chest shook with guffaws. "Then

well might'st thou name it Whirl'd, for surely thee and all thy fellows needs must be whirl'd off so treacherous a surface.''

"Now, now, Grym, Orbix was round once," I reminded him. "Of course it was round the *sensible* way, with everyone living on the *inside* of the planet so we couldn't get spun off into space."

"Aye, so 'twas." Grym nodded. "The Dark Ages."

"I give up," Scandal said. He started following the stream again.

Grym and I trotted after him. "I thought you wanted to know how Orbix got to be this way," I said.

"I changed my mind," Scandal replied, keeping his eyes on the path. "I'm *happier* not knowing. I'm *saner* not knowing. I'm telling myself it was the Plate Tectonics Fairy who did it."

"Who?"

"Yeah, she got together with Tinkerbell and Glinda for a wild party one Saturday night, downed a few too many tequila-and-pixie-dust shooters, then went home and zapped Orbix so every few aeons it gets the geological hiccups."

"Gee, that's amazing!" I was really impressed. "Except for the names, you got it right!"

Scandal stopped dead. "I what?"

"What happened to Orbix. Except it wasn't a *she* who did it, it was a *he*—two he's: Master Uvom and Master Murps. They were the two greatest wizards Orbix ever knew. Some people say that Master Uvom was the first man to learn how to gather and tame wild Majyk. Darned if I could understand how *magic* could ever be wild, unless the rappid you're pulling out of a hat hasn't had all his shots. He could even control it well enough to make himself live forever."

"Immortal?"

"No, just unprincipled." Scandal groaned, but he was doing that a lot, lately, so I just went on. "Of course, he wound up with a lot of jealous enemies. Master Murps was one of them. He studied hard and became almost as great a wizard as Master Uvom; then he challenged him to a duel, winner take all. It was awful. Whole continents were destroyed. The seas boiled. The stars stood still. Animals caught on fire. Women wore short skirts. And then, in a final burst of Majyk unleashed—it was over."

"Five says Master Uvom won."

"Nobody won," I told him. "Master Uvom lasted a few seconds longer than Master Murps, if that counts for anything. It was a disaster that almost wiped out the whole planet. The few wizards who survived called it the Big Accident, and even today we don't like to talk about it. Every wizard on Orbix has to carve Master Uvom's last words, 'Let That Be A Lesson To You,' over every hearth in his house so we never forget what can happen if we abuse the power of Majyk. Word of this got out through their servants and pretty soon having that saying carved over your hearth became the fashion with almost every householder on Orbix—the ones that had hearths, anyway. Not that they really know what it meant." Not that I did, either, until recently.

"Murps and Uvom sure learned it the hard way," Scandal mused.

"Some lesson. They both died horribly, and in the backlash from their last battle, Orbix got so saturated with Majyk that from then on it couldn't even control its own shape."

"Now, who does that remind me of?" the cat said casually.

I knew he meant me, and I didn't like it. He was right, of course: If Orbix couldn't straighten itself out so many ages after the Big Accident, what chance did I have of ever getting back to normal? That still didn't mean I needed him to remind me.

All of a sudden, I was tired. I found a tree—pretty easy job, in a forest—and sat with my back against it, my head resting on my knees. The Big Accident, big deal. Mine was bigger. I didn't look up until I felt something warm and furry rubbing against my ankles.

"Cheer up, sport!" Scandal's whiskers curled up. "You're forgetting: Orbix didn't have *me* on its side."

"What a comfort," I said.

"Aw, come on, kiddo! I said I'd help you out."

"Sure, as long as it helps you out, too."

Scandal folded his ears back and put on a gravelly voice. "Dammit, Jim, I'm a cat, not a philanthropist!"

"My name's Kendar, not Jim. And I don't know what a philanthropist—"

TZING!

The arrow flashed so close that its feathered fletch cut my right ear lobe before imbedding itself in the tree behind me. Scandal hissed. Grym's sword scraped from the scabbard. The barbarian growled and went into a fighting stance.

A dozen tall, slender bodies dropped from the trees. They all held loaded silver longbows aimed right at us. Pointed ears and huge, slanted leaf-green eyes peeked out through golden hair so long and flossy I was amazed they could see to aim their weapons. One of them spoke to us in a musical language I couldn't understand.

Well, not exactly musical. More like chirpy. Squeaky. Like the time we put mice in Lady Inivria's pipe organ.

"Who are they?" I whispered.

"And how the hell did they hide in the trees when they're all wearing bright pink leotards?" Scandal whispered back. "With sequins, yet."

Grym seemed to have the answer. "Aiiieee!" he cried. "*Welfies!*" Graverobber fell from his hands. "We are all dead men."

CHAPTER ——————— 12

"WOULDST THOU MIND TURNING OFF THAT LIGHT?"
Grym demanded. He sounded really mad. "Albeit we must perish
on the morrow, I should like to get a good night's sleep."

"Aw, put a sock in it," Scandal snarled. "He'd turn it off if he
could, and you know it."

"No, I wouldn't," I put in from my corner of the little blue
mushroom house. (Actually, there aren't any corners inside a
mushroom, but you know what I mean.) "If I could control the
way I keep lighting up with this stupid Majyk, I'd make it shine
bright enough to burn your eyelids off."

"Someone woke up on the wrong side of the fungus," Scandal
remarked, covering his eyes with his paws.

Grym grunted and rolled over onto his left side, taking all the
blankets. I didn't care; Welfie blankets were only made of spider
web and they didn't do a darned thing to keep you warm. The
pillows Welfies gave their prisoners were no better: the round
yellow center part of day's-eye flowers. Every time I put my head
down, I got a noseful of pollen and sneezed like crazy.

I hugged my knees and wished I knew what time it was. My
head said it was time to think about how to escape from the
Welfies, my feet said it was time to run first and think later, and
my stomach said it was time for breakfast. Meanwhile my Majyk
decided it was time to light me up like a moonfish. Deep in the
Fearsome Forest of Euw, time is relative.

I don't like most of my relatives.

Scandal and Grym were asleep again. I don't know how they
could just drop off like that when we were going to be killed the
next day. Maybe they decided the Welfies had no more idea of
how to tell it was daytime than we did, so they were safe. Safe for

now, sure, but even a Welfie's going to figure that eventually it's got to be daytime *somewhere*.

And when it was daytime, that was it for us. Escape? Nice thought. Too bad it was impossible. From the moment the Welfie archers got the drop on us, we'd made seventy-three different escape attempts, individually and as a group. Every one of them failed. If we ran, they caught us. If we ran faster, they shot arrows after us. If we ignored the arrows and kept running, they shot arrows with dragnets attached and that stopped us. And that was only how they thwarted the escape attempts we made on our way to the village.

I sighed and leaned my head against the wall. The mushroom house was nice and spongy—better than those gold-dusty Welfie pillows. It was too late to try to get away and I was too tired. Maybe my Majyk would protect me from whatever nasty surprise the Welfies had waiting for us tomorrow, but what about my friends—?

Friends? Now, why was I thinking of Grym and Scandal that way? Neither one of them liked me, not really. They were just stuck with me, that was all. Yeah, stuck with me until we could find a way to make my Majyk give them what they wanted— Grym a new face, Scandal a way home—and then they'd leave me. Some friends.

That's what I could use: some friends.

I was just drowsing off when I heard a scratching at the wall near my ear. I jerked awake and stared into the dark. The Majyk had stopped making me glow, but suddenly there was a fizzling and a sputter and I flared on.

"Oooooh," said the wall. "How do you do that?"

I touched the springy surface. "Can you talk?"

"No," the wall replied. Then it giggled. It had a very pretty laugh. The scratching started up again. After a short time, it stopped and the wall said, "This would go a lot faster if you ate from your side."

"Ate what?"

"What's right in front of your nose, silly: the mushroom. It's not poisonous, but it's not as good as the green kind. I've heard it tastes better if you fry it up with a little butter and a big, juicy beefsteak." I heard a soft dripping sound from the wall. That was ridiculous; walls don't drool.

But whoever—or whatever—was on the far side of the wall did. And whoever it was, wanted to reach me and was willing to eat a way through to do it. The least I could do was help out. I plunged my fingers into the soft prison wall and tore out a big chunk. It was woodsy, with a nice nutty aftertaste.

For a long time, the only sound inside and outside the mushroom house was chewing. Then, when I made a grab for another handful of wall, my fingers went right through and touched other fingers. They were long, slim, and cool as moonbeams. Without thinking, I tried to pull them towards me.

"Hey! What are you doing? I can't fit through a hole that size!" The fingers tugged out of my grasp. I put my eyes right up to the hole in the wall and peered out.

All I saw was night and forest and mushrooms with doormats in front of them.

"Psst! Up here. Get your hand out and reach up here."

The voice was coming from overhead now. I obeyed it, munching up a few more mouthfuls so that the hole was large enough for me to slide my whole arm out and up. I couldn't see, but I felt something settle onto my hand.

"All right, now close your fingers—*carefully*, for Sylvan's sake! I don't want to end up squashed like a jugbug. There, that's the way. Now bring me inside slowly, slooowly . . ."

I did what I was told. Something small and warm was squirming in my palm. It tickled like crazy, almost the same way Grym's Majyk-soaked sword made me feel. Then I uncurled my fingers, saw what I'd been holding, and started tickling in a whole new way.

It was a girl, a beautiful girl no bigger than a grasshopper. She was wearing a very short tunic that seemed to be made of dragonfly wings. Speaking of wings, she had a pair of them sticking out of her back. They were multicolored and shimmery, but when she tried to stand up on my palm they kept snagging on her long, gossamer-fine golden hair.

"Oooohhhhhh, I *hate* these! I wouldn't have to put up with them if I were a *male* Welfie. *They* don't have wings. It's not fair." She stamped her tiny foot and tossed her head while I watched, fascinated. I'd never seen anything so pretty. Then she looked up at me and said, "Well, what are you waiting for? Put me down. Or do you want me in your lap?"

Honestly, I didn't know what to say.

She made an angry face. "All right, you asked for it," she said, and the next thing I knew I was flat on my back with a fully-grown winged girl sitting on my stomach. Boy, you'd never think someone so slim-looking could weigh so much! It must've been the wings.

"By Buxomia's many mountainous mammaries, *now* what transpireth?" Grym roared, tossing aside the spider-web blanket. He rubbed his eyes and got a good look at our visitor. "Oh. Little know I how thou didst manage to conjure up such a morsel of maidenly beauty for thy pleasure, O Kendar. It may yet be that thou shalt redeem thyself in mine eyes. Carry on." He yanked the blankets back over his head and snuffled off to sleep.

"I like your friend," the winged girl told me. "He's cute."

"Get off my stomach," I told her.

She slid to the ground carefully, so as not to rouse Grym a second time. A mushroom house isn't that big—most of the space is overhead storage under the cap—so we were all cramped up together. If not for the wings, I would've liked it.

"Who are you?" I asked her. Actually what I said was "Who are y-*ungph!*" when I got a mouthful of iridescent wing in the mouth.

"Oh dear, I'm sorry. They are such a bother, aren't they?" She gathered in the loosely flapping wing the way I once saw Master Thengor's laundress pull a bedsheet off the clothesline. Her smile was—well, I'm not used to having pretty girls smile at me, so I didn't have anything to compare it to, but I guess it was one of the best out there.

"My name is Mysti," she said. "I'm here to be rescued."

"Uh-huh," I responded. This was *not* the right answer.

The smile was gone. "Maybe you didn't understand me," Mysti said, her high, pale forehead wrinkling up like a walnut. "I want to be rescued. Saved. Snatched away from a fate worse than death."

"Yeah, well, uh—" One look at her expression and I knew I'd have to do better than that. Fast. "I'd like to help you, Mysti, really I would, but you see, I've got this little problem."

"And what's that?"

"Who's going to rescue *me*?" Scandal mewed in his sleep and I corrected myself: "I mean, who's going to rescue *us*?"

Mysti's winged shoulders heaved with a tremendous sigh. "Oh, you men. Honestly. Do I have to think of everything?" She pointed at the hole in the wall. "For starters, you could try crawling out through that. You'd better. I didn't eat all that mushroom plain and raw for nothing."

I looked at the hole like it was the first time I'd ever seen one. "Mmm yeah, that might work for starters, except for one thing: We tried it. We tried it five times. Every time we tried it, they caught us and brought us back."

"Don't tell me you're a quitter," Mysti challenged me. "I hear from the Council of the Undying Wise that you're the greatest human wizard they've ever seen. You made a really big impression on the Elders. They were all squeaking and squawking about how much Majyk you had and how they'd never seen anything like it in ages. In fact, Lord Turalu was actually seen to twitch a whole finger while they were discussing what to do with you. The last time he moved anything, he was being chased by a giant horned hamster."

I didn't know Lord Turalu from a turnip, but I guess he knew me. "So . . . since the Council thinks so highly of me, what did they decide to do?"

"Kill you." Mysti shrugged and I got another mouthful of wing. "Mortals with Majyk make them nervous."

"Thanks," I said. "Thanks a lot. You can't imagine how much better you've made me feel." A thought struck me. "They're not going to be able to do it, though. My Majyk won't let anything kill me."

"That's what they all say." Mysti wiped off the edge of her wing where I'd gotten some spit on the velvety surface. "We're Welfies; when it comes to Majyk, we manage. Majyk is part of us, so all the wild Majyk out there, and the Majyk you human wizards tame, generally gets out of our way when we want to do something. It's—what do they call it?—manners."

Great. The one useful thing my Majyk ever did for me, and now I heard it was going to step aside and let the Welfies kill me because that was the polite thing to do.

"Majyk's a part of me, too," I countered.

She just laughed at me. "Listen, it's like swimming. A fish can swim and a human can learn to swim, but it's not the same thing at all; swimming's part of what makes the fish a fish."

I folded my legs under me and rested my chin on one hand. "If you're made of Majyk, why do you need me to save you from a fate worse than death? *You* should be saving *me* from a fate worse than—well, right now just plain death sounds bad enough to me."

She shook her head, and her silky hair danced around her shoulders like sunbeams. "I won't have to save you. You're going to do it yourself, and this time it's going to work."

"You sound mighty sure of yourself. Can you read the future?"

"I can't even read my own name. But I do know it's what I want you to do, and I always get what I want."

I'll bet she did. "Let's say I try one more escape. How do you know it'll work? How do you know they won't just catch me again and bring me back to this Council of the Wiseguys or whatever you call it?''

She twiddled her fingers in the air and then next thing I knew, I was facing the serious end of a silver dagger. ''Because if it doesn't work, you're not going to have to worry about the Council of the Undying Wise killing you. I'll do it myself. I'm one desperate Welfie.''

I licked my lips; they'd gone all sandy. ''You must be. I mean, you can fly, you can change your size, maybe even change your shape too, you can pull knives out of thin air, and you still need my help? Just what is this fate worse than death of yours that you can't face alone?''

''I'm a Welfie.''

''Yeah, a desperate one, you said. But what I want to know—''

''That's it.'' Her face was solemn as stone, if stone could have dimples. ''That's the fate worse than death I'm fleeing: I'm a Welfie. *And I hate it!*'' The way she screamed that last sentence turned her bright red in the face, made the veins on her neck stand out like a rope ladder, and knocked me over backwards on top of Grym before I could even ask her *Why?*

''That doth it,'' the barbarian snarled, reaching for me.

I crab-walked away from him fast. ''Ah, ah, ah! Mustn't touch! Majyk bite!'' I warned, wagging a finger.

Either Grym wasn't thinking or else the dirty rat had been eavesdropping on the whole Welfies-and-Majyk part of my chat with Mysti, because he picked up his pillow and smacked me right in the face. The pillow was Welfie-made, and Welfies don't *use* Majyk, they *are* Majyk. I guess a little of that passes over into the things they make. All I know is the pillow connected hard and I started choking on a throatful of pollen.

''There, there,'' said Mysti, pounding me between the shoulder blades. She scowled at Grym. ''Do you mind? We were trying to have a private conversation.''

''And I wast trying to sleep,'' Grym returned stuffily. Nobody can be as pompous as a barbarian.

''Getting all rested up so you'll have lots of energy for your execution?'' Mysti sneered.

Grym folded his arms across his magnificent chest. ''I shall not perish without an honorable struggle. Yea, I shall take a goodly number of the accursed Welfie foe down into the dark house of death with me.'' It was only then that he noticed her wings. ''Oh. I crave thy pardon, lady; I knew not that thou wert an accursed Welfie. I thought but that thou wert a bed toy of Master Kendar's conjuring.'' He gave me one of those scornful looks I was really getting to hate. "Forsooth, thou weakling, I did not think that thou hadst the magical skill nor the manly inclination for such frolics.''

That did it. That flaming well did it. I spat out the last of the pollen and glared at him. My whole face was covered with yellow dust, but all I saw was red. I felt hot from the pit of my stomach all the way to the tips of my ears. Something was bubbling inside me, and it wasn't Majyk. My mind seethed with furious thoughts like: *How dare he talk to me like that!* and *What does* he *know about my frolics?* and—finally, fatefully—*Why doesn't he pick on someone his own size?*

Mysti squeaked as my body doubled in bulk and popped out in muscles all over. I was still glowing, too, so the effect was even more startling. I heard Grym gasp as his hand instinctively went for Graverobber's hilt. (Only the sword wasn't there; the Welfies had taken it away as soon as we reached their village.)

I was still in a red rage. "You want a sword?" I shouted at him in a voice as deep and rolling as an avalanche's roar. "*Have* a sword!" I threw my hand high and a gleaming blade appeared in the barbarian's grasp. It was pure flame, the hilt covered with a knot of live, hissing, open-mouthed serpents. He took one look and dropped it immediately. My laughter made the mushroom quake. "So you think I'm a weakling? Not manly enough? How about if I were *twice* your size? Would I be manly enough *then*?"

Grym flung himself backward and Mysti shrank back to grasshopper dimensions as my head burst through the roof, my shoulders thrust the walls apart, and my legs shot out the door, breaking down the outer locks like they were straw instead of iron. (Iron locks on a building you could eat your way out of? That's Welfies for you.) I heard something go *whap-splat-aie!*

"What was that?" I asked, distracted. The instant I stopped being so mad at Grym, I stopped growing. Before I could blink, I was back to my old puny size. My Majyk light flickered and went out.

Mysti fluttered out the open door, then returned to hover near my ear. "That was the guard," she said. She flashed back to human size. "He's not going to be happy. You ruined his hair."

I groaned. In the dark, Scandal stirred. "Did I miss anything?" he asked sleepily, shaking pieces of mushroom from his fur. The sound of many running feet drowned out my answer. A bunch of Welfies arrived, lighting up the ruined mushroom house like broad daylight.

(Welfies don't need fire elementals or illuminum globes or even plain old torches to see in the dark. They twinkle with their own light. It's pink and gold and peach and lavender with a few white sparks floating in it. It reminded me of the fancy dessert Velma Chiefcook once tried on us, except no one would eat it. When she threw it into the moat, the slimegrinds threw it back.)

My tantrum brought nine or ten Welfies to see what I'd done to the prison and the guard. More were arriving by the minute. Most of them wore long white floaty gowns covered with sprinklings of blue glitter. A crowd of Welfie archers stood over to one side, leaning on their silver bows, pink sequined leotards clinging to their tall, slender bodies.

A third group of winged female Welfies came swooping down out of the trees to surround Mysti and drag her away. They were dressed in outfits just like hers, and as soon as they got their hands on her I couldn't tell her apart from the rest. Then she hauled off and started punching, kicking, biting, and cursing anyone within range. They had to drop her, but that didn't mean she was free. There were just too many of them, so they settled for knocking her down and sitting on her. One of them managed to stuff a gag in her mouth. I was kind of glad: She was starting to remind me of my brother Basehart.

"Is it just me, or do they all look alike?" I whispered to Grym.

"'Tis not merely thee, O Kendar," the barbarian said solemnly. "In the tales my tribefolk tell, it is well known that none can tell one Welfie from his fellows, save by the name tags."

"What name tags?"

"See'st thou there, the place above the left bosom?"

I looked where his sword-roughened finger pointed. Yes, he was right: If you paid attention you could see a small line of embroidery, but—

"I can't read that."

"No more can I. Yet didst thou know the Welven tongue, thou couldst. Yon tags be but a cruel jest upon the part of the Welfies, for to learn their spoken tongue taketh a man's full lifetime, and to learn their written language taketh more. Aye, glad they are to have it so. 'Tis said that he who standeth in possession of a Welfie's true name may call himself the creature's master."

Here was news. Mysti had *told* me her name straight out, just like that. Didn't she know what she was doing? Maybe the stories Grym had heard were false. On the other hand, maybe they were true, maybe Mysti knew exactly what she was doing, and maybe she'd been telling the truth when she said just how desperate she was.

I'd worry about that later, if I got a later. Right now, the white-gowned Welfies were falling back to clear a path up to the mushroom house I'd singlehandedly wrecked. Four strapping Welfies were coming through, carrying a gold sedan chair on their shoulders. Riding high above the crowd sat the first Welfie I'd ever seen whose clothing didn't make my eyes hurt or my teeth ache.

His dark blue velvet gown was belted and banded with black, but if his taste in clothes was drab, his taste in jewelry made up for it. On his head was a scalloped silver crown set with a single diamond so big it kept pulling his neck forward. You couldn't see his fingers through all the rings, and when the sedan chair stopped and he picked up the hem of his gown to get off, you could see shoes worth a king's ransom.

Maybe more. No one would pay that much to buy back King Steffan of Grashgoboum.

I remembered what Grym had just told me and checked out the place where this Welfie's name should be embroidered on his gown. Yes, there it was, all done in silver thread, with a few diamond chips sewn on for good measure. It looked like a dragon trying to crawl into its own ear.

The stately Welfie walked toward the wreckage. The three of us got to our feet slowly, keeping an eye on the archers—I hoped they'd get the message that we weren't going to try anything stupid. Following behind the velvet-robed Welfie was an attendant who carried Grym's beloved sword on a white velvet pillow. I could feel the Majyk in the blade calling to me. I could also hear poor Grym whimpering with the desire to get his hands on Graverobber again.

"O Kendar," Grym hissed as we stood in the glare of a hundred cold green eyes. "Canst thou not use thy Majyk in our cause now? Mightst work merely enough of a distraction that I might reclaim my noble sword and skewer some Welfie guts ere we perish?"

"I thought you understood," I replied out of the corner of my mouth. "I *can't* control the stuff!"

"Nay, nay, 'tis not so," he insisted. "Think, O Master. 'Twas thy *anger* as didst summon up the power to serve thee. I prithee now, get thou riled with all haste that we may blow this Welfie scum to atomies and depart from this uncanny wood."

"My anger . . ." I'm not as dumb as everyone keeps telling me. I mean, I hope I'm not. I can figure some things out for myself. Grym was right—I'd tapped into my Majyk when I got angry—but he was also wrong. That time when we stood facing

Zoltan's demons and I conjured up the magical sword, I wasn't exactly *angry*.

But what the hey, if it would save our skins, I'd try anger. And I'd try to work up enough of it so that not only could Grym grab his sword back, but we could get out of there. I scowled fiercely at the Welfies and thought, *How dare they keep us prisoners! How dare they threaten our lives! How dare they—*

It's not going to work, the dark-robed Welfie said. His thin lips didn't move, but I heard and understood every word.

My scowl vanished. "Did you say—?"

Thought, came the reply. *I didn't* say, *I* thought. *I'm doing it all inside your head, Master Kendar.*

"Well, would you mind *not* doing it?" I snapped.

"Not doing what?" Grym asked. The other Welfies giggled.

"Not you; him." I pointed at the crowned Welfie. "He's talking in my head."

Grym gave me the sort of look you save for the local licensed village idiot.

The Welfie spoke again. *You have been a very rude captive, Master Kendar. You have tried to escape and now you have destroyed our prison.*

"Gee, excuse me," I replied aloud, putting a bitter twist on my words.

"Why?" Grym asked. "What didst thou do?"

"I'm not talking to you!" The Welfies giggled louder. I took a step towards the crowned Welfie, my hand knotting into a fist. I knew I'd get an arrow through my heart if I tried to use it on him, but I couldn't help wanting to punch him in the nose. "Let's talk about *rude*," I told him. "Who asked you to come barging into my thoughts with your stupid head-talking when—"

We call it telepathy, Scandal said. I looked down at him. *Yeah, that's it: real woo-woo stuff, but I guess it works.*

His mouth never moved. Not once. He winked at me. *Oh, did you hear that?* came the words inside my skull. *Neat! Ze experrrriment iss ein zuczess. You got any spoons you want bent? How 'bout any Welfies?*

Who speaks? the Welfie demanded.

It is I, Fuzzbucket the Foul, scourge of the seven seas and a B-plus in Intermediate Spanish! Scandal crowed. I held my head. It was getting *loud* in there. *Who do you* think *it is? Whose head is it, anyway? Get outa here, you pointy-eared hobgoblin, before I call Central Casting and sic a Romulan on you!*

A frown set in on the Welfie's high, pale brow. *What babble is this, Master Kendar? These words of power are strange to me.*

Quiche! Scandal shouted, and when someone's shouting inside your brain it really makes your ears hurt from the inside out. *Barcalounger! Holistic! Granola! Factoid! Televangelist! Infotainment! And there's more words of power where those came from, baby.*

How can this be? I know of no other mortal—wizard or no—who has mastered our manner of silent speech. The regal Welfie was looking more upset by the moment. *And these alien words—*

Cher! Vanna! Def Leppard! Van Halen! I could almost feel the cat gleefully bouncing up and down on my brain. *Cholesterol!*

"Enough!" This time the Welfie's voice was right out in the open for everyone to hear. He folded his hands, bowed his head, and gracefully sank to the ground before me. "You win."

CHAPTER ——————— 13

I STOOD IN THE DOORWAY OF OUR NEW PLACE AND LET out a long, low whistle of admiration. "How do they fit all this inside a mushroom?"

"All this" was a vast room that looked about four times the size of the mushroom's outside. The beds and chairs were twists of silver shaped like flowering vines, with cushions and mattresses as soft and inviting as a pile of flower petals. There were no more of those awful, pollen-filled pillows. The floor was covered with pictures of undersea creatures made from pearls, turquoise, jade, and gold tile; the walls were hung with tapestries of hunt scenes so fabulous that the people and animals looked ready to leap off the cloth and invite themselves to dinner.

"All this" was also dinner. It was laid out for us on a crystal table that rested on top of a dragon carved from one tremendous emerald. Grym took one sniff and shoved me aside in his hurry to get at the food.

"Hey, not so fast!" I cautioned. "How do we know this stuff is safe to eat?"

The barbarian chopped a whole roasted pig in two with one blow of Graverobber. (The Welfies had given him back his sword on their leader's orders.) He picked up half the beast and took a big bite of ribs. "'Tis safe," he said with his mouth full. "And if 'tis not, I trust thy mighty powers will avenge my death, O great Master Kendar."

"Now I'm 'great Master Kendar'? Not too long ago, the nicest thing you called me was a weakling."

Grym shrugged and tore another hunk of meat off the pig's bones. "A man who can subdue the evil Welfies must indeed be a great master of Majyk. I now do most firmly believe that all thy talk of being helpless to control thy powers is but thy simple, wizardly way of making a joke. Many are the tales told by my people of great wizards who hide their true might from common men, the better to test them. Yea, the greater the wizard, the more like a total idiot he acteth. By this alone, I figure that thou must be the greatest wizard of all time. If it be thy pleasure to test me thus, so mote it be.''

I joined him at the feasting table, Scandal trotting at my feet. ''Why would I want to test you?''

The barbarian lopped off one of the pig's hind legs and pitched it to me before saying, ''Thou wouldst learn if I be worthy of thy Majyk, O noble sorcerer. Once I have proved myself to thee, then shalt thou grant me my desire and undo the curse of this, my face.''

''You've got it right on the money, Arnold.'' Scandal sat up on his haunches and pawed Grym's leg. ''Now how 'bout tossing some of that little piggy down here to the cheap seats?''

The barbarian smiled and tore the pig's other hind leg off. He dropped it inches from Scandal's head. ''Feast, O thou worthy beast. It may be that thy gracious master doth here test mine kindness to lesser creatures.''

''Get one thing straight, Tarzan,'' Scandal shot back around a mouthful of pork. ''Cats ain't *never* lesser creatures to *nobody*.'' Grym just chuckled.

This was going too far. I didn't want to get into another mess with the barbarian over lies about my Majyk, even if they weren't my lies. I tried to speak up. ''Grym, I'm telling you—''

Oh, let him alone, boss. Scandal's voice barged into my head. *If that's what he wants to believe, let him. It's no fur off your nose.*

I closed my eyes, concentrated, and thought, *I hate when you do that. It gives me a headache.*

The cat's answer showed up inside my head as easily as if he were talking to me: *Tough noogies. You're forgetting that this is how I saved your salami.* Again, *might I add.*

How come you can do that telly—tel—whatever it is?

Telepathy. Scandal's thoughts came in a little faint and fuzzy, as if he was thinking half to himself, half at me. *You got me, bud. My old human used to say he thought cats could read minds. Especially when he was thinking about taking me to the vet. Funny, ain't it? On my world, cats can see in the dark, only we still need a little bit of light to do it. Here, I can see for miles in the dark, even when it's pitch-black. I wonder how much of the other stuff works like that here?*

What other stuff?

The stuff people say about us: We always land on our feet, we've got nine lives, about how curiosity killed—

Why did he stop short like that? *Curiosity killed what?* I asked.

The conversation! He leaped onto the crystal table and walked between the dishes, his tail held high. When he got to a platter of broiled fish he dived right in, making almost as much noise as Grym.

I looked at the piece of pig in my hand, then put it down. I didn't feel like eating. Scandal had bought us some time, but we weren't safe yet. I didn't trust the Welfies.

Maybe if I knew more about them . . . *Good luck with that!* In all my years with Master Thengor, he never mentioned Welfies in one single solitary lesson. I'd remember if he had; I would have flunked it. No surprise that Master Thengor didn't say a word about Welfies. I bet the old pimple was just jealous because they didn't have to work for their Majyk the way he did; it was just a part of them.

Grym polished off the last of the pig and eyed my portion greedily. "Dost not eat, O Master Kendar?"

"I'm planning all the ways I'm going to test you," I said. "Here, help yourself." I tossed him the leg. He caught it in midair. With his teeth.

He was slurping the last gobs of grease off his fingers when we heard a silvery trill of chimes outside our new house. *Knock, knock,* came a jolly voice inside my head. *May we enter, O honored one?*

"I'll handle this!" Scandal exclaimed out loud, raising a paw. Then he invited himself back between my ears and thought, *Come on in, but wipe your feet first.*

Our new place didn't have a real door the way the prison-mushroom did. Instead the doorway was hung with spider-silk, like our old blankets. The crowned Welfie pushed these airy curtains aside and came in, followed by an attendant, wind-chimes dangling from one hand, and—

"Mysti!" I cried. Maybe it was a mistake, but I couldn't help it. There she stood with her hands tied behind her back. I could tell it was Mysti: Other Welfies either smiled these sticky tra-la-la smiles or gazed at mortals with cool contempt; only Mysti could wear an expression that seemed to say, *Mess with me and you're history.* She had some ugly bruises on her face and arms, but I bet the other Welfies looked worse. "What happened to you?"

"What did you call her?" The chief Welfie was so startled, he forgot himself and spoke out loud. He had the world's weirdest accent. He might have sounded better if he wouldn't talk with his lips all pursed up like that.

"Mysti," I repeated. "Um, that's her name, right?"

He turned to her. "Is it so, then, maiden?" He was *not* happy. "The wizard knows your true name?"

Mysti hung her head. "His power is great," she responded. "He forced me to reveal it."

I was going to protest *I did not! You ate your way into my prison cell and dumped your name right in my lap!* I didn't. I still remembered how easily Mysti could pull a knife out of nothingness. Rule One: Never fool around with a desperate Welfie.

The crowned Welfie turned a cold face to me. "What is done is done. Servant, release her." His attendant said a few words in Welfish and the bonds on Mysti's wrists dissolved. Keeping her head bowed, she dragged off to sit on one of the silver chairs. She was trying to look downcast, but I heard her humming a merry tune under her breath when she passed me.

I looked from Mysti to her leader. He still had a face you could skate on. "You know, that thing about me knowing her name, it was an accident," I said. I didn't want her to be in trouble with her folks. For all I knew, this Welfie was her father. "She just, uh, tripped and fell into the middle of a spell I was practicing. I didn't know it would force her to tell me her true name. I'd be willing to forget I ever heard it."

The Welfie's frosty laugh made his expression seem hot as a bonfire by comparison. "You are pleased to jest with me, O Master Kendar. Ha, ha. Let us speak no more of unpleasant things."

"What are you going to do with her?" I insisted. He refused to answer my question.

"Your command of Majyk is truly awesome, for a mortal," he said, changing the subject. "I have reported the facts to the Council of the Undying Wise and they have agreed that we misjudged you. Generally, we Welfies do not like strangers."

Noooooooo. Gee, fooled me.

"However, your powers have impressed us mightily. We are willing to call you friend. This is a great honor, as every mortal knows."

I knew it now, I guess. "I am not worthy," I said, with a little bow. It was the nicest way I could say what I was really thinking, namely, *I don't want you to be my friend and I wish the feeling was mutual.*

Now the crowned Welfie had one of those gooey smiles plastered across his face. I liked him better when he was freezing me out; it felt more honest. That smile though—it reminded me of Zoltan when he was pretending to be my best buddy.

"Oh, how I rejoice to hear you say that, Master Kendar!" he exclaimed, clapping his long, white hands together so that the rings rang. "It is proof of your wisdom and shows me that we were right about you."

"I'm so glad."

Sarcasm doesn't register on Welfies. "Yes, yes, we are more than willing to call you Welvenfriend, honored one, with all the blessings that come with such a title—"

Get it in writing, Scandal said in my head. *This bird's slicker than a pound of greased eels.*

"—as soon as you do us one teensy-weensy little favor."

Bingo! the cat thought at me.

I put on a smile every bit as fake as the Welfie's and said, "I'll be happy to do it."

What? Scandal nearly had a telepathic fit. *Don't just agree! Ask what they want first, then bargain with them! Sheesh, what kind of a rube are you?*

The kind who wants to get out of this place and home in one piece, I thought back at him.

Listen, where I come from, we've got a word for people who sign blank checks.

I'd care more if I knew what a blank check is.

And will you care if the 'teensy-weensy favor' these pointy-eared yazoos have in mind is something like, oh, slaying a dragon? You do *know what a dragon is?*

I also know that if they want any favors done, they're going to have to let us go free first. And once we're free, we'll run so far from the fearsome Forest of Euw that the Welfies will never be able to find us.

I could feel the astonishment in Scandal's mind. Maybe telepathy was catching. *You mean you'd jump bail? Go AWOL? Promise them anything, give 'em the gate? Tell the Welfies to kiss your sweet—?*

Yup.

Scandal purred and bounded over to rub against my leg. *My kinda guy! There's hope for you yet, skinball,* he thought.

"So!" I said, patting the crowned Welfie on the back. "What do you say we get started on this favor you want my extreme Majykal magnificence to do for you?"

He shuddered a little and gracefully stepped out of my reach. His servant hurried up to brush off the spot on his robes where my hand had rested. Smiling wider than ever, he said, "It is a trifle. The Council of the Undying Wise will want to tell you themselves. We'll announce it after your farewell dinner."

"Dinner?" Grym and Scandal pricked up their ears with the same eagerness.

"Dinner?" I repeated. "Then what was that?" I pointed at the remains of the feast on the crystal table.

"Just a snack," said the Welfie, Scandal, and Grym all together.

I shrugged. "Lead on." We all headed for the door.

"Aren't you forgetting something, Master?" the crowned Welfie asked. He smiled and turned on his shimmery candy-colored radiance until he looked like a raisin floating in a bowl of rainbow gelatin. When I was still a kid at home, one day I got into the kitchen and ate two whole batches of sugarplums plus a fruitcake. He reminded me of all the syrup-soaked nightmares I had for a week after.

"What did I forget?" I paused in the doorway and looked back.

"You know." He nodded towards Mysti.

This was strange. Why was I supposed to bring her along? Couldn't she just get up and follow us herself? I went over to her, still puzzling it out, and said, "You heard him; dinner time." She didn't move. "Aren't you hungry?" Nothing. "Is anything wrong?"

Softly as a mouse on tiptoe came her whisper, "You have to take my hand."

"I do?" I whispered back. "Why?"

"Sshh! He's watching us. If he catches me giving you hints, we're both sunk. It's what he expects. Just do it."

Well, what was the harm? Maybe it was a Welfie custom for the guest of honor to escort a special maiden to dinner. I wouldn't want to look like I was rude or ignorant, and I certainly didn't want to get Mysti into any more trouble. Even though she'd pulled a knife, she'd been a lot kinder to me than some people. I stuck out my hand and said nice and loud, "Won't you join me, Mysti?"

She pounced on my hand faster than a voondrab on a stinkwallow. The air erupted with starbursts of pink and purple and white. I thought every drop of blood in my body was turning into firefleas. The top of my head lifted clean off, soared around the room a couple of times, barked, and fell into the middle of the leftover roast pig.

When I could see straight again, the crowned Welfie's smile was pulled so taut that the tips of his pointed ears almost touched around the back of his head.

"Lovely," he said. "That's the nicest one I've ever seen. It must mean that the omens are especially good for your future. My congratulations."

"For what?" I gasped.

"On the occasion of your marriage."

CHAPTER ——————— 14

NEVER GO TO A WELFIE PARTY. NEVER.

Go to a nice cheerful funeral instead. You'll have a better time, you'll meet livelier people, and you won't have to worry about being eaten by the appetizers.

Mysti picked up the tablecloth hem and looked underneath. "You can come out now," she told me. "Grym killed it."

"Are you sure?" I wasn't making a move until I knew it was safe.

Mysti made one of those clucking sounds that means I'm this close to being called You Fool Ratwhacker, even by someone who doesn't know that used to be my name. "I'm sure," she said. "Even a giant sludgebat can't live very long without a head. Come on out right now and say something to excuse yourself. Great wizards aren't supposed to be terrified of monsters. You'll ruin everything for me."

As if she hadn't ruined anything for me. When my mother found out I was married, she'd faint. Then she'd kill me. And when my father found out I'd married a Welfie with no dowry, no lands, and no hope of inheriting a fortune, he'd throw a puffy blue conniption fit.

I crawled out from under the dinner table and waved to the guests. "Just a little wizardly joke, there," I announced. "We masters of Majyk always like to liven up our wedding feasts. I don't know about you, but I laughed so much it hurt."

"Ha, ha," said all the Welfies together. No one with half an ear could possibly mistake the sound they made for laughter. They went back to sucking nectar and looking wise.

As newlyweds, Mysti and I were seated at the high table, where everyone could see us. It formed one side of a square with three other long feasting boards on the mossy forest floor. Grym stood in the middle of the square and waved back at us with the severed head of the giant sludgebat he'd just killed. The monster was twice his size, and Grym was up to his knees in blood. He was delighted.

The crowned Welfie sat to my right. He leaned over and remarked, "Now you're in for a treat. Sludgebat wings are delicious. We have a chef who does nothing but carve them into tiny strips. They're served raw on little mounds of cooked rice with—"

"I never saw a sludgebat that big," I said. It was true; back home sludgebats are small winged horrors, no bigger than a man's hand, who live in badly cleaned drains by day and fly around at night looking for libraries. They like to gnaw the glue out of bookbindings and lick the ink off any exposed pages.

The sludgebat the Welfies had brought to dinner was big enough to gnaw the glue out of the complete works of Raptura Eglantine (*How Tender My Troll*) and lick the ink off any exposed authors. They led it in on a spider-web leash which the repulsive creature snapped easily before lunging for the high table. I took one look down its gaping red mouth and dived out of sight, Majyk or no Majyk. Fortunately, Grym had Graverobber and leaped right on top of the first course. One slash and it was all over. I think he was happy to have the exercise.

The crowned Welfie didn't think it was at all strange that the sludgebat was so extraordinarily huge. "Master Kendar, surely you don't expect our chef to waste his time capturing enough *common* sludgebats to feed this crowd? It's much more efficient to take one, grow it to the proper size, and carve it at the table."

"But it wasn't *dead* when you brought it to be carved at the table."

He gave me the sticky-icky smile. "I like my food fresh, don't you?"

"Oh, yeah, sure, fresh, no question about it." I just hoped my food didn't like me the same way. "And, um, how fresh is the rest of our dinner gonna be?"

I needn't have worried. After the Welfie chef served us the giant sludgebat's wings neatly sliced into a pile of tender tidbits over rice, the Welfie women came in with the main course: Flowers.

"What's wrong, Master Kendar?" my host inquired. "You haven't touched your honeysuckle."

"I thought it was the centerpiece."

"You are funny, for a wizard. Ha, ha."

"Ha, ha," the rest of the Welfies echoed dutifully.

"Eat it," Mysti muttered in my ear.

"But it's—"

"*Eat it!*" She had the sharpest elbows, human or Welfie, my ribs ever felt.

I picked a carnation from the plate of assorted blossoms in front of me and bit off a few petals. They tasted slippery and fuzzy and mildly sweet, all at the same time. I didn't like the way they clung to my tongue and stuck to the roof of my mouth.

"Ork," I remarked softly. Mysti's smug smile was the genuine article. "Now you know why I hate being a Welfie," she said so only I could hear. "I hate the forest, I hate the company, I hate living in a mushroom house that keeps getting bigger every time it rains, but most of all I hate the food!"

"Maybe I could get you some of the leftovers from the guest house. There's plenty of solid food laid out there," I suggested.

She shook her head. "Only visitors get served *good* meat. Your scraps wouldn't satisfy me." She flicked away her serving of sludgebat wing with contempt. "My kingdom for a steak! *Rare.*" The way she said that, I could almost see the bright red juice trickling out of her mouth.

"Is being a Welfie that bad?" I asked.

"Bad? Ha! Bad's not the half of it. Day after day, nothing to do but flitter through the forest groves, frolicking with herds of butterflies and eating *this* slop. Night after night of footing it merrily upon the dew-kissed grass and singing sweetly with my sisters." She made an ugly face. "I hate my sisters."

"I've got a brother I'm not too crazy about," I put in.

She looked at me as if I'd lost my mind. "Who cares about you or your dumb brother? I just want *out* of this lousy forest, and you're going to help me, *husband.*"

So that was how it would be? I folded my arms. "Maybe I will and maybe I won't. I kind of like it here. It's peaceful. And they won't make *me* eat hedge-clippings. I think this is just the place for a great master of Majyk to settle down, *wife.*"

For some reason, nothing I said upset her. She was still smiling the same way Scandal did when he'd done something rotten and I was powerless to stop him. This worried me, even if I didn't know what I had to be worried about.

I found out.

After the plates of flowers were cleared away and we were all served golden bowls of nuts and honey, the crowned Welfie rose to his feet and motioned for silence. He didn't have to bother. No one at the party was talking, and you can't make much noise munching on a mouthful of violets.

"Free Welvenfolk of the jolly woodland," he proclaimed. His audience looked about as jolly as they were going to get, which wasn't much. "We are here foregathered to celebrate the marriage of the great and glorious Master Kendar unto one of our own unworthy womenfolk."

"Huzzah," said all the Welfies in chorus, except for Mysti, who mumbled something nasty about the crowned Welfie's mother.

"Let the Welvenmaid Mysti come forth," the leader commanded, making a series of sweeping gestures with his arms until he looked like a lunatic windmill. Mysti at once wiped all smirks, sneers, and smartymouth looks off her face. She stood up tall and pure as a lily, her hands crossed on her chest, her face tilted up just enough so that everyone could see her expression of perfect, joyful obedience.

It made my stomach heave just watching.

Scandal nudged my ankle, making me look down. "Get her!" he remarked. "They having tryouts for *Joan of Arc Meets Godzilla* or what?"

"Shhh. I think she's got to look like that when dealing with the king. She's probably afraid of him."

Scandal leaped into my lap, the better to watch as Mysti approached the crowned Welfie. "I don't think that babe's afraid of anything," he said. "I think the only contact she ever has with terror is when she's dishing it out. And you're married to her. Line your shorts with lead and run for your life."

"Why would I want to line my—"

A resounding blast of Welven horns got everyone's attention. Servants had tidied up the central area and laid down a fluffy white carpet where once the sludgebat bled. A few telltale red stains seeped up into the rug along its edges, but that didn't concern Mysti or her boss. They stood on it facing one another in plain sight of everyone. No one at that dinner party could claim later that he'd missed seeing or hearing what happened. We had witnesses to burn. I wish we'd burned them.

What happened was the Welven lord snapped his fingers, Mysti turned her back to him, and he tore her wings off. Pow. Just like that. The harsh ripping sound struck me right to the bone. Every male Welfie there jumped in his seat, even though the males don't have wings, and every female gave a little shriek. You put several dozen little Welven shrieks together and you've got an earsplitting, nerve-racking sound I don't want to hear again as long as I live.

I shot halfway out of my seat. My whole body was crackling with raw Majyk. Most of me was shaking with anger and pity for poor Mysti's sufferings, but one small part of my mind gloated with the thought: *Here it comes! I've got my power back where I can use it! Now I'll teach him to go tearing the wings off my wife!*

Before I could get a handle on that thought, it was all over. Mysti was wingless but—wonder of wonders—unharmed. No, better than that: She was unbleeding, unruffled, and most definitely *not* unhappy! My Majyk sank and went out like a candle flame before I could scoop up a fistful and fling it at anyone.

Mysti's torn-off wings melted all over the white rug, dyeing it with beautiful swirls of color. She and the head Welfie stepped back onto the grass while attendants hurried forward to roll up the carpet and hand it to their lord. He, in turn, passed it to Mysti, saying, "It's not much as wedding presents go, my dear, but it was all so sudden that you left us absolutely no time to go shopping."

Mysti bubbled over with Oh-you-shouldn't-have noises and came back to our table. She stowed the rug under her chair and grinned at me. "How's about a kiss?"

"How's about later?" I said.

"Later as in 'never'?"

"Later as in when donkeys dance."

"Fine. I don't mind waiting." Mysti didn't look at all put out by my lack of husbandly affection. Something was up. I just hoped it wasn't my number.

Now the chief Welfie was ushering a whole new set of players onto center field. Something was going to happen, and because all the Welfies involved were males, I knew it was going to be something flashy and useless.

When I first set foot in the Forest of Euw, I didn't even know that Welfies existed, but as time passed I was learning more about them than I really wanted to know. For instance, the males did all the fusswork while the females did the real labor. (Mopping up sludgebat blood was fusswork because it wasn't really that hard, it didn't take very long, and you could complain about it loudly the whole time you were doing it. Cutting up sludgebat wings into itsy-bitsy slivers was top-level fusswork because you got to do stuff like juggle the knives and get lots of applause. Cutting the thorns off the main-course roses was females' work because it was tedious and no one said anything to you about the job unless it *didn't* get done.)

Anyway, here were four male Welfies next to the boss, silvery-gold hair blowing in the breeze, each carrying a small crystal ball on the fingertips of his right hand. The four linked their left hands and began a stately dance on tiptoe—I don't think the Welfie's been born who knows the meaning of *stomp*—while His Welven Nibs motioned for Mysti and me to come join the frolic.

Oh joy. Oh rapture. I hate to dance. I can't do it right. There's lots of things I can't do right, but dancing's the one I never *wanted* to do right.

Like I had a choice. Mysti grabbed my wrist and dragged me into the center area. "Come on, Grym, join us!" she called over one shoulder. "This is going to be fun."

"Shall it be vouchsafed me that I kill another sludgebat?" he asked brightly.

"Better! You might get to kill a *man* this time."

Well, that was enough to convince my good barbarian buddy. He vaulted across the table and was standing behind the head Welfie before Mysti and I reached him. The Welven lord didn't seem displeased to have Grym there.

"A mortal witness?" he said. "It is good. And you, my children, have already joined hands without my so instructing you? May this auspicious sign herald long years of domestic happiness, peace, and agreement for you both!"

I got the feeling that any domestic peace and happiness I'd enjoy with Mysti all depended on me agreeing to say the magic words, "Yes, dear," a lot.

"My lord," I said. "What do we need a witness for?"

"Why, for the ceremony of Binding, Blessing, and Business which I shall now perform, O Great One. We already have enough Welven witnesses, so it's only fair. It is a most wondrous ritual. Surely you have read of it in your books of arcane lore?"

I tried to look casual about my ignorance. "Sorry; I got into a nasty flame war with a rival wizard and the cur burned up all the chapters on Welfie culture in my books of arcane lore."

"No great matter." His Welfinity waved it all away. "Our rites are short and simple. A magician of your immense learning will be able to follow along easily." He twiddled his fingers and a purple flame bloomed on the back of his hand. It sprouted yellow wings and flew through the air to alight on the four linked hands of the still-dancing Welfies.

Fiery, fuzzy spines of grape-colored light zipped up each Welfie's arm, around his neck, down the other arm, and hit the twinkling balls with enough force to send them popping straight up into the air like soap bubbles. They all fell down with a tremendous crash of shattering crystal and a rumble like a dragon with the colic. The shards splashed upwards the minute they hit the ground, forming a jagged, glassy wave that threw itself over Mysti and me before I could blink. I started to scream, but just when the knife-edged pieces hit us, they melted into fat, oily droplets that smelled like my mother's perfume collection. Mysti and I got soaked and stinking.

"Behold, you are Bound," the crowned Welfie intoned.

So far, so simple.

Maybe not so simple. As we stood there, drenched, the melted crystals hardened without warning, sealing us inside a skin of clear stone. We could breathe all right, but there wasn't any room to move. You don't know what this meant until I tell you that when the crystal balls exploded I got so startled that I leaped into Mysti's arms. I was still there, pressed right up against her. One part of me was dying of embarrassment, one part was praying for a quick escape, and one part was jumping up and down for joy, setting off firecrackers, and putting up a DO NOT DISTURB UNTIL DOOMSDAY sign on the door.

"Donkeys dancing yet, voondrab-face?" Mysti asked too sweetly.

"What? Am I supposed to kiss you now or something?" I asked.

"'Or something.'" She was making fun of me and I didn't like it. "Let's put it this way: At this point in the ceremony you'd better do *something* to show we're bound to one another. Something *physical*."

"So what if I don't? I didn't want to be bound to you in the first place. I'm too young to be bound to you. I'm too confused to be bound to you. I'm too not-a-Welfie—"

"Welfies sing," she replied. "A lot. We travel all over the land by night, just looking for good places to serenade mortals who're trying to get a decent night's sleep. Mortals who hear Welvensong never forget it, mostly because it keeps them up all night and throwing old shoes and cold water out the window doesn't stop us. We make up all our own songs. How would you like to be the subject of a soon-to-be-famous song about young Master Kendar, the only mortal man ever to be *this* close to a Welvenmaid and he didn't do a thing because he didn't have a thing to do it wi—"

I kissed her. All the Welfies cheered. I think what they said was, "Yay." Once.

As soon as our lips touched, the crystal skin sealing us together steamed off, leaving us covered with a sticky warm dew that still smelled like too many flowers in too little space. The head Welfie grinned. "Behold, you are Blessed."

He clapped his hands and a crew of winged female Welfies fluttered down with clean white cloths and silver basins of water. Mysti and I got cleaned up pretty well, although a little of the smell hung on. When we were done, the Welvenmaids flew away and His Welfitude motioned for us to come stand before him again.

"You have been both Bound and Blessed," he said. "There remains but one last portion of this sacred rite to be performed: Business." He smiled at me as if I *had* to know what he was talking about.

Sure I did.

"Uhhhh . . . Business?" I asked, stalling.

"In truth, Business is the only word we could think of that sounded good with Binding and Blessing," he explained. "Really it's just a little favor."

"A favor," I repeated. "Gee, you don't have to. You've done me more than enough favors already: not killing us, not sticking your nose in my mind anymore, not making us eat flowers at every meal, not—"

"This favor is one *you* must do for *us*." He looked like he expected me to be thrilled to death at the chance. "It is only a token of your gratitude for the honor of being given a Welven bride."

I looked at Mysti. For this I was supposed to be grateful? Maybe if I'd had any choice in the matter, but as things stood, she'd been dumped on me like a wagonload of sand. A very pretty wagonload of sand, with some very nice curves to it, but still—

(It was like the Wedwel's Wishday presents I used to get from Aunt Gloriana, every one of which was ugly or awful or both. Mother not only forced me to write Aunt G. Gee-I-love-it notes, she insisted I *use* the disgusting things. This went on until the year Aunt Gloriana sent me a winter cloak-of-many-colors *so* ugly and *so* awful that when Mother made me wear it to do my chores, all our chickens took one look and dropped dead. Dad said, "I love my family as much as the next man, but relatives can't lay eggs," and wrote Aunt G. a nasty Stop-sending-my-innocent-though-stupid-son-those-godawful-gifts letter himself.)

I cleared my throat. By now, not only the crowned Welfie was smiling but so was every other Welfie in sight. All those perfect white teeth, all those perfect faces, made me feel like I was standing in a bowl of buttered marbles. "So, um, what's this favor, my lord?" I asked.

"There's a witch who lives in the Forest of Euw," the Welfie said. "Only Welfies are supposed to live here, you know. We don't like her."

"You wouldn't. I bet that since I'm a wizard and she's a witch, you figure she'll listen to me. You want me to do you the favor of asking her to leave, right?"

"Wrong," said the crowned Welfie. "We'd like you to do us the favor of making her dead."

MYSTI SAT DOWN ON A FUNGUS-COVERED TREE STUMP near the eastern border of the Forest of Euw and said, " 'Divorce'? What's a 'divorce'?''

Scandal planted all four feet firmly in the moss and told her, "It's a large, hairy beast that comes in your choice of decorator colors and eight taste-tempting, mouth-watering flavors including new banana-raspberry and chocolate-chocolate-chip. What do *you* care what a divorce is? The bottom line is the kid wants one from you and he's got enough Majyk in his guts to knock your socks off, even if you Welfies don't wear socks." He stood up and stalked away from her, tail lashing proudly. "I rest my case."

Mysti aimed one finger at Scandal's rump and a baby bolt of Majyk frizzled his fur. The cat screeched and leaped ten times his own height, straight up. His own store of Majyk set off half-a-dozen blazing pinwheels that sawed down a clump of unlucky saplings in our vicinity.

"That's one," said the Welfie.

"Hey! You leave Scandal alone," I protested.

"Or?" She was laughing at me.

"Or—or—or else." It was lame, but it was the best response I had on hand.

Mysti yawned and linked both hands around one updrawn knee. "I'm shaking."

On the fringes of our little group of merrymakers, Grym the Great paced back and forth like a captive lion, one hand clutching an unsheathed Graverobber, the other arm carrying our wedding gift, the wing-dyed white rug. "Wherefore tarry we?" the barbarian demanded. "Was it not entrusted unto us to seek out and slay the wicked witch of the woodland?"

Scandal looked up from licking his frizzled fur. "So we drop a house on her first chance we get, Scarecrow. Izzat all right by you?" He was a very cranky cat.

It hadn't taken Grym and Mysti long to understand that they were *never* going to understand everything Scandal said. In fact, Grym decided that Scandal's weirdest words just had to be the voices of his tribal gods, keeping an eye on their beloved boy-barbarian. It was only fair: These were the same gods who had slapped him with what Scandal called The Face From Planet Cute, and now they felt sorry about it. That was why they had turned the cat into an oracle. I couldn't get Grym to explain how come, if his gods felt *that* sorry, they didn't just change his face into something seriously fierce or just plain ugly.

"It is not for mere mortals to question the gods," was what he said.

I was going to ask "Why not?" except every time I tried that during religious discussions at home, Mother smacked me. She said it was for my own good and when I was all grown up and properly religious, I'd understand. Then I could smack my own kids.

A simple smack wasn't life-threatening, so my Majyk wouldn't do anything to stop it, but a smack from Grym was bound to hurt a heck of a lot more than a smack from Mother. I decided to let Grym's gods have things their own way, always the best way of dealing with gods.

Now Grym sheathed Graverobber and unfurled the rug with one flick of his mighty wrists. He sat on it, legs folded under him, and closed his eyes. A soft moaning rose from his lips.

"What's the matter with him?" Mysti asked. "Did he eat a voondrab out of season?"

"Ssshhh." I motioned for her to hush up. "He's just going into a trance. It's all right, he knows how. He told me that he used to be a Junior Shaman Scout back home. He has to be entranced to interpret what Scandal said."

"What? That stuff about a divorce?" Mysti got a flinty look in her eye. "I can interpret it for you without any trance: Say it again and you're sludgebat slivers."

"Hey, what are you angry at me for? I don't know what a divorce is any more than you do!" All I knew was that if it was as big and hairy as Scandal said, I didn't want to meet one after dark.

"The gods speak," Grym intoned. "The beast hath uttered

words of mystic import, a sign from on high as to how we may best fulfill our noble quest to destroy the woodland witch.''

"He said we should drop a house on her." I shook my head. "Nope. Forget that. I'm not going to do it. Not even if I could.''

"Ignore him, O gods," Grym droned. "He shall yet be made to see the wisdom of obeying thy behests. The cat hath spoken: So mote it be.''

"The cat talketh just to heareth himself talketh," I said. "Grym, there's something you'd better know right now: We are not dropping any houses, fulfilling any quests, or destroying any witches. Witch, *ha*! You believe everything the Welfies tell you? For all we know, this 'witch' is just some poor old lady who moved into the forest because her family's all gone and it's the safest place she could find.''

Grym's eyes flew open in disbelief. "Safe? When it be full of *Welfies*?''

"Your friend has a point, there," Mysti said. "Lord Valdaree knew what he was doing when he told you to kill the woodland witch. Do you think he'd have ordered you to a task that was easy enough for him to do himself?''

"Wait a minute, honeybuns." Scandal stalked in between Mysti and me. Mysti's hard stare was nothing next to the cat's green-eyed scowl. "You mean you Welfies already tried to ice the old lady?''

"Ice," Grym echoed, slipping back into his Junior Shaman Scout trance. "We must first make pilgrimage to the ice mountains and find a flying house . . .''

"We tried," Mysti admitted. "We failed. Eight of our best archers shall arch no more. All that we found afterwards was a handful of sequins, a broken arrow, and a lot of dead bodies.''

"Right. That's it." I folded my arms. "As the nearest thing to a leader this mob has got, I hereby decide that we are definitely not going anywhere near this woodland witch. We're going home instead, which is all I've been wanting to do since Master Thengor died.''

They all looked at me. Even Grym came out of his trance long enough to give me one of those Thou-canst-not-in-sooth-be-serious looks.

"I mean *my* home," I explained.

"We know what you mean," Scandal said. "It's the part about you being any kind of a leader that's a gas.''

I screwed up my mouth in what I hoped was a stern expression. "And why, pray tell, is that?''

"Because to lead anyone anywhere, the first thing you've got to know is where you're going."

"I know where I'm going." I tightened my arms across my chest. "I'm going *home*."

"Home," the cat repeated. "Nice idea. For those of us who *can* go home."

His words hit me like an arrow in the throat. For the first time since we'd been sent on our way by the Welfies, I really looked at my traveling companions, and in all three of their faces I saw the same longing and the same loss:

Home.

Mysti had just been booted out of the only home she'd ever known. True, she said she was glad to escape, but that didn't make facing the big unknown outside world any easier. Somewhere under her hard exterior, she was all alone and afraid.

Grym didn't have a home the way I thought of one. He was a nomad barbarian. Home for Grym wasn't a building or a name on a map or a special piece of land. Home for him was his tribe, his people. He could track them down and find them again, but as long as he had *that* face, he'd never really be able to be a part of them.

Scandal's home was another world, another dimension, a place so incredible it shouldn't be able to exist. Well, it existed, all right, a world that was only a rat hole away from mine, but just try to find that rat hole!

Three lost souls, three beings who couldn't get where they wanted to go unless . . .

Unless I helped them. Unless I learned how to master my Majyk and used it to help them. They needed me. Me, Kendar Gangle, Ratwhacker. The knot in my throat untied itself and leaked down into my stomach where it sat like a lump of Velma Chiefcook's oatmeal. It got heavier and heavier the longer I looked at those three. I wished I could take back everything I'd said about being a leader. People need leaders, but being needed is scary stuff. I wished everything could go back to being just the way it was before I crashed through Master Thengor's Majyk. I wished the only one depending on me was me.

The trouble with Majyk is it doesn't grant wishes. Rats.

"Now look," I said, trying to sound sure of myself. "My idea's the best one we've got until one of you comes up with a better one. Why should we try to destroy a witch whose spells are so powerful she's got the Welfies running scared?"

"We promised." Grym sounded just as sure of himself, and he wasn't bluffing. "We are therefore honor-bound."

"Wrong! *We* didn't promise a thing; this whole witch-killing was assigned to *me*, Master Kendar, and no one asked me if I wanted to do it; it was just dumped on me by the Welfies."

"I am thy sword-sworn servant, yon beast is thy familiar, and yon erstwhile Welfie wench thy wife," Grym pointed out. "That maketh it *we* in my book, O Kendar."

"Anyway, *we* can't get out of it," Mysti piped up.

"It's a big forest and it's only one witch," I reminded her. "If we want to avoid her, I think the odds are on our side."

"Wrong!" She mimicked me exactly. I didn't like it.

"Care to explain?" I asked her.

"My pleasure. Remember my wings?"

"Uh-huh."

"Remember the ceremony of Binding, Blessing, and Business when Lord Valdaree ripped off my wings?"

"Uh—ouch."

"Remember how they didn't bleed?"

I glanced at the rainbow-colored carpet Grym still sat on. "They melted, right?"

"That's what it looked like to you." Mysti's voice grew tense. "It's no easy thing for a Welfie to be able to wed a mortal, Kendar. The ceremony of transformation must be fulfilled in all three phases. The wings that were torn from me were a symbol of the promise we both made, you and I, even if you didn't know you were making any promise. If Binding and Blessing are all we do and we leave our Business undone, that's when my wings will bleed."

Scandal nudged my ankle. "I think she's serious, boss."

"Serious—?"

"I think if we don't kill this witch, Mysti dies."

CHAPTER ————— 16

"BUT SHE'S NOT DRESSED IN BLACK!" SCANDAL PRO-
tested from the shrubbery.

"What's that got to do with anything?" Mysti whispered. We
were all cramped close together, sharing a gap in the tidy hedges
surrounding the witch's cottage. The witch herself sat on a little
split-log bench just under the cottage eaves, her eyes closed,
looking like any ordinary, plump, middle-aged woman taking a
rest from her household chores. She wore a coarse gown of
rose-pink wool trimmed with blue, and a white kerchief bound up
her hair; nothing even remotely black.

"Witches always wear black," the cat replied. "Funny hats,
too, like a huge upside-down ice cream cone with a big round
brim. And they've got warts, and sometimes they've got green
skin, and when they laugh they cackle, and ugly—? Boy, are
witches ugly!"

"How ugly are they?" Grym asked.

"They're uglier than a well-digger's hunchbacked cockroach."

"Forsooth, that be an overfull guerdon of ugly," the barbarian
agreed. He shaded his eyes and took another look at the lady in
question. "Beshrew me, but I think we hath not got the right
witch. Yon female is no great beauty, yet she would not cause a
man of my tribe to throw her out of the tent for eating crackers in
the bedroll."

"This is going to be difficult," I said.

"What is?" Scandal asked.

"Killing her."

"Listen, pal, it's not *killing* someone that's difficult, it's
deciding you're gonna kill 'em. Back where I come from murder's
so easy, even a child can do it. And believe me, they do!"

"No, what's hard is, well, I was expecting a monster," I explained. "You know, if the witch was so horrible she even had the Welfies on the run, I figured she had to be some kind of revolting, disgusting, loathsome—"

The cat gave me a you've-got-to-be-kidding look. "You're a sap. Either that, or you've never checked out a book of mug-shots. Evil doesn't always go around wearing a fright-mask, Bwana."

"You're right, I guess." I looked back at the witch. "It's just that she looks so much like my old *nanny!*"

Grym laid his hand on my shoulder. "If 'twould aid thee, O Master Kendar, I might eftsoons lop off her head. Thou needst not watch."

"I don't think a witch who fried a whole troop of Welfie archers is going to just sit back and let one barbarian swordsman lop off anything, eftsoons," I said.

"Thou forget'st that mine trusty blade Graverobber is now awash with Majyk."

"*Thou* forget'st, big boy," Scandal said, "that the Welfies practically *sweat* Majyk and the old lady still managed to waste them."

"True, true." Grym was crestfallen. "Eftsoons we need a plan."

Scandal butted me. "What is this 'eftsoons' stuff he keeps saying?"

"I think it's an ancient musical wind instrument," I replied.

"I think your mother dropped you in a big bucket full of stupid when you were little," the cat commented and settled down at the roots of the nearest bush.

"I think I've got a plan," Mysti said. "Step one is we get the heck out of this shrubbery. It's making me itch all over."

"That would be me, dear," the shrubbery said. "It's that *pushy* poison ivy. Gets all over me, root and branch, until I can't do a *thing* with my leaves and—"

Mysti didn't scream, she just sucked her breath in so hard it stripped several handfuls of leaves off the hedge. Scandal jumped up, back arched, one paw ready to slash. A tender sprout of new growth shot from one of the bushes and whipped itself around his belly, lifting him into the air before he could spit.

More spiky branchlets snaked around Mysti, pinning her arms to her sides. This time she did scream, but there was no one left in a position to help her. Grym and I had problems of our own. A whole new bush with very brambly limbs sprang out of the earth right under Grym's feet, the branches growing up quickly around

him until he looked like a big sweaty bird in a green, leafy cage.
He tried hacking his way out with Graverobber, but the bush just
grew out of sword's reach, then shrank back again so fast and so
small that he didn't have room to use his blade.

As for me, the proud master of the biggest payload of Majyk on
Orbix, I would have done better with a pair of plain old
hedge-snippers. A green cage just like Grym's popped up under
me, its branch-bars tying themselves into a pretty knot above my
head, and my Majyk didn't do more than keep away some of the
meaner-looking thorns. I could hear Scandal's terrified yowling,
but it was hard to see anything far past my prison, on account of
the leaves. All I could make out was Grym's cage next to mine.

Then I was looking into a big blue eye. "Oh my, Jawj, you
really are the silly one," said a voice as warm and comforting as
a spice cake fresh out of the oven. There wasn't a hint of a cackle
in it. "I ask you to keep a lookout for enemies while I take my nap
and you capture *children*!"

"Hey! Who are you calling a child?" I demanded, grabbing the
branches. That was a mistake. Remember those thorns? My Majyk
was supposed to protect my life, but if I wanted to do something
dumb like grabbing onto a bunch of vicious stickers, that was fine.

For the first time ever, my yowl was louder than Scandal's.

"Goodness me." The blue eye blinked. "Have you hurt
yourself, sonny?"

"Moong," I said, sucking one hand. Then I switched over to
sucking the other one and said, "Gurnf."

"Dear, dear." The blue eye made clucking sounds. "I'm going
to have to bandage that, I see. You'd better come out."

A thin line of sizzling red light started climbing straight up the
brambly wall of my cage. When it got to a good height, it took a
sharp right turn and went across for a while before making another
sharp right and heading down. I smelled green wood burning, and
a flap the size of a doorway fell out of the cage's side. I was free.

Free to face the witch.

"Hello, love," she said. "Come on out and I'll put some
porkerpine-fat salve on those cuts and we'll have us a lovely little
chat." The blue eye was one of hers; the other was the color of
dark amber, a fact which made me feel kind of nervous. Except for
the eyes, up close she looked more like old Nanny Esplanadia than
ever. I expected her to give me a swat on the backside for playing
in the dirt, then to give me a hug and a cookie.

Nanny Esplanadia never locked up anyone in thornbushes,
though. The worst she ever did was whack my brother Basehart

with a broom whenever he tried bullying me. She went through a lot of brooms before Basehart got smart enough to beat me up only when Nanny Esplanadia was somewhere else. I came out of my hedge-prison and saw that Grym, Mysti, and Scandal were all tucked inside leafy cages like the one I'd just escaped.

"I'm not having any lovely little chats until you let my friends go," I told the witch.

She clicked her tongue and looked at me the way Nanny Esplanadia did the time I petted my first reekworm (These miniature dragons are the only critters I know with stinkier breath than Basehart's).

"Well, of *course* I'm going to let them go," she said. "I know that *I* never wanted to have them jugged like that in the first place. That was all Jawj's idea."

"Who's Jawj?" I asked, looking around. "Your familiar?"

"My shrub. Well, *one* of my shrubs, anyway; the one who makes all the executive decisions. They're all alive, you know, my bushes. If you're going to go to the trouble of putting in a hedge, do it right and put in a watch-hedge. I've been fairly satisfied with this one, although there have been unfortunate cases like yours where Jawj mistakes some perfectly innocent passers-by for enemies and flies off the handle. Off the roots, I should say. Still, how much real judgment can you expect from a bush?"

"I do not, I do not," the hedge chanted. "The action I took was, as indicated by all data points that were, really, at this time available for my, to a great extent, information, prudent."

"Yes, dear," the witch said, not listening. "Now tell the others to let the nice boy's friends go."

"Not gonna do it."

"Pruning shears," said the witch.

Next moment, we were all standing in front of the witch, trying not to look guilty.

"Whatever is troubling all of you nice young people?" she asked, truly concerned. She even bent down to Scandal's level and added, "Even your sweet little pet seems to be unhappy about something. Would a nice cup of tea help? We can have our own private party. I know I've got fresh bread and butter, and some honey muffins, and a little potted rappid left over from last night's supper. Come with me." She started for her cottage door.

"We're not hungry," I said, feeling miserable. She was such a *nice* lady! And I'd seen nothing so far to convince me that she was a wicked witch. Sure, she had Jawj and his thorny family guarding her house, but if I lived so close to the Welfies I'd have a watch-hedge, a watchdog, and a double moat full of watch-slimegrinds around the place.

Why did we have to kill her? I knew the answer to that one: If we didn't, Mysti would die. Just because I didn't want her hanging around me didn't mean I wanted her dead. I wished I could manage Majyk better. If I could, I'd go right back after the Welfies and make them lift their spell from her, or else—or else—

Or else what?

Or else something messy. Huh! Some wizard I was! I couldn't even think up a really awful punishment for my enemies. Master Thengor never had that problem when it came to taking revenge. He even had one whole section of the library full of nothing but books with titles like *Making Them Sorry* and *Vengeance is Sweet* and *That'll Learn 'Em!* and *101 Ways to Kick Them When They're Down*. I just didn't have what it takes to be a real wizard, Majyk or no. But here I was, stuck.

I glanced at Grym. The big barbarian was just as unhappy with the situation as I was; it showed. Mysti wasn't looking anyone in the eye, and Scandal had his fur fluffed out as if to keep everyone at a distance.

"Children, you're dawdling," the witch called to us.

"Forsooth, 'tis as Master Kendar hath decreed," Grym replied. "The pangs of hunger gnaw not at our vitals. We had as lief not go to meat."

"Don't be ridiculous," she said from the doorway. "The only meat I've got on hand is that potted rappid, and there's hardly enough of that to go around. Plenty of muffins, though! Come along, come along, I can't wait for you forever; I must go inside. You can eat something while I watch my soaps. You really must, you know. You'll need all the energy you've got if you intend to try killing me."

She went into the cottage and left us staring at each other like a bunch of village idiots.

CHAPTER —————— 17

WE WERE ALL SEATED AROUND THE TABLE IN THE witch's house, except for Scandal, who was curled up in my lap, full of potted rappid. "So much for the element of surprise," I said, flicking a few muffin crumbs off my plate. One of the house-toads hopped up and swallowed it before it hit the floor.

"I'm just as glad," Mysti said, scratching furiously. She was starting to break out in red blotches from her tussle with the poison-ivy-covered watch-hedge.

"Glad? How mote it be?" Grym demanded. "Thy life be forfeit lest we fail to slay the witch."

"Oh, poo." Mysti stopped scratching long enough to finish her cup of tea. "That won't happen now."

"Hold it," I said. "Wait just one little minute, here. In case you've forgotten, you were the one who got us all worked up about how if we don't fulfill the Business part of that Welfie Blessing, Binding, and Blah-blah ceremony, you're going to start bleeding from the place where your wings were attached."

"I was." Mysti reached for the toad-shaped teapot and poured herself a fresh cup. Aside from having to scratch herself silly every now and then, she looked as cool and calm as a river-stone.

"Well, *what* in the name of a bushpig's behind happened to change that?"

"Nothing's changed," Mysti replied. "If you don't kill the witch, I probably will start to die, and I'm pretty sure it's going to be the way I said: seepage at the wings, you know. More tea?"

I fought back the urge to pick up a toad and chuck it at her. There were more than three-score of the knobbly creatures hopping and flopping around the witch's cottage. We'd been tripping over them ever since we entered, but none of us felt it would be polite to mention them. As a matter of fact, all these toads strewn around was the first really witchy thing I'd noticed about our hostess. It was kind of comforting, in a way, if you can call toads a comfort to anyone except another toad. Before I started making them fly through the air, though, I thought I'd try one last time to get a straight answer out of Mysti.

"If we don't kill the witch—"

"—which I really don't want to do," Mysti remarked, uninvited. "She's such a nice lady." She munched another muffin. "And a good cook."

"—we don't complete the Welfie ceremony. And if we don't complete the Welfie ceremony, *you* die—"

"—which I *certainly* don't want to do. I mean, here I am, finally free of that crowd of lippity-skippity forest fa-la-las, finally able to go live somewhere interesting, where they're not constantly rousing you out of a warm bed because it's time to foot it featly upon the dew-kissed grass by the light of the moon, yo-ho-ho and yee-haw, *finally* finally able to get my teeth into a serious piece of rare beefsteak instead of all that damn nectar. Die *now*? No, thanks; nope; uh-uh; I'd rather not, if it's all the same to you."

I let my head fall to the table. It would have hurt, but I hit a toad. "I'm *soooo* confused," I moaned.

Mysti stroked my hair. "Darling, didn't they teach you any Logic in that wizard's school?"

"They did; I failed," I said, my mouth full of toad. The beast gave a cranky *juggerruumph!* and hopped away.

Grym snapped his fingers. "By Buxomia and her ten thousand wrung-out lovers, methinks I've got it! A witch so powerful as to overcome the Welfies must indeed command power enough to overcome the most insidious of the Welfie spells. Slay we her not! She shall be of greater worth unto us alive than dead, if she will but granteth us the boon of freeing Mysti from her impending peril."

"Do you think she would?" I asked. "Why would she want to help us at all? She knows we came here to kill her."

Just as I said that, the witch stuck her head out of the little black door to the back room and said, "Do you mind keeping it down, dearies? I'm trying to watch my soaps." She ducked back inside, only to reappear an instant later and add, "Of course I knew you came here to kill me. Everyone comes here to kill me. It's just the way we get things done around here." Then she was gone, popped back into the mysterious room, leaving nothing behind but a cloud of strange-smelling smoke.

"What's she doing in there?" Mysti asked. "The moment we came in, she laid the table, served us tea, and flew off through that little black door. She never even asked our names. *Or* told us hers."

"Relax, sister." Scandal yawned and dug his claws into my thighs just enough to hurt but not enough for me to pitch him off. "She'll get around to it. You heard the lady: She's watching her soaps. Back where I come from, in the afternoon loads of people drop everything, turn on the TV, put their feet up, and watch their favorite soaps. No big deal."

"What's a teevee?" I asked innocently.

The effect on Scandal was electrifying. All four paws shot out in opposite directions; his tail pointed straight at the ceiling, his eyes went wide, his pupils dilated, and his whiskers crackled with small, hiccup-y bursts of Majyk. "*No TV!*" he squawked. "Holy moley, that's right!"

He vaulted from my lap onto the tabletop, scattering toads left and right. "Get up! Get up!" he shouted. "C'mon, move it before she gets wise! Run for your lives, lower the boats, women and tabbies first, damn the torpedoes, *run!*"

He was running, all right: around and around in circles. It took me three tries before I grabbed him by the scruff of the neck and made him face me. His paws were still flailing. "Is there a problem?" I asked, holding the thrashing cat at arm's length.

"She's a witch!" the cat yowled.

"We know."

"Don't you see?" he panted. "She's lying to us. She can't be watching her soaps because you bunch of Robin Hood rejects don't even know what a TV is! She's using this 'watching my soaps' as an excuse to sneak off into her secret laboratory and mix us up some grief on the rocks, with a twist. All this tea-and-cookies stuff is a ruse. It's like Hansel and Gretel, where the witch wins their trust by acting all ooey-gooey sweet to the kids, then changes them into gingerbread and eats them. My mama didn't raise me to be a macaroon!"

The black door opened just as Scandal said his last say. The witch's rosy face peered out, but for the first time she wasn't smiling.

"What is all this racket? I know I'm not being a very good hostess, but if I don't watch my soaps, it's going to get messy in here. Since you can't be quiet, you might as well come in and be helpful.''

"In there?'' Grym asked. I was glad he'd taken over my Stupid Question Asker job.

"Isn't it the bright one!'' The witch looked pleased. "Yes, yes, right in here, hup-hup. If I leave them alone for too long, there's no telling what they'll do.''

Grym's hand closed around Graverobber's hilt. "Doeth we now as she biddeth us, lest she suspect our own suspicions,'' he rasped out of the corner of his mouth. "I shall venture first; Master Kendar, do thou follow last, to shield our rear.''

"Right,'' I rasped back.

The witch sighed and tapped her foot. "If you boys want to cover your rears—and very cute ones they are, I'm sure—you'll have to practice whispering better than that. All that ridiculous rasping you're doing makes you sound like a pair of assassins in a stage-play—a very *poor* stage-play, the kind where the hero turns his hat back to front and his own mother can't recognize him for the whole second act. I can hear every word you're saying, you know; clear as a bell and twice the brass.''

Grym and I put on a *Who, us?* look. We'd learned it from Scandal.

"Yes, you,'' the witch replied, even though we hadn't said a thing. "I wasn't born yesterday, more's the pity, and I've been earning a fairly decent living in the witchery trade for longer than since *your* last bath.'' This was aimed at Grym, who blushed. "So don't hang around here thinking you can teach Mother Toadbreath to suck eggs. For one thing, I don't like eggs, and for another—''

We never did get to find out what that other thing was because just then there came an ominous bubbling from behind the witch, a sour burning smell, a crash as if something large had toppled over, and then a long purple tentacle whipped out the doorway, wrapped itself three times around Mother Toadbreath's plump body, and dragged her, screaming and struggling, into the back room.

Grym gave a hellish war cry and plunged through the open doorway after them. I dropped the cat and dashed in pursuit. Behind me I heard Scandal yelling something about crazy heroes and Mysti hollering at the house-toads to move their warty butts so that she could get at the fireplace poker. Then I couldn't hear anything anymore because my Majyk was setting up a loud, angry crackling that surged over me from head to foot like a cocoon of fire.

The cocoon cracked wide open when I ran headfirst into Grym's brawny back, and the Majyk fizzled out. I had time to take one breath before Mysti rammed into me and the momentum carried the three of us over onto the floor.

Well, all right, Grym stood his ground—he was hulking enough to stand his ground in the middle of a whirlwind—but Mysti and I toppled like duckpins.

"Get off the floor, dears," Mother Toadbreath's comfy voice suggested. "I don't know what's boiled over and it might do things to you you wouldn't like."

Mysti and I got up, brushing ourselves off quickly. There was nothing on us, but if a witch tells you to get up or you won't like what happens next, I say you trust her and *move*. Then we peered around either side of our friend the barbarian and saw what it was that had made him freeze in his tracks in mid-heroic charge.

Happy as a tiggy with a tummy full of cheerberries, the witch was seated on one coiled tentacle belonging to a purple, bag-bodied horror that had seven more to spare. Each one of these held a long-handled wooden paddle which the monster occasionally dipped into seven out of the ten cauldrons that were seething away, each over its own little hearth.

Bright rainbow bubbles rose from each black pot except the one which had tumbled over onto its side, putting out the fire underneath. The bubbles danced in the sunlight that came in through the huge smoke-hole in the center of the roof. The rafters were festooned so thick with bundles of dried and drying herbs, grasses, flowers, and reptiles that you could hardly see the thatch above. The air hung heavy with a smell midway between my mother's rose garden and a hog-wallow at high noon.

Besides the paddles, the saggy, un-shaggy beast also had two immense green eyes, a triangular pink nose, a pair of pointed ears set high up on its head/body/bag, and a mouth like an upside-down Y that opened up to say: "Mrow."

"Hush, Puss," Mother Toadbreath said sweetly, patting the ugly thing between its ears. "Mommy's not angry at you. It's all Mommy's fault for leaving you to watch the soaps alone. Mommy tried to get her guests to come back here and lend a hand, but they were just being a bunch of old sillies, thinking Mommy was going to eat them. Mommy's never eaten anyone in her life, almost, has she, Mommy's precious?"

"Purrrr," the monster replied and closed its eyes.

"You were a very, very, *very* good little octopussums to think up such a clever way to get them in here. Now maybe they'll be kind enough to help clean up the mess.'' The witch hopped down from her creepy pet's coiled-up tentacle to give us a stiff, fake smile and add, ''*Won't* you?''

She was right about the mess; it was awful. Mother Toadbreath made Grym sheathe Graverobber and handed him a mop. He used it to spread the muck all over the floor in a nice, uniform layer. She would have done better to let him try cleaning up with the sword. Mysti got a spare paddle and was sent to stir one of the unattended cauldrons. That left me.

''Well?'' Mother Toadbreath asked, giving her own cauldron a good mixing.

I wanted to ask right back, *Well, what?* only I didn't like the look of that paddle. It was pretty obvious that the witch expected me to do something—not stir, because all the paddles were taken—but unless she had a spare mop, I didn't know what that something was.

I felt a familiar nudge just above my ankle. Scandal had come in silent as a shadow. ''Soaps,'' he said. ''She was watching her *soaps*.''

''Of course I was, dear,'' Mother Toadbreath said complacently. ''Didn't I tell you so? You really ought to be more trusting. But then I expect that cats would need ninety lives instead of nine if they trusted everyone.''

Scandal cocked his head. ''You know I'm a cat?''

''I'm a witch,'' Mother Toadbreath replied. ''I learned all about the creatures of myth and legend when I was knee-high to a basilisk. Never did think I'd have the chance to see an actual cat, though. This is quite the historic occasion for me. I suppose I ought to memorialize it in some way.''

She set aside her paddle and trotted over to a rack of wooden shelves that took up one whole wall of the room. They were lined with row on row of little brown clay pots, all clearly and carefully marked with green ink on yellow labels. She found the one she wanted, popped the cork, helped herself to a sprinkling of whatever was inside, and came back to her cauldron. She tossed a pinch of blue dust over the churning gunk in the pot, then spit into it. Immediately a gigantic bubble formed itself on the surface, then broke free and bobbed across the room.

A perfect double of Scandal floated inside.

''Hey! That's me!'' the cat exclaimed.

''No, it's just your spittin' image,'' the witch corrected him. She guided the bubble to a safe place on the top row of shelves.

"There! Now I've got something to remember you by," she said, satisfied. Then she looked at me and was not.

"Young man, the reason that pot of soap boiled over was because you and your friends would not come to help me when I asked—very politely, if I recall. The least you could do is help your big friend with the tidying up."

"I'm willing," I said. "Just give me a mop and—"

"Do you think I'm made of mops?" Mother Toadbreath replied. "I've only got the one, and he's using it."

"Well, couldn't you—I don't know—" I waved my hands vaguely, "just sort of witch up another one?"

She gave me another dropped-on-his-head-poor-boy look and said, "I am a witch, not a wizard. Wizardry's the art of making something out of nothing; witchery's the art of making do with what you've got. I can make a pine cone sprout into a lovely set of pinewood furniture, I can capture the image of a cat in the reflective surface of a soap bubble, I can make a rock into a rocking chair, but I can *not* make a mop out of thin air."

"You could try," I suggested lamely. "How about if I got you a stick to get started with? For the mop handle."

The witch's warm voice got small and cold as a hailstone. "Young man, a short walk from this cottage is the revolting little village of Cheeseburgh."

"Cheeseburgh . . ." Why did that name sound so familiar?

"The people of Cheeseburgh are perhaps the most unhappy, unlucky, untalented crowd you could ever meet. They've turned bumbling into an art. They are so incompetent that they've even had to take on *three* village idiots because one alone couldn't do the job right."

Oh. Now I knew why that name rang a bell. Every time I did anything wrong at home—which is to say, any time I did *anything* at home—my father used to call me a Cheeseburgher.

"What's that got to do with mops?" I asked.

Mother Toadbreath planted her hands on her hips. "Making mops is the one thing the Cheeseburghers do *well*. They even clubbed together to put up a big sign at the entrance to the village which says 'Welcome to Cheeseburgh: We Are Mops.' It's not much, but it's the only source of pride the poor things have got, and if you think I'm going to hurt my neighbors' feelings by making my own mops, *well*!" She snorted and gave the soap cauldron a vicious stirring. "Where were you brought up that you've got such poor manners, I'd like to know!"

I was about to tell her that I'd been raised not too far from Cheeseburgh, as it turned out, but I didn't get the chance.

Mysti gave a strangled shriek and dropped her paddle. She was staring at her outstretched arms, horrified. There was plenty to stare at: One had turned blue with green checks, the other had sprouted from wrist to shoulder a row of roses all the colors of a mountain sunrise. Wide red and white stripes spiraled up both her legs.

Something told me this was *not* your ordinary case of poison ivy.

She turned her face to me and whimpered, "Not the wings, after all. Silly me." Then her eyes rolled up in her head and she keeled over. Grym dropped the mop and scooped her into his arms before she could tumble into the cookfire under the cauldron.

"The Welfie spell!" I cried. I whirled to grab Mother Toadbreath's hands. "Please, you've got to help us! Mysti's a Welfie—I mean she *was* a Welfie until—the Welfies forced us to—Blessing and Binding and—told us we had to kill you, only we never wanted to—especially not after we met you and—but if we didn't kill you, something would happen to—but Mysti said you were strong enough to stop it from—only now it *has* happened, and—*Help her!*"

"There, there, Kendar dear," said Mother Toadbreath, calmly breaking my grip. "Not to worry."

I was astonished. "How did you know my name?" I touched my head, but I didn't feel anything like Scandal's old invasion of my thoughts.

"Oh, I know all about you; all about all of you, from the moment the Welfies made you their prisoners, that is. I'm such an old busybody—only to be expected, living way out here on my lonesome—so I make it a policy to have one kettle of soap on the boil just to keep an eye on the Welfies. They *do* bear watching."

"You watched the Welfies?" I knew Mysti needed help right away, but I couldn't help asking, "In the *soaps*?"

The witch chuckled. "There's all kinds of soaps in this world, laddie. Each one's got its own special powers, all according to the recipe. If you want to watch what your enemies are up to, you take the basic brew and add eyebright, day's-eyes, and a little smart-weed if you need intelligence reports spelled out in the foam. Naturally it takes some time to prepare a batch, but if I'm in a hurry I just pop in some rushes."

"Then if you know what's wrong with Mysti, do you—do you have any brew that can help save her?"

"Don't you fret." She patted my cheek, then said to Grym, "Take her into the outer room. You'll find my bed in an alcove behind a blue curtain. Lay her down on that and I'll whip up something that will set her to rights before you can say—"

"*Kill the witch!*" came the sudden shout from outside the cottage.

"Mercy," said Mother Toadbreath, folding her hands on her cushiony bosom. "Isn't that always the way? They're early."

CHAPTER ——————— 18

I HUNKERED DOWN ON THE FLOOR BENEATH ONE OF Mother Toadbreath's front windows, watching her as she confronted the angry mob outside. Through the ripples and dimples in the thick greenish glass panes they all looked like fish under water. There were so many people, all of them chanting, "Kill the witch! Kill the witch!" and waving what looked like lances and battle-axes over their heads. Where was the watch-hedge? I smelled smoke and guessed that by now, Jawj and all his fellow-shrubs were a smoking ruin. Clearly the mob knew what to expect at Mother Toadbreath's house and had come prepared with torches. I didn't need a crystal ball to predict what they'd want to burn next.

I closed my eyes, reaching deep inside me for my Majyk. All I found was tea and muffins. But the Majyk had to be there. It just *had* to be! If I couldn't make it obey me now, Mother Toadbreath wouldn't survive the mob, and if she didn't survive . . .

"A word in thine ear, O Master," said Grym, tapping me on the shoulder.

"AAAAAAAA!" I shrieked, leaping out of my skin. When I landed I turned on the barbarian and snarled, "Don't you ever do that to me again!"

"Thy pardon, O steel-nerved wizard," Grym said drily. "I would but know if I might sally forth to lend mine arm and sword unto the defense of Mother Toadbreath."

"How's Mysti?"

"I have settled her with as mickle comfort as may be," the barbarian told me. "And yet mine heart misgiveth, for the wench is not of seemly hue betimes."

"He means she's turned orange on the starboard side," said

145

Scandal, popping his head through the blue curtain concealing
Mother Toadbreath's sleeping alcove. "Orange with white squiggles.
And on her left side she's breaking out in pink and violet
blobs that look like dead possums." He jumped out of the alcove
and trotted over to join us by the window. "I don't think she's a
well Welfie."

"Tell me about it," I said, teeth clenched so hard they hurt.

"What I'm telling you, fearless leader, is you'd better get the
witch on the case *fast*, before Mysti takes off for that big
mushroom house in the sky." The cat jumped lightly onto the
windowsill and looked out. "What's happening?"

"They're all just standing there," I said, puzzled. "Standing
there, waving their torches and their weapons and chanting 'Kill
the witch!'—but they're not making any move to actually *kill* her,
and it's been a while, now."

"Far out," Scandal commented.

"Ha!" Grym thundered, striking his palm with his fist. "Behold,
the gods have spoken yet again through the agency of this
most blessed beast! We tarry to our peril. *Far out*, quoth the gods,
and far out it behooves us that we go. Yea, even as far out as hath
gone Mother Toadbreath, into the teeth of her enemies!" He was
out the door, sword drawn, before you could say *Come back,
stupid*.

"Oh, for—! She *told* us to stay inside," I said. "Not even Grym
can take on that whole mob alone. I'm going after him."

"This is getting to be a habit with you. Moron see, moron do,"
the cat said. "There's at least fifty of those raving yokels out there.
If you go after Conehead the Barbarian, that'll bring the odds
down to twenty-five to one. Big help."

"You forget, I've got Majyk, and so does Grym."

"You can use your Majyk the way I can use a bicycle, and
Grym's Majyk's all tied up in his sword."

"Well—" I groped for some reason to justify what I was going
to do anyhow. There was no way I could just stand by and let
Grym and the witch fight the mob alone. "Well, my Majyk *does*
protect me. I'll go out and provoke the peasants until they attack
me. It'll be a diversionary tactic so everyone else can escape."

"Nice tactic," the cat commented, whiskers curled sideways.
"Your Majyk protects your *life*, and that's it. So the mob can beat
you to within a bloody inch of death, if they feel like it. I'll bet
they'll find that *very* diverting. And if Grym and Mother Toadbreath
do manage to run away, that still leaves us with Mysti."

"I don't see you coming up with a better idea," I grumbled.

"Me?" Scandal folded his paws under himself and curled up into a snug ball of fur on the sill. "I've got a super idea: I call it staying alive. I think it's pretty catchy, it's got a good beat, and you can dance to it. They may say cats have nine lives, but no one says I've got to prove it." He closed his eyes.

I glanced out through the window. With glass that crude, all I could see were blurry shapes, but I could pick out Grym by his height and Mother Toadbreath by the color of her dress. The mob had them surrounded and the chant had changed from "Kill the witch!" to just plain "Kill! Kill! Kill!"—in Grym's honor, I guess.

"Fine, stay put," I told Scandal. "Hide in here forever, you mangy coward!"

"Never had the mange in my life, pimple-puss," the cat replied with a yawn as I strode bravely out the door.

"Halt!" I cried on the doorstep. "Unhand them at once, else feel the wrath of Master Kendar, greatest wizard in all the realm!" I threw my hands high in a dramatic gesture.

(Once when I was still living at home, a bunch of traveling players came to Uxwudge Manor and put on *The Tragicall Historie of Doctor Festus*, the story of a wizard who sells his pet demon for a mess of pottage, whatever that is. The actor playing the part of Doctor Festus was always making dramatic gestures like that. Real wizards like Master Thengor don't bother with them; they just fry you where you stand and go back to whatever they were doing before you got stupid enough to annoy them.)

"Coo! Lookit th' loony," said one of the mob.

"He's a few sheep short of a spindle," said another.

"Not got all his lampreys in the lingonberries," a third agreed.

"There's more'n one cracked cup in his cubby, that's certain," a fourth put in.

"Bonkers as a bushpig in a bed warmer."

"Crazier than what Eunice said to the tinker's baffle."

"Mad as a marsh hare!" cried a pudgy little man the color of filth.

"Here, now!" his bearded companion objected. "Hares don't live in marshes."

"Awright, Lorrinz, mad as a marsh voondrab, then. How's that?" the roly-poly fellow snarled.

"Not much better, Wot." Lorrinz stroked his beard. "Voondrab's is much content to live in marshes and doesn't hardly go mad at all if you leave 'em there."

"Ver-ry well," Wot replied slowly. "Since you've gone and

promoted yerself from third village idiot to critic, how would *you* say it?''

''I say he's just plain loony,'' Lorrinz said, which seemed fair enough, even to me.

I felt loony, Wedwel knows. Standing there on Mother Toadbreath's doorsill, striking the proper Enraged Wizard pose, bravely challenging the fearsome might of—

—a bunch of Cheeseburghers waving mops. No torches, no battle-axes, nothing but mops.

Grym was looking at me like I'd gone 'round the twist. The watch-hedge was still standing—the burning I'd smelled came from several pipe-smokers in the mob—and I felt like even the bushes were whispering about me behind their leaves. I dropped my arms back to my sides. ''Uh, hello, everyone,'' I said with a sickly smile.

''Don't pay any mind to Kendar,'' Mother Toadbreath told the mob. ''He's mostly harmless. But he does have an awful lot of Majyk, so I wouldn't go teasing him too much about being crazy if I were you. No telling what he'll do. Now, where were we?''

A man who looked like Wot's twin brother sidled up to the witch, cap in hand. ''We had just got to the point where we was all worked up into a killing frenzy as was about to rend you limb from limb, ma'am. If you don't mind.''

''Oh yes, Evvon, of course, so we were. Well, carry on.'' The witch made encouraging motions. No one did a thing. ''Excuse me,'' Mother Toadbreath said, sounding put out. ''I asked you if we couldn't *please* get on with it. I have a sick girl in there who needs my help and if she dies because you people shilly-shallied around, I am going to be *very* cross.''

Evvon scuffed up a small pile of dirt with the toe of his boot. ''Beggin' yer pardon, ma'am, but it's not all that easy to go bang into a killing frenzy from a cold start if you know what I'm saying. We got to warm up to it some. Else we needs some inspiration, like.''

''How about if I turned you into a toad?'' the witch offered with that awful, gooey smile. ''Would that be inspiring enough?''

''Hey! You can't turn Evvon into no toad!'' Wot protested. ''Do one of the others, if that's your pleasure, but you do him, and Lorrinz and me'll have to go scare us up a third partner. Think that's easy?''

A straw-haired man in the crowd snorted. ''What's so hard about it? He's only a village idjit.''

''*Senior* village idjit,'' Wot corrected him. ''With all official forms and licenses writ out proper, *and* a spotless record. Hasn't done one single intelligent thing in years!''

''Aye,'' Lorrinz agreed. ''We're proud of our brother, we are. He keeps this up, he might even get gov'mint work some day.''

''I'm going to turn all of you into the toads *and* the government, too, if you don't get cracking here,'' Mother Toadbreath said.

''Awright, awright, don't get your mop in a tangle.'' Lorrinz stepped up and started mumbling, ''Kill the witch, kill the witch, kill, kill, kill the—No, wait, that's not how it goes. I think we did about twenty kill-the-witch's before we started in on the plain kill-kill-kill. Right! That's it. Everyone, on my signal we do three more kill-kill-kill's, like that, and then it's alas-we-cannot-she-be-too-powerful-for-we, and then it's *her* turn. Ready?'' He raised his hand and brought it down in a beautiful sweep.

''Kill! Kill! Kill!'' the mob chanted on cue, then stopped, gasped all together, and intoned, ''Alas, we cannot, she be too powerful for we.'' They sounded about as bloodthirsty as a bunch of my former fellow-students back at Master Thengor's Academy reciting the Periodic Table of the Elementals.

Mother Toadbreath didn't seem to mind. She cleared her throat and replied, ''Oh, foolish villagers to have challenged me. Now you must pay for your foolishness by—''

''Ma'am?'' It was Evvon.

''*What* is it?'' the witch snapped.

''No, ma'am, I'm Evvon, he's Wot,'' the senior idiot said very politely. ''And *you're* supposed to say 'Now you must pay for your *rashness*.' Not 'foolishness.' See, you already called us foolish villagers just a bit before, and if you say 'foolish' again, there ain't no what you'd call *variety* to it and it don't seem like you're putting a lot of thought into—''

Mother Toadbreath stuck her hand into a little belt-pouch and handed Evvon a cake of green soap. ''Here, hold this,'' she said. He took it without thinking, which was what you'd expect a senior village idiot to do. Next thing anyone knew, there was a fat toad sitting on a bar of green soap at the witch's feet. ''Any more problems?'' Mother Toadbreath asked. There weren't.

She was able to get through her part with no further interruptions. It was all very simple: The villagers had supposedly showed up to kill the witch, the witch could not be killed and was angry, but by a lucky chance the villagers had just happened to bring lots and lots of gifts to prevent the witch from turning Cheeseburgh into Toad-in-the-Hole.

''Goodness,'' said Mother Toadbreath as the people piled up

sacks and crates full of fresh fruits, vegetables, meats, and other supplies in front of her. "Yes, yes, this will do. I'm not angry anymore. You may all go away in peace and safety."

The Cheeseburghers backed off, dipping their mops and tugging their forelocks respectfully. Lorrinz paused long enough to kick the bar of green soap out from under his brother idiot, restoring Evvon to his former self. The witch did not object.

"Oh, wait a minute!" she called after them. "If you go down the *left* fork in the trail that goes past Goligosh Pond, you might just happen to find a box full of soaps and potions and such that will take care of those awkward little health problems some of you poor dears have been suffering. Just a guess. I'm not saying you *will* find such a box, and of course I haven't the faintest idea how it got there, but—"

Dawn fell on my head like a ton of toads.

"It's all a *trading party*?" I burst out. "All of this 'Kill the witch!' stuff was just so you people could swap groceries for potions? Wedwel's mercy, *why*?"

"*Why*?" Evvon repeated, giving me a suspicious look. "Say, you're not here to try and do me and my brothers out of a job, are you? 'Cause we don't hold with no freelance idjits here in Cheeseburgh."

"It's death for any of King Steffan's subjects to buy and sell with witches, dear," Mother Toadbreath said gently. "And it's strongly discouraged for anyone to so much as associate with a known witch. That's been the law ever since that unhappy little incident with King Steffan's cousin and her stepmother and that silly old apple. All a misunderstanding, but still, there you are. Royalty always does overreact."

"Aye," said one of the non-idiot villagers. "Poor old Mother T. can't just walk into town an' buy what she's needing, no more'n we can come strolling out here to pick up any o' her remedies. But 'tis perfectly legal for us to try and kill a witch every so often, and if we ain't got what it takes t' actually *kill* the witch, who's t' blame us?"

"I *am* a very powerful witch," Mother Toadbreath said demurely. "It would be false modesty to deny it."

"Just so," the villager agreed. He was a swarthy man whose curly black hair was liberally dusted with white powder. Bright jam and jelly stains blotched his apron and he smelled strongly of sugar. He was either the village baker or a very messy eater. "So after we comes 'round and fails t' kill her again, she gets angered of us and we've got t' calm her down with gifts. Makes sense, don't it?''

"You always make sense, Goodman Bobbo." Mother Toadbreath smiled at him. "Also the best rolls in the neighborhood. I do hope you've included the extra dozen I asked for?" The baker nodded, proud of his product's popularity.

"I see," I said. "And then after they leave the gifts, if they just *happen* to find a crate of witch's potions on the road home, who's going to say anything about it if they take it back to Cheeseburgh?"

"Right!" Goodman Bobbo patted me on the shoulder in a friendly way, leaving white handprints. "Mighty careless creatures they is, sometimes, witches."

"What I *don't* see," I went on, "is how the people know what supplies *you* need and how you know what potions *they* need."

"Oh, that'd be th' toads, young sir," the baker said. He reached into the big pocket on his apron and handed me a flour-speckled toad. "This be th' one as come t' town yesterday."

I looked at the beast's back and saw Mother Toadbreath's shopping list neatly spelled out in warts.

"As for how I know what the villagers need," Mother Toadbreath said, "it's all in the entrails."

"Entrails?" My stomach lurched. All good wizards are taught how to read entrails: You take a poor, innocent animal, give it a tidbit, pat it on the head, then split it open, spread its insides out on a board and read the future in the twists, curves, colors, and markings of your victim's guts. Given a choice, I'd rather just wait for the future to get here. I always cut Introductory Entrails. "Mother Toadbreath, how could you?" I blurted.

"There, there, dearie, it's not so bad," she reassured me. "I don't go *killing* anything. Why should I? There's a lovely royal highway on the far side of those hills over there. Whenever I need to read the future, to see what the Cheeseburghers will be needing from me, I just pack myself a little picnic lunch, walk to the highway, settle down on the grass, and wait for a chariot to run over something for me. They always do, you know. Then I read that. It's very convenient, and the entrails are usually already spread out by the time I get—"

I felt all the blood plunge from my head to my feet. I clapped one hand to my mouth, spun around, and raced into the house.

CHAPTER ————— 19

"ALL I'VE GOT TO SAY IS THAT IT'S A GOOD THING THE Cheeseburghers left me an extra mop as one of their gifts," said Mother Toadbreath, watching while her octopuss swabbed away at the floorboards.

"Murf," the beast agreed, giving me a baleful look.

"Sorry," I said, blushing. "I tried to find a bucket."

"No harm done, dearie," the witch responded. To her pet he said, "That's good enough, Norris."

"Rrrow!" said the octopuss. He finished with the floor, wrung out the mop and put it away, then slithered back into the other room to tend the cauldrons.

Mother Toadbreath got back to me. "Now if you're feeling up to it, we still have that little business to take care of."

"What little business?"

"Your wife."

"Who?" It was still hard for me to think of Mysti that way.

"That sweet little Welfie girl. She's turned zig-zaggy all over. Black and gold zigzags. Oh, and did I mention the fish?"

"What fish? Mysti's turned into a fish?" I wouldn't have been at all surprised.

"No, but she seems to have sprouted a fish on top of her head. A salmon, I believe." ·

"'Tis a trout," Grym said from behind the blue curtain.

"Well, I never claimed to be an expert on the subject of fish," Mother Toadbreath called back to him. Then she grasped my wrist and said briskly, "Come along. It's past time you put that Majyk of yours to good use."

I felt an ache in my chest. "You mean . . . use it to cure Mysti?"

152

"*If* you're in the mood to save her life," the witch said with a nasty, sarcastic bite.

"But I thought—I thought *you* were going to do that. Couldn't you—don't you have the right potion? If you can defeat Welfie archers, you've *got* to be able to overcome Welfin spells."

"I've got to, do I?" Mother Toadbreath's face was inscrutable. "And what if I can't? Are you just going to let her die?"

"I don't want her to die," I said quietly. "But there's nothing I can do."

"Nothing," she agreed, "if you don't try. I'm very sorry, but I can't permit that. Come with me." She dragged me behind the curtain.

Grym and Scandal were waiting for us in the alcove where Mysti lay on Mother Toadbreath's bed. The cat perched on the headboard, which was carved in the shape of an owl with outstretched wings. Grym had his sword in his hand, as if he intended to fight death itself hand-to-hand, if he had to. The witch lifted the covers a bit to check on her patient's condition.

It didn't look good. Mysti had stopped changing colors and there was no fish anywhere I could see, but she was lying there very white and very still. Mother Toadbreath reached inside the pillow and pulled out a tuft of feathers. When she held them under Mysti's nose they hardly stirred. "It's almost over." She sounded resigned.

"What can I do?" I wailed. "*Tell* me! All the Majyk I've got is useless. I don't know how to make it do what I want. If I did, Mysti wouldn't be dying, I swear it! She wouldn't even be *married*!"

"He's telling you the truth," Scandal affirmed. "Just 'cause you own the horse don't mean you can ride it to win the Derby. Take my word for it, Kendar is no big-league Majyk-jockey. He gets off a lucky shot now and then, but you know what they say about busted clocks: They're right twice a day. If he did know how to use what he's got, Mysti wouldn't be here, and neither would we."

"Is that so?" Mother Toadbreath was perplexed. "Truly so?" She looked to Grym for confirmation.

"By my sword, dost think I would still be afflicted with this face were Master Kendar fully able to command the sum of Majyk he doth possess?" the barbarian asked.

"But—but it's such a *cute* face," the witch stammered. Grym gave her a dirty look. "Oh dear," she said. "Oh my. I didn't really believe anyone could have so much Majyk and not know the first thing about making it work. As a witch, you see, I don't use Majyk at all. My spells are performed using only the finest natural ingredients, strictly organic. Even so, I like to keep an open mind. I've managed to pick up a few second-hand texts on basic Majyk management and I've even got a little dab of the stuff put by as a curiosity, but I never thought—Oh dear.'' She glanced at Mysti's bloodless face and repeated, ''Oh dear.''

Grym gave me a cuff in the back. ''A murrain befall thee, also thy cattle if the wench perish. Thou laggard, thou couldst make thy Majyk obey thee didst thou but try harder!''

I'd heard that one before, mostly from Master Thengor and my father, about everything from potions to posture.

''You think it's that easy?'' I shot back at the barbarian. ''You think the answer to everything is always just 'Try harder'?''

Grym shrugged. ''Thou may'st accomplish much, in sooth, dost thou but make the proper effort. In willpower lieth all.''

''Suuuuure,'' Scandal drawled. ''Believe hard enough and you can do anything, right? So if you want to fly, just climb the tallest tree around and *believe*. Then jump off. When you go splat on the ground, it's not because people aren't birdies, it's because it's all your own fault that you didn't *believe* hard enough.'' He laughed. ''What a racket!''

''But this is awful!'' Mother Toadbreath exclaimed. ''I know how to manage Majyk, but to help this Welfie, what I need is some Majyk to manage.''

''By my sword, 'twill take more than *some* Majyk to heal her, I trow,'' Grym said.

''Why, yes, dear, you trow quite right.'' The witch patted the barbarian's hand. ''After all, as I said, I do have *some* Majyk put by—just a smidgin that I was able to catch by way of experiment last summer, after the blueberry harvest but before the unicorn stampede; I'm keeping it in a gravy boat in the cupboard with the good dishes, if it hasn't gone stale—but this case will most definitely take *scads* of Majyk to put right, and plenty of push besides.''

'' 'Push,' quoth'a?'' said Grym. ''If thou dost speak of marrow, of brawn, of strength, then I am thy man!''

''Ooh, wouldn't that be nice,'' Mother Toadbreath said, letting her eyes wander up and down Grym's impressive physique. ''But I'm afraid I was speaking more of *spiritual* push. You know: drive, desire, the will to win.''

''Hath I not already said that such strength of will is mine?'' Grym roared.

"Is it? Well, that's nice. Now if you've also got those scads of Majyk I mentioned, I think we can get Mysti on her feet in time for—"

"Be a sword's-worth of Majyk scads?" Grym asked, holding out Graverobber for Mother Toadbreath's inspection.

The witch fished into the neckline of her robe and pulled up a pair of wire-rimmed reading glasses on a silk cord. She set these on her nose, studied the sword, then said, "I'm afraid you're several bushels short of a scad, let alone *scads*, plural. You haven't even got enough there to make up half an oodle."

Grym's shoulders slumped. "Pox on't," he grumbled. "Thou hast the way, but not the will, I own the will, but not the way, and both of us do lack the means, which Kendar hath got but hath neither the will nor the way to use!"

"What we need is a *real* wizard," I said.

"What you need," Scandal remarked, "is a real camel."

"A what?" we all said at the same time.

"A camel." The cat closed his eyes. "That's a horse made by a committee."

Mysti opened her eyes and sat up in bed. "Oh, I feel wonderful!" she exclaimed, stretching her arms high overhead. "I feel like a new Welfie." She kicked back the covers and stared at what she found there. "Who put a trout in my bed?"

"It fell off your head," I said from up near the ceiling. "Anyway, I think it's really a carp."

Mysti looked up at me, blinked, rubbed her eyes and stared again. Then she decided to scream.

"Put a sock in it, sister," Scandal ordered. He sounded cranky, and for a good reason. He was being held around the middle in one of Norris' tentacles while another rubbed his fur the wrong way with a piece of silk. He was spiky as a thistle and twice as ready to sting, but he wasn't the only one in the octopuss's clutches.

"Feeling better, dear?" Mother Toadbreath called from her place in the coils of Tentacle No. 3. Her pet monster used it to hold her several feet off the floor while Tentacle No. 4 clutched a book called *Majyk Made Manifest: Everything Thou Didst Ever Desire to Wot of Majyk, Yet Didst Fear Ye True Wizards Would Find Out and Destroy Thee.* Norris held the book open so that Mother Toadbreath could check it every now and then. The witch couldn't do it herself; holding onto that gravy boat took both hands.

"I'faith, she doth look better," Grym remarked from Tentacles Nos. 5 and 6. One was wrapped around the barbarian's waist, the other helped him hold Graverobber steady at just the proper angle called for by the witch's book so that the Majyk-soaked sword acted like a focus for the healing power we generated.

"She *is* better," Scandal spat. "Now lemme go!"

"Let him go, Norris," Mother Toadbreath agreed. "And thank you, dear kitty. Without all those nice sparks from your fur to heat things up, it would have taken much longer."

"Yeah, yeah, yeah, the check is in the mail," Scandal said, jumping from the tentacle to the floor. He started licking his coat smooth again.

"While we're on the subject of letting people go—" I began.

"Of course, lovey." Mother Toadbreath tickled Norris' tentacles. "All done, sweetie-pussums. Let'ums Mommy go. Oh, and let 'ums go the nice barbarian swordsman and 'ums dear ittoo wizardums, too."

"*Wait!*" Mysti leaped out of bed with nothing but the top sheet to cover her.

Mother Toadbreath put away her reading glasses. "Yes, dear?"

"Before you tell your pet to let everyone go, aren't you forgetting a few things?"

"Like what, child?"

"Well, for one, you're still pouring that funny, glowing goo out of that gravy boat all over Kendar's head."

"Am I?" Mother Toadbreath glanced at her hands as if she'd never seen them before. "Mercy. So I am." She righted the gravy boat and wiped one last shining drip off the spout. "And it's not just any kind of funny, glowing goo, dearie; it's Majyk. I was priming the dear boy's pump. Now if that's all, I think we can allow Norris to—"

"—drop Kendar on his head," Mysti finished for her. "He's hanging upside down, you know."

"Oh, ah?" The witch got out her glasses again and checked Mysti's report.

It was true. I was hanging upside down from Tentacles Nos. 7 and 8, my hands making a this-way-please shape, aiming down at Grym's sword which in turn was aimed at the bed. For the past hour the four of us (with a little help from Norris) had been ganging up on Majyk. We bullied it until it trickled out of me into Graverobber, Scandal's sparks heated it up, Mother Toadbreath's knowledge told it what it had to do, and Grym's willpower shot it out the sword and all over Mysti until she was well.

"Don't you look funny, though, upsy-daisy like that." Mother Toadbreath chuckled while she made the octopuss release her and

Grym and put me down rightside up. My head was spinning badly. I staggered over to lean against the carved owl headboard, scowling at everyone.

"Here, now! You just wipe that ugly look off your face this instant," the witch ordered. "It's your own fault, you know."

"It always is," I muttered.

"You'll get nowhere fast with that attitude, young man. Quit before you start, that's your way. Just give up when the going gets rough and walk off, don't you?"

"That's not true!" Scandal said hotly. "Sometimes he runs."

"Well, I, for one, am not going to indulge you in your silly snits. Your darling little wife nearly died because you hadn't the foggiest idea of how to save her."

"Mysti is *not* my darling little wife!"

"I am until we put about a hundred leagues between me and the Forest of Euw!" Mysti hollered at me. "You're not getting rid of me until I'm safely out of my relatives' reach!"

"Good for you, dearie." Mother Toadbreath nodded her approval, then lit into me once more. "You won't always have other people around to clean up your messes, my lad! The sooner you learn how to take care of yourself, the sounder we shall all sleep, I'm sure."

I had to smile. "Now you even *sound* like my old Nanny Esplanadia."

"I sound like myself, which is not as old as all that and has always been good enough for me, thank you." The witch puffed up like one of her own toads. "And where would *I* be today if I'd taken your quitter's attitude? I shudder to think! Why, it was years and years back that I first knew what my life's goal was. Ever since then, I have devoted myself utterly to achieving it. Have I been successful so far? No. Would it be easier to give up? Oh, yes! Will I?" Her eyes narrowed and shot fire. "*Never.*"

"What is your life's goal, Mother Toadbreath?" Mysti asked, tying the ends of the bedsheet over one shoulder to make herself a very pretty white gown.

The witch seemed surprised. "Why, it's the same as for every proper young woman, of course: to kiss a toad and have him turn into a handsome prince who will marry me and take me away to his castle where we shall live together happily ever after." She picked up one of the mass of toads hopping and squatting on the cottage floor and gave it a kiss. When nothing happened, she let it drop and said, "It's just a matter of finding the right one."

"At least now we know why they call her Mother Toadbreath," Scandal whispered.

The witch didn't hear him, or pretended not to. She had other fish to fry, not including the carp that was still flopping around in the bed. "You, young man, are going to learn how to manage your Majyk or I shall know the reason why! Here." She shoved a book into my hands. "Now I want you to begin by studying the first five chapters. Do the exercises and essay questions at the end of each one. The answers are in the back, but don't cheat by looking at them until you've made an honest effort to come up with your own."

I dropped the book to the floor. It hit a toad, but luckily for the toad he was bigger than the book. "I was a student of wizardry at Master Thengor's Academy for years," I said. "I never learned how to use Majyk in all that time. Why should now be different? This won't work."

"Correction," said the witch. "*You* won't work."

"It's no use," I said. "I just don't have the brains for wizardry."

"Hmph! Who told you that? Master Thengor, I'll be bound. I've heard quite enough about these wizards to tell you that if you didn't learn a lick from him, it's small wonder. Once a pupil learns what he's come to learn, he's got no further reason to be lollygagging around the school, does he? And once he leaves the school, he takes his money with him. Wizards are no fools when it comes to money. They don't need Majyk to make *yours* disappear, I can tell you! The slower you learn, the longer you stay; the longer you stay, the longer you pay. And nothing makes a child learn more slowly than being told he can't learn at all."

"That's—" I was going to say *ridiculous*. Then I remembered something:

Every year we'd get one or two new students who came to the Academy on a royal scholarship. (King Steffan liked to support the arts.) The wizard who accepted scholarship pupils got a lot of royal favors, but he also had to sign a contract promising to teach the scholarship pupils until they were ready to receive their official pointy hats—the next step up after the robe, but one step away from getting the wand, which only the Council can award. However, the scholarship *money* that these pupils brought in was only enough to pay for two years of study.

Funny, but every single scholarship pupil at Master Thengor's Academy always got his pointy hat in less than two years' time.

Mother Toadbreath was smiling kindly at me. "Well, dearie? Are you game to try?"

I felt my mouth and eyes harden. "Just give me the book," I said, "and stand back."

"Get it yourself," said the witch. "You dropped it."

CHAPTER —————— 20

THE FIRST TIME I READ THE CHAPTER ON BASIC LEVITA-
tion, I got eight out of ten problems wrong.

The second time I read the chapter, I got five out of ten wrong.

The third time I read it, I got three out of ten wrong.

The fourth time, I decided to stop counting the ones I got wrong
and pay more attention to the ones I got *right*. That was a good
thing: There were nine of them.

I was holed up in the shade of the watch-hedge, trying to make
it a perfect ten when Scandal found me. The watch-hedge towards
the back of Mother Toadbreath's cottage was my favorite place for
studying, mostly because the poison ivy kept Mysti far away.
"How's it going, Houdini?" the cat asked.

I aimed two fingers at him and said, "Sysopbitglitch." Scandal
floated straight up to the top of the hedge. "How does it look like
it's going?" I grinned.

"Very funny. Put me down." After I did, Scandal fluffed his
fur the way he always did when he was annoyed. "You're a riot,
Alice, a regular riot."

"Some day you're going to call me by my right name," I told
him. "The shock will kill us both."

"Promise?" Scandal asked with a wicked smirk. He came and
rubbed against my legs.

"I don't understand this," I said, putting the book down.

"What don't you understand? Tell Uncle Scandal. I'm supposed to have nine lives. I can afford to be bored to death a couple
of times." He sank down onto his side and rested his chin on my
foot, purring.

"You."

"You're not supposed to understand me. Me, cat; you, human. If you understood me, I'd have to turn in my union card."

I sighed. "Half the time, I don't know what you're talking about."

"Only half?" Scandal cocked his ears forward. "I must be losing my touch."

"The funny thing is, it doesn't matter. Most of what you say makes sense."

"*Sense?*" The ears went back flat. "*Sense?* Brother, them's fightin' words. I'm a *cat*! A creature of intuition, of unfathomable depths and mystery. You want an animal that makes *sense*, you go get yourself a dog." He climbed into my lap, curled up into a ball, and appeared to go right to sleep.

"See, *that's* what I mean about I don't understand," I said. "One minute you're angry at me, or making fun of me, or calling me stupid—"

"Never called you stupid," the cat mumbled. "Called you *human*. Oh. Right. Never mind."

"—and next thing I know you're purring, or snuggling up to me, or rubbing against my legs. I don't get it; it's too confusing for anyone to understand. Do you like me or don't you?"

Scandal lifted his head and looked me in the eye. "I like you. Happy? Now drop dead." He went back to sleep.

I decided this was the perfect time to get that tenth Basic Levitation problem right. I held my right hand up the way I used to when I'd make shadow-duckies on the nursery wall for my sister Lucy; then I had the hand-puppet say the mystic word, "Dryginonnarox." Maybe I finally got the accent on the right syllable, because it worked! Scandal rose slowly from my lap and began to twirl in midair. He started off slow, then went faster and faster until he stopped pretending he was asleep and started howling for mercy.

I let him spin around a dozen times before I called off the spell and brought him back to earth. His fur shot off hissing fireworms of Majyk as he stumbled back and forth saying, "That is the last time I take a nap in an open clothes dryer." He tilted against me and added, "When I get my health back, I wouldn't put on my shoes without checking what's in them first if I were you, bozo."

"All I want is an honest answer," I said.

"You want honest?" Scandal lay down and dug his claws into the soil. "Okay, you'll get honest. I like you, pal, and it's scaring me out of four and a half lives."

"You like me?" I couldn't help smiling, even if I did feel

puzzled at the same time. "But—but why does that scare you?"

Scandal rolled onto his back, batting at some fallen leaves. "Because the last time I made the mistake of liking a skinball, he up and booted me out of his life the minute he found a soft, warm, huggy-wuggy skinball of the female persuasion, that's why. I told you about my software wizard, right?"

"Right," I said. I still didn't know what kind of Majyk software was, but it sounded very comfortable; probably used for making robes and slippers.

"First time the geek finds someone who doesn't shriek or laugh out loud when she sees him naked, the woman's allergic to cats and it's *hasta la vista*, kitty. *Ciao. Shalom. Aloha.* Here's your hat, what's your hurry. One day I'm fussing if I don't get canned tuna, the next I'm fighting rats for empty tuna cans." Scandal rolled rightside up. "Lots of people think cats don't have hearts. Well, we do. I had mine broken once; I'm not going back for seconds."

I reached out and scooped him up, holding him against my chest. "I'd never do anything like that to you."

"That's what they all say." Scandal stiffened his legs and pushed himself out of my arms. "Right now you *need* me. I'm still carrying around part of old man Thengor's shattered Majyk, remember? But thanks to Mother Toadbreath's moldy old book, you're finally learning how to use the Majyk you've got. Pretty soon you'll figure out how to collect all the pieces, including mine. You won't need me any more then. You won't need anyone."

I looked into the cat's eyes. He looked so proud, so independent, even after he'd just come out and told me he was hurt and afraid. You wouldn't know it to look at him. A boy could learn a lot from a cat.

"Majyk or not, I'll need you," I said.

"Mouse-turds. From what I hear you telling the old lady, you're taking to Majyk like a duck takes to orange sauce."

"You let Mother Toadbreath hear you calling her 'old lady' and you'll be the one in orange sauce," I warned him. "Anyway, all I can learn from this book is the basics; nothing fancy. A little levitation, a little illusion, elementary shielding spells that are only good for keeping off soft, blunt objects . . ."

"Goody. Next time we're attacked with custard pies, I'll feel so much safer, knowing I'm with you." Scandal sneered. "Not that you're gonna keep me hanging around with you much longer."

"Hey! I thought *you* were only hanging around with *me* until we could find you a way back to your own world."

Scandal turned his eyes away, embarrassed. "Chngdmnd."

"What?"

"*I said I changed my mind!*" the cat yelled in my face. "What, do I gotta have a license for it or something? I like this world of yours, okay? It's a lot cleaner and a lot quieter than my old stomping grounds and I won't have to go around half my life afraid of getting squashed by a Toyota."

"A toy what?" I asked.

"I rest my case." He folded his front paws one on top of the other.

"You really don't want to go?" I asked.

"Naaaah. This place is cool. Mother Toadbreath told me you don't have any really big dogs here."

"We used to," I admitted. "They kept running off into the swamps, and the slimegrinds ate them."

"Well, a cat's got enough smarts to stay out of swamps. Yeah, this is the life." He stretched so that I could see the faint stripes on his belly. "No cars, no dogs, just peace and quiet and—"

"*Kill the witch!*"

"—and the occasional witch-hunt." Scandal jumped to his feet at the familiar cry. "Let's go watch the fun."

We took our time going around to the front of the witch's cottage. We'd spent almost a week and a half with Mother Toadbreath, time enough for Mysti to make a complete recovery and for me to get on with my studies. In that time we'd gotten used to the Cheesburgh witch-hunts which happened about once every three days, just enough time for Mother Toadbreath to need a fresh supply of Goodman Bobbo's famous rolls.

(We'd also had a one-man witch-hunt when the senior village idiot, Evvon, needed some complexion lotion before he could go courting the village madwoman of nearby Sumpton. He stood outside Mother Toadbreath's door chanting, "Kill the witch!" and waving his mop all by himself for about an hour before anyone noticed he was there. Later we heard that the madwoman of Sumpton turned him down. She said she was mad but she wasn't crazy.)

The routine was old hat to us by now. Scandal and I knew there was no need to rush. A witch-hunt didn't get down to business until they stopped chanting "Kill the witch!" and switched over to plain old "Kill! Kill! Kill!"

We were just turning the corner of the cottage when I heard someone shout, "Hang her!"

I stopped in my tracks. "Something's wrong. They never say *how* they want to kill the witch."

"Burn her!" came another shout, as if to prove my point.

"Sure you're not just overreacting, boss?" Scandal asked, tugging at me with his claws.

"Sew her in a sack with that cursed octopuss of hers and throw 'em both in Goligosh Pond!" a third voice bellowed.

That was enough for Scandal. "Whoa! When they get that specific, they mean business! What gives?"

"Sshhhhh!" I motioned for him to be quiet while I peeked around the corner.

The village mob had gathered in front of the witch's house, as always, led by the three village idiots, but instead of mops they were holding pruning hooks and scythes and sickles and all sorts of sharp-edged farming tools. The women in the mob had scissors, and one of them—probably the village schoolteacher—was waving an ugly-looking ruler still covered with old bloodstains.

Mother Toadbreath was standing on her doorsill, toads swarming over her feet, facing the mob just as calmly as if it was business as usual. Grym, Mysti, and Norris were nowhere to be seen. My guess was they were still in the back room, watching the soaps. A witch-hunt was nothing to get upset about.

"I think there must be some mistake here," Mother Toadbreath said. "I don't remember having ordered a grocery delivery for today."

"There's been a mistake, all right, and you made it, witch!" Lorrinz yelled, waving a scythe. "For too long has our innocent village suffered, living in fear under the yoke of your sorcerous tyranny and—and—um—" He rested the scythe carelessly against his shoulder and dug around in his belt-pouch for something while the people standing near him dodged the swinging blade. At last he pulled out a piece of paper, unfolded it, read it through while moving his lips, then went on to say, "—sorcerous tyranny and opossum!"

A ball of blue fire whizzed from the back of the crowd to thunk Lorrinz a good one in the head. "That's tyranny and *oppression*, you idiot!" came a holler that I knew much, much too well.

The mob parted to let a dark-robed figure through. I cringed. It was Zoltan.

Lorrinz stood rubbing the back of his head. "I just read it like it's wrote," he grumbled, holding out the paper. "Can't blame me does you have bloodygodawful handwriting."

Zoltan grabbed Lorrinz by the front of his oatmeal-stained tunic. "In case you're forgetting who I am, I am not merely one of your noddy-headed old hedge-witches; *I* am a wizard."

"That's right!" Wot called from his place in the crowd. "So he is! It's writ down on his calling cards an' evr'thing!"

"Still not writ so's a person can read it," Lorrinz said, under his breath.

"Well?" Zoltan demanded, turning to the crowd. "What are you all staring at? Get on with your business! You came here to kill the witch. What's stopping you?"

There was a lot of uneasy muttering from the Cheeseburghers, punctuated now and then by a loud "*Ow!*" as someone cut himself on his neighbor's sickle. At last it was Evvon who came forward to say, "Beg yer pardon, sir, but when you came by the Wheeze and Garnish tavern, buying everyone a drink like the gent you are, you said that we wasn't actually to *kill* the witch. Just sort of come 'round here and stir up a fuss and use her as bait, like."

Zoltan rattled off a spell that made a large, pink bird appear over Evvon's head. The creature squawked once and laid an egg that smashed onto the senior idiot's skull; then the bird vanished.

"Was I speaking out of turn, sir?" Evvon asked, wiping yolk out of his eyes.

"It's not like we *can't* kill the witch," Wot piped up. "When I was at school our Mistress Cosh told us there ain't nothing you *can't* do in this world." He craned his neck and asked the ruler-waving woman, "Ain't that right, Mistress Cosh?"

"Did I see you raise your hand before speaking, Evvon?" the teacher shrilled, threatening him with the ruler. The idiot quailed. "Did I call on you to recite, young man?"

"I am surrounded by idiots," Zoltan said between slowly grinding teeth.

"Oh, no sir, not really," Goodman Bobbo broke in. "Only just those three."

"Soon t'be only just them *two*," Evvon said proudly. "Master Zoltan's been and offered me a chance to work for the gov'mint. I'm gonna be a bureau rat!"

"So much natural talent." Zoltan shrugged. "What more can I say?"

"Here! You can't just come among us and make off with one of our idiots!" the baker protested. "Leaving his poor brothers in the lurch, what with all the idiot work there's to be done around this town. It's not as if they were born Cheeseburghers. Those lads there are genuine *imported* idiots, with all taxes paid on 'em and everything! It isn't fair, that's what it's not." A storm of agreement rose up from the crowd, especially from Lorrinz and Wot.

Still in hiding, I stole a glimpse at Mother Toadbreath's face. The witch was growing more irritated by the second. Her hair, normally hidden under her headwrap, had escaped in long, damp strands of black streaked with gray. She tucked it behind her ears, knotted her fingers together, and said, "*If* you people don't mind, would you kindly take your bickering elsewhere? Some of us are not your high-and-mighty spangles-and-lace wizards, we're not. Some of us have to put in an honest day's work for an honest day's spellcasting. I've left eleven pots of soap on the boil, and while Norris and my assistants can handle the stirring, they don't know when to add which ingredients to the brew. So if you will excuse me—"

"Seize her, you fools!" cried Zoltan. Lorrinz, Wot, and Evvon very obligingly rushed up to grab Mother Toadbreath by the arms and bring her before the wizard.

"There you are, sir," Evvon said, tugging his forelock. "Although strictly speaking, me and my brothers ain't specifically 'fools,' like you called us."

"You're much too modest," Zoltan said smoothly. He stroked his moustache as he confronted the witch. "Don't be alarmed, my good woman. It's not you I'm after."

"It's not me you'll have," Mother Toadbreath countered. "I'd sooner settle for one of the toads."

Zoltan laughed. "Dear lady, you're almost as funny as you look."

"If I could get my hands on a bar of my best soap, you wouldn't be saying such things to me," the witch shot back at him.

"Your best soap? Oh, I tremble," said Zoltan, who didn't. "You'll never get to pull any of your petty enchantments on me. My Cheeseburgher friends have forewarned me of them all. Just out of professional curiosity, though, what would you have done to me if you had that soap to hand?"

"Wash your nasty mouth out, like your mother should have done! I expect she was too busy trying to remember your father's name."

Zoltan grasped Mother Toadbreath's chin and jerked it up so hard her whole headwrap came off. The mob gasped: There was another toad sitting on top of her head, this one smoking a pipe and reading a book. I could just make out the title: *Beyond the Kiss: Amateur Spellbreaking Made Simple*. As soon as he was exposed, the toad dropped book and pipe and hopped away to mingle with the others.

"Where is he?" Zoltan growled in the witch's face.

"Where is whom?" Mother Toadbreath countered.

"Where is *who*?" Mistress Cosh shouted from the crowd, starting a new argument.

"Your *assistant*." Zoltan made the word sound wormy.

"I have more than one of those."

"Very well, then: Your *stupid* assistant. Where is he?"

"He's right here," I said, stepping into view while Scandal scampered into the house. "Whom wants to know?"

CHAPTER ——————— 21

A HUSH FELL OVER THE CROWD. THE AIR WAS HEAVY with the weight of two great wizards' barely bridled Majyk. Eye to eye, we faced each other, neither one blinking. Tension seeped up out of the very ground on which we stood.

"Fuzz-face," I said.

"Ratwhacker," he replied.

"You were always kissing up to Master Thengor."

"You were too stupid to know *what* to kiss."

"Cod brain."

"Nematode."

"What toad? Where?" Mother Toadbreath struggled in her captors' grip and looked around eagerly.

"*Nematode!*" Zoltan shouted at her. "It means a *worm*, you old goose-spit!"

Mother Toadbreath settled down. "Well, there's no need to be rude," she said, primly straightening her shoulders.

"Hey, *Zollie*," I said, deliberately using Bini's special nickname for him. "Why don't you pick on someone your own size? Someone your goons don't have all tied up."

"Beg pardon, sir, but we ain't goons," said Lorrinz. "We're idiots."

"*Imported* idiots," Evvon corrected him. "Come all the way from Vicinity City, we did, before the Troubles."

"Ah yes, the Troubles," said Wot. All three of them shook their heads and made tsk-tsk noises.

"*I'll* give you troubles if you don't let her go," I told them. "Well? Go on and do it. *He's* got what he paid you for." I jerked my head in Zoltan's direction. "I'm out in the open. You can cut bait."

"Not on your lives!" Zoltan roared at the idiots. "This is not the Ratwhacker I once knew. He's changed somehow since he entered the fearsome Forest of Euw. I don't like it. Hold the witch fast and keep something sharp at her neck. This situation may require some study." He fell back a step and struck a thoughtful pose.

"Let her go," I repeated, "or you'll all require some funerals."

Mother Toadbreath's book didn't cover Destroying Your Enemies (Elementary, Intermediate, Advanced, and Party Tricks) until the twelfth chapter. I'd only gotten as far as the fifth, but I'd done very well with the chapter on Illusion. Scandal had run into the witch's house to get help, but until he came back I had to stall Zoltan. I did the warm-up breathing exercises to let my Majyk know I'd be wanting to use it soon; then I cupped my hands, wiggled my fingers like a nest of nematodes, and said, "Morganaticdithyramb!"

It was a very nice dragon, standing twice as tall as Mother Toadbreath's cottage. I was especially proud of the red horns and gold scales. It uttered one small, polite roar. (The book said that it's the little details like color and sound that make all the difference between a good illusion and mass panic in the marketplace.)

The dragon lowered its head and gave the crowd a casual once-over, like a lady about to pick one favorite candy out of an assortment box. The village mob exploded with shrieks, screams, and Mistress Cosh hollering that the dragon had not raised its paw before roaring and was going to get slapped on the talons with a ruler if it tried that again.

"Don't you men have someplace else you'd rather be?" I asked the idiots holding Mother Toadbreath. Their mouths hung open as they goggled at the dragon, but they weren't running away. I thought I'd encourage them. "She's hungry. *Very* hungry. I don't think she'll stop after just one of you."

"Don't move!" Zoltan ordered. "Can't you tell the beast is only an illusion?"

Wot licked his lips. "Uh . . . no, sir. Looks real enough to me." He dropped his hold on Mother Toadbreath and took off through the crowd like a crossbow shot.

I made the dragon roar again. That decided Lorrinz, who scampered after his brother faster than a greased lamprey down a drain. A large part of the mob joined him, leaving all their shiny scythes and sickles and pruning-hooks behind.

Zoltan cursed, then took a deep breath of his own, getting ready to unleash his powers. Whatever he had in mind was going to be something special, something really rotten, or he wouldn't need so much warm-up time. Knowing Zoltan, his spell might not be aimed at me. More likely it would be aimed at Mother Toadbreath. Somehow he'd tracked me to her home and figured out that she was helping me. Any friend of mine was dogmeat to him.

What was keeping Scandal? I had to scare off the last man holding Mother Toadbreath, and I had to do it before Zoltan worked himself up enough power to let loose that big spell. I must have panicked, because I think I overdid it. First I made the dragon's teeth longer and sharper; they seemed to grow while you watched. Then I added some drool—long, slurpy strings of it pouring from the monster's jaws. The dragon's eyes went from black to glowing blood-red. Pieces of dripping meat appeared in its claws. Spikes sprang up at the tip of its tail. I even added a row of human skulls on top of the spikes.

When I made the skulls start to moan *Evvon . . . Turn back, Evvon . . . Go home, Evvon, you idiot . . .* —Well, a good wizard is a good artist and a good artist knows when to stop. I never said I was a good wizard. The illusion scared Evvon all right; it scared him too well. He was petrified, frozen, unable to move a muscle, stiff as an icicle, and rooted to the ground as solidly as a boulder.

Did you ever see a boulder let go of a witch and run away? Me neither.

Zoltan was starting to make wizardly gestures. This was definitely going to be something bigger than a simple fry-you-where-you-stand. Besides, he knew better than to waste one of those on me. No question now that he was going after Mother Toadbreath, and if he happened to blast Evvon into Wedwel's Selective Paradise too, what was one less future bureau rat?

"Zoltan, *stop!*" I cried.

Zoltan lowered his hands. "Any particular reason?" he asked. He spoke like a man who had plenty of time to get back to the big-time Spell of Obliteration he was working on.

I nibbled my lower lip. Where *was* that miserable cat? It couldn't take him this long to fetch Grym. "Your quarrel is with me, not her. Have your man release her and we'll settle this wizard to wizard."

"Haw!" Zoltan jammed his hands on his hips. "Look what's calling itself a wizard, these days. Master Thengor would roll over in his grave, if he had one. I wouldn't dirty my Majyk by casting it at the likes of you."

"Yeah, not if you're *afraid* to," I sneered. Here was my chance. If I could provoke Zoltan enough, he'd hurl a bolt of destruction at me and my Majyk would make it shatter like glass. About a third of the original Cheeseburgher mob was still there, watching. If they saw me survive a full-blown attack of sorcery, they'd hail me as the winner, turn on Zoltan, and leap to Mother Toadbreath's defense.

I hoped.

"Afraid?" Zoltan raised one eyebrow. "Of you?" He snapped his fingers and my beautiful dragon illusion melted into a puddle. The human skulls on its tail-spikes turned into fluffy yellow ducklings, quacking merrily.

"I see your game," he went on. "It won't work, Ratwhacker. These simple peasants are behind me one hundred per cent of the way. Isn't that right, simple peasants?"

"Hooray," said the remaining Cheeseburghers with all the enthusiasm of a pile of wet laundry.

"Is one hundred per cent more or less than a half?" someone asked.

Zoltan didn't really need to have the Cheeseburghers behind him. He'd always been his own biggest cheering section. "As I see it, you have two choices," he told me. "Let the witch meet her fate, or give me your Majyk."

"Sure, just *give* you my Majyk. There's only one way for you to get it off me, and I don't much care for it."

"Oh, *that*." Zoltan disdained my objections to being made suddenly dead, just so he could help himself to all that power. "There'll be no need for you to die. I intend to enlist the witch's aid in stripping you of Majyk. With two experienced practitioners of the hidden arts working together, we can do it."

"*If* Mother Toadbreath agrees to help you," I reminded him.

"Which I won't." The witch spoke up. "Sir, you may be an acquaintance of Kendar's, but I'm bound to tell you that you are *not* a person I'd care to know socially."

Zoltan winked at her. "You'd be surprised what a little torture can do to make a body change her mind."

"If you lay one hand on her—" I began.

"Me? No need. She's a witch. There are laws in this kingdom about witches." Zoltan gave me one of those smiles that made me want to break his neck. "There are even rewards given for the capture, conviction, and execution of proven witches."

"Horrid trumpery laws, they are!" Mother Toadbreath was

indignant. "Forced on our good King Steffan by a bunch of self-serving wizards afraid of a little honest competition."

"I am proud to say that Master Thengor was one of the strongest proponents of the anti-witch laws," Zoltan said.

"Master Thengor was an old gunnysack rascal," Mother Toadbreath snapped. "Witchcraft's the only career in the hidden arts that's open to girls. The wizards say we ladies haven't the talent to manage *real* magic, then they fly clean off the handle when our homemade spells outdo their great, grandstanding enchantments."

"I don't think she's going to help you, Zoltan," I remarked. I hoped my smile was just as annoying as his. "And neither will I."

"With your help or without it, then," Zoltan responded. "I *was* merely going to summon the king's Justice with a fireball and turn the witch over to the proper authorities, but why wait? I can just kill her myself, since the two of you don't appreciate the favor I'm trying to do."

"What favor?"

"Helping you get rid of all that nasty, cumbersome Majyk. You might as well: You can't handle it."

"Oh yeah?" I countered. "If I can't handle Majyk, how do you explain *that*?" I pointed at the dragon. Then I realized that the dragon was gone, so I pointed at the ducklings instead.

Zoltan chuckled. "You've got some basic notion of how to use your Majyk, but there's a world of difference between your skills and mine." He began rolling up the sleeves of his robe as he spoke. "A child can scribble stick-figures with a piece of charcoal, yet give that same charcoal to an artist and he can create a masterpiece."

"If anyone gave you a piece of charcoal, you'd try to stick it up your nose," I sniped.

Zoltan put on a look of false pain. "Ratwhacker, you hurt my feelings! And after all I've gone through just so I could see your lovely face once more."

"You didn't go through the fearsome Forest of Euw," I said scornfully. "You're too much of a coward to challenge the Welfies."

"Why should I bother? If you survived, you'd come out again and I'd be watching the borders. And if you didn't survive— Majyk that's been freed by the death of its former master tends to stick together for a while. It would have drifted out of the woods sooner or later, and I'd be watching for that, too." The ghost of a crystal ball twinkled at the tips of his fingers for an instant. "I've had my eye on you for a while, Kendar. I suppose I could have made my move sooner, but the thought of getting these simple villagers to do most of the work for me was too appealing to pass up.'' He raised his hand high and gave poor Mother Toadbreath a meaningful look, with the accent on *mean*. ''Now it's my turn.''

''Young man, we do *not* raise both hands at once. One is quite sufficient. Put it down. You heard me, I said put-it-*down*!''

Mistress Cosh stormed out of the remaining crowd, waving her ruler, and gave Zoltan a swift whack across the knuckles of one hand. He let out a yelp and grabbed his sore hand, jumping up and down where he stood. The schoolteacher folded her arms and peered down her nose at his antics.

''Don't carry on in that childish manner, young man,'' she directed him. ''You aren't impressing anyone but yourself.''

''You miserable old lizard,'' Zoltan gritted. ''I'll kill you!''

He got another one with the ruler for that, this time somewhere that he didn't have knuckles.

''Aw, now, Mistress Cosh, why'd you want to go and do something like that to the nice gent for?'' Evvon inquired piteously. ''He's not even one of your old pupils.''

''Hush, Evvon,'' the formidable teacher commanded. ''If he were one of my old pupils he'd have better manners.''

I'd never sailed the sea in my life, but I could tell which way the wind was blowing. I raised my hand.

''Yes?'' Mistress Cosh called on me.

''May I please leave the roo—I mean, may I please go *into* the room?'' I asked.

''Permission granted. Don't dawdle.''

I didn't. I dashed back into Mother Toadbreath's cottage and bashed my head against Grym's chest just as he was coming *out*.

''Sorry for the delay, boss,'' Scandal said from between the barbarian's ankles. ''Mighty Joe Young here said he'd given sword-oath not to leave his soap-kettle until it stopped cooking.''

''Even so,'' said Grym, brandishing a wooden paddle. Grave-robber was nowhere in sight.

''You gave sword-oath for a lousy kettle of soap?'' I couldn't believe my ears. ''I thought sword-oath was only for important things.''

''Soap is important,'' Grym said. ''Moreover, Mother Toad-breath didst compel me thus to promise. Mysti yet abideth within, aiding Norris with the cauldrons which simmer even yet.''

''If you don't move, Mother Toadbreath won't be needing any more sword-oaths or soap,'' I told him. ''Zoltan's back.''

"Thine ancient foe?" Grym's jaw line hardened. "Hath he summoned more of the abominable fiends whom he commandeth?"

"Right now he's making do with a load of Cheeseburghers, but he might call in reinforcements any minute now. We've got to stop him!"

"Aye!" Grym shook the paddle angrily, then realized what he was holding. "Oops. Tarry thou, O Master, whilst I fetch mine own true blade, anon."

"No time!" I shouted, shoving him out the door.

Zoltan was cursing Mistress Cosh from here to Grashgoboum when the three of us burst out of the cottage and threw ourselves on him. We all tumbled over, thrashing in the dirt.

"Don't let him gesture! Don't let him talk!" I hollered. "It's the only way he can work Majyk."

"Can't talk while he's screaming," Scandal remarked. He dove under Zoltan's robe. Immediately the air turned blue with the sound of purely non-magical curses and shrieks as the cat's claws and teeth dug in.

I struggled to get a grip on Zoltan's hands, but Scandal was doing his job too well. Zoltan flapped like a sea gull in a noose, arms and legs flailing. He even managed to launch a few arcs of green fire, singeing my hair when I tried to hold him down.

Meanwhile, Grym was locked in deadly combat with Mistress Cosh, who was berating him for showing up barechested in public. "Were you raised by barbarians?" she demanded, and when he gave her an honest answer she got mad. Paddle against ruler, they slugged it out. It was a battle of giants, with the Cheeseburghers hanging around putting loud side-bets on the teacher.

I took a deep breath and launched myself so that I landed flat across Zoltan's stomach. Scandal let out an enraged squawk—I'd landed on him, too, but that didn't matter; this was my chance. Zoltan had the wind knocked out of him. Quickly I followed up my advantage, straddling his chest, using my knees to pin his arms to his sides.

Scandal crawled out from under Zoltan's robes just as I finished gagging him with a strip of cloth torn from the bottom of my tunic. "There!" I said happily, wiping sweat and grime from my brow. "Done. What do you think of that?"

Scandal opened his mouth to answer, but before he could get a word out, the whole cottage shook with a thunderous voice that bellowed, "*Think*? I think it was a waste of good coin sendin' you to that hoity-toity wizard school if this is how you end up, that's what *I* think!''

I winced, not wanting to look, knowing that I had to, sooner or later. A black horse stood before me, a ferocious stallion with a blue-cloaked rider on his back twice as ferocious and twice as wide as the horse he rode in on. I stared up into the face of doom and forced a smile.

''Oh . . . Hello, Dad.''

CHAPTER ———————— 22

"DARLING, I DO WISH YOU'D STOP PACING," MOTHER said without even looking up from her knitting. "You're making me nervous."

"Lady, he's not pacing," Scandal said. "He's sitting right here in this nice, plump armchair right across from you, with a handsome cat (that's me) on his lap."

"Oh, is he?" Mother blinked her big, blue eyes, but never took them off the half-finished whateveritwas in her lap. "That's nice."

"He's also sulking."

"Stop sulking, Kendar dear," said Mother automatically.

For what felt like the thousandth time, I tried to get my mother to pay attention to what I had to say. "Mom, *please*; it's not like I'm asking for anything much."

"No, dear. You always were a thoughtful child." She held up the whateveritwas. "Do you think I should do this next row in blue or white?"

"That woman Dad's got locked up in the dungeon is my *friend*. She hasn't done anything wrong and she shouldn't be treated this way."

"You know you're always welcome to bring your friends here for a visit, darling." Mother made up her mind and reached for the blue wool. "I don't mind. Did I say one little word when without so much as a letter of warning you showed up with *three* of them, and one not quite human?"

"I resent that," said Scandal.

For the first time in the conversation, Mother looked up and smiled at the cat. "I wasn't talking about you, dear."

I took a breath and let it out slowly before I said, "I know you're mad about Mysti, Mom, but I keep telling you, it was an accident.''

Mother's smile vanished. "People do not marry other people by accident.''

"Well, like you said, Mysti isn't exactly people. She's a Welfie. I mean, she *was* a Welfie. I'm not exactly sure what she is now.''

"Now she is your *wife*.'' You could've made snowballs out of the last word.

"No, she's not; not really. We haven't even—uh—'' Mom was giving me a flinty look. ''—kissed. I mean, hugged. I mean, we haven't even held hands.''

"He lies like a rug,'' said Scandal, half asleep. "It was a lovely ceremony. You couldn't get the bride and groom apart with a chainsaw. We had to send out for three truckloads of crushed ice to cool 'em down. They melted glaciers at the polar regions.''

"No one asked you!'' I shouted. "And we don't *have* polar regions.''

The cat just snuggled more deeply into my lap and flexed his claws. "Sshhhh, I'm asleep,'' he said.

"Kendar darling, you're being rude to our guests,'' Mother said, attacking the whateveritwas again. "We're just simple country nobility here at Uxwudge Manor, but we do pride ourselves on our shining reputation for hospitality.''

"Is that why you put Kendar in the bedroom next to yours and Mysti in the towers?'' Scandal murmured. Asleep, my foot.

"Listen, Mom, I don't care if Mysti's sleeping on the second moon from the right! All I want is to get Mother Toadbreath out of the dungeons and back in her cottage where she belongs.''

Mother picked up another knitting needle and jabbed the whateveritwas through the heart. "I can't help you, dear. You know I never meddle with the dungeons. You want to speak with your father.''

No, I didn't.

"I thought—I thought maybe you could speak with him about this for me,'' I suggested. "He listens to you.''

Mother's laugh was as brittle as old leaves. "Wedwel forgive you for being such a charming liar! Lord Lucius doesn't listen to anyone except his chief huntsman, his head gamekeeper, his master of hounds, and sometimes your sister Lucy.''

"I'll bet he listens to Basehart, too,'' I grumbled.

"Yes, I suppose he would listen to your brother,'' Mother agreed. "Although Basehart doesn't say much, as a rule. Except when he's hungry, or when he's killed something. Or when he *wants* to kill something.''

Ah, home! Nothing had changed. Damn.

I decided that maybe Mom was right: Like it or not, I'd have to talk to Dad if I wanted to do Mother Toadbreath any good. I stood up, dumping Scandal on the floor. For a sleeping cat, he managed to flip over and land on his feet with no trouble and no surprise.

''Where can I find Dad, Mom?'' I asked.

''Hmmm. It's not meal time. Killing something.''

I went down to the stables with Scandal trotting after me. Dad's favorite horse, the black stallion Slaughter, was being rubbed down after a hard ride. I spoke to the grooms, who told me that Dad had just returned from the hunt and was probably in the kitchens, helping skin and gut the kill. I thanked them and tried to pat Slaughter. Slaughter tried to bite my hand off. No, nothing had changed.

I found Dad up to his knees in blood and happy as a tick. He swung a huge gutting knife and sang a traditional hunter's ballad as he worked:

> ''Oh, we spotted the deer, the merry, merry deer;
> Oh, we spotted the deer so merry, merry-o!
> Oh, we spotted the deer, the spotted, merry deer,
> And we shot 'em full of arrows in the morning-o!''

I stood in the kitchen doorway, waiting for him to notice me. That was stupid. I'd been waiting sixteen years for him to notice me and no luck yet.

''Dad!'' I called.

''Eh?'' He spun around, almost decapitating one of the servants with his knife. ''Oh, it's you.'' He went back to slashing open dead animals.

I came into the kitchen, trying to avoid the puddles of blood. ''Dad, we need to talk.''

''No, we don't,'' he said.

''Dad, *please*—''

This time he whirled so fast that he nicked a servant's ear badly. ''Now look here, Kendar, I've got nothing to say to you,'' he growled at me.

''Fine, then maybe you can *listen*, for a change,'' I growled right back.

Dad gave me a peculiar look. I guess this was the first time I'd ever talked back to him. Still, old habits die hard, and ignoring me was a very old habit with Dad. "Hmph! Listen to what? To your puny excuses for comin' home a failure? An expensive failure, too! When your mother got it into her head to waste my coin sendin' you off to become a spell-slinger, I never said a word. Wedwel knows, you weren't showin' signs of makin' anything else out of your life, so it might as well be wizardry, that's what I thought. At least it'd get you out from underfoot."

"I was only a little kid when you sent me away to Master Thengor's!" I protested. "What did you expect me to make out of my life by that age?"

"Your brother Basehart killed his first deer when he was six years old." Dad's moustache bristled with pride. "Just a fawn, it was, but he strangled it with his bare hands and I said to all my friends, 'Now there's a child of *destiny*!'"

"Couldn't pronounce 'homicidal maniac'?" Scandal asked.

"Eh? What's that?" Dad tensed like a hunting hound. His eye lit on Scandal. "What in the name of nightmares are you?"

"I'm no fun to hunt and I'm no good to eat, so what do you care?" Scandal replied.

"Oh. Right." Dad signaled the servants to bring him a fresh carcass.

I grabbed his knife-hand on the downswing. "I'm not here to talk about me. We're going to talk about the witch and we're going to do it *now*."

Time slowed down as my father turned to look me in the eye. All three of his chins were trembling. Little white blotches started to show on his face. I could feel the muscles in his arm tense and untense under my fingers until I let go.

"Talk," he said.

I tried. I couldn't. He made a face like someone who's been given a birthday present that turns out to be mud.

"Don't waste your breath, O noble Master Kendar," Scandal said, bounding between Dad and me. "It will be my honor to explain matters to your father." He twitched his whiskers at Dad. "Hey, big boy, I'm not gonna shout. Bend over. If you can."

Dad was taken aback. He bent forward as much as he could to hear what Scandal had to say.

"Now pay attention, because it's cheap and so are you: Your son Kendar is *not* a failure. Not unless you think it's no big deal that he's now the top Majyk-man in the kingdom. The kingdom? Heck, the whole *world*."

My father was suspicious. "Is this true?"

"Puh-lease, Porky, have I ever lied to you? I'm ready to swear on a stack of Bibles that when the great wizard Master Thengor died, he didn't give one scrap of his Majyk to anyone else.''

That was true; Master Thengor didn't *give* anything to anybody.

"What's a Bible?" Dad asked.

"No fun to hunt, no good to eat, so—"

"—what do I care? Quite right. Proceed."

"Look, my point is, your little boy's doing okay for himself. Maybe he can't stab dinner to death like his brother, but with Majyk he can just *blink* at a deer and two seconds later—kazowie!—roast venison for everyone."

My father turned from the cat to me. "Is what the creature's sayin' so, boy? You really gone and made a wizard of yourself?"

"Welllll . . ." I felt mighty uncomfortable. "The Council hasn't given me my wand yet, but—"

"Kazowie," Scandal repeated. "It doesn't take a piece of wood to make a wizard."

"By Wedwel's teeth, the beast is right!" Dad guffawed, pummeling me on the back. "So we've finally got a wizard in the family, eh? Good, good. It'll take a wizard to fix up the trouble your sister's gotten into."

"Trouble? Lucy?" For a moment I forgot all about Mother Toadbreath's predicament. "What's the matter?"

"Haw! Nothing the strong hand of a loving father can't fix."

I was afraid of that. "It's not—? She isn't—? All those horrible stories Nanny Esplanadia used to tell her about men and she still went and—?"

"*Men?*" Dad roared, his face turning the color of the fresh deer blood splashed everywhere. "If I so much as *sniff* a man sneaking around anywhere near your sister, I'll—I'll—I'll—!" He didn't say exactly what he'd do, but he made some very explicit gestures with his gutting knife.

"Then what's she done?"

My father made a gurgling noise in his throat, threw down his knife, and clapped a bloody hand around my wrist as he dragged me out of the kitchen. We crossed the great hall of Uxwudge Manor where the mounted heads of twelve generations of murdered animals gazed down on us with glassy eyes. We went up the main staircase and down the portrait gallery where twelve generations of Gangles watched us pass. We wound up in Dad's library, a room that held the Gangle family's entire book collection. It was called *Wyld Animauls I Haf Kill'd*, written by Sir Theofric Gaungelle, the founder of our house.

Something was wrong in the library. There was a second book on the shelf.

"There," said my father, pointing at it with a bloody finger. He refused to touch it—not because he didn't want to get it all gooey, but because the only thing Dad ever did with books was squish spiders. As I picked it up, he went on to say, "I found it in your sister's possession."

"*How Passionate My Paladin,*" I real aloud. "By Raptura Eglantine." Behind me I heard Scandal gagging on a hairball.

"She's . . . *readin'*," said Dad, his voice choked with shame. "My little girl, readin' *books*. How could this have happened? Where'd your mother go wrong?"

"How long have you been married?" Scandal asked. I shushed him. Things were starting to click in my head. A plan for saving Mother Toadbreath was actually forming unaided in my own personal brain. It was a light, wonderful feeling, especially since in all those years at Master Thengor's Academy I'd always been told that the only way I'd ever have an original idea was if someone beat it into my skull with a stick.

"Reading," I echoed, trying to sound just as shocked and disappointed as Dad. "You know, if news of this gets out, you'll never find a man willing to marry Lucy." My father groaned. "And if no one marries her, you'll have to support her for the rest of your life." He groaned louder. "And if she never marries, you'll never be able to get your hands on the groom's bride-price, or any spare pieces of land he might throw into the bargain, or his family's wedding gifts to us, or all the holiday presents they'd give you, or—"

It was the first time I'd ever seen my father cry.

Somehow, Scandal and I got him out of the library and back down to the kitchen, where we found a table and a couple of stools in a private nook. Our old family cook, Maisree, took one look at the poor man and brought out a bottle of Dad's special nerve tonic, then left us alone. The stuff was called Old Cocklebur and it smelled like moldy bread, but a glass of it cheered him up pretty quickly.

When my father was in a sunnier mood, I made my offer. "Dad, if Lucy's reading, she's got to be reading *something*, right?"

"O' course she is!" Dad was indignant. "Showed you the book myself, didn't I?"

"Ah! But how can you be sure that's the only one she's got?"

"What? D'you mean to say there might be more?"

"It is a possibility." Now that I was playing the part of a great and powerful wizard, I tried to look wise and all-knowing. "Does Lucy know that you've got this one?"

"I caught her with it out in the herb garden when she should've been doing her needlework. Tore it out of her hands, I did!"

"I'd say she knows, then," Scandal remarked. "Thanks to Mister Subtle-as-a-Brick-in-the-Head."

That was just what I wanted to hear. I steepled my fingers and said, "Since *she* knows that *you* know, you *must* know that she won't want *you* to know if she's got any more books like that. You know?"

"I do?" Dad looked like I'd dropped a stag on him.

"Of course you do!" Scandal butted in. "And you must also know that you're never going to be able to find out where she's got them all hidden."

"I won't?"

"Dad," I said, not unkindly, "when was the last time you ever found anything in this house when Mom was the one who put it away?" While he was chewing that over, I bent down to whisper to Scandal, "You know what I'm trying to do here?"

"No," he whispered back. "But I can play along."

I straightened up again. "The way I see it, you've got two problems. One: Finding the books Lucy already has, and two: Finding out where she's getting them from in the first place." I leaned across the table. "That's where I can help you."

A little while later, Scandal and I were in my room, washing up for dinner. That is, I was washing up, he was just sitting there, staring at me with real admiration in his eyes.

"I can't believe you pulled it off," he said. "You really sold the old jerk a bill of goods."

"Scandal, be careful what you say. That old jerk's my father. We may not see eye-to-eye on a lot of things, but underneath it all, he's still basically a good man."

"Friend, someday you're gonna learn that there's nothing more dangerous in this world than a good man who's positive he's doing the right thing for all the right reasons."

"Dad *is* doing the right thing," I reminded him. "He's not going to put Mother Toadbreath on trial for witchcraft until after I use my great wizardly powers to find out where Lucy's been getting those books. That buys us time."

"If he's *really* doing the right thing, how come he won't just let the lady go?"

I sighed. "He can't do that. Too many people know that Lord Lucius Parkland Gangle, in his capacity as the king's Justice in these parts, has caught a known witch. If he lets her go free without a trial, he'll get in trouble with the royal authorities.''

"Who's gonna tell the royal authorities?" Scandal demanded, lashing his tail. "Not the Cheeseburghers! They didn't even have the backbone to put on a real witch-hunt until our pal Zoltan stirred them up, promising to use his own powers to protect them from Mother Toadbreath's magic. Then he dangled the king's reward for catching witches in front of them like a catnip mouse and the poor suckers jumped.''

"Speaking of which, where is Zoltan?" I asked.

"Search me. Last I heard, he vanished as soon as your dad threw Mother Toadbreath in the dungeon. If she gets out, the villagers will be too scared to rat on her, *or* your old man.''

"But Zoltan would." I caught a glimpse of myself in the mirror, looking grim.

"I don't know how your laws work, buddy-boy, but I'm guessing that if it only took one man's word to call someone a witch, Zoltan wouldn't have bothered with getting the Cheeseburghers on his side.''

"That's right." I brightened a little. "He can't do anything legal against her without witnesses to back him up. Maybe I'll get to work on Dad after dinner, promise him to find Lucy's book *and* her supplier *and* a husband in the bargain, if he lets Mother Toadbreath go.''

"That's the way, kid!" Scandal beamed at me. "Think big. Now let's go get some chow.''

Dinner was in the banqueting hall of Uxwudge Manor, a room almost as big as the great hall, only without the animal heads on the walls. Instead, there were dozens of paintings of such lovely scenes as "Wild Boar Goring of the Hounds," "Still Life with Gutted Weasels," "Man Massacring Partridges at Sunset," "Waterfall with Two Bears Rending a Headless Swineherd," and "Last View of the Metheglin Fox-Hunt as it Goes Over a Cliff.''

Scandal and I were the last to arrive. Mom sat at one end of the table, Dad at the other. Lucy usually sat on Mom's right side, Basehart on Dad's, only tonight they were seated across from each other, halfway down the long sides of the table, leaving the places of honor for guests. I blushed a little to see that the empty seat at Dad's right hand was obviously mine. Basehart gave me a dirty look for taking it, but I hardly noticed, even if he was sitting just one chair down from me.

In spite of the honor my father was finally paying me, I knew this wasn't going to be a nice, calm, family meal. It wasn't that I was worried about Mysti, who scowled at me from her seat next to Basehart, on Mom's left. It wasn't the fact that Grym, across from me on Dad's left, had laid his unsheathed sword Graverobber on the table. It wasn't even the fact that my sister Lucy, to the left of Grym, was making sugar-eyes at the big barbarian. It was the guest I saw seated in the other place of honor at Mom's right that gave me a bellyful of voondrabs.

"Pass the rolls," said Zoltan.

CHAPTER —————— 23

EVERY BITE I ATE AT THAT DINNER TASTED LIKE STRAW.
(Of course the way old Maisree cooked, most meals at Uxwudge
Manor came out tasting like straw. I think she used a cookbook
called *Boil It 'Til It Stops Twitching*.) I didn't enjoy a bite, keeping
my eyes on Zoltan through the whole meal.

I wish I could say that my companions shared my anxiety—
things are always easier to bear if you know you're not the only
one who's miserable—but no such luck. Scandal leaped onto the
table, pounced on a whole roasted rappid, and ran out of the hall
to devour it, growling happily to himself.

Grym was too busy stuffing his face with big pieces of meat to
worry about what Zoltan was doing there. Every time he came up
for air, Dad filled his platter again and said it was a pleasure to see
a real man "doin' some real eatin'."

As for Mysti, trapped between my mother and my brother, she
had her hands full, and I don't mean with that huge slab of steak
she'd always dreamed of. Mom kept jabbing at her with questions
like, "Is that your real hair color?" and "Why is it that everyone
says welven women have fat thighs?" while Mysti kept jabbing at
Basehart with her salad fork because my beloved older brother
refused to keep his hands to himself.

Meanwhile, Zoltan smiled through it all and gave his exclusive
attention to my sister Lucy.

My sister . . . When had she stopped being the cute little girl
I remembered? Where did all that long, golden hair come from,
and those big, blue eyes just like Mom's, only intelligent? And
why in Wedwel's name did Mom and Dad let her wear those
clingy gowns? You could see every curve she had, and she had
plenty. I knew my sister had to grow up some day, but did she also

have to grow *out*? Yes, but *that* much? No wonder Zoltan didn't have a word to say to anyone else!

We had just finished dessert when a horrible caterwauling started up outside the manor house. The noise was so hellish that it almost made our family butler, Genuflect, drop his tray of after-dinner drinks. "Oh dear," he said with a sigh. "That creature is still out there."

"What creature?" my father demanded.

"A large, purple beast with eight legs, sir," said Genuflect, offering Dad a glass of *calabash*. "Rumor has it that it belongs to the, ah, lady presently enjoying the excellent hospitality of your dungeon."

"That's Norris!" I exclaimed.

"OrowrowROW!" Norris agreed from outside.

"Perhaps." Genuflect's face was about as expressive as a stone wall. "I did not inquire after the animal's name. It haunts the house and refuses to go away, in spite of Maisree having tossed a bucket of cold dishwater over it. Shall I have it shot, sir?"

"You can't shoot Norris!" I protested. "He's Mother Toadbreath's octopuss."

"Quite right, Genuflect," Dad said. "Don't you go off shootin' the beast."

"Very good, sir."

"I'll do it myself."

"*Dad!*" I howled.

"Eh?" My father tossed back his *calabash* and let Genuflect pour him another. "Want to kill it yourself, then? Good boy. Will you be needin' one of my bowanarrers, or would you prefer to go at it with a lance?"

"I don't want to do either one."

Dad shook his head. "Beast's got eight arms, that's not sword-work, boy. I guess we might have a javelin or two somewhere about the place, but—Abstemia! Where's my good javelins?"

"Where did you leave them, dear?" my mother asked brightly.

"I'm not going to kill Norris with *any* of your weapons," I said.

"Scared?" Basehart sneered. He leaned over in front of me, grabbed the *calabash* bottle off Genuflect's tray, and guzzled. Our butler was used to Basehart's manners. He just went to the sideboard, got a fresh bottle, and went back to serving as if nothing had happened.

Mysti joggled Basehart's elbow so that the bottleneck clinked against his teeth and *calabash* splashed all over his shirt. He wrung it out into his glass and drank it.

"Haw! I see what you're drivin' at," Dad said. "Grand old wizard like you doesn't have any use for a plain man's weapons, eh? Just like your furry little friend said, all you've got to do is look at the beast cross-eyed and—kafwoom!—it's roast thin-gummy for everyone."

"You don't want to roast it, Kendar dear," my mother said. "You only want to make it properly dead, then give it to Maisree. If you cook it yourself, you'll hurt her feelings and she'll quit. You have no idea how hard it is to hire a decent cook these days."

"I'm not going to cook Norris and I'm not going to kill Norris," I said, speaking slowly. "He belongs to Mother Toad-breath. I don't go around killing other people's pets."

"I do," said Basehart. He waved the empty *calabash* bottle at Genuflect, signaling that he wanted more. Our butler went suddenly blind and only served the people on the far side of the table.

I tried to make them understand. "Listen, the only reason Norris is hanging around the house is because he misses his owner. If you let her go, she'll take her octopuss home with her and you won't be bothered by either of them anymore."

"Let her go?" Dad snorted, making his moustache ripple. "Can't do that, boy! It's against the law, and I'm King Steffan's Justice throughout all the lands of Uxwudge Manor, includin' the village of Cheeseburgh. An accused witch must be brought to trial, then hanged or something."

"An *accused* witch." I leveled a finger at him. "But who's accusing her?"

"I am." For the first time all dinner long, Zoltan looked at me instead of Lucy.

"That's right, dear," Mom said. "This nice young man ran into your father while he and Basehart were out hunting this afternoon and said that he'd like to make an official accusation of witchcraft against the lady we've got in the dungeon. Your brother took him to give his statement to the bailiff while Lord Lucius took care of cleaning the day's kill."

So that was it. While I'd been down in the kitchen with Dad, Zoltan had weaseled his way into the house.

My brother spoke up next. "After we see the bailiff, him and me gets to talkin'." Basehart had an ugly leer. Basehart had an ugly *face*, but the leer made it uglier. "Turns out he went to school with you. When I hears a couple o' the tales he's got t' tell, I invites him to dinner so's he can share a few of 'em with everyone . . . *Ratwhacker*.''

Mom beamed. ''Wasn't that nice of your brother?''

''Wonderful.'' I was seething inside, but resolved to hold onto my temper no matter what. Getting Mother Toadbreath out of trouble was more important than paying my brother back for this, or settling accounts with Zoltan. I knotted my fists in my lap and went on as if Basehart hadn't said a word.

''One accuser isn't enough,'' I said. ''Even if he is an old school *friend* of mine.''

''The boy's right.'' Dad said it like it was a big surprise to him. ''Law says you need at least two witnesses willin' to swear out a complaint of witchcraft.''

''And a very fair law it is. Don't you agree, charming Mistress Lucy?'' Zoltan simpered.

My sister gave him the look she usually saved for creamed spinach.

''Well?'' I could hardly keep the note of triumph out of my voice. ''Where's your other witness?''

''In Grashgoboum,'' Zoltan said smoothly, reaching into his robe for a rolled-up piece of parchment. He gestured and it floated down the table to my father's place. ''His new job prevents him from being with us, but I think you'll find his sworn statement to be in order.''

Dad unrolled the parchment and read, '' 'I, Evvon, formerly senior village idiot of Cheeseburgh, only now I'm living in Grashgoboum and have got me a nice job as a bureau rat not doing too much of anything, do hereby swear that Mother Toadbreath's a witch and I can lick any man what says she ain't. She turned me into a toad just because I told her she was saying the witch-hunt words wrong. What's this world coming to if you can't take a little constructive criticism, I'd like to know.' ''

My father put the scroll down. ''Signed and sealed, all proper. The word of a government worker and an idiot. You can't ask for more than that.'' He actually looked sorry as he turned to me and said, ''I'm afraid the lady will have to stand trial.''

CHAPTER —————— 24

GRYM POKED ME IN THE BACK WITH THE POMMEL OF HIS sword. "Art thou certain that this way lieth the Welfin wench's room, O Master?"

"Sure, I'm sure! I grew up in this house. I know where everything is. Mom's got Mysti in the eastern tower and that's this way."

"If thou sayest so." Grym didn't sound too confident.

"I was born in the bottom of a linen closet in Malibu, but even I know that *tower* means *up*," Scandal said. "We've been going *down* this same flight of stairs for hours."

"It hasn't been *hours*," I replied. "You don't know Uxwudge Manor at all. It started out as Theofric Gaungelle's favorite hunting lodge—nothing fancy, just a mud hut with a good spring of water nearby. Over the years it became a wooden fort, got turned into a hilltop castle, and now it's just a big, sprawling, messy maze of a house."

"In other words, you can't get there from here," Scandal said.

"Trust me. I know what I'm doing."

When we ended up back at the door to my room, I had to admit that I didn't.

We started off again, this time with Scandal promising to hunt out Mysti's room by smell. We crisscrossed the great hall three times, wandered up and down the portrait gallery, and finally found ourselves at the foot of a narrow, winding staircase.

"By the sacred scalp-drying racks of mine ancestors," said Grym, "this looks like the same stairway we traversed before."

"It *is* the same." I frowned at Scandal.

"So sue me," the cat responded. "Only this time howzabout we go *up* the stairs instead of *down*."

It was worth a try. *Anything* was worth a try. We had to reach the dungeon before dawn. Earlier that night, right after dinner, I'd decided that we had to go see Mother Toadbreath and warn her about her upcoming trial. I could get Dad to delay it, but not forever; not with two witnesses ready to stand against her.

Clever Zoltan. He'd gotten Evvon out of Cheeseburgh and set him up in that government job so that the former idiot could send in his testimony without fear of the witch striking back. I wasn't guessing; I knew, because when I went back to my room after that awful meal, I found a note from Zoltan waiting for me on my pillow. He spelled out what he'd done, what he wanted from me, and what he'd do if I didn't cooperate. I could sneak off with him quietly and let him try to remove my Majyk, or let Mother Toadbreath take her chances with King Steffan's anti-witchery laws.

I'm sure we can find a painless way to rid you of your accidental inheritance, he wrote. Painless? Would he care if it wasn't? *Come to my room secretly, without those ragtag friends of yours, and we will leave. If I am gone, that leaves only the idiot's testimony. With one witness there can be no trial. Your Majyk, or the witch's life; it's your choice.*

Without those ragtag friends of mine . . . *Friends.* I already counted Scandal as a friend, but to have more than just one—! Would Grym and Mysti agree with Zoltan's assumption? Were they my friends? I wasn't going to run off without finding out.

There was also the matter of my "accidental inheritance," as Zoltan put it. Thanks to Mother Toadbreath's book, I was starting to get the hang of Majyk—nothing fancy yet, but good enough so that I'd stopped lighting up uncontrollably. I wanted to see how far I could take my lessons. What I *really* wanted to see was whether there was finally something in this world that I could do well enough to make me special.

Something besides ratwhacking, I mean.

Too bad the book didn't cover Majyk tricks like making a witch disappear from a dungeon and reappear in the next kingdom, but maybe Mother Toadbreath herself had heard how it was done and could teach me. As second best, she might know how I could use my Majyk to turn her dungeon door into sawdust. At the very least, who better than a witch would know the anti-witchcraft laws, including where to find the loopholes?

When I mentioned this last plan to Grym, he looked at me like I'd lost my mind. "By the iron loincloth of Andromium the

Untiring, dost thou mean to leave a matter of justice in the hands of the *law*?"

"Only as a last resort," I assured him. I hoped it wouldn't come to that.

We took Scandal's advice and started up the winding stair. It was an easy jog for Grym, who had thigh muscles like a pair of tree trunks, but it wasn't long before Scandal demanded to be carried.

"Just keep going," the cat directed when he was settled in Grym's arms. "Only one way you can go, you know."

We climbed some more, sometimes passing arrow-slit windows that let in moonlight, but mostly finding our way in the dark. It was tiring and tedious. Pretty soon I was wondering if Grym could carry me, too. Before it could come to that, we reached the top of the tower. There was a landing, a little alcove where a night-candle burned low in its glass holder, and a door.

"Dis mus' be da place," said Scandal. "Put me down, Tarzan." He jumped out of Grym's arms and sauntered over to give the door a deep sniff. "Yup," he pronounced. "Fee, fi, fo, fum, I smell the blood of"—he paused and crinkled up his nose, puzzled—"your *brother*?"

"That's—" I began. I didn't get to say *impossible,* because the door flew open and something big and stupid flew out. It was Basehart, clutching a bottle of *calabash* to his chest. I saw him make a determined effort to hit the oncoming wall face-first rather than risk smashing the precious drink. He succeeded.

"Basehart, what are you doing here?" I demanded, glaring down at him.

"Nothing," he replied, sounding like he had a mouthful of spider web. His nose was bloody, maybe broken, and a few of his teeth wobbled when he spoke. It didn't hurt his looks at all.

" 'Nothing'? Ha!" Mysti stood in the doorway, wearing a thin, clingy white nightgown. Her shimmering hair fell down her back in silky waves, with just the tips of her pointed ears sticking through. The longer I looked at her, the harder it got for me to breathe. She stalked out of her room and stood beside me, giving Basehart a look that could kill, skin, cook, and serve him on a platter.

"I was sound asleep in the first decent bed I've had in my life when this slug comes oozing into my room and wakes me up, all ready for a cozy little party. When I told him to get out, he just chuckled and told me that I'd thank him in the morning. Then he tried to *nothing* me! He tries any more *nothing* like that and I'll feed his liver to the—Well, maybe I'll just eat it myself and save the bother.'' She drew back one bare foot, ready to give Basehart a kick in the head.

''Desist,'' said Grym, picking her up and holding her too far off the floor for the kick to connect with anything but air. ''It ill behooves thee, maiden, to kick a man when he is down.'' He showed his teeth and added, ''Leav'st thou that to the professionals.'' He set her down to one side and got ready to use Basehart's head for a football.

''No!'' I held up one hand and stepped between the barbarian's foot and Basehart's head. My fingers were glowing with the golden light of Majyk.

''Wow,'' Basehart marveled from the floor. ''Do another.''

I gave him a disgusted look. ''You've got three breaths to tell me why you're up here, bothering Mysti, or I let Grym play kick-the-cantaloupe with your skull.''

Basehart rolled over and used one hand to drag himself up the wall. The other was still holding tight to the bottle. He took a long, gurgly drink, then said, ''Ain't fair.''

''What ain't fair?''

''Her.'' He jerked the bottle at Mysti. ''You. Dad. Mom always liked you better'n me, but leastwise Dad was smart. Used to was, anyhow.''

''Smart? Because he liked you better?'' I asked.

'''Course!'' Basehart was genuinely surprised by the question. ''Wouldn't anyone?''

''Well, scratch *him* from the Inferiority Complexes Anonymous meeting,'' Scandal said.

''Then, top o' all that, you go an' come home a big deal wizard. *With* a wife looks like that.'' Basehart leaned back against the wall as his knees began to fold up. He skidded down slowly, grousing about how he was the one who deserved Mysti, not me.

''He's got a point there, boss,'' Scandal said. He smiled at Mysti. ''Your big dream's to get your teeth into a healthy hunk of meat at every meal, his hobby's killing meat-things. Babe, can I interest you in a marriage made in heaven? Well, if heaven's got a slaughterhouse on the premises, that is.''

Basehart's eyes brightened. ''Oh, *would* you?'' he exclaimed, grabbing for Mysti's hand. She backstepped and he fell over. ''Marry me,'' he told the floor, ''and I'll make you the happiest wench at Uxwudge Manor.''

''I'll marry you when pigs fly,'' Mysti said.

''Swell! It's a deal!'' Scandal said quickly. ''Bwana, you warm up those levitation spells and I'll help your brother Quasimodo here get a pig and—''

"No one around here is getting married or *un*married," I said in no uncertain tones. "Now, go away, Basehart."

My brother lifted his head from the floor. His eyes were two burning slits full of anger. "No one tells me what to do," he snarled. "'Cept Dad. And Mom. And Nanny Esplanadia. Think you can throw your weight around 'cause you're a wizard, but I can still knock you around so's your head buzzes like a nest of mousekitters."

"Try it." My hands became fists. "Just try."

Basehart shook his head. "You'd like that. Give you an excuse to frizzle me up with your powers. I'm not stupid."

I bit my tongue.

"The way to fight wizardry's with wizardry," my brother continued. He stood up and headed for the stairs. "I'm gonna go get my good ol' buddypal Zoltan. He's a woozard. Wizard. Better one'n *you* ever was. He's went an' told me all 'bout *you*." He paused at the stairhead, turned, and spat, "Ratwhacker!"

Scandal darted in front of Basehart just as he took the first step down. He caught his foot on the cat, pitched forward, lost his grip on the *calabash* bottle, let out a yelp of alarm as it smashed on the stone stairs, windmilled his arms wildly, and tumbled right over in spite of it all. We heard him thump, bump, thunder, rumble, and roll all the way down, then silence.

"I killed him," Scandal said, proud of himself.

"Cat, you'd better be wrong," I gritted, leaning over the stairwell and straining my ears for some sound of life below.

"Huh? What's the beef?" Scandal was bewildered. "That bozo was a truckload of trouble waiting to happen, all of it with your name on the label."

"That bozo is my *brother*," I retorted. "Just because we hate each other doesn't mean I want him dead."

The cat sniffed. "Picky, picky, picky."

"Dost think the varlet hath his quietus made with a bare catkin?" Grym asked.

"I don't know," I said, "but I'm going to find out."

I skittered down the stairs, not caring whether the others followed. Down and down I went, but I didn't find Basehart anywhere. At first there were only steps, steps, and more steps, corkscrewing down into the dark from the landing at the top of the tower. After a while some other landings cut into the tower stairwell. I stopped at each of these and looked out to see whether my brother had crawled away from the stairs to die in the halls beyond. He wasn't on the first floor I reached or on the next one down. I was ready to check out the third when everyone else caught up with me.

"You could have waited," Mysti said. "I had to get dressed." She wore a gown so shapeless and heavy that it defeated even her curves. I didn't know whether to be disappointed or relieved. "Your mother took my old things away to be washed and gave me this," she said, spreading the coarse cloth. "Like it?"

"No one told me the circus was in town," Scandal piped up. He nosed under the hem. "Wow! Stalagmites!"

"Get out from under there," I ordered, dragging him back. "And stop all this fooling around. I've got to see if my brother's all right, then we've all got to find Mother Toadbreath's cell. And," I said to Mysti, "I don't have time to care about your ugly dress."

"Oh." Mysti's voice got very small. "Then let's find your brother, by all means." I couldn't see her face when she said that, but I heard a catch in her throat that sounded like tears being held back.

"Mysti, I'm sorry if I hurt your feelings, but—" I never got to finish the sentence. A brawny hand clamped itself across my mouth and a strong arm bearing a sword came up in front of my face. "Hist," Grym whispered harshly in my ear.

"Grmph," I replied.

"Hist!" the barbarian insisted. He let me go. "Not a word. I hear voices thither." He motioned towards the corridor beyond the stairwell landing. "We must proceed with caution, lest it transpire that thine oafish brother hath by his late misfortune roused the house, to our peril."

"Oh, no!" I groaned (quietly). "You mean he woke Mom?"

"*Hist!*" We histed. The hall beyond the stairs was well lit with many small beeswax candles. When I peered out, I just missed being spotted by a pair of guards standing watch at the far end of the corridor. Guards and beeswax candles cost a lot of money, especially if you want to keep them going all night. I wondered what was in this part of the house that was so valuable.

One of the guards stretched and yawned. "Wedwel's toes, but I'm bored. Where's our relief when we need it?" He cast a longing look down the large staircase to his right.

"Bored?" the other guard repeated. "After all that to-do with Basehart? When he come a-tumbling feet over forehead down those tower stairs, I thought we was under attack for sure!"

"Aye, you jumped high enough," his companion agreed. "But when you've been working for the Gangles as long as I have, you'll know that young Basehart falls down stairs so regular you can set a clock by it."

The younger guard clicked his tongue. "All that rumpus, I thought he'd broke all his bones. Not a mark on him! There's still miracles."

"Oh, he'll have bruises enough to show for it tomorrow," the veteran said. "But as for breaking his bones, he hasn't before, so why should he start now? We did all we could for the lad, pointing him down the main stair and telling him to find his own bed."

"He fell down the main stair, too."

"Well, these Gangles do love their little family traditions."

"There!" Mysti whispered fiercely. "Basehart's fine, worse luck. Now let's find Mother Toadbreath."

"Hist!" Grym said for the fourth time. He blocked Mysti's access to the stairs. "Stir we not hand or foot until yon guards do meet their relief, lest they harken unto our footfalls and I find myself compelled to slay them right bloodily."

"I wish you wouldn't," I said. "Mom will blame me."

"Tarry we until there cometh other guards, that we might depart under cover of their greetings to their fellows," Grym suggested. He had a point. We didn't want to draw any attention to ourselves. Silently I let him know that we would follow his plan. We all settled down on the stairs to wait.

Time passed slowly. Scandal curled himself up and went to sleep in Mysti's lap, but the rest of us didn't have his talent for taking naps whenever we liked. Every so often I would take a quick peek into the corridor, just for something to do. Soon it got to be a game. I'd see if there were any clues in the hall that would help me guess what was in that room the guards were protecting so dutifully.

It couldn't be the treasury. Dad kept his money in a room that lay below dungeon-level. Once he'd taken me there and we had to find our way by touch. He refused to bring even a candle with him, as a safety measure. You can't steal what you can't see.

It wasn't the armory. Dad loved his weapons, but he liked to have them within reach. Over the years Mom had grown used to tripping over spears, swords, and crossbows at every turn. I gazed at the row of pink and purple unicorn tapestries hanging on the corridor walls, while I tried to imagine what else we had at Uxwudge Manor that Dad would want to keep so well guarded.

Pink . . . and . . . purple . . . unicorns?

I knew.

My guessing game ended just in time. The sound of armed men came clanging and clashing up the stairs at the other end of the hall. The two guards snapped to attention as a pair of cloaked and hooded figures emerged from the main staircase.

"Halt!" said the older guard still on duty. "Give the password."

"Marry your son when you will; your daughter when you can," said the taller of the two new men. The *much* taller, I should say. He was about twice his partner's height, but only because the second fellow looked tiny enough to walk under a table without messing his hair. If I knew Dad, he'd hired that one for half-price.

"Pass, friend. It's about time you got here." The older guard shook some kinks out of his legs, then called to his partner, "Come on, Horst, let's see if there's anything in the kitchen for two hungry men."

Horst didn't move. He was eyeing the small guard closely. "Aren't you a little . . . *little* for this line of work?" he asked.

"It's not polite to make personal remarks," the tiny guard replied, giving him the cold shoulder.

That didn't discourage Horst. Still suspicious, he said, "I don't recall seeing anyone your size down in the guardroom. What's your name? Where do you come from?"

"I'm no one you'd remember," the little man replied. "You see, I'm not one of Lord Lucius' regular guards. Someone called in sick today and he hired me as a temporary. My name's Milkum, if that's of any real interest to you."

Horst continued to scowl, but his partner wasn't going to help him investigate. The older guard was too eager to be on his way. "Come on, come on," he urged. "He's all right. I've seen him around here a time or two before this, but he don't stay. A temporary, like he says." Pounding Horst on the back, he herded the younger man down the big staircase.

"Thank goodness," said Milkum. "I thought they'd never leave. Well, if we're to make a night of it, we'd better get going." He opened the door he was supposed to be guarding and bowed to his partner. "She'll want to use you first. Take off your clothes."

I leapt forward, a half-choked scream on my lips, just as the door swung shut behind them. Though Grym seized the back of my tunic, I kept lunging, like a leashed dog that smells meat. "Let me go! Let me go!"

"Boss, you're gonna wake the whole house," Scandal protested. "You're gonna wake the whole neighborhood. You're gonna wake the whole blinkety-blank-blunk *kingdom*! What about Basehart? What about Zoltan? What about Mother Toadbreath? What about *hist*?''

"Wedwel's Democratic Hell take all of them!" I shouted. "That's my *sister's* room!" I went limp in Grym's grasp and squirmed out of my tunic. Stripped bare to the waist, I raced down the hall. The door wasn't locked—good thing, or I would have broken some bones trying to knock it down. I flung it wide, then gasped at what I saw.

There was my sweet little sister, swept off her feet in the arms of a man who made Grym look puny. She was draped in thin, filmy cloth as sturdy as a soap bubble and almost as transparent. Two hooded cloaks lay discarded on the floor. Little Milkum sat on the chest at the foot of Lucy's bed, kicking his heels and smiling merrily.

"Oh, that's good!" he crowed. "That's very, very good! And who's the skinny one in the doorway supposed to be? Your husband?''

"I'm her brother!" I declared.

Milkum pouted. "Husbands are better."

Lucy sat up straight in the big man's arms—not easy, but Lucy always manages—and gave me a withering frown. "Not now, Kendar," she said. "I'm right in the middle of a good book."

"YOU'RE *WHAT?*" I COULDN'T BELIEVE WHAT MY LITTLE sister had just told me. It was too shameful. It was too horrible. It would kill Dad when he found out. It would kill Mom when the neighbors found out.

"Stop making such a fuss, Kendar." Lucy leaned back among the pillows on her bed and yawned in my face. "I'm a big girl, now."

"How long has this—this—this *thing* been going on?" I waved at the bench where Lucy's two midnight callers now sat.

"Please don't call Milkum a *thing*." My sister didn't even blush when she smiled at the little man. "I know he's not much to look at, but he's one of the best. And as for Curio—" She nodded at the blond, muscular "guard" who'd been holding her in his arms when I burst in. "We've done this together so many times, for so many years, just thinking about it makes me feel old." She giggled.

"Old?" Scandal popped out from under Lucy's bed. "Spare me, Grandma Moses. Back where I come from, you'd be selling Girl Scout cookies instead of hot buns."

"Scandal, shush," Mysti said. She and Grym were stationed by the door, taking turns keeping a lookout. They wore the cloaks Milkum and Curio had discarded and were ready to take the fake guards' places outside Lucy's room if they heard anyone coming.

"I still can't believe it," I said. "What Dad thought you were doing—This is a thousand times worse."

"What *did* the old boy think Pollyanna was up to?" Scandal asked.

"He caught her with a book by Raptura Eglantine. He thought

she was *reading.*" No matter how hard I tried, I couldn't make the word sound as sinful as Dad did.

"Well, I can see where a Neanderthal trainee like your daddy would think that reading's dangerous—it might actually lead to *thinking*, God forbid—but what could be worse than—?"

"Writing," I said. "She *is* Raptura Eglantine."

Scandal howled.

Milkum hopped off the bench and edged up to me. "And as Raptura Eglantine, your sister has a duty to her public. Why, even King Steffan himself is a devoted fan. As soon as he read her very first book, *How Wild My Wizard*, he recognized and rewarded her talent."

"The king *knows* that Lucy Gangle is Raptura Eglantine?" Oh, the shame of it!

"Certainly not." Milkum tugged his collar straight. "That would destroy the air of mystery and romance surrounding Orbix's favorite author."

From under the bed, Scandal said, "You're kidding. You mean she's the top writer not just for this cockamamie kingdom, but in your whole twisted *world*?"

"Those parts of it that can read, yes. The works of Raptura Eglantine have been translated into all the languages of Orbix. We are currently negotiating with the Bards, Players, and Mountebanks Guild for the rights to recite, act out, or juggle her books in public." Milkum rubbed his hands together. "Oh, it does give me such satisfaction to know that I was the first to discover her."

"It gives you more than satisfaction, Milkum," Lucy drawled.

"Well, I am her agent," the little man admitted. "Also her publisher."

"And who's he?" I jerked my thumb at Curio, who had taken a small leather flask from his belt and was smearing oil all over his bulging muscles. "Her editor?"

"Curio is my inspiration, Kendar," Lucy said. "I thought you knew: Before I can write all those love scenes, I have to live them first." Then she laughed at me. "Oh, don't be an old silly. Curio just poses for pictures."

"What pictures?"

"In my books. *On* my books. Milkum has many skills, but when it comes to art, he can't even draw a conclusion. So when it's time to illustrate *How Fierce My Freebooter—*"

"The latest Raptura Eglantine smash-hit," Milkum chimed in.

"—he hires an artist from the Street of the Starving Illuminators in Grashgoboum, Curio poses, and there we are. When you broke in on us, I was using Curio to show Milkum the scene I thought would look best on the new book's cover. Now do you see?''

"What I see is that when Dad finds out, he's going to give a whole new meaning to 'smash-hit.' '' I turned to Milkum. "I hope you can swim, because my father's going to drop you in the moat.''

"Kendar, we don't have a moat at Uxwudge Manor," Lucy said.

"For this, Dad will build one.''

"Your family should be flattered," Milkum protested. "Didn't you hear what I said about the king himself adoring Raptura Eglantine? He insisted we change the name of our publishing house to reflect his royal patronage.''

"Which is?''

"Full Court Press.''

"You're not going to tell Daddy, are you, Kendar?" Lucy wheedled.

"I don't know.''

My sister's face fell. "All right, tell him, if you insist. Then just go on your merry way. *You* haven't had to spend your whole life stuck in this house, waiting for some chinless geek with a load of land to marry you. Oh, and don't think they'll ask me if I *want* the chinless geek or not. If he's got enough land, Daddy and Mummy will make sure I want him. Or else.''

"They can't force you to marry.''

"Can't they?'' Lucy's eyes flashed. "If I don't marry, I'll be stuck here forever. It's so easy to tell a prisoner to be patient when you're outside the prison. You got to go away to school. You don't know how boring it is, living here in the country, with all these *wholesome* things to do. Wholesome makes me sick. There are just so many flowers a girl can pick before she goes crazy.''

"You said it!'' Mysti agreed, uninvited. She abandoned her post by the door and came to sit next to Lucy. "And when you tell them you're tired of picking day's-eyes and you want to do something *interesting* for a change, they say, 'Why don't you go out and frolic upon the grass and dance and sing with the gentle woodland creatures?' Am I right?''

"All except the gentle woodland creatures part," Lucy told her. "Basehart and Daddy killed off most of them.''

"I hated the singing part the worst," the former Welfie complained. "They never let me sing anything with lyrics. It was all tweedle-deedle-dee and lilly-lolly-lo until this thick coating of solid sugar formed on my tongue.''

"At least they didn't make you learn to play the lute." Lucy made a face like she'd bitten into a cockroach. "The lute and the harp, because those are the *proper* instruments for a lady. Plinkety-plinkety-plankety-plunkety-plink until you're ready to tear off one of the strings and strangle someone. Once I asked if I could have trumpet lessons. Mummy had a sick headache that lasted for a week and Daddy said no."

"They make you embroider, too, I'll bet."

Lucy nodded. "The next person who hands me a needle is going to get it right back, point first." Her glance slued over to me as she added, "And the *first* person who tells Daddy what I've been doing up here will get the complete works of Raptura Eglantine right where the sun—"

"I'm not going to say a word," I promised. "I've got enough troubles of my own without playing tattletale."

"Troubles?" Lucy's eyes went from me, to Mysti, to Grym. "I understand," she said. She didn't, and she proved it. "Now, Kendar, just because your wife appears to feel a mad, glorious, all-consuming passion for this man—"

"I do?" Mysti said, puzzled.

"She does?" Grym asked, mortified.

"—doesn't mean that she doesn't love you, her true husband. In reality she's only using this to make you jealous."

"I am?" Mysti looked at me. "Is it working?"

"Soon you will be driven to the point of desperation by this charade," Lucy forged on. "Your suspicions will eat away at you until you stumble upon a scene to rend your soul: Your wife! Your best friend! Caught together in an embrace of burning desire!"

"Hey, *I'm* his best friend and all I ever did was take a catnap on her knees," Scandal objected. "You're not pulling the old badger game on me."

Lucy didn't hear him. Her face was transformed, shining with a strange radiance. She was clearly in the grip of a force even more powerful than Majyk.

"Heartbroken, you will turn away from the spectacle of her slender, milky arms entwined about his mighty, sun-bronzed neck, her soft lips crushed to his in a kiss whose raging fires seem to melt them both to the very bone!"

Grym groaned and hid his face in his hands. Curio went over to him and said, "She gets like this sometimes. I cannot wait to see what the cover for this one will look like. Here, have some oil."

"But I haven't kissed *anyone*!" Mysti wailed. "Not for a long, long time, anyway, and definitely not Grym."

Her words didn't matter. My sister was off in a world of her own. Her skirts and long sleeves swirled around her as she posed, gestured, and darted from me to Mysti and back again. "You burst into tears and run from the room. She pursues you, calling your name, swearing by all she holds dear that it was only a trick to make you notice her. Deaf to her pleas, blinded by your tears, you don't watch where you're going and plummet off the castle battlements."

"What castle?" I demanded. "What battlements?"

"You plunge into the moat!"

"*What moat?* We don't *have* any moat!"

"But just as you are about to drown, her faithless yet adored name on your lips, she dives in and rescues you, almost dying herself in the attempt. You take her into your arms and gaze into her eyes. The fires of unbridled love—long smoldering beneath the thin surface of a polite marriage of convenience—surface suddenly, in an overwhelming surge of torrid tenderness that takes you by surprise and sweeps you both away on the crest of wave after thundering wave of—!" She stopped cold.

"Go on, go on!" Mysti begged.

Lucy shook her head. "No, no, that won't work. It's got to be the man who rescues the woman."

"Why?" Mysti was peeved.

"Because it's always the man who rescues the woman," Milkum put in. "And if that's what the public's been buying up until now, we mustn't upset them, must we?"

"Well, speaking of rescuing women," I said, "that's what's really my trouble." I explained to my sister about Mother Toadbreath and Zoltan's threats. She looked disappointed.

"So you want to break her out of Daddy's dungeon?"

"I want to, but I can't do that now," I said. "When Zoltan got Evvon safely tucked away in the capital, he made sure that the government people knew Lord Lucius Parkland Gangle had a witch on his hands. They'll want a full report about how he handles the situation, and if the witch just vanishes before she can be put on trial, Dad will be held responsible. I need to speak with her to see if she's got any ideas about how we can get her out legally, with no one getting hurt."

"Only Hawkeye can't find the dungeon," Scandal said, finally coming out from under the bed and planting himself at Lucy's feet.

"If that's all you want, I'll have Curio show you the way," Lucy offered. "He posed down there once for a scene from *How*

Carnal My Captive.'' A canny glint came into her eye. ''He'll even hang around to show you the way *out* of the dungeon if you promise not to tell Daddy one word about my books.''

''What makes you think we can't find our own way out?''

''That's just what the artist said who went with Curio the first time. He finished painting the scene, then told Curio to take it back upstairs and he'd be along later, after he did some sketches of the cells. He hasn't been seen since.''

''The price of his pictures has gone up nicely, though,'' Milkum said cheerfully.

I gave in. ''Fine, it's a deal. Your secret's safe with us. Anyhow, if people *do* find out about Raptura Eglantine, no decent man will marry you, and since you don't want to get married—''

''I never said that.''

''Right, you didn't. But I *know* you don't want to be forced to marry someone you don't love—''

Mysti burst into tears and ran from the room. I pursued her, calling her name. No one fell in the moat. When I caught her and asked what was wrong, she punched me in the arm and spat, ''Nothing!'' I'll never understand Welfies.

By the time I brought Mysti back, Curio was ready to be our guide to Mother Toadbreath's cell. It's a surprisingly short distance from here to there in Uxwudge Manor when you know where you're going. Before long we found ourselves standing in a row outside the witch's iron-barred door. There were no candles and no torches, so I cupped my hand and summoned up some Majyk to give us light.

''My, my,'' Mother Toadbreath said after I'd explained how matters stood concerning her trial. ''And you say it's to be soon?''

''Dad said he'd try to stall it for a while if I helped him find out where my sister Lucy has been getting books to read.'' I sighed. ''There's no way I can tell him the truth about that, and he's a man who likes results. There's also the trouble with Norris.''

''Oh, my poor darling octopussums!'' the witch exclaimed. ''Is he all right?''

''He misses you and he's letting the whole house know it. I'm trying to keep Dad and Basehart from killing him.''

''You won't be able to do that forever.'' Mother Toadbreath sounded somber. ''If I am found to be guilty of witchcraft, they will hang me, and under the law they will destroy my pets.''

''Why? Because they think Norris is an evil spirit who helps you work dark spells?''

''No, because it's impossible to find good homes for full-grown animals, and the government can't be bothered. Little baby octokits and hushpuppies are easy to place, but once they're no longer cute, well—'' She shrugged. Then she got a glimpse of Curio through the bars. "Speaking of cute—Young man, were you ever a toad?"

"Mother Toadbreath, how can we help you?" Mysti asked.

"I could always give Zoltan what he wants," I said.

"I won't hear of it!" The witch was firm. "Give a bully an inch and he'll take a kingdom. I would sooner die than see all that power fall into Zoltan's hands. At least while you've got it, Kendar, we know you won't use it for wicked, selfish purposes."

"We also know he can barely use it at all," Scandal remarked. He winked at me.

"For now," the witch countered.

"We have to do *something*." Mysti was determined. "I won't just let them kill you."

"Neither will I," I said. "My father's a grown man. He can take care of himself. What's the worst the government people could do to him for letting a witch escape?"

"Punish him in the same way they would have punished me," Mother Toadbreath said softly. "He would hang."

My lips were suddenly dry. "Maybe—maybe I could use Majyk to whisk all of us away, far away to the other side of Orbix. You, me, Dad, Mom, everyone, maybe every*thing* in Uxwudge Manor, and—!"

"Kendar dear, you're babbling." The witch's voice was gentle and kind. "You can't do that. You lack the skill. You lack the *power*. I may not use Majyk myself, but I do know that it has its limits, even when someone's got as much of it at his command as you do. The fanciest transportation spell any wizard can work is making things float, and even then you can't keep it up forever."

"It's hopeless," I moaned.

"There, there." Mother Toadbreath tried to comfort me. "If worse comes to worst, I suppose you can put in a good word for me at the trial. Mysti could stand up and tell everyone how I helped heal her. Perhaps if I can show that my magic is a help to people—"

"I'm not exactly people," Mysti mumbled.

"Oh? Goodness, that's true. Although strictly speaking, you aren't exactly a Welfie either. I hope you aren't planning on applying for any licenses. The bureau rats just hate it when you can't fill out the forms one way or the other. By the book, by the book, that's the only thing they understand."

"Buy the book is the only thing Milkum understands too," said Curio. "Could you please hurry? Time is passing. Soon the real guards will arrive and he and I must be gone. It is a long journey back to the capital."

"The capital!" Mother Toadbreath clapped her hands for joy. "Why didn't I think of that? Kendar dear, come closer. I've just had an idea."

She began to whisper to me.

CHAPTER ──────────── 26

IT WAS A FINE, BRIGHT, BREEZY MORNING WHEN WE prepared to leave Uxwudge Manor. Dawn was only a hint of light in the distance. No one had come to see us off or wish us well on the road. That was because no one was supposed to know we were going and we weren't taking any road to get there.

Scandal and I were the first ones up. After last night, with all our wanderings through the manor halls and the discovery of Lucy's shameful secret, I felt too exhausted to sleep. The cat was bright-eyed, cheerful, and ready for anything, which made me even more short-tempered. To keep myself from worrying about what was keeping the others, I decided to use the waiting time for practice.

"All right, then how does *this* sound?" I asked Scandal. Kneeling on the roof of Uxwudge Manor, I bowed my head and declaimed, "Your Majesty, in the name of truth and justice I do implore thee to throw the mantle of thy mercy over thine unworthy albeit loyal servant, Mother Toadbreath." I looked up to see the cat's reaction.

Scandal was leaning over the edge of the roof, making a retching sound, shoulder blades heaving violently.

"No good?" I sounded touchy because I was. The cat stopped convulsing and gave me a skeptical look. "Oh no, it was *very* moving. I was particularly inspired by the part about throwing up on the king's mantle."

I took offense. "I suppose you could do better?"

"You know it, Chuckles. But from what I've gathered, King Steffan's court is not the place to spring surprises. A cat's bad enough, but a talking cat? No way. Your people believe in cats the way my people believe in unicorns. I show up and start pleading the old girl's case and the first thing they'll do is act like I'm not there. It doesn't hurt to be a little crazy when you do government work, but if you're really nuts they might transfer you to the army. If they *do* decide that they all see me, next thing they'll do is check the liquor cabinet. And if they discover that they're not crazy and they're not drunk, *then* they'll decide that sane, sober, honest folks shouldn't have to put up with such things and they'll run me out of town on a rail. *If* they let me get away alive.''

"Do your people do that to unicorns?" I asked. "How do they get them to balance on the rail?"

"Never mind. Go back to working up a good, groveling speech for when we see King Steffan.''

I paced the roof. "This isn't easy. I've never had to ask for a royal pardon before.''

"It's the only thing that'll save Mother Toadbreath," Scandal reminded me.

"I know, I know. How about this: O grand and mighty monarch—!''

"Oh, brother." Scandal snorted. "Why don't you just tell him: King, I've got the biggest hog's-load of Majyk this realm has ever seen and I know how to use it. Now, you hand over a pardon for my friend Mother Toadbreath and repeal your dumb anti-witchcraft law and maybe—just maybe—I won't turn you into a flamingo. There! Simple.''

"I can't turn the king into a flamingo," I said. "I don't know what a flamingo is.''

"I do. We can work together on that one," Scandal reassured me. "If we're lucky and the king's smart, it won't get down to flamingos, but if he wants to play hard ball, he'll be standing on one leg straining shrimp through his nose before you can say *lawn ornament.*''

Every time Scandal got tough, I got nervous. The cat was all big plans, but guess who got stuck putting them into action? And guess who got the lumps if the big plans didn't work? Scandal said it was because he was the executive type. All I knew was that "executive" sounded an awful lot like *execution.*

I sighed. "I wish I had a real wizard's robe, at least. That way it'll sound more believable when I threaten to turn King Steffan into a flamed dingo.''

"*Flamingo.* It's a big, ugly pink bird with legs like stilts and a beak like an upside-down canoe. People see them lots of places on my world.''

"They do?" I scratched my head. "And they've still got a problem with plain old common *unicorns*?"

The trapdoor in the roof opened as Mysti climbed out, tossing a small traveler's sack up ahead of her. She had gotten rid of the ugly tent-dress Mom wished on her and was wearing a set of my old clothes instead. The britches fit her fine, though the tunic was a little tight here and there. So was my chest when I looked at her. "Well, I've got it," she said, patting the belt-pouch at her side.

"Got what?"

"Mother Toadbreath's gravy boat. Grym and I sneaked out of Uxwudge and went to her cottage to get it. We locked up Norris in one of the spare rooms, too, so we won't have to worry about your family killing the poor thing while we're gone. Mother Toadbreath said you should study Chapter Twelve in your book; it's got a paragraph or two about how to capture wild Majyk."

"He's supposed to catch some wild Majyk by pouring gravy over it?" Scandal asked.

The one-time Welfie rolled her eyes in the identical way that Scandal rolled his whenever he wanted you to know you'd said something dumb but he was going to be patient with you. The cat didn't like getting a taste of his own medicine at all.

"You can't learn how to catch wild Majyk just by reading the book," Mysti said. "That secret's passed down only from wizard to wizard."

"How come Kendar and I got lucky with old Thengor's stash, huh?" Scandal challenged her.

"And Grym's sword, too," I added.

"That wasn't truly *wild* Majyk," Mysti countered. "Thengor's hoard was used to being tamed, mastered, and domesticated. It wanted a new home, a new master—not just the portions that stuck to you but all the scattered pieces. If it had been left alone long enough after his death, it would have gone back to its wild state and run free; then you wouldn't have caught it so easily."

I thought about her words. "Wild, tamed, running free, caught because it *wanted* a new master? You make Majyk sound like it was alive."

"Worse: You make it sound like *me*," Scandal said.

Mysti shrugged. "All I know is what Mother Toadbreath told me. That includes the part about what you're supposed to do with the book and the gravy boat. Just in case you run into any more of those bits of Master Thengor's original collection that will be attracted to you anyway, Mother Toadbreath said you could try draining it off the way it says in Chapter Twelve and use the gravy boat to hold it until you learn how to absorb it yourself.''

''A force that was strong enough to turn your planet into a pretzel and you want the kid to store it in a piece of dinnerware that doesn't even have a cover.'' Scandal snickered. ''Yeah, right. If it was one of those plastic dishes where you burp the lid before sealing, I could see it.''

''Burping dishes? I never heard such nonsense! And you scoff at me, creature?'' Mysti looked ready to start her all-red-meat diet with Scandal. ''Ha! That shows all you know. This is an *enchanted* gravy boat.''

The cat laughed so hard, he almost rolled down the trapdoor when Grym opened it and joined us. The barbarian had a large, tightly rolled bundle slung over one shoulder and a covered wicker basket in his other hand.

''Forsooth, the beast doth make full merry,'' he observed. ''This bodes well, for it doth signify that the gods are in a mellow, antic humor, perforce.''

''It signifies that the cat has the brains of a sliced radish, perforce.'' Maybe it was the weather, but I thought I saw steam rising from Mysti's pointed ears. ''Here.'' She shoved the gravy boat into my hands. ''You do what you want with it. I've delivered Mother Toadbreath's message; I'm through. Listen to the cat, if you think he's got all the answers.''

Scandal strutted between us. ''You know, Fairycakes,'' he said, whiskers tilted at an arrogant angle. ''That's the first sensible thing I've ever heard you say. Okay, time's catnip; let's get this show on the road.''

We worked silently. There wasn't too much to do. Grym unrolled the big bundle, which turned out to be the wing-stained white carpet Mysti and I had received for a wedding gift. He placed the wicker basket dead center on the rainbow rug. ''Breakfast,'' he explained. I stowed the enchanted gravy boat in the basket, then riffled through Mother Toadbreath's book, re-reading the chapter on Levitation. It was a long way from Uxwudge Manor to Grashgoboum and King Steffan's court if you didn't cut through the Forest of Euw. Overland it took four days, with luck. Dad couldn't delay the trial any longer than two days at the most.

We had no choice: If we wanted the king's pardon for Mother Toadbreath, we'd have to fly.

Scandal picked his way around the perimeter of the rug, sniffing it cautiously. ''It'll never get off the ground,'' he said. ''It's too big. In the flying carpet stories, they send up a one-man rug. This is a broadloom space station!''

"It *will* fly." Mysti was ready for a fight.

"It ought to fly," I said, a little less sure of myself than Mysti. "In the book it says it's always easier to make an object float when it's something that belongs in the air in the first place."

"That makes sense." Scandal's eyebrows twitched with amusement. "When it comes to buoyancy, balloons beat baboons ten to one. But since when does a rug belong up in the clouds instead of down on the living room floor?"

"Since that rug soaked up my wings," said Mysti.

"Look, at least we've got to try." I stepped onto the carpet and closed my eyes, calling the Majyk in.

"Eh, what's the worst that can happen?" I heard Scandal say. "Us cats always land on our feet." I felt a small, warm body come to stand against my leg. "Contact! Chocks away! Curse you, Red Baron! Tower, do you read? Roger, wilco, over and—"

"Shut up," said Mysti. My eyes were still closed in concentration, so I only heard her words and caught a whiff of her sweet, flowery scent near me.

"Hey, who invited you?" Scandal hissed. "We don't want a whole committee tagging along to the capital. It's gonna be tough enough getting Kendar in to see the king. Someone's gotta stay here to keep Zoltan from pushing Mother Toadbreath's trial ahead before we can get back with the pardon. Someone's gotta make sure the kid's Mommy and Daddy don't catch wise that he's missing."

"Someone's got to help Kendar fly this thing," Mysti replied.

"What?" I opened my eyes. The former Welfie maiden was seated cross-legged on the rug.

"They were *my* wings," she said. "Even now they serve their original purpose. When they were stripped from me at our Binding and made a part of this rug, it was only so that I could share the gift of flight with my new husband."

"Won't it need Majyk to make it fly?" I asked.

"Welfies *are* Majyk. My wings were Majyk. If you were my real husband, Kendar, you could command the carpet to fly you anywhere you liked, with or without me. The way things are—" There was a lot of bitterness in her smile. "This rug will fly without you, Kendar, but it will never fly without me."

"Dread naught," said Grym. "I will remain behind to stand as sword and shield unto good Mother Toadbreath, and a burr in the breeches of that most heinous wight, Zoltan. Also, I shall feed the octopuss."

So it was settled, even if it did put Scandal's nose out of joint. I closed my eyes again and performed the spell for Simultaneous Levitation of Several Large Objects letter-perfect.

Not a darned thing happened.

"Maybe we've got too much weight aboard," Scandal remarked, staring hard at Mysti.

"No, that's not it." I sank down onto the rug. "It's the Majyk. I don't feel it working. I don't understand; I did this spell before and made it work!"

"Yeah, but what were you trying to float then?" the cat asked. "We are talking major poundage here." His whiskers flicked towards Mysti, who made a gesture of unknown meaning back at him. "Look, why should you sweat? She says the rug can fly without you. I say you let her prove it."

"Very well, I will!" Mysti snapped. She closed her eyes and made lifting motions over the rug. She made it rise twice as high as I'd done, which was still twice nothing.

"By this blade!" said Grym. "I am but an humble barbarian, yet methinks it might serve thee well didst thou unite with the wench, O Master."

"What?" I gaped. "Here? In public?"

"Thy powers, thy powers only, need'st thou unite." It was Grym's turn at eye-rolling. "Forsooth, 'twas even so that Mother Toadbreath did effect the wench's cure by joining the Majyk pent within my blade, thy body, and the august person of the oracular cat. There is a saying amongst the hordes of mine late, long-lost, lamented chieftain, Uk-Uk the Unspeakable: 'Dispute ye not with past success, lest I chop off your worthless head.'"

You can't argue with that.

Grym made us stand on the rug in an arrangement that was as close as possible to the way we'd done it at Mother Toadbreath's cottage without having to use Norris. Mysti knelt with the enchanted gravy boat in her lap, I stood in front of her holding Graverobber with the point aimed straight down into the dish. It cost Grym dearly to part with his sword, but he said I needed something to focus my powers.

"I can bear this sorrow if it meaneth swifter aid and succor shall be brought anon to our good friend the witch." He tried to sound brave about it.

I ran through the spell again. A thin streamer of bluish light flowed down the length of the sword into the enchanted gravy boat. This time the rug quivered with life and began to rise slowly—too slowly—from the rooftop. "It's taking too long," I said. "By the time we get high enough for me to make the rug move forward, it will be broad daylight and Dad might spot us when he goes out to kill breakfast."

"Speed shalt thou have," Grym promised. "Now lightly, good Scandal, dost thou rub thy fur eftsoons against the grain, that sparks therefrom might generate."

"Eftsoons thy mama," said the cat.

"Scandal, please." My arms were getting tired from holding Grym's sword, but by using a minor levitation spell, I took off most of the blade's weight. I spoke the words to lower the rug back to the rooftop and rested the sword. "The energy you gave off at the cottage really sped up my Majyk. We need that now."

"I know, I know, but no cat in his right mind likes having his fur rubbed the wrong way."

"No?" This was news to me. "But if you don't like it, why did you call it ecstatic electricity?"

Scandal wrinkled up his nose. "Whether I like it or not, I can't do it for myself. We cats are built to only rub ourselves the right way."

"I could do it," Mysti offered.

"Nay, thou must keep charge of yon vessel upon thy lap," Grym said. "When thou art airborne, perforce thou must lay hold thereto, lest it tumble from ye rug and all things goeth splat. Thy hands shall be full."

"I could put the gravy boat down on the rug."

We tried it that way. It didn't work; the rug wouldn't get off the ground. Then we tried it with the gravy boat back in Mysti's lap and we floated up just fine.

"This is so weird," Scandal said. "It's like we're all forming a giant electric circuit that'll only work when all the elements are hooked up one way. Kendar supplies the Majyk, Grym's sword conducts it into the gravy boat—so that's kind of like a storage battery—Mysti conducts it from there into the Welfin magic of the rug, and Kendar's standing on the rug so that closes the circuit."

"Marry, forsooth?" Grym's brow furrowed.

"Or something. Hey, don't ask me, I'm just the catalyst." Scandal licked a paw absently. "All I know is, if one contact point breaks so someone can muss up my fur, the whole thing fizzles."

"So mote it be. The gods have spoken, albeit the half soundeth like most pure divine gibberish."

"Hey, no one's asking you to be Conan Alva Edison, but you

saw for yourself: One way, it works, the other way . . . *nada*!"

"Aye, verily." Grym nibbled his thumb in thought. "Willingly wouldst I fare forth in thy company, that I might provide hands to lay upon the beast's back. Yet dare we not. One must remain behind to ward the welfare of the witch."

"We sure could use an extra pair of hands," Scandal agreed. "Even if they will be rubbing me the wrong way."

"Too bad Curio left," Mysti said. She sounded a little too sad about it, which annoyed me.

"Too bad *Milkum* left, too." There was a definite sneer in my voice. "He'd have been just as good."

"Oh, no." Mysti fluttered her eyelashes at me. "I think Curio had *much* better hands. Do you think we'll be able to find him when we get to the capital?"

"No." I was curt. "They left Uxwudge Manor before us, but they're going to Grashgoboum on horseback. We'll be there and back before—"

The trapdoor flew back with a bang. "Aha!" my brother bellowed, waving a shortsword. "I thought I heard someone up here! What're you doing, eh?"

"How could you have heard us?" Basehart's sudden entrance had me in shock. "Your room's four storeys down."

For an answer, my brother grabbed his head and groaned. "Don't shout, for Wedwel's sake. Haven't you got any pity for a man with a *calabash* hangover? And you—!" He pointed at Scandal. "Stop stomping about."

"Look, Basehart, no one's shouting here but you. Why don't you go back downstairs to bed? I promise we won't disturb you again."

"Oh, no you don't." Basehart wagged his sword at me. "I see what you're up to. This is some sort of evil magic you're working up here. Zoltan warned me about how you can't use your powers and how you're always using 'em to call up vicious demons."

"How can I call up vicious demons with my powers if I can't use them?" I thought it was a reasonable question. I forgot I was talking to my brother.

"Trying some of that fast wizard-talk, eh? You don't fool me. You're gonna call up a vicious demon and make him tear the walls off Uxwudge Manor so's your friend the witch can get away."

"Basehart, if I could call up a vicious demon, the first thing I'd have it do is shake some sense into your skull. You actually believe—?"

"Wait, O truly evil Master Kendar!" Mysti sprang to her feet, the gravy boat clutched to her bosom. "In the name of all dark sorcery, I beg truce!"

"Huh?" She made a go-along-with-this face at me. "Oh. Oh, sure. Truce. Yea, verily. Go ahead."

The former Welfie now spoke to my brother in a voice like warm honey. "Noble warrior, I can see that it is useless to try to conceal anything from your all-seeing wisdom." She glided closer to him, eyes aglow. "That is why you are my only hope. Nay, the sole hope of all Orbix!"

"You bet," Basehart said readily. Then: "Hope of what?"

For answer, Mysti melted into his arms and pressed her lips to his ear. Whatever she was telling him made the blood rise to his face and the sword drop to his side. When she finally stepped back, he swayed dizzily. "*Really?*" was all he asked. She nodded. "Wow." He almost dived headfirst through the trapdoor.

"What did you say to get rid of him?" I demanded.

"I didn't get rid of him," Mysti replied. "He'll be back as soon as he brings us another basket of food."

"What!"

"He's coming with us," she said demurely. "We do need someone to rub the cat, and Grym can't be spared."

"Ye gods!" Grym exclaimed. "By what arts hast thou convinced yonder bully-boy to throw in his lot as witch's advocate and aid?"

"I didn't do that. He's still looking forward to seeing Mother Toadbreath hang. Like the good cheesehead he is. If you tell Basehart something is evil, he'll believe you without a second thought."

"Without a first thought, either," Scandal said.

"So I just told him that yes, Zoltan was right about you, Kendar. You're a powerful, evil wizard who was trying to summon a demon to destroy Uxwudge Manor, except I was using my own powers to prevent you."

"And why would you be doing something like that?" I wanted to know. "I *am* your husband."

"Oh, are you?" Her mouth quirked up at one corner. "Well, I also told him that ours is no true marriage. Are you going to give me any argument on that?"

I was silent. I don't know why, but I was also ashamed.

"It's so simple," Mysti said. "As we stand here, the forces of nameless Evil hover over Orbix, waiting to overwhelm the powers of eternal Good."

Grym brightened. "Uk-Uk the Unspeakable cometh?"

"*Cosmic* Evil, you twit." She grinned. "And guess who is the master of all the dark forces?"

Grym didn't have a clue. Scandal did. "*Him?*" he yowled, staring at me. Mysti nodded. "*He's* the leader of the Let's Trash the Universe for the Heck Of It gang? *He's* gonna spray-paint 'Kendar Rules' on the side of Eternity?"

"Only if Evil triumphs over Good," Mysti said. "Or Chaos over Law, either one."

"I bet you also told him that you were riding on the side of Good, huh?" Scandal said.

"Even so, O beast." Grym didn't give Mysti a chance to respond to the question. "Canst thou not see that she hath fair golden tresses?"

"Blond hair and white hats, yeah, they do go together," the cat admitted. "The pointy ears don't hurt, either. You *can* tell the good guys without a scorecard."

"Yet how mote it be that he hath accepted thy marriage to the Lord of Evil, wench, an thou be'st on the side of Good?"

"Oh, I only married Kendar to slow him up." Mysti pressed the back of one hand to her forehead and pretended to swoon. "It was a hideous sacrifice, but if I had managed to buy even a day's help for the forces of Law, I can die happy." She collapsed in a cloud of giggles.

"Great!" I paced the rug. "Just great! Now you've got my idiot big brother convinced that I'm some sort of epic villain who's going to destroy the world when before he didn't think I could find my way out of an open door."

"Better than that, I've got him convinced he's the chosen hero who is the only one capable of saving the world from you and your hideous plot." Mysti was calm. She could afford to be.

"Sis," said Scandal. "I hate to bust your bubble, but do you have any idea what these chosen heroes *do* to the villain when they corner him? I'll give you a hint: *En garde*, thrust, thrust, parry, lunge, thrust, hack, slice, stab, bleed, bleed, bleed, die."

"Basehart won't kill you, Kendar." Mysti's complacent smile was starting to get on my nerves. "In the first place, he can't; not with your Majyk on guard. In the second place, there's the prophecy."

"*What* prophecy?" It was the logical question, but I didn't sound very logical shouting it.

"Ah, cheez, there's *always* a prophecy, boss! Lemme guess." Scandal raised a paw. "The great and ancient prophecy that hath slumbered long in Welven halls and doth speak of how the chosen hero shall overcome the evil lord and get the girl, only he won't actually *kill* the villain so we can all get jobs when they make the sequel?''

''How did you know?'' Mysti asked.

''My first wizard had bad taste in books.''

All of which meant that a few minutes later we were flying swiftly towards the towers of Grashgoboum on a wing-stained white rug with me holding the sword, Mysti holding the gravy boat, and Basehart rubbing the cat the wrong way as he dreamed of the cheers he'd get when he saved the world from his little brother.

cHAPTER —————— 27

WHEN I WAS STILL A NEW STUDENT BACK AT MASTER
Thengor's Academy, sometimes when the weather was fine I'd
lean out an upper-storey window, stare off at the distant towers of
the capital, and dream about the day when I'd be a great wizard
and travel there to seek my fortune. It didn't take me long to learn
that if going to Grashgoboum depended on my becoming a great
wizard, I wasn't going to get any closer to the city than in my
dreams.

Funny things, dreams. They have a way of coming true in ways
you never dreamed.

Grashgoboum is called the City of Towers. No other city in all
King Steffan's realm has so many of them, so tall or so beautiful.
That's because there's a very strict royal law on the books that
says any city caught trying to build a tower will be burned to the
ground and turned into a *knoblop* playing field. There is another
royal law which says that the towers of Grashgoboum may only be
constructed of a particular kind of stone—a rare stone that's a
lovely, light shade of amber flecked with gold. Some people say
that this law is thanks to the good taste of the royal family. Others
say it is thanks to the fact that the royal family owns the only
quarry in the kingdom where this rare stone is found. Still other
people say nothing, and they get to live longer.

Whoever owns the quarry, the effect of the golden towers is still
magnificent. It is said that travelers from all over Orbix stand in
silent awe when they get their first glimpse of those majestic
structures.

I guess they never traveled with a cat.

"It looks like a bunch of pencils stuck in the ground!" Scandal
exclaimed when we flew in sight of the city. "A whole bunch of

pencils and the ground's all covered with soap bubbles. Dirty soap bubbles."

"Those are the towers of the royal palace," I told him. "And those 'bubbles' are the other city buildings."

"Ugh. This is the best you people can do? Pencils and soap? Nothing in between? Where I come from, we try to get a little variety into our cities. You got your posh skyscrapers, you got your high-rent high-rises, you got your apartment buildings and your townhouses, and then you got your slums. Oh boy, I'll say you got your slums!"

"Those bubble-shaped buildings are the slums. The only decent place to live in Grashgoboum is the palace. That's why they built the palace so big. If you want to live in the capital, you either have a government job—with a palace apartment—or you've got nothing."

"That's—why, that's awful! That's barbaric! That's—" Scandal was sputtering, and I don't mean just the sparks flying from his fur where Basehart was roughing it up. "That's—Actually, that's a lot like we run things back home. Never mind."

As we flew nearer, I explained as best I could all that I knew about the history of Grashgoboum. Master Thengor never taught us anything about it, which is probably why I knew so much. Strange, whenever I had something to learn that wasn't going to be graded, I wound up almost an expert on the subject. But tell me that what I knew was going to be on an exam and I'd turn around and fail it, hands down.

"Grashgoboum was founded shortly after the War of the Two Cousins Once Removed and Their Aunt Pooki," I said. "The last king in the direct line died accidentally during a friendly game of *knoblop* when his chicken escaped the scoop-net and flew up into his horse's face, causing the beast to stumble, step into one of the goal-buckets, and throw his rider. Because it was third *hork* of an exhibition game, he had just taken off his helmet so he could balance the mince pie on his head for extra points. Unfortunately, mince pies don't help much when you hit a stone wall headfirst. It was very tragic. The game was being held in honor of the king's engagement to Princess Sluice of Wend."

"Is this gonna be another story with giant horned hamsters in it?" Scandal asked. "Because if it is, I'm gonna jump."

"Kendar's not telling it right," Basehart said. "There's a lot of good bloody parts in it. Let me handle them."

"Handling bloody parts? Wouldn't you just love that," the cat said drily.

"*I* know this one!" Mysti piped up. "The two cousins once removed were the closest living heirs to the throne, only neither one of them wanted to marry Princess Sluice. One of them had a strong dislike for women with moustaches longer than his and the other was *very* devoted to his sword-brother, Ingbard the Well-Developed. So they fought a war that lasted ten years, loser take all, and they both had the good luck to get themselves killed at about the same time at the Battle of Ingbard's Sandal.

"That was when Aunt Pooki took over as Queen Pooki, the first independent female ruler your kingdom ever had. The first thing she did was announce that there was a new god named Kimberli who had given her the crown and said that if anyone tried to take it away from her there would be a plague of something ugly that left stains. All the nobles were sick and tired of war, so they built a temple to Kimberli, declared a week-long festival with plenty of free *calabash* until everyone was walking into walls, and then went off to have a nice, long lie-down."

"How come you know all this?" I asked. "I thought Welfies didn't care anything about mortal affairs."

"Lord Valdaree had a bet going with Lord Babalu about which cousin would win the war and pretty soon everyone had some gold riding on it, so we all kept up with the news from outside," Mysti explained. "Of course when Queen Pooki was crowned, the entire Welfie nation went into debt with a dwarf named Joblot and we haven't paid any attention to you mortals ever since, except to kill you. It's cheaper."

"Awwww, you left out the good stuff," Basehart protested. "What about all the battles and the assassinations and the part where Princess Sluice got her hands on Ingbard and—?"

"I know I'm going to hate myself for asking this," Scandal interrupted, "but what did happen to juicy Sluicy?"

"Queen Pooki set her up as the first virgin high priestess of Kimberli if she promised to donate her dowry to the temple. Sluice agreed and moved in right away with her six children and devoted personal servant, Ingbard."

"I see," said the cat. "Well, I'll just go and plunge to my death now, if you don't mind." He was joking, but no one had warned him that my brother had a sense of humor that was limited to jumping out of dark corners and yelling "Boo!" at elderly relatives with bad hearts.

"No! Don't!" Basehart shouted, making a grab for the cat. His outburst startled Scandal, who had been sitting placidly on the rug, allowing Basehart to rumple his fur so the sparks (and the rug) would fly. Scandal jumped, hissing, teeth bared, legs stuff, claws out. He was small, but when he got angry he looked dangerous.

Without thinking, Basehart knew what to do with dangerous animals. Basehart knew everything without thinking. He seized the nearest sword, which happened to be the one I was holding, and took a slice at Scandal. He missed, but he still did more than his share of harm.

With Graverobber out of my hands, the current of the Majyk stream was cut off abruptly. The rug gave a sickening lurch, pitching me on top of Mysti. She screamed as I knocked Mother Toadbreath's gravy boat out of her hands. It rolled right to the rippling edge of the carpet where it teetered over emptiness.

"I got it, I got it, I got it!" Scandal yelled, springing forward. The rug gave another shudder and jerk while he was in midair. The gravy boat toppled to safety, but the cat found himself looking straight down at a whole lot of thin air. "I don't got it," were the last words I heard him say before he plummeted from sight.

I didn't even have time to feel shock. It was like Scandal was a candle-flame accidentally blown out by an approaching whirlwind. You don't think about what happened to the flame; you just concentrate on saving your own skin from the coming storm. The cat wasn't the only thing hurtling towards the ground. Without the Majyk circuit, the flying carpet was only flying straight down, fast.

Mysti clung to me with one hand, the other holding the gravy boat. Basehart clung to Mysti. The ends of the carpet flapped up around us as we fell. Both lunch baskets and Mysti's traveling bag slipped off into the abyss of sky. All I could see was a fluttering rainbow curtain, all I could feel was wind, all I could hear were the terrified voices of my brother and my wife begging me to do something.

All I could say was, "Ow." Something hard and cold with a wicked edge was cutting into my foot. I looked down and saw Graverobber pressed against the side of my shoe. I grabbed the sword and desperately chanted the spell of levitation.

We continued to levitate in the wrong direction.

"The gravy boat," Mysti gasped. "Aim it at the gravy boat." I did, with no luck. Basehart stopped begging me to save him and started cursing me.

"A fine Lord of Evil you are! Can't even make a simple rug stop falling out of the sky! Good's goin' to triumph over Evil by bloody *accident*, that's what!"

"Rrrragh! Who asked you? This is all your fault, Basehart!

Why, I ought to—!'' With that weird strength you sometimes get in hopeless situations, I raised Graverobber over my head and swung the sword wildly around and around.

And around and around it continued to go. The blade glowed with Majyk's golden light and gave off an unearthly *chud-chud-chud-chud* noise. The carpet slowed its fall, then stopped and hovered peacefully in midair beneath the whirling blade.

"Wedwel's leftmost eyebrow, what happened?'' Basehart asked, teeth chattering.

"I don't know, but I can tell you what's going to happen if you don't move your hand,'' Mysti informed him. They were still arguing about whether that was any way for a beauteous Welven agent of Good to talk to the chosen hero prophesied of old, when I brought the rug gradually to land.

We were on a level stretch of ground not too far from the royal highway. I didn't even need to shade my eyes to see the crowds coming and going to and from Grashgoboum. A few trees stood between us and the road, though nothing like a real forest. If we wanted, we could walk to the city from here, see the king, and maybe even convince him to dispatch one of his own messengers to take Mother Toadbreath's pardon back to Uxwudge Manor in time.

From here on, it was going to be easy. Then why did I feel like a rock was rooted in my heart?

"Kendar!'' Mysti waved to me from a clump of bushes a short distance away. "Look what I found!'' She whipped out the plain brown dress Mom had forced her to wear to Uxwudge Manor. "My bag came open when it fell off the rug and everything else is scattered to the winds, but I found this caught in some branches. Isn't that lucky?''

"You *want* to wear that thing?''

"No.'' She yanked it over my head before I could say a word. "*You* do.''

"I do not!'' I managed to say as soon as I got my mouth clear of the neck-hole.

"Yes, you do. Remember, you're a wizard, and a real wizard needs to wear a real wizard's robe.''

"Real wizards don't wear brown—Oh, forget it.'' I felt tired and sad. Scandal was gone. I'd never had a friend before, so I never knew that losing one would hurt this much.

Mysti reached out to touch my cheek. "What's this?'' she asked when her fingertips came away wet.

"Nothing." I wiped my face dry with one sleeve. "Let's roll up the rug and go."

Basehart and Mysti shouldered the bundled rug between them. We all decided it wouldn't look right for a mighty wizard to enter the gates of Grashgoboum hauling a carpet. I got to carry the enchanted gravy boat, which was shining full to the brim with Majyk and made a nice, creepy, wizardly impression on ordinary people. I'd stowed Graverobber inside the rug; my arm was still aching from swinging the big sword overhead for so long.

The royal road to Grashgoboum teemed with all sorts of travelers. There were Squal tribesmen from the Newtgriddle Desert, wearing their coin-trimmed robes to show off their wealth. (Among the Squal, they use the same word for "millionaire" and "extreme lower-back problems.") There were the limber merchants of Askwat, whose stock-in-trade was contortionist acts and law books. A brightly painted caravan with yellow wheels and a red top rumbled by, driven by a sullen-looking bear swaddled in gaudy silks and drawn by a matched team of eight golden-haired little girls.

"Undersiders," Basehart whispered. Like him, I'd heard the stories about how life was . . . *different* once you traveled around the Big Bend in our world, but I'd never seen the proof of it until now.

The bear saw us staring and immediately slapped on a toothy grin as fake as any human merchant's. "Grrreetings, gentlefurs! Interrrrest you in some nice, frrrresh porridge today?" When we politely declined, he lapsed back into his original grumpy expression and drove on.

As crowded as the king's road was, the other wayfarers made room for us as soon as they glimpsed my robe and the enchanted gravy boat. I'd added a little something extra to the Majyk glow by reciting the spell for Simple Fireworks to Amuse Your Friends. Every so often small spurts of glittering red, blue, and yellow sparks would leap from the gravy boat and fall back to earth as fiery flowers.

"Ho, make way! Make way for the king's own unicorns!" A strident voice cut through the mixed hubbub of the road. I heard a thunder of hoofbeats coming up fast behind us. Already the other travelers were scattering to either side of the highway. The royal white unicorn is the wisest, most beautiful creature on all Orbix. The problem is, he knows how wonderful he is and doesn't see anything wrong with trampling lesser beings stupid enough to stand in his way.

I moved quickly to the roadside, but not so quickly that I looked like I was running away. I had my image to think of. A wizard must remain dignified in all situations, or so Master Thengor told us the day a crowd of my classmates caught him in the wine cellar with Velma Chiefcook and no clothes. Basehart didn't have to worry about his image. He just yelped and dove for the bushes, leaving Mysti standing there trying to hold up the rug by herself.

It was an awfully big rug. She tried tugging it out of the way of the approaching herd and only succeeded in losing her footing. She fell over backwards and the rug fell across her, pinning her down. The unicorns were coming on at a brisk canter, their horns catching the sunlight like the lances of an invading army.

I had no choice. I raced back into the middle of the road and took a stand between Mysti and the unicorns, holding the enchanted gravy boat to the sky. "Halt!" I cried, making the multicolored sparks shoot higher than ever.

The unicorns didn't so much as slow to a trot.

"Way, there!" came that harsh voice again. "Make way, ye young fool! I've no wish to be scraping your hide from the king's pavement." Out of the dust rising on all sides of the snow-white herd, a single dapple-gray unicorn with a broken horn came galloping towards me. On his back was a wrinkled, sun-browned man whose silver hair was almost as shimmering as the unicorns' manes. He rode bareback, carrying a blue and white pennant at the end of a thin bamboo pole. As he came nearer, he shifted the pole so that it became a lance aimed right at my chest. All the time he kept shouting. "Way! Way! Get the stinking blazes out of the way!"

I could hardly believe my eyes. "Uncle Corbly?"

The man blinked and dug his knees into the gray unicorn's flanks, jerking the poor beast's mane to make it turn sharply left. The unicorn bleated and reared, pawing the air. "Kendar?" he said when his steed calmed down. He didn't wait for me to answer, but wheeled right around and bawled at the oncoming herd, "Halt!"

His "Halt!" worked a lot better than mine. The unicorns stopped dead. It was amazing: Not one of them took another step. Unicorns in the back of the herd didn't bump and bumble into those ahead of them. Unicorns on the flanks of the herd didn't stray off to crop the grass alongside the road.

"Hey! What's the holdup?" someone called from the rear.

"Nothing, Torse!" Uncle Corbly called back, cupping his

hands to his mouth. "Just some daft boy without the common sense to get out of the way."

"Why didn't you run 'im down, then?" Torse hollered.

"Can't! He's my cousin Abstemia's boy, she what married Lord Lucius Parkland Gangle even after what her father warned her."

"Oh." There was a short silence from the back of the herd. Then: "A Gangle, eh? That'd explain the daft part all right."

Uncle Corbly chuckled, then dismounted and patted the gray unicorn's neck. "This *is* a day for rare meetings. I thought you was still in wizard school, but from the look of you, you've come out with honors. I never did see a brown-robed wizard before."

"I'm a special case," I said. It was no lie.

"Is that so? And didn't they teach you special cases that it's dangerous to stand between a herd of the king's unicorns and—" He stopped and the breath caught in his throat as he stared at something just behind me.

I looked over one shoulder. Mysti had rolled the rug off her and was standing up, brushing the dust from her clothes. Her tunic and breeches were ripped, but somehow this made them look better than ever.

"Uncle Corbly," I said, "I'd like you to meet my wife. Mysti, this is Corbly Guzzle, unicorn-keeper to His Majesty, King Steffan."

Mysti's smile lit up her face, even through the grime. "I'm *so* pleased to meet you, sir," she purred. "Goodness! Unicorn-keeper to the king! Isn't that a coincidence? Kendar was just saying to me, 'Mysti, our only hope of speaking to the king is if we can find my favorite relative, Corbly Guzzle. Everyone knows King Steffan relies on him and would never, ever refuse to see us if he asked.'" She pulled her tangled hair behind her ears and added, "All Kendar could talk about this whole trip was Corbly, Corbly—"

"*Welfie!*" Uncle Corbly shrieked, pointing at Mysti's telltale ears with a shaking finger. He vaulted onto his unicorn's back and hollered, "Turn the herd, Torse! Turn the herd and run before—"

It was too late. A wind came up behind us and blew towards the herd. Their nostrils flared, but they didn't move. As I watched, I saw the change begin. Slowly at first, then with sickening rapidity, a blush of pale lavender began at the tip of the lead unicorn's muzzle and spread all the way over his body. The animal to his right whinnied as a wave of daffodil-yellow washed over him; the one to his right turned a frosty blue. The tide of pastel colors moved on from one unicorn to the next. Some turned petal-pink, some minty green, but none escaped. A howl of anguish from the rear of the herd told us that Torse had seen what was happening and knew he had no power to stop it.

Mysti gaped at the rainbow sea of once-white unicorns. "Did I do that?" she asked innocently.

"Miserable Welfie female!" Uncle Corbly's voice trembled with rage. "Where are your wings? If I'd seen so much as a wink of 'em, I might've saved the herd from this!"

"Her wings—They took her wings away from her when we—when we were married," I stammered.

"Married? Then it's true when you called her wife?" Uncle Corbly's bushy brows shot up. "Have you thrown in your lot with the treacherous, unicorn-tinting vermin?"

Basehart chose this moment to come stumbling out of the bushes. "That's no way to talk about the pure and beautiful maiden who's the agent of Eternal Good and Law helping me fight the Lord of Shadows and Evil and Chaos and stuff."

"Basehart." Uncle Corbly was an animal-lover. He uttered my brother's name the same way a minstrel would pronounce *music critic*. "What's all this twaddle you're spouting? Finally fall down one staircase too many, hey?"

"Him!" Basehart jabbed a finger at me. "He's the lord of what I said. And I'm the chosen hero, what the ancient Welven prophecy foretold, who's goin' to kill—Well, maybe not *kill*, him being my brother and that'd upset Mom so bad she'd never let me hear the end of it—but who's certainly goin' to stop him."

Uncle Corbly spoke softly, but we still managed to hear him, even though the traffic on the king's highway was starting up again, skirting the stalled unicorns. "Stop him from doing what?" he asked.

"Um," said Basehart.

"Taking over the universe," Mysti supplied. "Or at least Orbix. Definitely this kingdom."

"And is that why you need to see the king?" Uncle Corbly sounded very calm and pleasant. "To let him know you're the Lord of Dark Thingie?"

"Uncle Corbly, I'm not really—"

"Because I can guarantee you that you *will* be seeing the king. I will take care of it myself. As soon as we pass through the palace gate, I'm going to use my position as chief unicorn-keeper to His Majesty to make sure you're all taken directly to the king's own rooms—"

"Gee, thank you, Uncle Corbly!"

"—*so that King Steffan himself can have the pleasure of sending you all to his darkest dungeon for the crime of exposing royal unicorns to a Welfie!*"

Mysti, Uncle Corbly, and I were in a three-way shouting match, arguing about why only *white* unicorns had to be royal unicorns when I became aware of a second gray unicorn standing beside us. The man riding it was built like a barrel. His face was longer than one of my father's hunting stories. He had to be the herd's rearguard, Torse.

"What happened, Corbly?" he whimpered. "What's come over all our purty white unicorns?"

I didn't hear Corbly's reply. I could only gaze at the sleek, smiling, furry ghost Torse held in front of him.

"Scandal!"

"Hi," said the cat. "I landed on my feet."

THE DRAGON ROSE OUT OF THE SEA OF FLAME. HIS mighty head swayed this way and that, seeking his enemy. Huge jaws gaped wide as green fire poured from his mouth. Smoke the color of blood streamed from his nostrils.

The knight wore shining golden armor and carried a glittering green sword. He strode bravely over the fiery sea to challenge the monster. The dragon's mouth opened in a silent roar. A jet of flame shot out to overwhelm the knight, but the warrior's golden armor didn't show so much as a singe. The knight leaped forward, leaving little trails of sparks behind him, and swung his sword. The dragon's head fell, severed at the neck, to land with a splash of red fire in the sea.

"Whee!" said the king, and clapped his hands. "Do another."

"Yes, Your Majesty," I said wearily, passing hands over the enchanted gravy boat. The tiny, burning images of victorious knight and slain dragon sank beneath the surface of the miniature Majyk sea that had spawned them. "I'll try."

"What my noble and fearsome lord means," Mysti said hastily, "is that he'll try not to disappoint Your Majesty."

"Oh, Master Kendar could never disappoint me," King Steffan replied with sincerity.

"Never," said Scandal, who was curled up in the king's lap, "is, like they say, a hell of a long time."

King Steffan smiled and stroked the cat. "What a smart creature it is. I'll wager there's not another king on all Orbix who owns such a marvelous beast."

"Yeah, us legendary monsters don't come cheap," Scandal informed him. "Behind the ears, Your Kingitude; scratch behind the ears.'' The king obeyed, cooing over the cat like a deranged treacledove.

The royal coach rumbled on over the king's highway, heading for Uxwudge Manor. We would reach home in a little less than two days thanks to the swiftness of the unicorns pulling it and an order from His Majesty sent ahead down the road that all other traffic clear out of our way. Unicorns can cover the same distance as horses, only twice as fast. Fortunately, their speed is unaffected by their color, because every single unicorn that came within sniffing range of Mysti turned a pale pastel shade. One poor animal sprouted a rose at the tip of his horn.

We pulled into post houses along the way several times to change unicorns. As the king's chief unicorn-keeper, Uncle Corbly was also our chief coach driver. I could hear him groan every time he hitched up a fresh team of royal white unicorns and Mysti's uncanny Welven influence turned them all the colors of the rainbow right before his eyes. It broke my heart to hear him.

''But I'm not doing it on *purpose*!'' Mysti protested. ''When they tore off my wings, I thought I was through as a Welfie.''

''You know what they say,'' Basehart said. ''Once a Welfie, always turning unicorns funny colors.''

''There, there, my dear,'' said the king, leaning forward to pat her hand. ''No one is blaming you.''

''You don't mind?''

''Oh, I suppose that when Guzzle shows me his bill at the end of this month for purchasing so many new white unicorns, to replace the ones you've spoiled, I shall mind terribly. But for now I am too happy with this delightful beast to care.'' He tickled Scandal under the chin and beamed like a child when the cat purred. ''Such a find! Such a treasure! What is the loss of a hundred common unicorns next to the gain of a single cat?''

''Does this mean I get sardines without having to beg?'' Scandal asked.

''This means you shall have anything your heart desires,'' the king replied.

''Bingo,'' said Scandal, and settled down to sleep.

The king's coach was an incredible piece of work. As long as we rode in it, we didn't have to stop on the road at all, except to change unicorns. There was seating inside for eight—seating that converted to comfortable beds so easily that even a king could do it. The king's special traveling chef rode in the rear of the coach, where he would prepare elegant meals and snacks in a tiny kitchen. The king's steward served us where we sat, first pulling out ingenious little folding tables from the armrests between our seats. The ride was so smooth, the king's butler could pour our wine and Scandal's cream without fear of spilling a drop. Most convenient of all was a small cubby behind the kitchen, which Scandal kept calling "the skinball litter-box."

It was hard for me to take my eyes off the cat. I kept expecting him to vanish. I kept telling myself that there was nothing spooky about his surviving that terrible fall. Cats are legendary monsters and have their own set of rules. One tale says they always land on their feet. I'd just happened to see the proof of this, that was all.

So why did I still feel miserable?

I tried to take my mind off Scandal, and relax. Everything was going to be all right now, although things hadn't started out so happily back in Grashgoboum.

Uncle Corbly and Torse cut three unicorns out of the herd for us to ride into the city. Unicorns don't need to be broken to the saddle, like horses; they're smart enough to know what you want them to do and to do it with a minimum of fuss. However, another reason they don't need to be broken to the saddle is that they will never *wear* saddles, not ever, take it or leave it. Also, they'll only allow themselves to be hitched to coaches and chariots and wagons if there's at least a king, a queen, a prince or a princess going for a ride. Load up a duke and they balk.

Like Uncle Corbly says, "Unicorns are worse snobs than dragons, and dragons are so snobby some folks say they died out altogether. If you're only going to eat royal virgins, you're looking at a mighty empty table most days."

It wasn't easy riding bareback. Another thing about unicorns is you can't use the horn for a handle. If you try, the unicorn will buck you off his back and show you what the horn's really used for. I held on the best I could, clamping my knees to the beast's light orange sides, and hoped we'd get to Grashgoboum fast.

As soon as we entered the palace courtyard, word of our arrival raced through the halls and found the king in no time. (You can't make a quiet entrance when you're leading a herd of candy-colored unicorns.) He came out on a balcony overlooking the courtyard, swore all kinds of oaths when he saw what had happened to his unicorns, and ordered his men to arrest everyone and he'd sort it out after lunch. Guards flooded the courtyard, dragging us off our unicorns with shouts of "It's the dungeon for you, me proud beauty!" One of them tried arresting the unicorns. The king leaned over the stone railing to shout at the overeager guard. Then he caught his first sight of Scandal, and it was love.

We were hustled into the throne room instead of the dungeon—Mysti, me, Basehart, Uncle Corbly, and Torse still holding the cat. I set off some minor fireworks in the enchanted gravy boat while Mysti pleaded for Mother Toadbreath's life, but the king wasn't paying any attention to us. All he could do was stare at Scandal and smile.

"I will give you pardons for fifty witches if you'll only tell me how you got that astonishing animal," he said.

Torse tried to pretend that Scandal was his, "raised from a pup," but the cat himself soon put an end to that.

"King, you wanna know anything about me, Master Kendar's your man."

"You mean he is your master?" King Steffan asked. He was about ten years older than me, but he had a face that made him look younger. Everything you said came as a surprise to him. His dark eyes would get wide, his weak chin would wobble, and he scratched his head until clumps of coarse black hair were standing up straight all around his jeweled crown.

Scandal snickered. "My master, he says. A cat with a *master*? Naaah, he's just the mightiest wizard Orbix has ever known. Whoa, Kingie, do you ever have things to learn!"

We found out that King Steffan had been a fast learner from the time he was a prince. The first lesson he'd ever been taught by his royal daddy was: *I am the king and you're not.* The second was: *In this kingdom there is* my *way or there is* no *way.* He picked those up right away. Between the two he knew all he needed to know.

"Cat, you will be very happy living with me," he said.

"Now hold onto your royal pants, Your Bozoness—" Scandal began.

The king clapped his hands and the throne room was immediately invaded by a horde of servants, all carrying trays overflowing with a wealth of tantalizing foods. At a gesture from King Steffan, they approached the cat and set their trays down on the floor around him. Scandal looked at heaps of roast meats, mountains of glazed partridges, piles of plump fish. His eyes seemed to grow bigger and bigger the longer he looked. At last, with a happy snarl, he threw himself onto a broiled salmon twice his size and dug in. He only stopped tearing off hunks of fish long enough to look at the king and say, "You know, a cat could get used to this."

Between petting and feeding the cat, King Steffan managed to give us everything we'd come to him seeking. Almost everything.

"I shall deliver my pardon to the witch in person," he announced.

"But Your Majesty, it takes four days to reach Uxwudge Manor—maybe more, if you travel in royal style," Mysti said, trying to make him see reason. "That will be too late. Her trial takes place tomorrow."

"Tchah!" The king waved off her objections. "I'll see about that." He immediately summoned a messenger. "I shall send him on ahead to Uxwudge Manor with a letter marked with the king's own seal. This says Lord Lucius Parkland Gangle is not to begin the witch's trial until I get there," King Steffan said, showing us the document. Then he passed it to the keeper of the king's own seal who in turn held it so that the king's own seal could mark it with his needle-sharp teeth.

"Good boy," said the keeper, tossing the beast a fish.

"Ark, ark!" the king's own seal replied, clapping its front flippers together before it waddled out.

(Anyone can carve a seal out of soft stone and use it to stamp hot wax with the king's device, making a paper legal. That's the trouble: *Anyone* can do it. But no one can forge the unique pattern one special animal's teeth make, which is why the monarchs of Grashgoboum will always live in palaces that smell like herring.)

"And be sure to ride one of my unicorns," the king instructed his messenger. "We can't have them starting the trial without us." After the messenger bowed and left, King Steffan turned to us and smiled. "I've never seen a real witch before. This is going to be *fun*!"

Fun. I suppose it was fun to ride in the royal coach. The king had his servants tie Mysti's rug to the roof, then ordered his guard of honor to follow after us on horseback. It didn't matter to him that we would reach Uxwudge Manor well before they did.

"It's not as if I need protection," the king said. "My people adore me. Besides—" His hand fell on my shoulder. "I'll be safe enough traveling with the greatest wizard Orbix has ever known."

"When's he gettin' here?" Basehart asked. Mysti gave him an elbow in the stomach.

"Your Majesty does my noble lord Master Kendar too much honor," she said, fluttering her eyelashes at the king.

"Hey!" Basehart objected. "He's not the greatest wizard like what you said. He's the Evil Dark Chaos Lord of—of—of Dark Chaotic Evil!" That earned him Mysti's other elbow. She jerked him aside, but not so far that I couldn't hear every word she told him.

"Look, nitwit, Kendar is *supposed* to be named the greatest wizard on Orbix!" she whispered fiercely.

"Ah?"

"Yes, and after we get Mother Toadbreath taken care of, the king is then supposed to give Kendar his very own palace and a steady job and new clothes for everyone and enough money to buy many, many beefsteaks."

"Oh?" Basehart frowned. "How d'you figure?"

"It's part of the ancient prophecy." Mysti seemed to think that settled that. She didn't know that sometimes my brother can be surprisingly—Well, *intelligent* is too strong a word. Let's just say he can pick the most annoying times to stop being led by the nose and to start asking questions.

"How's that ancient prophecy go, exactly?" he wanted to know.

"What? All of it?"

"Just the part that covers the things you were just talking about."

"Oh. Ummmm." Mysti bit her lip. "You wouldn't understand it. It's all in Welfish."

"Translate, then."

Mysti took a deep breath, then began: "There once was a mage named Nantukit . . ." I had to admire her. By the time she was through, she even managed to work in the part about the beefsteaks.

Beefsteaks and all, there we were, hurtling over the highway to home. We passed the time with me doing all sorts of fireworks scenes in the gravy boat. It was tiring and I was running out of ideas for scenes. There had to be a dragon in every one, or the king sulked. There are only so many stories you can do with dragons before it gets to be more of the same.

"Well, Master Kendar?" the king inquired, peering into the glowing depths of the gravy boat. "Aren't you going to do another?"

I was tired. I was so tired of conjuring up dragons in a gravy boat that I said so, right to the king's face. "And I'm not going to 'do another,'" I said firmly.

I could feel Mysti stiffen with horror beside me. She wasn't human—not if she could still make white unicorns change color—but she still knew you don't say no to kings. Not unless you want to try breathing out the top of your neck. "What my noble lord Master Kendar means, Your Majesty, is that he is tired of using his own unworthy imagination to make up these tales. It is his dearest hope that *you* will suggest the next scene.''

"Sure it is," I said.

"Oh, goody!" Kings don't hear sarcasm. Kings only hear what they want to hear. "How kind of you, Master Kendar. I wish I had mentioned your generosity in the letter I sent to the Council of Wizards." He left his seat to open one of the overhead storage bins, Wedwel knows why.

I felt all the blood dive from my face to my feet. I must have looked awful, because Mysti whispered, "Kendar! Are you all right?"

"Not for long," I whispered back. The king was too busy rummaging through the bin to overhear. "He's written to the *Council* about me! As soon as they reply, he'll know I'm not the great and mighty Master Kendar. I never got my Master's wand, I never got my pointy hat, I'm not even wearing a real wizard's robe!"

"So what? By the time their letter gets to him, Mother Toadbreath will be pardoned and we'll be long gone."

I couldn't believe how little she knew of the Council. "Eleven of the most skilled wizards in the realm and you think they'll send a *letter?*"

Before Mysti could say either *Don't worry* or *We're dead,* the king was back in his seat, holding a pile of books in his lap. "Here, Master Kendar," he said, giving me the top one. "I'm sure you'll find plenty of inspiration in here."

"How Loving My Leprechaun," I read. My throat knotted. "By Raptura Eglantine." Yes, there was Curio's unmistakable face and body on the cover. He looked good in that giant shamrock loincloth. I gave King Steffan a sickly smile. "You want me to do *all* of this book?"

"Mercy no!" The king reclaimed his beloved book. "I just wanted you to see how the hero's supposed to look. I can tell you which are the best scenes to do. I've got all her books by heart." To prove it, he began to recite:

"'Amberthral lay back amongst the rumpled glory of her red silk sheets, her tawny hair falling in undulating ripples of gilded splendor over the creamy wonder of her proud breasts. She reached for the golden mirror with the jeweled face of a mermaid and a fishtail handle. Had last night's delicious storm of tender passion changed her? She could scarcely believe that all Corrazo's skillful yet infinitely patient lovemaking had not left some mark upon her enormous, luminous green eyes, her full, generous, rosy lips, her delicate, finely arched eyebrows, her lush, thick black eyelashes, her slender, elegantly upturned nose. 'I never dreamed I could abandon myself so utterly to a pixie,' she mused aloud, before sinking once more into completely satisfied slumber.''

I was still working on the part where Amberthral and Corrazo are cruelly separated during the war with the nectar pirates, when the royal coach came to a halt.

''We're here,'' Uncle Corbly announced. ''Looks like they got your message, Your Highness.''

''Did they?'' said the king absently. He was gazing eagerly at the gravy boat. There was no way he would let either of us have a look out the windows until Amberthral and Corrazo were saved.

''Aye, right enough. There's a crowd of curly-haired peasant children waiting with baskets of flowers to throw at ye—I'd dodge 'em, was I you, judging by the sulky looks of most. There's a nice banner across the front of the manor house, says 'Welcome, Aunt Grativa' with 'Aunt Grativa' painted out and 'King Steffan' put in. There's a table of refreshments under the big elm, and—wait a minute—Yep, as I thought: There's a half-naked warrior battling for his life against a demon.''

I shoved the gravy boat into King Steffan's hands and burst out of the coach. Without me there to control the scene, Amberthral and Corrazo got chopped into bite-sized pieces by the gleeful nectar pirates, but I didn't care. I had to see if what Uncle Corbly said was true.

It was.

''Hail, O Master Kendar!'' cried Grym, waving a bloody sword.

''Woof!'' said the demon.

''What took you so long?'' said Zoltan.

CHAPTER ————— 29

"NO FAIR!" BASEHART BAWLED. "I GO AWAY TO SAVE the universe and he stays home and has all the fun!" He ran from the coach into the house, probably to fetch a sword.

"My, what's all this?" the king asked, looking out the open coach door.

"Unhealthy," Scandal told him. "Let's keep out of the way."

The king was happy to do exactly that, holding the cat to his chest and staying inside the royal coach, while Grym and the demon fought back and forth across the lawn. The demon's talons tore up huge chunks of turf. Grym's sword sometimes overswung, lopping down flowering shrubs and small saplings. The air was thick with the barbarian's curses, the demon's hellish roars, and the angry sobs of Strunk, our family gardener.

"Grym! Catch!" Mysti yelled. She had clambered onto the roof of the coach, grabbed Uncle Corbly's belt-knife, slashed open the ropes holding her rolled-up carpet, and unfurled it. Graverobber whipped through the air.

I rattled off the Levitation of Small-to-Medium objects spell and pointed at the sword, hoping that was the correct gesture for making it go where I wanted it to. Graverobber zoomed straight to Grym's waiting hand. The barbarian uttered a cry of triumph, tossed aside his borrowed blade, and renewed the attack against Zoltan's demon.

My former school-chum had summoned up a real prize this time. This fiend had it all: Scales, horns, claws, talons, forked tongue, spiked tail, fangs, poisonous breath, and body odor. Half its face was naked bone with one googly green eye leaking blood from the socket; the other half was striped black and red with no eyes at all. Instead, five small mouths scattered from forehead to chin said mean things about Grym's mother.

Grym shut them all up with one sideways slice of Graverobber's blade. Along with the blood, a geyser of toads spurted from the demon's severed neck and hopped away into the crowd.

"Oh, catch them! Catch them! You never can tell!" Mother Toadbreath cried in anguish. She was standing on a small scaffold that had been hastily nailed together and placed beside the refreshment tables. If you didn't mind having a hangman's noose around your neck, it was nice to have a place in the shade.

Basehart emerged from the house, sword in hand, and saw that it was all over. "Awwww!" He flung down the blade and stomped off to join my father, who was seated at a long table set up under a big elm. Dad wore a strange hat that looked like what happens if your drop a chocolate layer cake off the top of the East Tower. He didn't seem to be comfortable or happy.

"Yoo hoo! Your Majesty!" Mom came running out from the midst of the curly-haired, surly-faced village children. She pounded on the coach door. "You can come out, now. It's all right. That was just the prosecution and defense lawyers summing up Mother Toadbreath's case."

"Whose case?" The king's head popped out the window, scarlet with anger. "The witch's case? You mean you've gone and had the trial, even after—? I say, didn't you get my message about not starting it until I got here?"

"Yes, Your Majesty," Mom said, making a deep curtsey. "The prosecution lawyer ate your messenger and his mount."

"Aye," Dad confirmed from his place under the elm. "And had the gall to lounge around afterwards, picking his teeth with the unicorn's horn. Demons, *bah*! What's more, that grinning whippersnapper with the beard and the silly hat—the cheeky beggar who's been eating *my* food and enjoying *my* hospitality while making wolf's eyes at my little girl Lucy every chance he gets—that stinking blister said he'd have the bloody lawyer eat us, too, if we didn't get the witch-trial under way."

Zoltan made an ironic bow to my father. "You're too kind, Lord Lucius. I merely thought it was cruel and unusual punishment to make poor Mother Toadbreath wait so long to be brought to trial. The anxiety might be too much for her. Justice must be speedy, in case kings are not."

"We thought that if we got the trial over with and the witch hanged before you got here, you'd understand," Mom said, clasping her hands prettily before her. "Lucius gave the servants special orders: While you were listening to the children sing their little song of welcome, they were to cut down the body and throw a nice tablecloth over the scaffold so we could use it for an extra refreshment table.''

"That was very thoughtful of you," the king said. "However, since I am here now, we shall have no more of this witch-trial nonsense. The lady has my royal pardon." He stepped out of the coach and took in the whole scene while all present bowed low. The good Cheeseburghers from the regular weekly witch-hunts were present, and more besides, all in their finest clothes, all looking mighty nervous.

King Steffan's eyes lit upon Zoltan, still standing there with that obnoxious smile on his face. Zoltan had bowed as nicely as everyone else, but there was something in the way he did it that made it seem more like he'd just thumbed his nose at the king.

"Your Majesty is most gracious," Zoltan said. "Might I ask why you have decided to pardon Mother Toadbreath in spite of the laws against witchcraft?"

"I felt like it," the king replied.

"Yeah, and he also feels like yanking that dumb law off the books altogether," Scandal jeered from the shelter of the king's arms. "Just because some princess has the brains of rice pudding and takes poisoned apples from strangers, you don't all of a sudden arrest a bunch of nice old ladies and hang them from every vacant tree branch like they were Christmas decorations!"

"You don't?" the king and Zoltan asked simultaneously.

"Who's an old lady?" Mother Toadbreath huffed from the scaffold.

"You know what else?" Scandal went on. "When we get back to Grashgoboum, my good buddy King Steffan is going to go over the laws of the kingdom and get rid of *all* the stupid ones."

"I am?" The king was surprised to hear it. "How am I going to tell which are which?"

"Gee, just a wild guess, Kingie, but you could try hiring a good lawyer."

"The cat speaks well!" King Steffan beamed. He beckoned to Grym. "You, there! You in the loincloth. Come here." Grym wiped sweat and black demon-blood from his forehead and trotted over. "You look like a good lawyer to me. You're hired."

"Out upon it!" Grym replied. "What cozening is this? Albeit I did most willingly engage to stand in defense of Mother Toadbreath, I vow and swear by this, mine own true sword, that the whole of my legal strategy was to slay any who attempted to take her life. Ne'er hath I heard myself a good lawyer named. In sooth and verily, I am a barbarian!''

"Sounds like a lawyer to me," Scandal said. "Half the time, you can't tell what the heck he's saying. Like the kingpin says, you're hired."

Grym rubbed his chin. "Beshrew my heart, this misgives me much."

"You know that little problem you've got with your face?" Scandal wheedled. "I guarantee you, no one ever calls a lawyer *cute*."

"Thou speakest with the very tongues of the gods, O oracular animal, and yet I hesitate . . ."

"Palace apartments, three meals a day, and I'll grant you a fresh loincloth every Feast of the Plucked Vulture," said the king.

"Done!" Grym grasped the king's hand and sealed the bargain while almost snapping the royal fingers.

"Besides, cutie," Scandal put in, "you be a lawyer long enough and I guarantee we'll find someone willing to rearrange your face for you."

Grym fell to his knees and blessed the king.

"Your Majesty is a never-ending source of astonishment," Zoltan said through a grin gone stiff. His fingers were twitching, curling around an invisible wizard's wand. I got the feeling there was going to be a brand new demon among us any second.

"I wouldn't do that if I were you," I said quietly, moving to stand behind him.

"Do what, Ratwhacker?" he snapped, whirling to face me.

"Knowing you, anything. Don't try it. Grym's got a sword that can handle all the fiends you want to summon up, and my brother will be thrilled to help him."

"So I saw," Zoltan said drily. "Nor would it hurt your warriors' cause having a Welfie and the witch on their side. No, Ratwhacker, I'll call up no more fiends today. Word gets back to the infernal regions when a demon doesn't come home after a job. The others know who summoned him, and pretty soon you get a reputation for being a dangerous man no sane demon wants to work for. I'd rather not have that happen to me."

"Smart. Take your marbles and go home, Zoltan; it's over. The king pardoned Mother Toadbreath, so you've lost your biggest bargaining chip with me."

"The witch is free," Zoltan admitted. "Now you want me to go away, letting all of Master Thengor's Majyk stay trapped inside you to rot, useless?"

"Oh, I think I'll put it to some good use," I countered. "I don't hold *all* of Master Thengor's power, remember? There's plenty of his original Majyk hoard scattered out there, waiting for me to bring it home. I'm kind of looking forward to the adventure of finding it before it goes back to being wild Majyk again."

Zoltan's face turned pinched and white. "You *know* about how mastered Majyk can turn wild?"

It was my turn to wear the obnoxious grin. "I've learned a lot about Majyk, thanks to Mother Toadbreath and my friends, and I'm going to learn more. I still don't know if I want to be a wizard. Maybe some day I'll get rid of the whole lot, but I can tell you this: When that day comes, I won't be giving any of it to a greedy, power-mad Majyk-guzzler like you!"

I expected Zoltan to throw a curse in my face, or at least some spit. I expected him to growl and snarl and slink away muttering darkly. Instead he simply blinked and said, "I see." Then he turned and strolled casually over to the crowd of village children.

I wondered what he was up to. I was about to investigate, when I was seized from behind and spun around into a gigantic hug. "Dear boy!" Mother Toadbreath gushed. "I knew you'd come through for me!"

"Are you all right?" I asked.

"Never better, child. Your father runs one of the better class of dungeons."

"He'll be happy to hear that. I guess."

"Goodness, I do hope this royal reception won't take too long," the witch said, surveying the crowd. "I'd like to get back to my cottage. I've got so much catching up to do on my soaps, and dear little Norris must be frantic to see me again."

"Surprise!" Grym shouted. He lifted the cloth covering one of the refreshment tables and leaped out of the way as Norris shot out, waving his tentacles and meowing with uncontrolled joy. Mother Toadbreath was bowled over in an avalanche of purple suckers and whiskers.

It was pretty clear to me that I wasn't going to get to resume my conversation with the witch for a while. That didn't matter. I enjoyed having some time to look around and see what my family had done to welcome the king, besides repainting Aunt Grativa's banner.

Now that the trial was over, the front lawn of Uxwudge Manor was overrun with servants in a flurry of activity. Some were carrying out the biggest, fanciest chair we owned, others were dragging the scaffold over to make a stage. I saw Mysti deep in a heated argument with Thorgit, our major-domo and *knoblop* instructor. He wanted to use her carpet to drape the king's platform; she wanted to tear his nose off if he tried. Strunk and his two assistant gardeners loaded the demon's body into a wheelbarrow and hauled it away to the mulch pile.

"There you are, Kendar!" Mom's hands fell on me like twin thunderbolts. "What were you thinking of, running off that way *and* taking your brother with you? How could you leave your poor father and me to run a witch-trial all by ourselves? And then to invite the king without giving me any warning—!"

"Mom, I—"

"Oh, don't even bother trying to explain. A mother gets used to ungrateful children. I've done my poor best, that's all, and it will have to do." She reached into her sleeve and dabbed at dry eyes with a lace handkerchief.

"It looks fine, Mom, honestly."

"Do you really think so? There was so little time between when we got the king's message and the moment Zoltan's fiend ate the messenger. I can't say I much care for that young man, Kendar. I hope he isn't a close friend of yours. Although to do him justice, he was a tremendous help to me in getting the village children to memorize the little song of welcome I wrote for King Steffan."

"You wrote a song, Mom?"

"It's nothing, nothing at all." Mom tried to look modest, but you could tell she was proud of herself.

The platform was finished, the big chair pulled on top of it, and a few horse blankets dragged out of the stables to cover the bare wood. It wasn't very grand, but like Mom said, it would have to do. Thorgit sported a black eye, and used the other to shoot dirty looks at Mysti, who was seated solidly atop her carpet, arms folded.

King Steffan mounted the platform with the help of several Cheeseburghers, who got down on all fours to make a human stairway for the royal feet. He was still carrying Scandal.

Scandal . . . I felt like someone had punched me in the stomach. *When this is over, Scandal's going to go away with the king. He'll live in luxury all his lives in the royal palace of Grashgoboum and I'll never see him again.* My eyes started to sting. I tried to stop being stupid. It wasn't like the time I thought he'd died, falling off the flying carpet. He'd be alive, he'd be pampered, he'd be spoiled rottener than he already was, he'd have everything his heart desired—

He wouldn't need me anymore.

I was so unhappy, I missed the first few words of King Steffan's speech of thanks to my parents. ''—awfully kind of you to go to all this trouble,'' he was saying. ''And I give you my word as your adored and beloved king that when my army catches up with the royal coach, they won't steal any chickens or burn your crops. My ministers tell me that whenever an army goes anywhere, that's the first thing people complain about—stolen chickens and burnt crops. You'll all be pleased to know that my guardsmen are not just any military riffraff. They are all given a thorough examination. When they get to the question that goes 'Do you like to steal chickens and burn crops?' they had better answer 'No' or out they go! I'll grant you we do have one sergeant in the ranks who likes to steal crops and burn chickens, but ever since we made him the army cook everything has been—''

''Your Majesty, the children have a little song of welcome for you,'' Mom spoke up suddenly. The villagers cheered at the top of their lungs so that the king couldn't say another word about the burnt chickens.

The chorus of curly-haired children came forward, dragging their flower baskets, and bunched up in front of the king's platform. Mom fluttered around, pushing them into two lines. They kept sticking their tongues out at her and shoving each other. One angelic child sat down and began to sniffle. Another little darling loudly announced, ''Milgrub's wet hisself!'' The unlucky Milgrub howled and punched his accuser in the shoulder. A fight broke out. Curly hair is just as good for yanking as straight.

While all this was going on, I noticed one child still standing among the adult villagers. He was one of those children always called ''big for his age,'' which means he was as wide as he was tall, and all muscle. The little brute had narrow eyes that must have been keen enough when it came to picking out smaller children to bully. He had a face like a cranky dragon and a temper to match, but he did have a lovely head of curly golden hair, so Mom had drafted him for her children's choir. He looked like he'd rather be holding a big stick or a rock instead of a flower basket.

Zoltan was patting him on the head and smiling. The brat smiled back, like the fierce lowyena does before it rips the throat out of a hyena, its mortal enemy. I didn't know Zoltan liked children. Maybe this one reminded him of one of his pet fiends.

''Percival!'' Mom called. ''Percival, you are keeping His Majesty waiting. Kindly join the rest of us, won't you, dear?''

Percival snarled, but he jogged right over to take his place in the crowd of children. It was amazing. The moment he arrived, the other kids stopped fighting, fidgeting, and fussing. You'd probably get the same effect if you dropped a large snake into a roomful of rappids. Everyone froze, staring uneasily at Percival, ready to duck, dodge, or run like hell the instant he made a threatening move. As for Percy, he coolly took his place in the front row and held his flower basket primly in front of him. He was still wearing that blood-chilling lowyena smile.

"Isn't that nice?" Mom simpered. "Now, my darlings, just like we rehearsed it! And a-one, and a-two, and—"

Twenty grumpy faces lifted towards the king. Twenty squalling voices began to sing the same words to twenty different tunes:

> "Welcome, welcome, good King Steffan,
> Unto Uxwudge welcome be.
> Welcome, welcome, good King Steffan,
> To this place we welcome thee.
> Welcome, welcome, welcome, welcome,
> We do sing so happily.
> Good King Steffan, please be welcome.
> We have flowers to welcome thee."

Then the children all reached into their baskets and scooped out handfuls of grubby day's-eyes and cowslips and newts-lie-bleeding, and tossed them at the king. I've never understood why pelting someone with dead plants is supposed to make him feel welcome, but there's a lot I don't understand.

For one thing, I didn't understand why Percival wasn't tossing his flowers at the king. He seemed to be the sort of kid who'd enjoy any excuse for throwing things. Instead, he just stood there waiting, his head cocked to one side, one eye closed, one arm stretched out straight in front of him, thumb up. What was he doing?

I got my answer when the children began the second verse of Mom's song:

> "Welcome, welcome, good King Steffan,
> We are here to welcome thee.
> Welcome, welcome, good King Steffan,
> With a hearty welcome free.
> Welcome, welcome, oh yes, welcome,
> W-E-L-C-O-M-E.
> Good King Steffan, we sing welcome.
> With more flowers we welcome thee."

While the kids hurled the second wave of blossoms at the helpless king, Mom scampered up to me and whispered, "Did you like my song, dear?"

"Very, uh, welcoming."

"I knew you'd like it." Mom's dimples showed, then vanished when she saw Percival standing idle while the rest of the children were doing their best to bury the king under a mountain of wilted greens. "Percival, what *are* you waiting for?" she snapped.

Percival winked at her. "A clean shot, Lady A.," he said, and reached into his basket.

The flower looked like any other day's-eye, except it was as big across as a man's hand and it sparkled in the sunlight. Percival grasped it by the petals, drew back his arm, and with one smooth move threw it. It sailed up and over the edge of the platform, sliced through the other flying blossoms, and struck King Steffan right in the middle of his forehead.

The King stood up shakily, dropping Scandal. "Ladies of the Society for the Preservation of Voondrabs," he said, a rigid smile on his face, "I can't tell you how happy I am to be here, because I'm not."

Then he keeled over, off the platform.

THE CHILDREN SCATTERED, EXCEPT FOR POOR MILGRUB;
King Steffan fell on top of him when he toppled off the platform.
The villagers gasped, then ran. They knew that when kings start
keeling over, the safest place for a peasant to be is Far Away.
Zoltan went with them.

All these escapes made it easier for the rest of us to reach the
king. Mother Toadbreath and Norris got there first. She instructed
the octopuss to roll His Majesty off of little Milgrub, who stared
at us with terror-stricken eyes before taking to his heels without so
much as a thank-you. Father stood beside His Fallen Majesty
bellowing for hot water and clean sheets.

Basehart poked Dad in the ribs. "Hot water and clean sheets is
for when the hounds have pups."

"Well, if it's good enough for my hounds, it couldn't hurt the
king," Dad snapped back at him.

"Basehart! Daddy! Kendar! Yoo hoo!" We all saw my sister
Lucy waving from the great stone balcony that ran across the front
of Uxwudge Manor. "Someone come inside and I'll give you the
proper things for helping King Steffan."

I cupped my hands to my mouth and shouted, "Why can't you
just bring them out yourself?"

She cupped her hands to her mouth and shouted back, "Because
Daddy's an old silly who says a witch-trial is no place for a proper
young lady so I've got to stay in the house! I've been watching
from up here the whole time. I saw Zoltan give young Percy a bag
of candy and do something funny with the ugly brat's flower
basket. If I were you and I wanted to know what happened to the
king, I'd hunt down that miserable wizardling and—"

"Anon!" Grym cried, brandishing Graverobber and taking off after Zoltan. "Eftsoons!" We knew he meant business.

"Wait for me!" Mysti called out, and sprinted gracefully after the barbarian.

While Basehart went into the manor house to fetch the first-aid supplies, my mother hovered nearby, watching Mother Toadbreath examine the king. "Is he alive?" Her voice trembled.

The witch laid her ear to the royal chest, then uttered a sigh of relief. "He is."

"And did he like my song?" Mom asked eagerly.

Mother Toadbreath gave her *that* look.

I felt a familiar nudge at my ankle. "What the heck happened?" Scandal demanded.

"King Steffan got hit in the head with a flower," I told him.

"No, seriously."

"I'm telling you the truth. It was a day's-eye."

"For real?" The cat sniffed disdainfully. "What a wimp."

"Whatever that is," I said. "Not that it's going to matter much once the king's guardsmen get here and find him like this."

"Why? What's gonna happen?"

"Not much: They'll just burn Uxwudge Manor to the ground and kill us all. *Try* to kill us all," I corrected myself, remembering how well my Majyk protected me from death. Too bad it wouldn't also protect my family and my friends. Would I want to live, only to watch them die?

"No problem," Scandal said. "I've got a plan."

"What?"

"We run away."

"That's no plan!"

"We run away very, very *fast*."

"That's better. Too bad it won't work. Dad would never abandon Uxwudge Manor, and Mom would never abandon Dad."

"Aw, that's sweet," said the cat. "On my world, we've got a special name for people that loyal."

"What?"

"Dead."

I grew grim. "No; not while I'm here."

"Kendar, baby, cookie, sweetie, doll, trust me; you can't use your Majyk to stop a whole army," Scandal wheedled.

"I can try."

"That's just what my uncle Fluffy said when Aunt Cuddles told him he couldn't cross the Santa Barbara Freeway. We buried him in a pizza box."

The crowd around the fallen king got thicker by the minute. Uncle Corbly and Torse came to kneel beside His Majesty, weeping and wringing their hands. Sometimes, for no good reason, one of them would exclaim, "Wurra-wurra!" and the other would respond, "Lackaday!" They were up to thirteen *wurra-wurras* and twelve *lackadays* before Mother Toadbreath told them to make sense or shut up.

Basehart appeared, carrying a bowl of fragrant, steaming water and some fresh white towels just as Grym and Mysti returned, dragging Zoltan along between them. Maybe it was my imagination, but I thought my old schoolmate wasn't putting up that much of a struggle.

I didn't have the chance to think about it. While Norris propped up His Majesty, Mother Toadbreath soaked a towel in the water, wrung it out, folded it neatly, and patted it over the king's forehead. He moaned and twitched. The witch sniffed the water and smiled at Dad.

"Ah! Your daughter is a very bright young girl. She's taken almost the exact herbs I would have chosen and steeped them in this basin: crushed mint, feverfew, dotage, hamsterbane, wake-me-when-it's-over, and just a hint of parsley. This will bring His Majesty around soon enough."

She applied another compress, then held the bowl under King Steffan's nose. The king moaned louder and opened his eyes with a jerk. "Where am I?" he asked.

"You're at Uxwudge Manor, Your Majesty," Mom said with a dainty curtsey.

"I am? Good gods, *why*?"

Before anyone could explain, we heard the thunder of tramping feet coming up the road and the sound of many manly voices raised in song:

> "Oh, we march, march, march,
> Yes, we march, march, march,
> And we march, march, march
> For good King Steffan!
> While we march, march, march,
> As we march, march, march,
> We all march, march, march
> For good King Steffan!"

Scandal looked at my mother. "Someone's been stealing your material, lady."

The first ranks of the king's guard came into view, spears held high, banners flying. Their leader wore a helmet shaped like one of Mother Toadbreath's soap cauldrons, except it was gold, upside-down, and topped with three plumes of the rare demantante bird—red, white, and blue. As soon as he laid eyes on the king, he didn't like what he saw at all. He barked orders to the men, who quickly spread out to form three sides of a square around us. The fourth side was Uxwudge Manor itself.

Dad surveyed the mass of spears, arrows, and drawn swords, all of them pointed at us. "Something wrong, Officer?" he asked the head guard.

"You've got His Majesty on the ground," said the leader. "And that's Captain Bamf to you."

"It's perfectly good ground," my father replied evenly. "And that's nuts to you, Bamf."

"*Captain* Bamf." The head guard crossed his arms. "And I don't care how good your ground is, sir, it still don't do to leave kings laying about on it. They gets all dirty and then there's no decent use to be had from 'em 'til they're washed."

At a word from Mother Toadbreath, Norris set the king upright. His Majesty still looked dazed, but he managed to smile and wave weakly at his army. "Hello, hello, I'm so glad you could all join me for the opening of this troll bridge," he said. "Now if someone will toss the troll a piece of raw meat, I think I can safely cut the ribbon and the first pedestrians will have a fifty-fifty chance of getting to the other side without being eaten."

Captain Bamf gave Dad an accusing glare. "He's crazy!"

"And?" Dad was unconcerned.

"We can't have us a crazy king!"

"Come, come, Captain, we've done it before, Wedwel knows."

"Yes, but those kings as we had that was crazy, they was crazy to start with. A man knew where he stood with 'em straight off. As captain of the king's guard I'd go see one of 'em and he'd tell me, 'Bamf, today I want the men to go and conquer all of Orbix.' I'd bow all sharp and proper and I'd say, 'Yes, Your Majesty,' and I'd leave the room and come back an hour later. The king'd ask me, 'Well, have you conquered all of Orbix?' and I'd tell him, 'Yes, Your Majesty, and I brought you back a nice little present from our trip.' Then I'd give him a toy boat or a wooden sword or something. *He'd* be happy and *I'd* be happy."

The captain sighed mightily. "But when you takes a perfectly good working king and goes and turns him crazy—Well, a man don't know whether His Majesty's going to *stay* crazy, does he?

One day he might up and tell me to conquer Orbix, only this time he'd really *mean* it, and to hell with all the toy boats in the kingdom! Where'd I be then, eh? I'm a career army man and I won't stand for this. It's *undependable*, that's what it is!''

"Now, now, my good man," said Dad. "No need to sputter so. King Steffan is perfectly crazy now and I'm willing to give you my word as a gentleman that he'll stay that way."

Captain Bamf's expression turned suspicious. "Here now! Did he get like this from you leaving him laying about on the ground?"

"He's just had a little knock on the head is all," my father said, trying to brush the whole matter aside.

"With a day's-eye," Scandal put in. "Right spang in the middle of his forehead."

"What? He got hit with a *flower* and that's how it left him?" Captain Bamf was so shocked, he didn't even notice that he was speaking to a cat. "I always said the royal family's been marrying their own cousins for too damn long, but no one listens to me!"

"Hey, soldier boy, it wasn't a *real* day's-eye. See that bearded geek over there?" Scandal nodded to where Zoltan was being held by Grym and Mysti. His pointed wizard's hat had been crushed and broken and his robe had some minor rips, but he was taking it all calmly. Too calmly.

"Aye, I see him." Captain Bamf had the face of a battle-hardened veteran, the nose broken in several places, the skin sun-browned, scarred, and bristly with stubble. When he frowned it felt like there was a storm getting ready to break over your head. "Was he the one who struck down His Majesty?"

"Well, he's the one who magicked up the dandelion of doom," the cat said. "He bought off some midget caveman to do the actual flower-flinging, but it's his idea, his flower, and if you're smarter than you look, his neck."

"I confess it." Zoltan didn't even blush. "It happened just as the beast says."

"Hoi! Who're you calling a beast?" Captain Bamf demanded.

"Yo, G.I. Joe!" Scandal batted at Bamf's leg. "Don't bust a bandolier. He means me."

"Aye?" The captain regarded the cat. "And what manner of bad dream did you spring from, laddie-buck?"

"Los Angeles."

Captain Bamf blanched and made a hasty gesture meant to ward off evil. "Don't you go uttering no words of mystic power at *me*, you misbegotten spawn of a dragon's armpit! Lois Ann Jellies right back at you!''

"He's a cat," I said.

"Is that what he says?" The captain squinted one eye at Scandal. "Has he got a license for it?"

Zoltan's voice poured out over us, smooth as syrup and twice as gooey. "Please, Captain, let the beast be whatever he claims. This is not helping your king. The fault for his present condition, as I have freely admitted, is mine. You must understand, it was all an accident. I never wished to harm King Steffan. My real target was young Kendar Gangle, there." He nodded at me.

"Right!" Captain Bamf pulled a small pad and pencil out of his belt-pouch and began to write. "So that's one count of attempted assault, one count of *royal* assault, one count of conspiring and hiring to commit assault, and one count of hiring an amateur to do the job. I wouldn't want to be in your shoes when the Assassins' Benevolent League gets wind of this, my lad!"

"I feel simply awful about the whole thing," Zoltan replied with a cheerful smile. "Especially the part about missing Kendar. The spell I placed on the day's-eye was intended to turn him into a babbling idiot. We are mortal enemies, you know."

"That don't signify. What it comes down to is you've gone and damaged the king."

"Not irreversibly," Zoltan murmured.

"Eh? What's that?"

"I only said, Captain, that since it was my magic which left King Steffan as you see him now, my magic can also restore him to his former self."

"Why didn't you say so, man! You two!" the captain barked at Grym and Mysti. "Release him at once!" They hesitated, which made Captain Bamf impatient. "Come on, come on, let the man go. Where d'you think he's going to run to with my men all about?"

"Verily, 'tis so," said Grym. He nodded to Mysti and they released their hold. Zoltan stepped gracefully away from them, rubbing his wrists and arms.

"Now if someone will be good enough to fetch me the enchanted day's-eye which did this, I can proceed."

My own brother Basehart brought the flower. "This had better be good, wizard," he growled.

"Oh, it's going to be better than that," Zoltan purred. He set the giant day's-eye on top of King Steffan's head.

The king bobbed and bowed this way and that. "Yes, Lord

Bisto, it *is* a lovely day for a coronation, isn't it? I only hope this heat won't make the egg salad go all funny. Mayonnaise has no sense of loyalty.''

He was still talking to ghosts when Zoltan said a few choice words of power, did something fancy with his hands, and whisked the day's-eye off the king's head.

''Ta-da,'' he said with a straight face.

The effect was electrifying. King Steffan reacted as if someone had doused him with a pail of ice water. His eyes got wider and wider as he looked all around him, fully awake at last. ''Am I at—Uxwudge Manor?'' he asked.

''You are indeed, Your Majesty!'' Mom clapped her hands together with childish delight to see her king restored to his senses. ''And you'll be pleased to hear that we haven't used any mayonnaise at all on the refreshments.'' She gestured towards the tables that still sat undisturbed in the shade of the hanging tree.

''Uxwudge Manor,'' the king repeated thoughtfully. ''And I am King Steffan.''

''Well, at least he hasn't got magnesia,'' Captain Bamf commented. ''There's a mercy.''

''And I came to Uxwudge Manor because—because—'' He scratched his head.

''Because of Mother Toadbreath!'' Scandal piped up.

''Oh yes! Now I remember. *You* came to bring me here on account of Mother Toadbreath.'' He pointed at me. ''And you, and you, and you.'' He singled out Mysti, Basehart, and Scandal, then pointed at Grym and said, ''And when we got here, *you* were defending her. Chopped the head clean off the other fella.''

''Thou hast hit the mark, Majesty,'' Grym affirmed.

''Right!'' The king was extremely pleased with himself. ''That's the whole story, then. I remember it all. Mother Toadbreath—she's a witch, isn't she?''

''So I am, Your Majesty.'' Mother Toadbreath dropped an awkward curtsey to the king.

''I rather thought you were. Well, it's all quite simple, then: We've got laws against witchcraft in this kingdom. We've also got laws against people who try befriending witches.'' He turned to Captain Bamf.

''Hang them all, then we'll eat. I don't remember having lunch at all.''

CHAPTER ——————— 31

"WELL, IT'S BEEN REAL," SAID SCANDAL. HE HAD A
noose around his neck and was seated on the shoulders of a very
tall guard. The man didn't look happy. I wouldn't, either, if I'd
been picked to be the scaffold for a cat. Like Scandal told him,
"These little sharp things you feel digging into your shoulder are
called claws and I know how to use them. Feeling *lucky* today?"
But the poor man had no choice: After a lot of fussing and several
experiments, Captain Bamf decided that this was the only way to
make the beast hang.

The rest of us sat on five of the king's own unicorns under the
hanging tree. It was going to be a group-hanging and Mother
Toadbreath's original scaffold would never be big enough for all
of us at once. Besides, it was still being used as the king's
platform. Grym used his sharpest legal argument in our defense,
but there were too many guardsmen. They overpowered him and
took away his sword. Basehart got the same treatment. Mysti put
up a good fight, too. More than one of the king's men wouldn't be
walking straight for a week.

For all the good it did. We were still stuck on unicorn-back,
wearing rope necklaces and waiting to dance on air.

"This isn't going to work on Kendar, you know!" Mysti
shouted at Zoltan.

"If you mean this won't kill him, I already know that," Zoltan
replied. "But I don't think he'll enjoy hanging by his neck for a
couple of hours that much, even if it can't kill him. In the long run,
it might make him see reason."

"I don't know why he won't just give you his Majyk, Zollie."
King Steffan pouted. "After all, you *are* my Court Wizard and I
am the king and I *did* command him to do it."

251

I swear, every time Zoltan heard the king call him by his new title, it made his head puff up an extra size. The so-called restoration spell had given King Steffan a whole lot of memories he'd never had, including that bit about Zoltan being the Court Wizard.

"Never mind, Your Majesty, he'll come around," Zoltan said. "Or he'll twist in the wind until he does."

"*Imaginesia*," Mother Toadbreath whispered.

"Don't you mean *am*nesia, toots?" Scandal asked.

"I said *imaginesia*. What's wrong with the king. First you forget everything you ever knew, then you remember things you didn't ever know. I read about it a time or two in my books, but I never thought to see an actual case. My, this *has* been an educational day!" She looked pleased.

"I could use some education," I whispered back. "Did your books say anything about how to cure it?"

"Oh dear. I can't remember."

My heart sank. In a few minutes, the hanging would begin. There stood Mom and Dad on the lawn, surrounded by a crowd of guardsmen. Mom was crying on Dad's chest and Dad was trying hard not to cry himself. A little farther off, Mother Toadbreath's pet octopuss, Norris, was making the sky ring with his yowls of misery while eight men held his arms behind his back.

Uncle Corbly and Torse stood a little way off, keeping an eye on our unicorns. There was no danger of the animals bolting out from under us. They were too smart for such tricks. They would wait patiently for as long as it took until their keepers gave them the signal to run. Uncle Corbly and his assistant didn't look too happy with their new roles as executioners. Torse even said "Wurra-wurra" once, in our honor, but Uncle Corbly was too heartbroken to reply "Lackaday." The rest of the king's servants remained inside the royal coach where they had comfortable seats and a good view.

"Come on, come on," the guard who was supporting Scandal grumbled. "That's the army for you: Hurry up and wait. When're we goin' to get this circus on the road?"

"What's the rush, dogbreath?" Scandal asked sweetly and dug his claws into the man's shoulder until he yelped.

The only reason we weren't already dangling was up on the balcony of Uxwudge Manor. My sister was not behaving herself at all.

She'd started yelling nasty words at King Steffan and Zoltan

and all the king's men from the moment they attacked us. She
vanished from the balcony for a while and tried to rush out of the
house to help, but Captain Bamf had ordered the doors barred to
prevent our servants from racing to the aid of their master's sons.
(He didn't know our servants very well. Good Cheeseburghers all,
as soon as the trouble started they all went and hid in the wine
cellar.) We heard Lucy pounding on the doors and using words
that made Captain Bamf himself blush.

When Lucy discovered that she couldn't get out of the house,
she reappeared on the balcony with one of Dad's longbows. The
guards retreated from Uxwudge Manor, raising their shields in a
protective formation around King Steffan. They didn't have to
bother. Remember the nectar pirates from *How Loving My
Leprechaun*? In the big battle scene, Amberthral picks up a sword
from the dead body of one of the sailors and kills about
seventy-five pirates, even though she's never held a blade before
in her life. Lucy didn't just write that nonsense, she believed it.
She used up four quivers of arrows without hitting anything but
air, then had a tantrum and broke the bow into a million pieces by
bashing it against the balcony railing.

Now she had dragged out a box filled with all of Mom's
perfumes and cosmetics and was throwing them at the guards. She
was a much better shot with a scent-bottle than with a bow. No one
was getting killed, but the men she hit had to scamper away and
wash, or die of embarrassment when their comrades teased them
about how pretty they smelled. There was no way we could have
a nice, dignified hanging until something was done about Lucy, so
we sat and waited.

"By Prodromia's lean and muscular thighs, O Master Kendar,"
I heard Grym mutter. "If thou art awaiting the fabled last minute
ere thou wilt snatch our bacon from the flames, I humbly suggest
that it hath arrived."

"But the king's guards took my gravy boat away. Look, there
it is on the refreshment table."

The barbarian cocked his head and saw that I spoke the truth.
There sat the enchanted gravy boat, glowing brightly amid
the trays of cookies and cream-cheese sandwiches, just out of
reach.

"Dost thou truly need such gewgaws to manifest thy powers?"
Grym asked.

"Maybe, maybe not. Using the gravy boat seems to make it
easier for me, but what's the use? Gravy boat or no gravy boat, I

can't work any spell with my hands tied behind my back like this." My voice was low and tense. "It's not just the words, it's the gestures."

"Forsooth? Meseems that such gesticulation was mere folderol and stage-dressing wherewith to beguile the gullible."

"The book says that when you're using Majyk, the words are to get its attention and the gestures are to point it at the job you want done."

"I am but a simple barbarian, and yet it striketh me that after so many centuries you wizards might have come up with some more efficient manner of commanding this force on which you do so much rely."

"A force . . ." I thought about it. "I think there's something more to Majyk than that."

"Even so? And what might that be?"

"I don't know, but I think I'd like to study it and find out."

"May the gods grant thee a quick mind, then, for methinks thy chances for an education shall eftsoons run out at the rope's end."

I decided not to remind him that, thanks to Majyk, I couldn't be killed. He could. It was awful enough that Grym was going to die without making him feel bad about it.

"Kings!" Scandal's guard snorted. "Look at him, just a-sittin' up there, pretty as you please, not a care in the world, while honest sojers is forced to get theirselfs all a-stink fightin' off that wildcat on the balcony."

"If I had this damned noose off, I'd show you what a real wildcat can do," Scandal hissed.

"Huh! Makin' us all lollygag about like this ain't right. Do you want *my* opinion. I'd say as how he's just a-waitin' for the problem to go away!"

"That's my sister," I said. "She won't go away."

"And a lovely, high-spirited girl she is, young man. But even in a house that grand, she's bound to run out of ammunition soon or late, and *that's* when you'll hang. A disgrace, that's what I call it!"

"You'd free us?"

"I'd hang you. But I'd do it in short order and have done! Our king sits around on his royal backside much longer, he'll forget about the hangin' entire, you mark my words. You'll be left a-sittin' on these point-horned ponies until Orbix shifts shape again."

''Perchance someone ought remind him of our presence,'' Grym suggested.

''The way his mind's been muddled?'' The guard gave a sarcastic laugh. ''It'll take more than a few polite words in the royal hairy ear to make *that* crowned cuckoo remember anything.''

''*That's it!*'' Scandal exclaimed, bouncing so suddenly that he almost lost his grip on the guard and hanged himself without royal permission. ''It's like with amnesia! It's got to be! On TV, every time someone gets a knock in the head and loses his memory, all it takes is another knock to get it back! What we've got to do is give King Steffan one good, hard clunk in the noggin and he'll remember about pardoning Mother Toadbreath and letting us go and making Grym his lawyer and giving Zoltan a kick in the tail. It's the shock that does it.''

''Good idea!'' Basehart said eagerly.

''Great idea,'' I said with a lot less enthusiasm. ''And how are we going to do it?''

We all exchanged looks. We were *here* and the king was *there*. Our hands were tied. So much for that.

''Ninnies,'' Scandal's guard muttered. ''Even could you do it, you'd only be buyin' the purchase of more trouble. It's a hangin' offense to whack kings in the head, whether or not they needs it.''

Scandal's whiskers drooped. ''Aw, nuts,'' he said.

''There, there, dear,'' Mother Toadbreath comforted him. ''It wouldn't have worked, anyway. When you mentioned giving the king a shock to restore his memory, you helped mine. Imaginesia is different from amnesia. A knock on the head won't help at all. False memories have pushed the true ones clear out of the king's mind. We'd have to come up with some of his true memories and force them on him until they manage to shove the false ones out again.''

''We tried that!'' Mysti objected. ''All the time I was fighting the guards, I kept yelling at the king to remember all the promises he'd made about you and Kendar and—''

''A tap on the head with a feather won't cure amnesia,'' the witch said. ''You've got to use a rock. And when it's *imaginesia*, you can't use just any old memory. It must be one that the patient treasures most.''

''How can we know what that is?'' the Welfie demanded.

''We can't,'' said the witch, and bowed her head.

"Oh, yes we can!" Scandal's whiskers perked up. His eyes glittered and his fur gave off short bursts of Majyk sparks.

"Ow! Cut that out!" his guardsman protested. "You've gone and singed my best uniform, you have!"

Scandal didn't care. The cat was trembling with energy. "Lucy!" he shouted. "*Lucy!*"

My sister heard him. She lowered the perfume bottle she'd been about to fling. "Yes?" she called back. "What is it?"

"The book! Say something from the book!"

"What book?"

"*Yours!*"

My sister is a smart girl. She didn't hesitate a moment. She took a deep breath, held onto the railing to steady herself, and began to recite at the top of her lungs:

"'Wave after wave of searing passion crashed over Lyriana as she felt Bruno's hot breath at her throat. His paws were skillful yet gentle, lifting her already dizzy senses to new heights of sheer rapturous abandon. She seized his shaggy head and whispered urgently into his pointed ears, "Yes, *yes*, my darling! I am yours!" Their mutual pleasure mounted into a universe-shaking climax. At the supreme moment of all, Lyriana tossed back her mane of silvery hair and, joining voices as they had already joined bodies and souls, howled at the full moon with her beloved.'"

There was a stunned silence. "Ick," said Zoltan, breaking it.

"What do you mean 'Ick'?" King Steffan demanded indignantly. "That was the most beautiful scene from one of the most beautiful books ever written: *How Wondrous My Werewolf* by Raptura Eglantine." The king then rubbed his forehead and added, "And what are you doing here?"

"I'm your Court Wizard," Zoltan said.

"You are *not*! Kendar Gangle is supposed to be my new Court Wizard. Where is he?" The king looked around impatiently.

"He's over there, Your Majesty," one of the guards said. "Waiting to be hanged with the rest."

"What rest? What hanging? There wasn't supposed to be any hanging!"

"There was, according to *this* bird, Your Majesty." The guard jerked his thumb at Zoltan. "He said you wanted to hang the Welfie, the witch, and the warrior. Also your new Court Wizard and the whatd'youcall'em—the one in the loincloth—the lawyer. Oh, and the cat."

There was a minor earthquake in the general vicinity of the

king. When the dust settled, Lucy was off the balcony and out on the front lawn with everyone else, Zoltan was in chains, and we were free.

Scandal sat in King Steffan's lap and grinned. "Well, like they say, no noose is good noose."

Zoltan wasn't the only one to curse him for that.

CHAPTER ——————————— 32

IT WAS A LOVELY PARTY. THE KING'S GUARDS ALL SAID they'd never eaten such delicious cream cheese sandwiches. Captain Bamf had to scold several of them for hiding extras down the front of their uniforms "for later."

"There's only one thing an old sojer loves more'n a good cream cheese san'ich," Scandal's former scaffold said, giving Mom a roguish wink. "An' that's a nice, hot piece of—"

"Oh, please, *don't*!" Mom's cheeks turned red and she fled to the shelter of the refreshment table.

"What's wrong?" the guard asked. "'Twasn't like I expected *her* to give me a nice, hot piece o' cheerberry pie." He crammed the rest of the sandwich in his mouth and stalked off, mumbling about women.

Dad was so happy to have his sons saved from hanging that he didn't say one harsh word to his daughter about the balcony scene.

"These book-things," I heard him remark to Captain Bamf. "Just a passing fad. Girls will be girls. She'll get over it. It's best not to make a fuss or she'll keep on reading just to spite me. Ignore it and it'll go away, I always say."

"That's what we say in the army, too," Captain Bamf agreed. "Especially about dragons."

I found Lucy helping Mom at the refreshment table, serving punch to the guards. I was able to drag her away and whisper, "Dad still thinks you only *read* books."

"King Steffan doesn't suspect a thing either," she told me. "He believes I'm just another Raptura Eglantine fan. Let's keep it that way."

"You're sure?" I teased. "He'd ask you to marry him in a second if he knew who you really were."

"No thanks."

"Why not?" I never did learn when to let go of a joke. "King Steffan is young and not too bad-looking, for a king."

"I'm not blind, Kendar." Lucy gave me a look that could have melted rock. "King Steffan is a very handsome man."

"He's no Curio."

"Neither are you," she shot back. It hurt. "But there's still a girl silly enough to prefer your looks to his." Using only her eyes, she indicated a shady spot under some flowering pigwhistle bushes where Mysti and Mother Toadbreath sat eating lunch and scratching Norris behind the ears.

She didn't mean Mother Toadbreath.

"Mysti?" I exclaimed. It came out sounding stupid for a very good reason. "She thinks I'm handsome?"

"She thinks a lot of things. Why not try asking her what they are sometime?"

"Yes, but—but she doesn't *really* think that. She just latched onto me to escape from being a Welfie. She told me her name on purpose so the others would force her to leave."

"She could have told it to Grym just as easily," Lucy pointed out. "Grym looks a lot more like Curio than you ever will."

"So you're saying she really, really, *really* likes—?"

"I'm not saying another word about it. And neither are you. All I'm telling you is to pay a little attention to something besides Majyk sometimes."

I frowned. "This still doesn't explain why you won't tell King Steffan who you are. I mean, if you *like* him—"

"I'd rather have him marry plain Lucy Gangle and get to meet Raptura Eglantine later than the other way around."

I wandered off just like Scandal's former scaffold, muttering a lot of the same things about women.

"Master Kendar! Come and join us a moment." King Steffan waved to me from his makeshift throne. All the servants he'd brought along from Grashgoboum were milling around behind him, saying nice things about the cream cheese sandwiches. As I walked nearer, I saw Scandal sitting in the king's lap as if he owned Uxwudge Manor, Grashgoboum, and all Orbix. I felt a pang when I remembered that the time for us to go our separate ways was closer than ever.

"What can I do for you, Your Majesty?" I asked, kneeling on the lawn.

"First, you can tell your lovely mother that she makes the best cream cheese sandwiches I have ever tasted."

"Thank you, Your Majesty, but it's our cook who deserves the credit."

"Then please tell your lovely mother that she certainly knows how to hire good cooks."

"Yes, Your Majesty. Will that be all?"

"Well, there is one more teensy-weensy little thing." The king leaned forward and whispered, "What am I going to do with *him*?" He jerked his head at Zoltan.

My ex–school chum was standing to one side of the platform, his wrists shackled with cold iron cuffs. That old smug smile of his was gone. There was no room for it on a face so full of hate. Two of the king's men were assigned to guard him. They didn't look happy. They were missing all the cream cheese sandwiches.

What to do with Zoltan? I didn't have the faintest idea, but I bet I knew what someone like Grym or Mysti would say:

"Kill him." Or someone like Scandal. "Kill him very dead."

"Nice kitty," said the king. "You told me that already."

"You bet I did," the cat replied. "But I still see him wasting oxygen."

"I've never had to order the execution of a wizard before." King Steffan was troubled. "Besides yours, Master Kendar, and then I wasn't myself. I don't know whether I *ought* to kill him, you see. Generally speaking, I mind my business and the wizards mind theirs. It wouldn't do to get the Council of Wizards angry."

I had to agree with him there.

"So what's the problem?" Scandal insisted. "Look, Zoltan is bad news. Kill him first; then if this Council shows up and says you did the wrong thing, you say, 'Oops! My mistake. That's why they put erasers on the ends of pencils.' Then you make a big donation to the Home for Retired Wizards and everyone goes away happy."

"Everyone *left alive* goes away happy," I said. "Scandal, you don't know wizards."

"*I* don't know wizards? Ha! And what have I been hanging out with ever since I popped in on this orbiting loony bin?"

"All right, then you don't know the *Council* of Wizards," I corrected myself. "They are eleven of the oldest, wisest, sharpest, slyest, strictest, meanest, most merciless—"

"Don't forget snappy dressers," the cat said, his ears suddenly pricking up.

"What?"

"Turn around."

I did, just in time to see my sister Lucy offering a tray of cream cheese sandwiches to eleven white-bearded wizards in silver-spangled black robes. They had appeared on the front lawn of Uxwudge Manor without any warning, without even a puff of smoke or a clap of thunder. When you're a wizard of the Council, you don't need to show off or prove anything. People are afraid of you on principle.

The Council members ate three sandwiches apiece and four entire trays of cookies before they even came over to pay their respects to the king. Dad went half out of his mind giving orders to the servants to fetch chairs for the wizards. The servants weren't doing too well following orders. Remember how they were hiding down in the wine cellar? Well, they weren't just hiding.

One wizard, a mage called Master Walpole, stared coldly at the milking stool our servant Gunderslot offered him. Poor Gunderslot's nose was as red as a bloodshot rose, his eyes were blurry, he swayed back and forth like a reed in a gale, and he had a bad case of the hiccups.

"Chair?" he said feebly, holding out the stool.

"If you insist," said Master Walpole, and Gunderslot was turned into a big blue armchair with plenty of cushions. The wizard sat down with a contented sigh and said, "A footstool would be nice. Are there any spare children in the neighborhood?"

When all the members of the Council were seated, their leader, Master Starkadder, called for silence. Don't you just bet he got it.

"The Council of Wizards will come to order. I have here in my hand a letter sent to me by King Steffan the Good Enough." Master Starkadder made the letter flap up into the air, high above the roof of Uxwudge Manor. It then began to stretch and grow until it covered most of the sky and every word on it was as tall as a pitchfork.

Master Starkadder set a pair of spectacles on his nose and tilted his head back to read the gigantic letter for those unable to read it for themselves. "As you can see," he said, "the king writes to us about one *Master* Kendar. He says that since the death of Master Thengor, he has lacked a Court Wizard and would like to let us know that he has chosen this *Master* Kendar for the job. He then says that he hopes we are all well and that my lumbago is better." He snapped his fingers and the letter vanished. "It is."

"Oh, I'm *so* glad to hear that," King Steffan burbled. "Truly I am. I don't have lumbago myself, but I'm sure it must be very—"

"Shut up," said Master Starkadder.

"When we got the king's letter, we checked our records,"

Master Walpole said. "We found no *Master* Kendar anywhere." His eyes were as small and hard as two dried peas. When they swept the crowd, I felt as if a thousand mousekitters were nibbling on my spine.

"We think it is only good manners to meet this *Master* Kendar," said Master Starkadder.

"We think it is a wise idea, especially since, when we checked our records again, we did find a number of complaints made by several of the late Master Thengor's students, servants, mistresses, concubines, his widow, Lady Inivria, and his associate, Master Benidorm, against one Kendar *Ratwhacker*," Master Walpole said with a tight little smile. "What might you tell us about *him*?"

No one spoke.

"That's me," I said, taking a step forward. My voice sounded a lot louder than I expected. Instead of a meek, terrified peep, I'd admitted who I was right out, so that everyone could hear. "I'm Kendar Gangle of Uxwudge Manor, also called Ratwhacker."

"Also called *Master* Kendar!" Mysti shouted. "And don't you forget it."

Grym waved his recovered blade, Graverobber, overhead and added, "Likewise called with pride sword-brother unto mine own self, Grym the Great, once of the barbaric horde of Uk-Uk the Unspeakable, presently a lawyer unto His Majesty."

The Council members all made faces like they were smelling a pile of dead slimegrinds on a hot day.

One of them said, "I am Master Moondog, keeper of the records. An apprentice wizard may receive his robe and his hat from his teacher, but he may not be named *Master* until he has proved himself by examination before the Council. He then receives his wand and his name is inscribed in the Great Book. We also include a picture, although nine times out of ten it doesn't look a thing like him. I know that I had my eyes closed when they did mine, and no one told me my hair was sticking up like that. They refused to give me a second chance, which isn't fair at all. I mean, when the next keeper of the records takes over, he's going to think I looked like that all the time and so are all the other keepers who come after him and—"

"Master Moondog, you'll be dead by then; shut up, too," said Master Starkadder. The chief wizard peered at me. "So you are the one."

I forced myself to meet his gaze without showing any fear. Inside, I was hollering for my mother. Actually, I was hollering for my enchanted gravy boat; it was much more useful than Mom. Too bad that I'd left it on the refreshment table.

"Well, *Master* Kendar," the head of the Council said. I was starting to hate the snide way they all kept saying *Master* when they meant me. "How does it feel to be the proud owner of so much Majyk?"

"Now, or when it first happened?" I replied, looking him right in the eye.

Master Starkadder's fuzzy white eyebrows rose. "Is there a difference?"

"I think so. When I first got tangled up in Master Thengor's Majyk, I was terrified of it. All I could think about was how to get rid of it the fastest way possible. When I found out I couldn't give it away until I learned how to control it, I was even more frightened."

The old wizard's blue eyes glittered. "Am I to gather that you're not afraid any more?"

"Oh, I'm still afraid of Majyk. I always will be. So would anyone who's smart. Majyk's powerful stuff. It's made our world what it is, ripped it apart, and put it back together any way it wanted. Some wizards only think about what they can do with Majyk; they never worry about what Majyk can do with them. Yeah, I'm still afraid of it, but I'm not going to let it go."

"Very enlightening." Master Starkadder tapped the tips of his twiggy brown fingers together. "May I ask why any sensible young man would hold onto something that scares him so much?"

"I've heard about fires burning down whole cities, but I don't see anyone giving up cooked meat."

"Why are you listening to this claptrap, Master Starkadder? The puppy's gotten a taste of power and likes it, that's all!" Master Walpole snapped. "He's not as big a fool as he looks. All this talk about fearing Majyk is poppycock. Look at him! He loves it; it shows in his face."

The chief wizard's bright eyes never left mine. "What I see in his face is truth."

Master Walpole made a disgusted sound. "You're getting soft, Starkadder. I'm telling you, he's as greedy for Majyk's power as any of us. We wouldn't be where we are today if we hadn't fought and schemed and plotted and connived to gobble up as much Majyk as we could hold. Master Thengor was the worst of the lot, and I say that when this boy soaked up Thengor's Majyk, he soaked up Thengor's greed as well."

"You know what?" I said. "You're right."

That took Master Walpole by surprise. "I am?"

"If Master Thengor loved Majyk because of what it gave him the power to do, then I love Majyk the same way. If he wanted to get more and more and more of it so that he'd be able to *do* more, I'm just like him."

"Ahhhhh." Master Walpole's mouth stretched wide. "You see, Starkadder? I told you so."

Master Starkadder's lips twisted into an unreadable expression. "Come here, boy," he said to me. I approached the Council. My knees shook a little from holding them stiff so long. When I was almost in Master Starkadder's lap he said, "That's close enough. Now tell an old man: What is it that you've used your Majyk to do?"

I told him. I told him about using Majyk to help Grym fight Zoltan's demons and to save Mysti's life and to fly us all to Grashgoboum to get Mother Toadbreath's pardon. The whole Council listened.

When I was done, Master Starkadder said, "Thank you, young man. We will now deliberate and reach a verdict." The eleven wizards closed their eyes for the time it takes to breathe in and out once, then opened them. "We've decided."

"Oh yeah?" Scandal shouted from the king's lap. "Well, we're gonna appeal! This is a kangaroo court! We were railroaded!" He sprang down and ran to join me. "Perry Mason's gonna hear about this! And Rumpole! We'll take it all the way to the Supreme Court if we—"

Master Starkadder looked at the cat. "Marvelous," he said. "You really are a creature of legend come to life."

"Plus I've got a tidy little nest egg of my own Majyk tucked away, Grandpa, and I'm ready to throw it behind my buddy Kendar before you can say *hocus pocus*, so don't mess with us!" Scandal stalked back and forth stiff-legged in front of the Council.

"Your loyalty to your friend is admirable," the chief wizard remarked. "But wouldn't you like to hear our verdict before you decide to fight it?"

Scandal gave the wizard a look that said *I don't trust you.* "Okay." He spoke cautiously. "What *is* the verdict?"

A different wizard stood up and said, "I am Master Caxton, recording secretary of the Council. It is the decision of this august body that since Kendar Gangle, called Ratwhacker, has not passed any of the official mastery tests for high wizardry, he does not have the right to be called Master Kendar."

"Hey!" Scandal objected. Master Starkadder said one word

and made a brief gesture. A shining bubble of air sealed itself around the cat. Scandal pounded on it with his paws and butted at it with his head, but it wouldn't break. His mouth moved without a sound escaping.

"I didn't feel right telling a legendary beast to shut up," said Master Starkadder.

"Furthermore," Master Caxton continued, "since Kendar Gangle has not received his wizard's robe or hat from a recognized instructor of Majyk, he is forbidden to use his powers on his own."

I started to say something, but I didn't want to wind up in a bubble, so I kept quiet. It was the loudest quiet I ever knew, full of the sound of me screaming *It's not fair!*

"Instead, he is commanded to continue using Majyk in the company and with the help of any and all beings who possess some measure of their own Majyk."

"I'm *what?*" I couldn't help asking that. It just popped out.

So did Scandal. His bubble of silence burst and out he bounced. "I get it!" the cat exclaimed with glee. "He's a Student Driver!"

"I beg your pardon?" Master Starkadder leaned down to Scandal's level.

"When he's solo, Majyk's a no-no, but it's okay when he's got a keeper standing by."

The chief wizard was bemused, but not displeased by Scandal's explanation. "You have grasped the general idea, if a bit crudely. Since in the past he has used his Majyk for the greatest good when teamed with others who have Majyk too, we thought it best for him to continue doing so. It will be best for everyone, in the long run."

I could feel my face lighting up with joy. "So you mean it's all right for me to go on learning about Majyk as long as I stay with Scandal?"

"The king's new pet? Hardly. You can't stay in the royal palace forever. You've got all the rest of Master Thengor's strayed Majyk out there, waiting for you to collect it. In fact, the Council orders you to do so. It would be a terrible thing if so much formerly domesticated Majyk were to fall into the wrong hands. With you, at least we know it will be safe."

"But what about what you said?" I protested. "Scandal's got part of Master Thengor's Majyk in him, and you told me I can't use it without him!"

"Not without *him*," Master Starkadder corrected. "We said you can't use your Majyk without someone—*anyone*—who has some Majyk of his own. Or *her* own. Ah yes, you will have to forgive us, young man. We did hear the news—we always hear the news—but we have not yet had the chance to congratulate you. On behalf of the Council of Wizards, I would like to wish you every happiness on the occasion of your marriage." He beamed at Mysti. "I think that a Welven wife has more than enough Majyk in her to satisfy the ruling of the Council."

"I'm not his wife," Mysti said hoarsely. She wouldn't look at me. "I only got him to marry me so I could get away from my relatives."

"There, there, you're not the only one," Master Moondog said. "I get some of my best wives that way."

"You don't understand." The Welfie's voice broke. "He doesn't want me!"

"Well, he'd better want you. He can't take the king's pet cat with him on his quest and you're the only one who qualifies as a recognized P.P.M."

"Possessor of Personal Majyk," Master Starkadder explained.

"Let him take someone else!" Mysti sobbed. "Let him take Mother Toadbreath!"

"He can't take me, dear," the witch said, putting her arms around the Welfie's shuddering shoulders. "I don't use Majyk for my magic. Perhaps he could borrow Grym's sword instead? That's just chock full of Majyk."

"Although to part with mine true steel-brother, Graverobber, is as to ripping the living heart from out of my bosom and holding it, dripping with blood, before my dying face," Grym said solemnly, "I'll do it."

"No, no, that won't do." Master Caxton shook his head. "We said it must be a *being*, not a *thing*. Look, we're busy wizards. We've given you our ruling. How you work it out is your own affair. We have other business to attend to, so if you'll be good enough to move on . . ." He shooed us away like chickens.

We all drifted over to one side. I tried to speak to Mysti, but she kept turning away from me. I was making one more try when Master Caxton announced, "The next order of business is the apprentice Zoltan, called Fiendlord."

Zoltan was dragged before the Council. This time he did put up a fight, snarling all sorts of curses. None of them could work, of course; not with his hands shackled so heavily. The biggest gesture he could make was to wiggle his fingers.

"What have we here, Master Moondog?" Master Starkadder asked when the guards at last forced Zoltan to stand still.

Master Moondog consulted an apricot-sized crystal ball. "Falsely calling himself *Master* Zoltan when he hasn't got his wand yet, bribing a rather revolting child to attack King Steffan with an imaginesia spell and—" He looked up. "There is a letter of complaint from a non-wizard on file against him, too."

"Indeed?"

"Yes, from a former servant-girl of Master Thengor's called Bini. The subject is rather, ah, delicate. The girl feels that it is rather, um, *urgent* that Zoltan honor the promise of marriage he made to her before the, ahem, seven remaining months expire. If you follow me?" He blushed and tucked the ball away.

"We do, Master Moondog, thank you." Master Starkadder sat back in his chair. "Zoltan, what do you have to say in your own defense?"

"Everything I did, I did for the best of reasons," Zoltan replied proudly. "A tragic accident stole Master Thengor's Majyk from its rightful heir—or heirs," he added quickly, "and gave it to a bungling misfit who couldn't even learn the simplest spell while he was a student at the Academy. Since that time, I have devoted my whole life to recovering my late Master's hoard. If I have used questionable means to accomplish this, I ask your pardon."

Master Walpole tapped the arms of his chair. I hoped poor Gunderslot wasn't feeling it. "In other words, you meant well," he said.

"I had only good intentions," Zoltan agreed.

"Well, we all know where the road leads that's paved with those, don't we, gentlemen?" Master Starkadder said. The council nodded, and again all of them closed their eyes for the space of a single breath.

When they opened them, Master Caxton, the recording secretary, announced, "It is the verdict of this Council that since it is a shame to waste such a well-paved road, you shall depart on it at once."

"In other words," Scandal said with a gleeful leer, "you can go to—"

"I am *condemned*?" Zoltan roared. His face darkened with rage. "You old fools. I don't need you and your stupid examinations to tell me when I am a Master of Majyk! I refuse your judgment. I reject your authority. I'll show you all who you're dealing with!"

He rattled off a lot of ominous words, but he couldn't move his hands at all. I only saw his fingers twitch and curl very slightly. So did the Council. They knew as well as I did that you need gestures as well as words if you want to use your Majyk. There was no cause for alarm.

"Now, if you are quite through with your little tantrum," Master Walpole said drily, "perhaps we can—"

His words froze on lips that had turned suddenly blue. He slapped at his ankle, let out a moan, and slid out of his chair. The king's guard who rushed to his side just had time to say, "He's dy—" before he, too, froze in mid-sentence, his lips blue, swatted at his ankle, and toppled over with a horrible groan.

"What is this?" Master Starkadder demanded as all around him other members of the Council and the king's guard began to fall. "What's happening?"

Zoltan just smiled.

"NOW WILL YOU RECONSIDER YOUR VERDICT, GENTLE-men?" Zoltan asked the Council. "Or will you all lie in the same grave?"

The gathering on our lawn had turned from a party to pande-monium. The royal unicorns—no fools—all stampeded. The ones still in harness took the royal coach with them, the loose ones scattered every which way. Uncle Corbly and Torse took off after them.

Guards ran everywhere, mostly crowding around the king's platform. They darted their eyes suspiciously in all directions, trying to see an invisible enemy. Whenever another guard tum-bled, the ones left standing stabbed the air with their spears and swords. It didn't do any good, but it made them feel better. Until the next man fell.

"Let me pass! I'm a witch!" Mother Toadbreath cried, shoving her way through the mass of guards surrounding the Council. She flung herself on Master Walpole's body and made a quick examination. "He's still alive—just barely," she said. "He's been poisoned."

"Oh, I knew there was something fishy about those cream cheese sandwiches," Master Moondog whimpered.

"Not unless cream cheese sandwiches *bite*." The witch gave him a severe look. She lifted the hem of Master Walpole's robe to reveal a small half-circle of punctures on his ankle. It was no bigger than the mark I could make with my thumbnail. Everyone still left standing rushed to check the other victims. They found identical wounds on all of them.

"That doesn't look like any snake bite I've ever seen," Master Starkadder said.

"That's because it's no snake," Zoltan replied. "It's a fiend. One of my best fiends."

"Perdition take it for a cowardly demon!" Grym cried. "Doth it fear to face its death? I have slain full many of its brethren and this one shall I slay also. Lift thy spell of invisibility from it, Zoltan, lest I lift thy skull from thy shoulders!"

"And he doesn't mean eftsoons, he means *now*," Mysti said.

"Come, come, my beefy friend." Zoltan looked at Grym's drawn sword and only smirked. "Invisibility is one of the greater enchantments. By now even a lout like you must know that big spells require big gestures. The fiend I've summoned this time is completely visible."

"Then where—? *Agh!*" Grym dropped Graverobber and slapped his ankle, then crumpled to the ground. Like all the others, his lips were blue.

Mysti knelt beside him at once, laying her head to his chest to listen for the heartbeat. Suddenly her eyes flew wide open and she gave a piercing shriek. I expected her to fall over, blue-lipped. Instead she pointed wildly at the thick grass and exclaimed, "There it is! There is goes! Ugh! I never saw anything so ugly in my life. Oh, stop it, stop it, Kendar!"

"Stop what?" I saw nothing but a thin ripple in the grass. "Where?"

"*There!*" She jabbed her finger insistently. "It's heading for the refreshment tables!"

"It's heading wherever I tell it to go," Zoltan said. "Only a Welfie has eyes sharp enough to see a fiend so small." He raised his shackled hands and wiggled his fingers. "Big spells to summon big fiends demand big gestures, but sometimes it's the little things that count."

A demon so small it could race through the grass unseen. Why not? A bird in the sky can look down on the thickest forest and never know that a man is running through the trees below. A tiny demon, summoned by a tiny spell, but a demon whose bite was poison.

"Kendar, you must stop it." Mother Toadbreath echoed Mysti's words. "These men are dying. In my cottage I've got some soaps that might be the antidote, but if we don't hurry and bring them here—"

"Take one step toward your cottage, witch, and you will be the next to feel my little friend's bite," Zoltan snapped. The next instant he was smiling again. "Let's leave it to the Council. Free me, forget the charges against me, give me what I want, and I'll let the witch go fetch her antidote. Refuse and . . ." He let his voice trail off. There was no need for him to say what would happen if the wizards didn't give in.

"Your threats mean nothing," Master Starkadder said. "We can destroy your fiend."

"How?" Zoltan countered. "With firebolts? You can't hit what you can't see. Will you destroy this entire estate and everyone here, only to discover that my small helper has hidden himself under the hem of your own robe?"

Lord Starkadder said nothing. I could tell by his frustrated scowl that Zoltan was telling the truth.

"I say!" my father objected. "Wizards or whatnot, you lot had better not try that whatsit with the firebolts on *my* property. When a man offers the hospitality of his home in good faith, he doesn't deserve to have the guests burn the whole blasted place down around his ears! For Wedwel's sake, give the cheeky monkey what he wants and send him packing. Then you can hunt down the hooligan a week or so after and give him what for."

"Dad, I don't think that's going to work," I said.

"Why not?" Dad puffed out his moustache. "It's worked for me every time a fox got at my pigeons."

"In pity's name, do something!" Mother Toadbreath cried, laying a hand on Master Walpole's chest. "This man is almost dead."

Master Starkadder threw a dozen curses at Zoltan, but they were only angry words. "I cannot let the innocent die. Very well: You are free." He spat out the spell that melted the iron cuffs from Zoltan's wrists. "Now begone, and take your hellspawn with you. We have lives to save."

Zoltan rubbed his wrists. "Not so fast," he said. "There's also the matter of your sentence against me."

"We lift it. There. You have my word that the records shall show no past charges against you. As for the future, look out for that yourself." The old wizard's blue-eyed glare was enough to freeze a dragon's heart.

"Thank you." Zoltan raised one eyebrow. "And—?"

"What do you mean '*And—?*' you shameless, brazen, impudent, presumptuous, arrogant, saucy—"

"Dork," said Scandal. He jumped onto Grym's chest and announced, "What Houdini's trying to say is he ain't going nowhere until you give him what he wants. Three guesses what that is. The first two don't count and the third starts with *Kendar*."

"Well-guessed, cat," Zoltan said, untroubled by the animal's sharp tongue. "Would you like to try another?"

"Sure. Like how about I guess how long you could keep smiling if one of the king's men puts an arrow through you?"

"And leave my little friend all alone, with no one he has to obey?" Zoltan clicked his tongue. "He'd miss me. That would make him sad. When he's sad, he bites harder. Now here's a riddle for you: If *one* bite from my pet fiend leaves a man on the brink of death, what will *two* bites do?"

His mouth and eyes turned hard as he added, "Kendar, I'm glad you've learned some control over your Majyk. It will be easier for you to force it out of your hands and into mine. You can come away with me now, or you can stay and learn the answer to my riddle. I'll start with—"

Lucy screamed and leaped onto the refreshment table. "I felt something touch my leg!" she cried.

"The nerve!" Dad snorted.

"Oh, good, a volunteer," Zoltan said pleasantly. He called out to Lucy, "Staying up there won't save you, my dear. He can climb up after you any time he likes, unless . . ." He looked at me with hooded eyes.

It didn't take me long to make my choice. I never had a real choice to make. My home was a wreck, my friend Grym was dying, my mother was having hysterics, my sister's life was in danger, and my gravy boat was out of reach. I couldn't focus my Majyk fast enough without it. If I took one step towards the refreshment table, Zoltan would order the tiny fiend to bite Lucy; *twice*. Even if I could get my hands on the gravy boat, I didn't know any spells of destruction. Fireworks, yes; destruction, no. Besides, how could I fight what I couldn't see?

"I give up," I said, bowing my head. "I'll come with you."

Zoltan's moustache curled up just like Scandal's whiskers. "Very smart, Ratwhacker."

"I'll come," I repeated. "But first you've got to make that little demon go away and leave everyone else in peace."

"Fair enough." Zoltan wiggled his fingers and said, "*Verticillium japonica.* Done. Happy? Then let's not overstay our welcome." He linked his arm through mine and started to lead me away, saying, "Which way are the stables? I don't think your father will mind lending his own son a couple of his best horses."

As we walked past the refreshment tables, Lucy called to me, "Don't do it, Kendar! Don't just give in to him!"

I paused long enough to tell her, "Don't you see? I've got to."

"But once he's got what he wants, he'll kill you." I saw tears in her eyes.

"Why, what a thing to say!" Zoltan pretended to be shocked. He clapped me on the back. "Kendar will be the first to tell you, I've always been his dearest, closest, most trustworthy—"

"*Grrrrrrrrrr!*"

It was a sound like none I'd ever heard before. It made my bones feel hairy. I had to turn and see what could possibly make such a blood-curdling growl. At the very least it had to be a dragon.

"*GrrrrROWrrrrrROWrrrrrROW!*"

All right, a *flock* of dragons.

"*ROWlllllerrrrROWfffffzzzzgrrrrrROWROWROW!*"

Either that, or one very angry cat.

Scandal crouched on Grym's chest, snarling deep in his throat, his brightly burning eyes fixed on something invisible. *Whik-whik-whik* went his tail, lashing back and forth. Every other muscle in his body was tensed, wound up tighter than a snail shell.

"Trustworthy *this*, you midget Mephistopheles!" he screamed, and pounced into the grass. Growling and spitting, he swiped his bare claws at . . . nothing.

"It's the fiend!" Lucy cried. "Zoltan lied! He *didn't* banish it! The cat's small enough to see it! Oh, Kendar!"

Zoltan threw one arm around my neck in a headlock. "Move and I'll have it run away from that cursed beast and kill your sister *now*."

Could he do it? Was the small fiend fast enough? I didn't dare to find out. I could only watch and pray that Scandal would have better luck than me.

It looked that way, at first. The cat sprang forward, ears flat, paw jabbing, then sprang away. "Gotcha!" he crowed. I thought I saw a drop of something green fall from the tip of one curved talon. "Say your prayers, you hairball from Hades!" He crouched low, wiggled his hips, and leaped.

His shriek of pain shattered my heart. He jumped straight up, waving his front paws frantically as if something had wounded both of them. I heard Lucy gasp and Zoltan laugh out loud as Scandal rolled over and lay still.

"That's done," Zoltan said. "Now come, unless you'd like to stay and see me do the same for all your—*unk*."

You'd expect a man to make a much louder sound when he's been hit on the head with an entire glass punch bowl.

"Why, thank you, Master Thengor," Zoltan said. "I promise

you I'll find the perfect place to hide all of your Majyk.'' Then he lay down to sleep on it.

''Hurry, Kendar,'' Lucy said. She shoved the gravy boat at me, her hands still damp with spilled punch. ''The fiend has no one to tell it what to do, now. You've got to kill it before it runs amok.''

''My pleasure.'' There was a knot in my throat. When it came undone, I'd cry over Scandal's death, so I held onto it and turned it into anger instead. My cat—my *friend*—was small enough to see the fiend he fought. *Small* was the answer I needed. Grym's great sword couldn't stop the creature, but I knew someone's that could.

The surface of the enchanted gravy boat sparkled as the knight in burning armor emerged. He stepped out onto the palm of my hand, drawing his miniature sword. I spoke the words that told him what sort of dragon he was going to fight. All flame and fireworks, he saluted me as I knelt to put him down in the grass.

But then a strange thing happened. The instant before he stepped off my palm and set off in search of the demon, I heard myself utter other words, words I'd never learned from Mother Toadbreath's book. It was as if the Majyk itself whispered to me. My vision blurred and I felt like I was being swept into a whirlpool that spun me down and down into the depths of dark and secret waters.

When I could see, I was standing in the middle of a grove of green bamboo. The stalks towered above my head, bending and whispering together with every passing breeze. I looked at my right hand and saw the fine, bright blade I carried in an iron glove.

This was what I wanted: To be more than an onlooker. To be the one to kill the monster that had killed my friend. I tilted my visor down and followed the demon's trail, a path of broken stalks that was plain as black on white to my eyes.

I found the fiend within sight of Grym's fallen body. The barbarian was transformed into a range of rippling brown mountains. When Mysti bent over to listen for his heartbeat once more, her shimmering hair became a mass of clouds drifting over the peaks. The demon scampered through the grass, chittering with evil joy. Green-skinned and lumpy, it had a face that was mostly mouth and a mouth that was all teeth. It was headed back to give Grym the second, fatal bite.

I broke off a stalk of bamboo and slashed a crude point on the end. It wasn't a real spear, but when I threw it, it flew well enough to hit the demon right between the shoulders. The fiend shrieked and whirled to face me. Black venom dripped from its fangs.

Clumsily it groped behind until it was able to wrench the spear out of its back. Then, with a terrible, open-mouthed hiss, it charged.

I'd never used a sword before in my life, but the fiery knight my Majyk made had fought a dozen dragons for King Steffan's entertainment and won. Together we easily sidestepped the fiend's first attack, drawing blood from its side as it hurtled past. The monster relied on its small size and deadly bite, not on its brain. Foolishly it repeated the same tactics it used on its gigantic victims. It couldn't seem to understand that this was a battle on a different scale.

Once the demon did manage to topple me from my feet. Our fight had trampled many stalks, slick with the fiend's blood. I had the bad luck to step into a green, slippery pool of the stuff just as the creature attacked. A glancing blow from its shoulder was staggering enough to make my armored feet shoot out from under me. I rolled over and up onto one knee as soon as I hit the ground, in time to feel the wind whistle through the demon's teeth as its jaws snapped shut on the spot where my head had been. A splash of venom seeped through my visor, just missing my eye. My cheek burned even though I was inside a body that was itself a work of fire.

I scrambled to my feet and braced myself. There would be no more taunting my enemy, no more dancing out of his reach. The time for that was done. It rushed at me with claws high and mouth roaring. The skill with which I stabbed and slashed at the demon was the knight's, but the satisfaction I felt when the blade went into the creature's heart was all mine.

When I cut off its head, the green blood rose up steaming in a cloud of glittering white mist all around me. It smelled like lilacs and washed the demon's burning venom from my face. I sighed and closed my eyes with pleasure as the pain trickled away. All I wanted now was more of that delicious, healing scent. I took a long, deep breath into my lungs and smelled . . .

. . . fish?

"He's awake! Look, he's awake!" Mysti's voice filled my ears. "It's all right, you can stop licking him now."

Licking? I opened one eye.

"Hiya, boss," said Scandal with a smile. "Hey, did you get the little creep? Heck, what a question! You wouldn't be alive to tell the tale if not. Good work, *Keemo Sabee*. I always did say that if you want someone to kick serious demon-butt, Kendar's your man."

"You're alive," I stated, both eyes open and staring.

"You got a problem with that?"

"But weren't you—?" I didn't want to say it, so Scandal saved me the trouble.

"The D-word? Deader than disco, yup. Oh, by the way, while you were out, your brother and father brought back the soaps Mother Toadbreath needed. Everyone's gonna be fine, up to and including Tarzan."

"You were *dead!*"

Scandal shook his head. "You know, boss, you aren't gonna get anywhere in this world without a high-school diploma. Weren't you the one who told me that on Orbix that bit about cats having nine lives works just like the always-fall-on-our-feet stuff?"

"Nine . . . nine . . . nine . . ." I couldn't stop that idiotic repetition of the word, until the cat sat up on his haunches and patted my arm.

"Eight to go," he said. "Let's make them count."

If I continued to think about it, I was going to hear something inside my brain go *ping!* So I stopped thinking about it and instead asked Mysti, "Where's Zoltan?"

"Over there." The Welfie nodded towards the king's platform while she helped me to my feet. I saw Zoltan in the middle of the Council talking *very* fast.

By the time we reached him, he was saying, "—your own word of honor, Master Starkadder, and you know it!" His hands were not only cuffed, but covered with iron mittens to prevent him from moving so much as a fingernail. In spite of that, he looked triumphant.

"It is true." Master Starkadder sighed. "I did give him my word that we would lift his sentence."

"You see?" Zoltan gave everyone an insufferable smile.

"Do you *have* to, Master Starkadder?" King Steffan pouted. "It doesn't seem fair, him going and ruining a lovely lawn party and then not even getting a slap on the wrist for his shenanigans!"

"I gave my word," the old wizard repeated. "I gave it as head of the Council of Wizards. If I break it, no one will trust our judgments ever again."

"But for him to get off scot-free—!"

"Master Starkadder?" Scandal batted the wizard's ankle. The old man jumped, forgetting for a moment that the tiny fiend was dead. "Master Starkadder, could I have a word with you?"

The wizard looked dubious, but he nodded. I picked up the cat and held him near Master Starkadder's ear. As Scandal whispered, I saw the chief wizard's face slowly break out into a smile.

"*Good* kitty!" Then he said, "*Pronuba chuppah oikophobia!*" and made several curvy signs in the air.

"So *there* you are at last, Zoltan Fiendlord!" Bini exclaimed, stamping her foot. "And what do you mean by going off like that and telling me you'd be back in a minute? *I'll* give you a minute you won't forget!"

"Oh, dear," Mom sniffled. "I always cry at weddings."

EPilOGUE

"KENDAR?" MYSTI REACHED ACROSS THE BED AND shook me.

"I'm awake, I'm awake," I said, snorting and snuffling like an old bear.

"I've got something for you."

"Ummmm." I pulled the covers over my head and tried to go back to sleep. I heard Mysti sigh.

"I don't know what's wrong with you," she said. "You don't take an interest in anything anymore. Are you sick? Do you want a physician? Maybe a chiropractic healer would straighten things out."

I could see that I wasn't going to get any more rest until I paid attention to Mysti. "All right, I'm up," I said grudgingly. "Now show me what you've got."

She did. It was a fruit basket.

"Not another one!" I sank back into the pillows with a groan.

"Same kind, same source." Mysti twirled the big basket by its handle. "You'd think that by now Zoltan would catch on to the fact that you are not stupid enough to eat any fruit he sends you, especially not poisoned apples."

"Yeah, I know. They're always so *perfect*-looking." I sat up and took one out of the basket, turning it this way and that. "Real apples aren't this red and round and shiny. Who does he think I am? Some dumb princess?"

"Careful." Mysti perched on the edge of my bed and held up one finger in warning. "We've got a dinner party in the royal palace next week and that dumb princess will be there, only now she's a dumb *queen*."

"Do we have to go?" I whined. "All she can talk about is how much she misses the simple life in that woodland cottage, and all her husband can talk about is how lucky she was that he was brave enough to kiss her and break the apple's spell when everyone else thought she was dead.''

"I know," Mysti agreed. At the last dinner party in Grashgoboum, she'd been trapped by that boring man for hours. "If you want my opinion, he wasn't brave; he was desperate. No live girl would hold still long enough for him to kiss her. How anyone could ever give *him* a name like Charming—!"

"His parents had already named his older brother Prince Obnoxious. So let's not go."

"We have to go."

"Let's say we're sick."

"Do you really *want* King Steffan to show up here with another get-well gift?"

"No." I didn't even have to think about it. "Peacock noodle soup and the complete works of Raptura Eglantine. And I had to eat *all* the soup while he watched. 'We can't have anything nasty happen to our Court Wizard,' he said. If he wants to talk about nasty, he should try that soup!"

"What do you want me to do with the apples?"

"Throw them in the moat."

Mysti made a face. "I tried that. The slimegrinds threw them back. They also hired a professional letter writer to send us a note saying that if we try that again, they'll complain to the authorities. Then they ate the letter writer. The moat's gotten too awful even for them. They want some changes made."

I lay back down and yanked the pillow over my face. "Don't we all."

Mysti jerked it away. "What?"

"I said, maybe we don't belong here. Maybe we should move."

The Welfie gave me a hard look. "Are you crazy? The king himself gave you Master Thengor's old palace to live in for free, and you want to *leave*?"

"It's too big, it's drafty, it's hard to heat, it's impossible to get enough servants to run the place properly since I don't have that much cash, and there's still a big hole in the roof of the master bedroom."

"So it needs a few minor repairs." Mysti shrugged. "The heating problem will be solved as soon as you master the lesson on how to summon fire-sprites. Do the one about water-willies first, though: The plumbing is in awful shape and if we use the moat one more time, the slimegrinds are going to move out before you do."

I rested my elbows on my knees. "You like this place?"

"No," she admitted. "But where else do I have to go? At least it's big enough so you don't have to see me if you don't want to." She looked away.

A dozen different words came to my lips and died unsaid. I knew what Mysti was thinking: *You're stuck with me because of the Council's ruling. Ever since the king took Scandal off to be his pet, I'm the only Possessor of Personal Majyk you know left. You can't use your Majyk without me, and the king wants you to use your Majyk, so I've got to stay with you, whether you want me or not. That's why we live under the same roof and go to all King Steffan's silly dinner parties like real married couples. But I know that we're not. I know you don't want me at all.*

What she didn't know was that she was wrong.

What I didn't know was how to tell her.

"Maybe it would be better if you'd start searching for the rest of Master Thengor's Majyk, like you're always saying you want to do," Mysti went on. "You could still study while we travel, we'd see all kinds of interesting places, meet new people, and the fresh air would do us both some good." I didn't say anything. "Well, you think about it. I'll go out back to the swamp and try throwing this batch of apples to the voondrabs."

She closed my bedchamber door behind her. Her own was all the way at the other end of the palace. The room I'd chosen to sleep in used to belong to Velma Chiefcook. Although I had my pick of scores of big, beautifully furnished rooms, I felt most comfortable in this little place with just a bed, a table, a couple of chairs, and a nice view of the herb garden. I always think better in small, snug spaces, and ever since the king made Mysti and me move in here, there was plenty to think about.

Should I go out on the road with Mysti? It wouldn't be just the two of us. We'd have to take along all the awkward silences and the fake smiles. Would we ever be able to talk to each other without sounding stiff as parchment? At least when we stayed in Master Thengor's palace, Zoltan knew where to send the poisoned apples and that gave us something to talk about more naturally.

I almost felt sorry for my old schoolmate. His new bride had hauled him off to live in her old home town, a place that made Cheeseburgh look like Grashgoboum by comparison. The last I heard, the people had elected him mayor because he scared everyone. Everyone except Bini.

I leaned over the edge of my bed and felt around underneath until I found the box. I pulled it out and set it on my knees. It glowed with a faint golden light. If I took the lid off and tilted it over, I could pour Zoltan's Majyk into my lap. The Council had no trouble stripping him of most of the power he'd received as an apprentice. They left him with just enough to work a few minor spells—like doing simple home repairs, poisoning apples, and figuring out the income tax—and sent the rest to me as a palace-warming present. Mysti told me that she'd help me add it to my own Majyk, but I didn't know if I wanted to touch anything that Zoltan had been using.

Now I felt different. Maybe if I got enough Majyk together, I'd find the way to make things better between Mysti and me. And if not, maybe when you had enough Majyk, you didn't feel lonely anymore. I picked up the box, closed my eyes, and got ready to pour.

"Do you know someone's been feeding poisoned apples to your voondrabs?" Scandal threw a limp, spiny purple body onto the bed and leaped up after it. "Whoever it is, tell 'em to keep up the good work."

"Scandal!" I cried, shoving the box of Majyk onto the windowsill and grabbing the cat into my arms. "Scandal, what are you doing here?" I hugged him and stroked his sleek head and scratched him under the chin until the whole bed shook with his purrs.

"Whaddaya mean, what am I doing here?" he said at last. "You sleep through what the Council said or what? You can't mess around with Majyk unless you've got the paramedics standing by, right? So here I am. Don't thank me all at once. Small, unmarked bills will be fine."

"But the king—"

"He'll adjust. I'll send him a postcard. Look, Kendar, if I had to put up with one more *Oo's an icky-bicky-wicky iddoo legendary monster pussums tat?* from that dumb cousin of his—you know, the chick who took one bite of poisoned apple and hasn't shut her mouth about it since?—I was gonna jump out the window. Eight times." He stalked in a circle on the covers and settled down. "When do we eat?"

"Scandal, I thought—I thought if you stayed with the king, you'd have the chance to explore all of Grashgoboum and maybe find—maybe find the rat hole that can take you home again."

The cat rolled over, showing off his white belly. Looking at me upside-down, he said, "Bwana, there's a great line in this old movie—never mind what a movie is, just work with me on this one, okay?—where Dorothy says, 'Toto, I don't think we're in

Kansas anymore.' Only they cut out the part where Toto answers back, 'Fine with me, babe. Kansas ain't no bargain.' If I stick around here, I get three square meals, lots of fun, always land on my feet, nine lives, no chance of ending up as a freeway Frisbee, and—Oh yeah, one more thing—'' He rolled rightside up and looked me in the eye. ''I get a friend.''

''Gee, Scandal, I—''

''A friend who will move his lazy butt outa bed and get started on fixing the one thing this place needs before I give it the full feline seal of approval.''

A little while later, Mysti came looking for me. I wasn't in my room, I wasn't in the gardens, and I wasn't in the Academy library. There was only one other place I ever went in Master Thengor's palace: the kitchens.

I heard her calling my name. It echoed strangely off the stone walls. ''Kendar? Kendar, there's a letter from the king. He wants you to help him find that cat. Kendar, are you down here? Ken—''

''*Sshhhhhh!*'' said Scandal from on top of a barrel of onions. ''The boss is busy.''

I crouched in front of the same rat hole that had brought Scandal through into our world. I had a dead sardine in one hand and a net in the other. I dangled the fish in front of the rat hole and softly crooned, ''Heeeere, kitty, kitty, kitty. Niiiiiice kitty, kitty, kitty.''

''Giiiiirl kitty, kitty, kitty,'' said Scandal.

CRAIG SHAW GARDNER'S
FUNNY FANTASIES!

"A lot of fun!"—Christopher Stasheff

The Ebenezum Trilogy

On a road fraught with peril and dark magic, the mighty wizard Ebenezum and his hapless apprentice, Wuntvor, search for the City of Forbidden Delights.

__A MALADY OF MAGICKS 0-441-51662-9/$3.50
__A MULTITUDE OF MONSTERS 0-441-54523-8/$3.95
__A NIGHT IN THE NETHERHELLS 0-441-02314-2/$3.50

"A fun romp!"—Robert Asprin

The Ballad of Wuntvor Trilogy

With Ebenezum still suffering from his allergy to magic, Wuntvor sets off on his own to seek a cure. But before he does, he'll have to outsmart the dread rhyming demon Guxx Unfufadoo and Mother Duck herself!

__A DIFFICULTY WITH DWARVES 0-441-14779-8/$3.95
__AN EXCESS OF ENCHANTMENTS 0-441-22363-X/$3.50
__A DISAGREEMENT WITH DEATH 0-441-14924-3/$3.50

For Visa, MasterCard and American Express orders ($15 minimum) call: 1-800-631-8571

FOR MAIL ORDERS: CHECK BOOK(S). FILL OUT COUPON. SEND TO:

BERKLEY PUBLISHING GROUP
390 Murray Hill Pkwy., Dept. B
East Rutherford, NJ 07073

NAME_____

ADDRESS _____

CITY_____

STATE _____ZIP_____

PLEASE ALLOW 6 WEEKS FOR DELIVERY.
PRICES ARE SUBJECT TO CHANGE WITHOUT NOTICE.

POSTAGE AND HANDLING:
$1.75 for one book, 75¢ for each additional. Do not exceed $5.50.

BOOK TOTAL $ _____

POSTAGE & HANDLING $ _____

APPLICABLE SALES TAX $ _____
(CA, NJ, NY, PA)

TOTAL AMOUNT DUE $ _____

PAYABLE IN US FUNDS.
(No cash orders accepted.)

265

STEVEN BRUST

__*PHOENIX* 0-441-66225-0/$4.50

In the return of Vlad Taltos, sorcerer and assassin, the Demon Goddess comes to his rescue, answering a most heartfelt prayer. How strange she should even give a thought to Vlad, considering he's an *assassin*. But when a patron deity saves your skin, it's always in your best interest to do whatever she wants . . .

__*JHEREG* 0-441-38554-0/$4.99

There are many ways for a young man with quick wits and a quick sword to advance in the world. Vlad Taltos chose the route of the assassin and the constant companionship of a young jhereg.

__*YENDI*   0-441-94460-4/$4.99

Vlad Taltos and his jhereg companion learn how the love of a good woman can turn a cold-blooded killer into a <u>real</u> mean S.O.B...

__*TECKLA* 0-441-79977-9/$4.99

The Teckla were revolting. Vlad Taltos always knew they were lazy, stupid, cowardly peasants...revolting. But now they were revolting against the empire. No joke.

__*TALTOS* 0-441-18200/$4.99

Journey to the land of the dead. All expenses paid! Not Vlad Taltos' idea of an ideal vacation, but this was work. After all, even an assassin has to earn a living.

__*COWBOY FENG'S SPACE BAR AND GRILLE*
0-441-11816-X/$3.95

Cowboy Feng's is a great place to visit, but it tends to move around a bit—from Earth to the Moon to Mars to another solar system—And always just one step ahead of whatever mysterious conspiracy is reducing whole worlds to radioactive ash.

For Visa, MasterCard and American Express orders ($15 minimum) call: 1-800-631-8571

FOR MAIL ORDERS: CHECK BOOK(S). FILL OUT COUPON. SEND TO:	POSTAGE AND HANDLING: $1.75 for one book, 75¢ for each additional. Do not exceed $5.50.
BERKLEY PUBLISHING GROUP 390 Murray Hill Pkwy., Dept. B East Rutherford, NJ 07073	BOOK TOTAL $ _____
	POSTAGE & HANDLING $ _____
NAME_____	APPLICABLE SALES TAX $ _____
ADDRESS _____	(CA, NJ, NY, PA)
CITY_____	TOTAL AMOUNT DUE $ _____
STATE _____ ZIP_____	PAYABLE IN US FUNDS.
PLEASE ALLOW 6 WEEKS FOR DELIVERY. PRICES ARE SUBJECT TO CHANGE WITHOUT NOTICE.	(No cash orders accepted.)

315